Mistake Me

Cassie Gordon

ISBN: 978-1-7353583-1-4 (Paperback)
ISBN: 978-1-7353583-0-7 (EPUB)

B4EE254E01AEF59DC60FB35026248423ABEDFB
EE82828F2897264475B7AD615B
F2F9A424714DA648458D8232C8146286EB0EF14FA
A178DA764B667AD75F26129

A note to you, dear reader,

This book contains elements that may be triggering for you. If you are sensitive of death, kidnapping, abuse, sexual assault, or the like, please be even more careful. This book also contains some graphic violence and content. As always, continue at your own risk.

Thank you to By the Book Editing for editing services. And thank you to all my beta readers for your contributions and help!

I give thanks to Jesus Christ for allowing me to write this book. He's been so good to me, and I thank Him for what He's provided for me. I pray this book touches you, makes you think, and makes you consider God.

~Cassie

I tried and died the very same day
To be my own way of escape.
I tried in vain to make it alone,
But found that in me, I have no hope.
But there is One who is more powerful than all,
Who guides my steps, is not created,
And won't let me fall.

~Cassie

1

"I'm alone!" A distant cascade of thunder erupted through the sky, barging its way through the thin walls of the tiny, vine-covered house. Ennis jumped at the sound, dropping her keys onto the cream-colored counter with a little more power than she had planned. Releasing her workbag that was filled to the brim with files onto the grey tile floor, she kicked the door shut with a bang. "A full weekend alone, away from the horrors of part-time desk life."

Rubbing at an ache in her chest, she took a deep breath. *A weekend alone. Parents are on their way to the Caribbean. I'm okay now. I can do this.*

Immediately, she caught a whiff of something. Sniffing the air, she followed the scent to the kitchen and opened the fridge, pulling out one of many reusable containers stacked on each other. A note fluttered to the floor, and she reached down for it and straightened up again. The note blackened, and she shook her head, focusing her eyes.

"'We'll be back on Thursday. Call Vici if you need anything in the mean time! She's always next door. She'll check on you periodically. And I restocked the fridge and freezer. Don't forget to eat! ~Mom.'"

Opening the freezer, she saw a tall column of reusable containers amidst an array of salty prepackaged meals and other similar reusable containers. The corner of her mouth lifted. Shaking her head, she stuck the container back in the fridge.

She shrugged off her favorite green jacket, taking a moment for herself in the living room. Stretching her aching fingers, she chuckled. "Maybe I can finally make some real progress on the last draft. I should publish it soon." Tapping a finger to her chin, she felt like she was forgetting something but shrugged it off, continuing on to the bathroom.

When she reached down for the bar of soap on the sink's ledge, her mind was assaulted with a foolish comment she'd made to a co-worker earlier that afternoon in the workplace bathroom, and she shook her head. *It wasn't too terrible, was it? Should I apologize, God?*

After spending several minutes weighing the idea and the slippery ocean-scented soap in her hands, she didn't think she'd done anything wrong, and the recipient hadn't seemed to think anything of it. *Maybe it wasn't that bad... It's probably just OCD. But... it really could have hurt them and—*

Taking a deep breath in, she clenched her fists. "We're not going to worry about that. We've already thought about it, and there's nothing we need to do. It's time to rest and get refreshed, not get bogged down by OCD. The facts. Look at the facts." She shrugged, thinking maybe that was the thing she'd forgotten. She turned on the faucet and scrubbed absentmindedly.

Looking up, hazel eyes stared back at her. Her short, dark hair looked a mess but complemented her pale skin, which seemed even paler with her dark green long-sleeved shirt.

Leaning closer towards the mirror, she narrowed her eyes. "Yep, my complexion speaks of my habits." The corner of her mouth lifted.

As she walked away without another glance, a frown dipped her smirk. Shuffling into her bedroom, she lifted the blinds ever so slightly. A stream of smoky sun filtered through the window. Squinting, she let the blinds fall back. "Sun but not in it. Just the way I like it." She blinked hard a couple of times. "Weird that there was thunder. Must be off in the distance." Stretching out her limbs, she gazed out her open doorway into the hall. No one was home. There was no one around. No cat. Not even a fish. She nodded.

Shifting her weight to her other leg, she tapped her fingers idly, her brow furrowing, and she frowned again.

She shook her head and took a deep breath, walking towards the living room. "Okay, me, time for a little relaxa—"

A wave of music flowed through the tiny house and bounced off the white walls, filling the space with life that the simple, used furniture could not supply. She whipped her phone out of her pocket and looked at the screen. Her brow furrowed.

She cleared her throat and answered. "Hello?" she said in a thick Scottish accent.

"Ennisssss, hey youuuu…" Ami's overly friendly voice spilled out of the phone.

Ennis exhaled. "Oh no…" She dropped the accent.

Ami chuckled. "You know me too well. And nice Scottish, by the way. You've been practicing."

Something that sounded like children screaming erupted in the background. *Is she at an amusement park?* A siren wailed, and a sound of falling trees boomed in the distance.

"How else will I entertain myself? You could've been a telemarketer. I didn't recognize your number. What's up? Is a bomb going off?" Ennis squinted and gave a nervous chuckle.

Ami's voice crumpled slightly. "Look, I know it's short notice but..."

Ennis's shoulders straightened. "Ami, what is it? What do you need? I know that voice. What's wrong?"

Indistinguishable sounds tore through the background, and a string of angry shouts rose up amidst heartless laughter.

"It's my... well, it's my family reunion."

Ennis's eyes widened. "Oh no..."

"Yeah, I've avoided it for like two years, but my family actually made me come along this year. I mean, I'm an adult but they dragged me into it like a cat on a leash! They kidnapped me this morning! I couldn't find my phone either before we left, so I'm borrowing my cousin's."

Sounds like she's uneasy...

"Coverage is spotty here too, so I'm glad this call even got through." Ami sighed and gave a humorless laugh before her last shred of sanity broke. "I can't stand my family! I mean, it's like a war zone here, and they do nothing but fight." She paused to take a breath. "I thought if you came along, at least I'd have someone on my side. You know," she said in a muffled tone, "also someone I can use as an excuse so I don't have to play their terrible pool table tournament or endure their torture they call a 'kayaking contest'?"

Ennis huffed a laugh as she walked to the kitchen and took a seat in a carved wooden chair. "Yeah, because you can say I'm afraid of water for both of those."

"How would that be for both?"

"The water. Pool?"

"What?"

Ennis smirked. "Never mind. It was a joke.

"You should just tell them you don't want to participate. Be clear." Her eyes focused unseeingly on the swaying yellow and orange trees through her kitchen window.

Shutting her eyes, Ennis winced. "Where's it at?"

"Ennis Athrú, you are my best friend in the world! I love you so much!"

"Yeah, yeah. You love me. Cut the fluff," she said sarcastically, rolling her eyes with a smile. "Where are you?"

"Heehee! Okay, well, I'm in Mount Onus. You know where that is?"

Ennis looked at the tile floor. "No."

"There's only one family retreat in this town."

"Okay, I'll look it up."

"You are the very best—"

Ennis held the phone away from her ear as the enthusiastic voice exploded. After the din died down, she shook her head, smiling. "Well, you're worth it, Ami. What are friends for anyway?" While her voice was sweet, her eyes were faraway.

"Well, any good friend of yours would know you'd rather be spending your weekend alone working on your new book, but it makes it all the more meaningful that you're coming."

Ennis smiled a little. "Okay, Ami. I have to pack for my little vacation adventure this weekend."

"Okay, pack for cool weather. It's mid-October, after all. The winds in these mountains can get pretty cold at night."

"Right-o."

"Oh, I wondered if you wanted me to help you move those boxes to storage next weekend? I know you've been wanting to do that for forever."

Ennis didn't hesitate. "No, it's okay. But thanks." Her eyes caught the heavy stack of fresh boxes shoved against the wall in the kitchen. She shrugged a shoulder.

"You sure? Those old books are like rocks. I don't think your wee little body can carry—"

"*Okay*, Ami, I get it. But I've been... eh, cracking down on the strength exercises and," Ennis looked at her straining arm muscles that hardly changed as she flexed them, "you wouldn't want to run into me in a dark alley."

"Uh-huh... Well, I bet your *muscles* could win the kayak contest then."

"Of course they could. Mwah."

"Did you just kiss your bicep?"

"And if I did?"

"Never mind. But really, if you need any other help, just let me know, okay? As always?"

Ennis stared at the floor for a moment. "Yeah, I know..."

Clearing her throat, she glanced around the tiny kitchen. "I need to start packing."

"You're the best!"

"Bye." Ennis hung up, stuffing her phone into her pocket, and looked from bare wall to bare wall. Her house was the same as she'd left it this morning: untouched and lifeless. With her parents now gone on vacation, there was no one around, and no one to make the drive with her. "I should make more friends." She caught herself and slapped her face. "No! Not after what happened before. Don't let anyone get too close. You know

12

what happens." She stared at the floor. "It always does."

Sighing, she pulled out her phone again. "Let's see... Mount Onus, where are you?" She studied the screen and huffed. "Nine hours." She blinked. "Well, okay then. Ami, this really says something about how much I love you as a friend... Please get me through this, God."

She tossed her phone onto the faded sea-blue couch and walked into her room after making sure some upbeat instrumental music was playing. Backing up, she picked up her phone and paused the music, closing her eyes to listen. Silence. She looked up the weather on her phone. A high chance of rain this weekend in Mount Onus. But it looked like a small cell of rain would sweep over her line of travel some hours from now. Frowning, she bit her lip. "If it gets too bad, I'll just stop somewhere and wait for it to pass. Or if I get too tired." The music returned.

After lugging down an ancient black suitcase from her closet shelf, she hauled it up onto the bed, humming to the strains of the refrains. She beat the dust off its exterior and then began to gather her belongings with shaky hands and distant eyes.

~

"And an extra pair of warm trousers... And another shirt and..." Ennis pulled out the next drawer, exposing her swimming gear, "absolutely not." She shut the drawer and placed an extra pair of socks in her black suitcase. Her laptop rested on her bed, a notepad on top with a pencil askew.

The side of her mouth turned down a little. "Oh well. There're other weekends. I've got an important mission this weekend. Writing can wait."

She zipped up her suitcase and reached for the laptop, resting it on her bedside table. She smiled, and then her face became stern as her voice slipped into Scottish. "Better not bring ya, lest ya die in the rage of battle. Plus, Mount St. Onus is supposed to get a lot o' rain this weekend. And if they put me out in a tent... Best not to risk ya. And it's only a couple days."

She looked around the room again, hands on her hips. "Okay, Ennis. Let's start this trek." After slipping on her black waterproof boots, she grabbed a black trench coat off a wall hook and shrugged it on over her green jacket. Spotting her keys, she swiped them off the counter. Her hand hovered over the doorknob that led to the front porch. "I can do this... Come on, body." Her hand shook. "She's worth a trip to the moon!" A small smile reached her face but then faded. "My only friend, and she knows me best. Yet I still don't trust her..."

She turned the knob. "I can't rely on anyone."

Sweeping out of her house with a frown, she clicked the door shut silently.

2

Ennis switched on her blinker and turned onto a twisting highway. The curvy grey road was absolutely abandoned. The highway in her rearview mirror bustled with evening drivers.

"Huh. Well, I don't like traffic anyway."

She smirked, taking in the wide scenery. The trees lined the road like a golden wooden cage. The farther she drove, the more the trees morphed together, becoming one passing heap of brown with a top layer of multicolor blur. She smiled to herself as the colors whipped by. Her phone was lying on her car's middle section, the illuminated directions giving off an unnatural glow.

"Stay on 34 for... 99 miles!" Glancing at her dashboard clock sent a frown to her face. She looked back to the desolate road.

She sighed. "You can do it, Jay Jay. I know you're old and have seen a lot of miles, but we can do this!" She patted the steering wheel and sighed again.

"This is insane. I've already been driving for four hours. I've never even heard of this highway."

Her car lurched as the road veered left. "If you can call it that," she muttered.

A few more minutes slipped by in silence. No music, no radio. Just car noise and the sound of her slightly increased breathing rate.

And then a monstrous rumble.

"Whoa. That sounds... ominous," Ennis said, looking up towards the sky. A sheet waited to confront her on the horizon, making the pass from her fading blue night into the ominous grey imminent. "That doesn't look like a little cell to me."

As time rolled by, so did the clouds, overtaking her front view. "Looks like I have a date with a storm tonight." Ennis laughed to herself, settling more comfortably into her seat as her grip tightened. "This is going to get pretty bad..."

~

As some more time passed, an out of place, pretty dark blue blue sky speckled with stars revealed itself before the clouds overtook it and her car. The dark puffs swirled maliciously, asserting their cloudly dominance with pangs of thunder and spears of lightning. And yet, no rain. She caught sight of her phone and pulled off to the side of the highway. She took a picture to commemorate the truly terrifying storm and then got back on the road, driving straight towards the chaos.

~

Finally, she decided to start playing some music since each turn had become synonymous with the last, almost inseparable. Not to mention the storm was beginning to get her anxiety rolling. She wanted to keep her mind off the inevitable. She bopped her shoulders as she sang to her favorite playlist.

And then something gave a thunderous crack.

A flash of pure white enveloped her vision, and she screamed, somehow managing to keep the car straight. Her heart yelped for escape from her chest with rapid pleas. "Lightning! Whoa, I think it struck my car!"

Pulling off to the side of the road, she parked her car and stared out the windshield. "Oh. I'm okay... I'm still alive..." she told herself, taking deep breaths as best as she could. She tried to pry her white knuckles from the steering wheel with one hand, but they remained firmly affixed. With her one free hand, she ran her fingers through her short hair and found that they were trembling. She shook out her restless hand. Once her heart had stopped palpitating, she took a deep breath. "Keep moving." Pulling back into the road, she rolled along.

Then the horizon became fuzzy... And she could see the fuzziness getting closer.

The sheets of torrential rain finally enveloped her, attacking the windshield.

"No, no, no. I can't see!" The panic that had been pushed down reemerged like an angry fountain. "God, please make the rain stop." She scrambled for her phone. The signal was nonexistent. "Perfect..." Driving at a pathetic speed, she tried to make out the upcoming exit.

"Is that a two or an eight for how many miles until the next exit?" She passed the blurred sign. "Definitely an eight. Figures." She huffed, rubbing her arms.

After several minutes of crawling through tight turns and curves that didn't belong on a highway, the exit sign appeared. Before turning off, she saw a blank attractions sign.

She sighed in aggravation as the sign slowly rolled by. "Great."

She looked again, squinting this time. "What's that?" A "Cindy's Diner" sign clung desperately to the metal below the actual sign, swaying in the gusts.

"Okay, that's a start," she said, exiting and turning right towards the direction of the diner.

After about a mile, she saw a blob of red light on her watered-down windshield. As she drove on, the blob morphed into what she could only guess was a red "open" sign. She sighed in relief as she pulled into the gravel lot, surprised to see two other cars there. The place looked closed, only dim lights lit inside. "I'm so glad I decided to wear boots." Standing water filled the muddy parking lot. Flipping up her trench coat collar, she got out, slammed her door shut, and made a run for it.

Letting out puffs of breath, she was surprised to see that the breaths weren't visible since the cold bit into her flesh.

At the door, two people were about to walk out of the darkened establishment. She pulled the door open for them, standing in the torrential rain. They shuffled out without thanks, both wearing brooding looks.

She walked in and could feel warmth seep back into her bones some. Despite being outside only a minute, she had been chilled nearly to her core.

The lightning revealed loads of empty tables in the dim, shanty diner. Chairs were stacked on top of the tables, adding more shadows when the lightning flashed.

"Hello?" Ennis called. The diner replied with her voice. Light flooded the eating area when a swinging door opened from the back, exposing whom Ennis assumed was "Cindy." The plump, middle-aged woman smiled, looking like a cheery aunt and beckoned Ennis in.

"Oh, you poor, crazy thing. You're driving out there on a night like tonight?"

"Yeah, I'm helping out a friend," Ennis said politely.

"Oh, well, I'll be glad to serve you. But know that we closed ten minutes ago. It's after eleven."

"Sorry about coming in like this. I'm not actually here to eat. I need directions."

"Oh, baby, sure thing! By the way, where's your accent from? You sound charming!"

"Delaware."

"Oh, isn't that classy?"

Ennis laughed uncomfortably, adding a hushed, "No."

"I've always wanted to go to Europe."

Ennis blinked blankly, staring at the aproned woman. *Europe?*

The waitress called out something over her shoulder and then hobbled energetically up to Ennis. "Oh, and my name's Cindy, dear."

"Sam," Ennis replied, nodding her head politely. *Okay, I guess I'm "Sam" this time. Nondescript enough. She shouldn't be able to trace me in case she's a psycho.*

"Well, Sam, where do you need to get to?"

"Do you know Mount St. Onus?"

"Hmm... it doesn't sound familiar."

"I think it's northwest of here."

"Dear, I don't think you should be driving out in that rain. I can tell you where a hotel is though. Let me check with"—she yelled out over her shoulder—"John! Where's Mount Onus?"

An unintelligible, disgruntled reply came from the kitchen.

"Yeah, thought not. Anyway, a hotel's nearby. I know I set up this diner in the middle of nowhere,

19

but practically everyone who travels 34 stops here. No competition." She laughed at herself, and Ennis joined in politely. "The hotel is another 50 miles farther northwest on 34, I think." *Whoa, that's a lot of extra miles. Is it worth it? Hmm... I don't really have much of a choice. Either the hotel or sleep in my car.* Ennis frowned.

"But I don't advise it, sweetie Sam. This storm isn't supposed to let up all week. And maybe even then!"

Ennis chuckled. "I know the conditions are less than ideal unless you're trying to get away with murder."

Cindy twittered and looked towards the kitchen.

Ennis's laugh quickly died off, and she cleared her throat. "But, uh, I really don't have much of a choice, do I?"

"I guess you're right. Well, then, get on 34 again, go 50 miles, and then you'll take a left onto East Road." Ennis whipped out her phone and started typing. "Then a left onto Yulley, and then you should be able to follow the signs from then on, I think."

Ennis typed the last few words hastily and showed them to Cindy.

Cindy took a quick glance at the phone as the man in the kitchen hollered something unintelligible, and then she huffed. "Yeah, I know," she called back to him. "Thanks!" She shook her head and turned back to Ennis.

"Yeah, I think that's it. Hold on... It's actually a B&B, so it won't be some big building."

"Ah, okay. Well, thank you for the directions. Have a nice night." Ennis waved, edging towards the door.

"Okay. It was nice meeting you, Sam! Take care on the roads. We don't have a police station, hospital, or fire station around here for about a hundred miles or something, so you better be careful!" She yelled out over her shoulder, her hands on her hips. "And you too, *John*!"

Ennis's eyes were wide. "Got it. Thanks." With that, she slipped out the door and pulled up her collar once more, running to her blue car.

"Okay, Jay Jay. Time to get revving," Ennis said, shutting the door. Her dark bangs dripped languidly on her cheeks and eyelashes. Without brushing them aside, she started the engine. The deafening rain beat intensely on the car, and she could barely hear her own voice over the constant drumming. "Please help me get there safely, God." She swallowed thickly, pulling out her new directions. Then she plugged her phone into the charger.

"She said to get back on 34 and go 50 miles first. So let's do that." She shivered, rubbing her damp arms. Shifting into drive, she slowly pulled out onto the road again.

~

The car crawled along the highway for a long time before she reached for her phone. Still no signal.

"Murphy..." she grumbled. "First Jay Jay gets struck by lightning, then my phone loses GPS signal, and I didn't even print out directions. I did write down the address though... But why didn't I print directions? Or even screenshot them? Ugh..."

Her head fell back against the headrest. She sighed, setting her phone back on the middle console. "Serves me right, I guess."

She glanced at the clock. "Okay, it's half past midnight. I could keep going..." Ennis's hands gripped the steering wheel a little tighter. "Not that I have much of a choice." The thunder, which had previously taken a break for tea, began to rev up again in full force.

BOOM. CRACK!

"I don't even remember the weather calling for thunderstorms!" she lamented.

The road took a dip and skewed left. Ennis checked the written directions on her phone and then examined the odometer. "What the... It's been 50 miles. Where's East Road? There've only been numbered exits. No road names." She squinted to see out her window, but her attempt was futile against the grey waves gushing down the glass. However, she thought she saw a silhouette of a sign that included more than just numbers. She rolled down her window with a growl, letting in wet lashes of attack. Cupping her eyes, she made out a sign but still couldn't read it. "Close enough," she muttered, rolling up her window.

Peeling left across the road, she prayed that no one was coming the opposite direction at this hour. She was barely able to stay in her lane as it was. Crossing safely would be a miracle. Rolling down the passenger window, she edged across the road. "Thank You, Lord, for helping me cross safely. Thank You no one is crazy enough to drive out here like me."

Discovering that Yulley was almost immediately right after the turn off of 34, she had to back up and turn left.

"I guess this was the exit! Now for those signs she mentioned..." She scanned the drenched, autumn landscape. Her car crept along the road, not wanting to make any tortoises feel bad.

A few lights fizzed in the distance, and her tight throat loosened a little. "Civilization..." She felt like she could cry. "Population?" She drove by the small streetlight that highlighted the end of a road with a left or right turn sign. "Zero..." She sighed, bringing her attention back to the possibility of signs for the B&B... and life.

~

She drove for what felt like hours on Yulley. "This cannot be right." She hesitantly looked at her phone, dreading that her fears would be confirmed.

No bars.

"Lovely..." Her body shook. The damp had now thoroughly reached her bones, plunging her into a relentless ice bath.

She looked agitatedly at the dash. Half-past two in the morning. *That's over three hours I've lost.* "Should I even turn back now? Maybe I missed the sign? I mean, it'd make sense to... But maybe a sign'll show up in a mile. Who knows? What do I do, Lord? It's looking pretty bad." Her sopping clothes clung to her body, and she sighed, knowing her car's seat felt it too. She suddenly realized that the road signs, when they did appear, no longer read Yulley, but some obscure road number. *I guess the road name shifted. I know I didn't turn onto another road.* She looked at the indeterminable landscape. *Right?* Chastising herself again for not printing directions, she reluctantly continued her drive in the deluge.

As she glanced once more at the clock, the radio caught her eye. Turning it on, she found static on the first couple of stations. "I guess the towers don't reach out here in the middle of nowhere." Each time she progressed to the next tuning position, her heart fell a little more. She sighed as the last possible FM station yielded static. Nothing but static on all accounts. Out of curiosity and desperation, she flipped to AM and started filtering through the channels. Eventually, she discovered a station that played one *very* staticky banjo song on repeat and then one station she could barely make out. Bypassing the banjo fest, the second station was relaying some ad. Listening very carefully, she made out the words "—road 933. The second left on road 466 northbound. Stay with us." The ad cut out and her head flew up to look around. *Is that an ad for the B&B?* As she continued to scan the soaked tree-lined road, her heart sank. There was no road sign for 466. She felt like death as her exhaustion reached a peak. *Maybe I should just spend the night in my car.* Palpitations wracked her heart every now and again, and she knew she needed to sleep ASAP. On top of everything, she desperately needed to use the bathroom. There were no homes that she had passed since she first got on 34, and no buildings since Cindy's Diner. The trees outside started to look extremely inviting.

She took the next left she found and pulled off to the side of the road. "Desperate times call for desperate measures." Taking a deep breath, she opened the door. She walked some ways into the forest and dug a hole with shaky hands.

It was the worst bathroom experience she'd had yet. But seeing as there had been no civilization in the past couple hours, she hardly worried anyone would see her.

After she was done, she started her way back to her car, now freshly drenched in the chilly rain. The wind had battered her further. She looked up and saw a small brown sign on a post, too small to be government-issued. "Road 466. Wait... Isn't that from the ad?" she asked herself, her voice drowned out in the relentless pounding. A hand flew to her forehead, and she squeezed her eyes shut. "And the... second left on road 466. That might be... the B&B!"

Walking furiously the rest of the way to her car, she jumped in, still very aware that she had thoroughly soaked her driver's seat in rainwater. She drove at a roaring pace of 15 miles per hour and made the second left.

It felt like another hour, but her dash now read a little past 3:30 a.m. Her heart jolted as she saw a driveway. It wasn't labeled, but she saw half-washed away tire tracks.

"People!" she cried and turned down the driveway. She returned to turtle speed as she was now on a deep forest adventure. The road led back into the woods, deeper and deeper. However, the tire tracks remained like a guiding light. The woods encroached on her, but her determination overpowered trepidation at this point. The wind had swept a fresh wave of red and brown over the road, making the tracks seemingly invisible. Or were they still there at all? Thunder shook the air, and she could feel it rumble in her bones. Undeterred, she powered through, her wheels slipping a little on the wet leaves.

"Please get us there, God..." She looked at the gas tank. "Quarter of a tank... I'm so thankful I filled up before getting on 34! Maybe this place also has some spare gas." Her heart hammered as lights twinkled to life in the distance. "Yes!" As she pulled up farther, a large house with a white-tan exterior materialized. Massive, but ancient. Mellow light beckoned from inside the house, lighting a few windows on the ground floor. She didn't see any power lines or telephone lines. "Hmm..." The adrenaline wore off, letting trepidation and hesitation creep in.

Stopping in front of the house, she chuckled, peering at the lofty four-story building. "This looks like a house you'd get murdered in. But... I need to sleep." She was afraid she'd faint and no one would be able to get help. Cutting the engine, she stepped out into the rain and stared at the front door, wanting to assess her new situation. She hadn't seen any signs of life despite the light in the windows. She squinted at the house, the trees cutting off her view as her eyes travelled left and right. *This house is huge. Or maybe my vision's going blurry.* She rubbed her eyes and huffed. *It might be some old, historical house made into a B&B or something.* Taking a deep breath, she pulled up her collar.

3

Ennis sprinted through the rain to the front door and stopped on the smooth cement porch. At least the overhang offered some shelter. The dark green door looked welcoming, despite the outward appearance of the rest of the house. A bright light scorched her vision. Her arms flew up over her eyes, and she turned away. A tall, lanky man with medium black hair, wearing a blue suit vest and white dress shirt, held the door open, looking interestedly at her. She got a whiff of musty book smell. "You're here from the ad?" he asked carefully. She couldn't make out the rest of his appearance since the sudden light was still causing her to see stars.

"Y-yes," she said, shielding her eyes.

He stepped back farther into the house, and she peered into the searing light. Biting her lip, she inspected the dull white walls of the house's exterior. The man standing some ways inside the door turned around and looked at her. Once her vision cleared some, her heart jumped as she realized his deep green eyes were searching hers. *He doesn't* sound *like a murderer... But they never do.* She looked blankly through the door, taking in the light grey interior, and then turned back to look at her car. *Should I get my bag?*

He smirked to himself and slightly bowed with his head. "Where are my manners? Please, do come in," he said, stepping forward and offering his ivory hand. Her eyes widened a little more, her face looking blank. He let his hand fall to his side as she stepped into the house, avoiding his strangely interested gaze.

Looking down, she realized her muddy boots had tracked in puddles of mud. "Oh, sorry."

He waved a hand at it. "We'll get it cleaned up. It's not a problem."

Rubbing her hands together, she peered around the house. The hall she was in was lined with a few bookcases. Multiple paintings hung farther in the hall, and there was a standard-looking sitting room to her left. The house smelled slightly dank. Thunder rumbled the large house, and lightning cast new light over everything, resurrecting shadowy figures that vanished the same moment they came to life.

"Is... there a room available?" she asked, seeing another head in the room to her right. Some unidentifiable food smell wafted from somewhere close by. *Must be the kitchen.*

The man nodded. "What's your name?" he asked politely, holding out a hand. She shook it.

"Ennis." Ennis gritted her teeth, immediately wishing she hadn't given her real name. After all, she knew nothing about the man or the B&B. Exhaustion had eroded her senses. *Nice one, Ennis...*

"Hey, Saeva," the tall, muscular man called without taking his gaze off her, "why don't you come over and greet our new guest?" Ennis could see a ruffle of medium-length brown hair move from behind the kitchen entryway towards her. The man had pale blue eyes, a stony expression, and skin a little tanner in color than the first man's. *Why does blue-eyes look like he's assessing me?* After a few seconds of him staring at her, a smile lit his face, one that made him look like he knew something she didn't. His body, although shorter than the first man's, was still tall and even more muscular. She supposed she could ram into him, and he would hardly budge. He wore a brown leather jacket and dark jeans. *They both look like they're in their 30s.* She was never good at guessing ages but knew they were definitely older than she was. She shifted her weight onto her other leg.

"Hello," she said neutrally.

"Well, hello there," the second man said. His gaze inspected her. Ennis shifted again, looking around the house. *Ooookay. Where's the nearest exit?* She sensed the first man had moved behind her, and a sweat broke out over her body. But with the rainwater already soaking her, it just piled onto the mound of growing discomfort.

"Benedict," Saeva said, "who is our new guest? Is she...?"

"Yes, Brother. Everything has checked out."

"Perfect."

"Uh..." Ennis said, creeping back towards the door at an angle. She heard a step behind her. Her back hit Benedict's chest, and she felt his hands on her sides, catching her.

Ennis yelped and jumped, wild-eyed, her fists clenched at the ready. She side-stepped away. "I'm n-not sure that I'll be staying. And stay away from me!"

"Please don't get worked up," Benedict said, picking at his blue vest and looking at the water stain. He smiled, one hand in the pocket of his slacks, not caring to wipe the water away. "We would be honored to have you stay," he said naturally.

Saeva smirked and slid up before her. "I do hope you'll stay with us. We even have a room prepared for you," he purred, stepping back. "If you're hungry, we can get you something." His voice echoed off the grey walls as he walked away.

Silence followed. Even the continuous thunder had gone still.

She looked up at Benedict, who smiled in reply, his green eyes glinting. "I'll get you set up in your room."

Ennis thought over whether she should stay or get out of there as soon as possible. Her limbs felt too heavy, and her clothes sloshed with each step. Her body was near collapse, and she couldn't stop internally shaking. *Ugh. I can't just continue on like this. It's not safe for me to drive right now. I'm so tired. And if I pass out, there would be no one to help me out. I'd have to drive pretty far if I wanted to escape these two... mildly creepy men anyways. And they haven't murdered me yet, so that's a good sign. I might just be overreacting. I guess it comes down to which is safer: staying here with creepy people who could turn out to be safe people or passing out with no chance of help. What should I do, God? Go and try to find other civilization? But I'm really in the middle of nowhere. I haven't seen any signs of human life since the diner!* Benedict cleared his throat, and Ennis snapped back to the present. "I'm not sure I'll be staying," she repeated, feeling his eyes on her.

"Oh..." came his cryptic reply. He looked out the window and a timely bout of lighting lit up the room. This aided the weak spurts of incandescence that clung to the walls. "You could go," he propositioned, "but it's pretty nasty out there. The roads are hardly drivable. I'd feel bad letting you go out in that." He bit the inside of his lip as he examined the pounding rain on the lattice window. Thunder erupted from the heavens, shaking the floor. She shifted towards the door, trying not to rock back and forth on her toes. Her vision was going black. *I'll buy myself some time to think.*

"Let me get my bag." She started towards the door, but Benedict held up a hand.

"Allow me," he said, stepping around her.

"But I'm already wet!" she called, but he was already out the door and in the rain. Her heart thumped wildly.

Saeva peeked his head around the wall. "Oh, if he's doing that, then I'll show you to your room. But please have lunch with us when you're done. I know it's a bit late for it."

"Lunch? It's way past midnight." Her brain was noticeably sluggish, and she found it hard to breathe. She tried to inconspicuously loosen the muscles in her throat. *I need to sleep. Now.*

"Call it tea then or whatever," he said with a short laugh, stepping in front of her. "This way."

He began making his way down the hall and went up a flight of the red carpeted staircase. His feet bounded up another flight, and Ennis trailed behind, clearing her throat, trying to swallow the feelings she was getting from this place. He led her down a steel-grey hall with wooden accents, until finally he stopped. They stood in front of a heavy, dark wooden door that seemed bigger than normal to Ennis. They'd passed several like it on the way. Saeva opened the door and welcomed her in. Ennis's heart was pounding, despite the crushing fatigue that was threatening to overtake her.

The walls were a slate grey. Wooden furniture and a standard queen bed with an ancient-looking green duvet lined the room. He pointed to an open door in the room's wall, which led to the bathroom. "This bathroom is yours. I know how you like your privacy," he said with a slight smirk.

That's weird... I never said anything about my love of privacy... She had to admit that he was right, but a shudder trickled down her spine. Something was off here. She could feel it. Like a chill that had settled permanently in her bones. Or maybe that was just the soggy clothes sitting on her body. She nodded, and he bowed his head slightly, striding to the door.

"The library is on the second floor. I'll show it to you tomorrow." With that, he closed the door noiselessly.

"Library?" she whispered.

Ennis stepped forward and gave the knob a firm push and turn. "Hmm." There wasn't any click, and she huffed, turning the lock a couple of times and opening and closing the door. "Huh." Walking back to the middle of the room, her mind was in overdrive.

"Strange," she whispered, "in more ways than one..." She fully intended to be up and out of there before dawn, but she knew her body would be unable to cope with so little sleep. Otherwise, she'd have driven through the night to reach Ami. If she could ever find her way back to civilization... She had to face that she was lost, hungry, and extremely tired with no one to help her if she needed to go to the hospital. This was her choice. To stay... for now... with the lesser of two evils.

Walking into the bathroom, something black caught her attention in the corner of her eye. Turning on her heel, she saw a black pile of folded fabric on the bathroom counter. Her brows furrowed. The fabric fell loose as she lifted it above her head. "What is this?" Shaking out the mass revealed a single opening on one side of the thing. "This is... bizarre." The black cape crumpled slightly in her grip. "Did someone leave it behind? Maybe it's waterproof." Shaking her head, she replaced the piece onto the counter, which brushed down her side and fell to the floor. She pulled out her phone and inspected the screen. No signal. No service. She dropped herself into the tub, planning to sit there until Benedict brought her suitcase.

It was a fair few minutes before she heard what sounded like her luggage being rolled down the hall. And a few seconds later, there was a tapping. She stepped over the tub's edge and walked silently to the door. Unlocking it, she found Benedict thoroughly soaked, his black hair sopping. He put her luggage on the ground and scooted himself inside her door.

"Thank you, but really, I could've gotten it. Now you're soaked."

"I don't mind the rain, and I'm happy to serve you," he said, bowing slightly.

Her nervous laugh was cut short. "Whoa, whoa. What's with the bowing? Both of you are doing it. There's no need."

"As you wish," he said before disappearing down the dim hall.

Peering around the edge of the doorway, she squinted. "Okay, this place is definitely creepy. I'm out at first light." She locked the door. "Or at least once this storm lets up."

Spinning around, she noticed that the curtains of her room were especially thick. She couldn't recall ever seeing black curtains that thick used as normal décor before... But this place was hardly normal. Overall, though, it did do the room a bit of a favor, just like the green armchair near the window. Besides those pieces and the bedspread, the rest of the room was wood or a slate color, like a solid mass of oneness. The curtains were at least different. She looked down. The ancient wooden floorboards were just jumping to give splinters. She turned back to the bathroom. Entering, she tossed her trench coat, green jacket, soiled green shirt, and trousers into the corner of the tub.

After taking a quick shower, she wriggled into a dry black long-sleeve and some trousers. She rummaged through her open suitcase on the floor, becoming increasingly violent in her search.

"Didn't I pack my salt tablets!" She shook out her suitcase. They weren't there. Sinking back onto her knees, she was exhausted. "Great... This isn't good." She sighed. "I must've forgotten to pack them. I was in a hurry to get in as much daylight as possible." She clenched her fists and then resigned to replacing her belongings into her luggage.

Once she was done, she held out a hand, and it was trembling. Closing her hand into a fist, she stood up slowly and sighed. "I guess I'll need to get salt from food then."

Her dark hair clung to her face as she stepped into the hall. Before she started to move, her stomach gave a nasty shudder. And then she began to move out.

Ennis stared at the many doors that lined the way. *This place is massive.* Hesitating down two flights, she found the long hallway she originally entered. Some scent that smelled edible wafted her way. As she turned the corner into what was apparently the dining room, she noted a fireplace burning behind the more muscular, blue-eyed brother. *Say-ee-vah, was it? Oh, why did he have to be here?* The open doorway to the kitchen was in the corner of her eye, being monitored for other insane residents.

"Ahh, there you are. We have so much to discuss with you," Saeva said, beckoning her to join him at the set dinner table. He sat comfortably at the head of the table in front of the fireplace. A book he was reading was casually set down with a smirk.

Okay, this is getting really weird. She gingerly took a seat in one of the high-backed chairs at the other end as far away from him as possible and closest to the front door. The massive wooden table could easily seat twelve people. Catching his probing eyes, she questioned her decision to stay. *Should I run for it? This guy is really creeping me out.* Her stomach growled, and she felt like she would faint. *But I'm out of food, right? I still need gas. Wait, should I even tell them I need gas? Makes me sound more vulnerable. But I do need it. I mean, besides being creepy, they haven't done anything to hurt me.* Her body shuddered. *I need to sleep.*

Ennis was jolted to her senses when she realized Saeva was staring at her. *What? Am I supposed to say something? Did I miss a question?*

"Thanks for taking me in on such short notice. I was hoping I'd find the place." *Not so sure that I hope that anymore...* She glanced out the window to her right. Not that she could really see anything with the water gushing down it. "The directions were a bit confusing, but then I heard the ad," she explained. Saeva stared at her, that slight smirk still on his face. Another shudder rippled down her spine.

A shadow passed by the entrance to the kitchen and moved down the main hall. She did a double-take to catch the shadow, but it vanished too quickly. Saeva looked past her, into the open walkway that led to the hall. The shadow was gone. "Ah, Ennis, that was Valentine, our semi-new resident *human* helper," he explained. "Valentine?" he called.

What's with the odd inflection of human? Ennis turned to see whom he was talking to. The shadowy figure reemerged. She stared at the man. He was tall, lean, yet muscular, had black hair that just passed over the tips of his ears, skin as pale as moonlight, and was decked out in a white shirt and an antique-looking silvery-grey vest with a pair of black slacks and shoes. She guessed he was in his mid-30s as well. Maybe. She wondered how she had thought he looked like a shadow a few seconds ago when he was clearly wearing light colors. His hands were folded lightly behind his back. He looked tense despite his neutral face.

Her heart leapt as Valentine turned his hazel eyes on hers. His gaze was steady and showed nothing but pure, quick analysis.

"Valentine, would you check on the food, please?" Benedict asked, appearing from the hall before disappearing again. Valentine nodded politely in Benedict's direction and swept off but not before catching her gaze once more right as he turned the corner to go into the kitchen. Her mind churning slowly, she couldn't fathom his gaze's meaning, but she felt like he was trying to tell her something. *Maybe it's my imagination.*

Saeva picked at his leather sleeve. "My brother and I are only too pleased to have you with us and are hoping you'll prove far better than our *last* guest." Ennis could feel the distaste associated with the "*last*" visitor.

"What, did he not pay the nightly fee?" she asked.

His head fell forwards, and he laughed. Ennis looked at the hall entrance. Eventually, Saeva's head fell backwards, still laughing. She thought she heard Benedict's voice from the other room ask what was so funny.

"You're funny. Nightly fee." Saeva smirked.

"But isn't this a B&B?" Ennis asked. Her heart started beating madly again as if it were angry with her and saying, "Foolish you!"

"Oh, well, I guess you could call it that. But no. I mean, our guests pay with their information and aid. You did hear the ad, right?"

"Part of it," Ennis said, wringing her hands under the table. "What exactly did the ad say? What do you mean 'information and aid'?" She breathed rapidly and reminded herself to calm down. *Lord, what do they mean? Please keep me safe!*

"Writing of course." Benedict answered, walking in with a tray in each hand. "Here's yours, Brother." He set down a tray in front of Saeva and lifted off the silver platter's lid.

Silver trays are weird to have nowadays. And writing? What is going on?

Benedict exposed a layered ham sandwich that Ennis thought looked particularly tasty. Saeva bent down to smell it. When she felt herself starting to drool at the fresh bacon and onion, she quickly swallowed. The sandwich was stacked high with lettuce and tomato as well, which she didn't even particularly like. But it looked very appetizing under a thick slice of crusty baguette. Saeva, still bent over, looked at her under his lashes. He tilted his head to the side, his neck at an odd angle. "Hungry? I bet you are," he said. Ennis felt a sour jolt in the pit of her stomach. *I wonder if the food will be poisoned...* Benedict placed a tray in front of her, simultaneously lifting the cover.

But there was no bread. No bacon. No ham.

She felt like she couldn't focus her eyes. Blinking hard, her stomach dropped as the image before her didn't change.

On the tray, there stood a tall glass of thick, red blood.

4

Ennis stared at the glass, unable to make anything of it. All that passed through her mind was that she was very, *very* much in trouble. Her mind reactivated when a peal of thunder violently lashed out overhead. Then her mouth started moving. "What... what is this?" The smell leached into the air, and iron threatened to overtake her. *Definitely blood.*

"It's B negative. I hope you don't have a preference. This was what we could get," Saeva said. "We're not exactly sure if different types have different flavors." He looked at her for a moment. "Do they?" he asked curiously.

Benedict looked slightly concerned as he walked over to his place on the left of hers. She felt a strong gag coming on.

"Is it not up to your standards?" Benedict asked, hovering over his seat, looking as if he'd snatch it away at any moment.

"Is this some sick joke?" Ennis snapped, bolting up from the table, her hands planted firmly atop the glistening wood. While she could hide the black that overtook her vision, she couldn't hide her body's shaking.

"Are you that offended?" Saeva asked, perking up with even more interest. His cold eyes almost looked amused.

"Yes! I don't know what kind of B&B this is, but I think I'm at the wrong place. I'll be leaving now. I should've left before I got here," she said, shoving her chair back and marching for the door.

"I'm afraid we can't let you do that," Benedict said, looming in the open section of the wall that

39

led to the hall. And the front door. *When did he get there!* She stopped and sized him up, debating whether to make a dash for the exit. He looked like he'd be able to snag her if she tried. Her heart was racing at an unhealthy pace, and her vision was still black. When breathing became increasingly difficult, her hand shot up to her neck.

Saeva rose as well, making his way towards them. "Our last guest tried to pull the same thing, you know. He came to us, what, Benedict, five months ago?"

Benedict nodded.

"He tried leaving, and it didn't end well for him. We have better defenses set up around the perimeter now. If you don't want to be staked, then I suggest you don't leave," Saeva said.

"Staked?" Ennis said, feeling a cold sweat overtake her body. "And... the blood..." She began to churn through these two items, and her mind came up with one answer. *Oh...* Her voice was monotone. "You think I'm a vampire." *They're crazy and potential murderers. This is not good.*

"You can drop the act. I think we all know what you are," Benedict chimed, stepping closer to her.

"If you say confused, you'd be correct," she replied, trying to keep the anger and confusion from making too much of an appearance. *Maybe they'll let me go if they realize I'm human.*

"Your act won't get you anywhere. The signs that you're a vampire are obvious," Benedict noted, his green eyes eager.

"Oh yeah?" Ennis said, her voice laced with sarcasm. Her usual gusto was crumpled by her fear. The urge to flee overwhelmed her, but that wasn't an option right now. She went with fight instead.

"Haven't you ever heard of liking the indoors?" she countered.

"It goes beyond your pale," Saeva leaned in a little, squinting, "*very* pale skin."

"Oh really?" she asked hotly, filled with more sarcasm.

"When you first came in, you didn't come in without first being welcomed." Saeva stared at her.

"I was debating whether to get my luggage!" she lamented.

"You heard the ad," Benedict added.

"My *radio* heard the ad," she huffed.

"Impossible. We play the ad at a frequency that human ears, nor radios, can detect," Saeva snapped.

"Well, *my* radio did!" she protested. "I'll go out there and prove it right now!"

"I already tried. It doesn't work. That's how our last guest came to us. He heard it being broadcasted," Benedict explained. "Oh, and Saeva, that reminds me, we should take the ad down again now that we've got our new resident," he said. "It actually just went up a few months ago. We took it down while we set up our new defenses," he murmured.

"But you don't have my keys. How did—" She patted her pockets, knowing that these weren't her original clothes she had on.

Benedict pulled her keys from his pocket, dangling them in midair with a smile. She lunged for them, snatching them out of his hand.

"Our last guest got a stake to the heart for trying to leave," Saeva said predatorily.

Her heart stuttered. *They* are *murderers!*

"But what was really telling was that tonight you looked at my brother as if you wanted to eat him.

You must be very hungry," Benedict stated. He was perfectly serious.

Her words came quickly. "I was looking at the sandwich, and then he leaned forward—"

"Save it, Ennis. You're here, and you'll be helping us whether you like it or not," Saeva stated, leaning towards her. "You *cannot* leave."

Ennis cast a hot glare towards him and then at Benedict. "Look, you're mistaken," she growled.

"If you were a human, you'd have to die. We can't have humans knowing about us here." Benedict chuckled as if her statement were completely ridiculous. "We're very sensitive about those things. So it won't benefit you to play human. But since you're not, then you don't have to worry about that," he said cheerily. "You'll live here and help us write our books properly and gather information. We need all your accurate knowledge on vampires. After all, that was our ad."

Benedict stepped in front of her and leaned in a little, assessing her. "I like you." He smiled at her and then shot a pointed look at Saeva, who returned a contemptuous glare.

They'd seriously *kill me if I were human. Which I am... So what does that leave me with?* She gave one last assessment of the front door. She desperately tried to feel more awake, but her body was shutting down, her brain no longer willing to compute much of anything. Judging by how the brothers were positioned, she didn't have a chance of escape right now. She looked around the room, not seeing any elements of distraction she could use either.

"I'm going to my room," she stated stiffly. Robotically, she walked towards the stairs, feeling their amused and curious eyes following her. She rounded the first flight's corner before her legs became like jelly. She clung to the railing and hastily made her way up another flight.

I need a plan. I really, really need a plan.

5

Ennis flung the door open to her room and slammed it shut behind her, triple checking the lock. Her eyes darted around the room until she spotted a heavy-looking wooden dresser. Her muscles strained, and she became breathless as the large chunk of wood scraped against the floorboards.

After two very long minutes, the dresser was snug against the doorframe. She sighed, crawling onto her bed. She curled up into a ball and hugged herself tightly.

"I'm alone… This isn't good. I thought they were creeps, and they turn out to be psychotic too." Her hand flew to her neck, digging into her skin. "Think of a plan, Ennis," she willed, squeezing herself tighter into a ball. She cast her gaze wildly around the room. What were the potential assets? Her phone sat on top of her suitcase. Sprinting off the bed, she dove for her phone and retreated to her previous spot, curling herself back up into a ball. She dialed a number.

"Please, please, please," she whispered. A piercing BEEP sounded and then went silent. Her heart sunk, and the phone hung up on itself. "No service… even in emergency mode." Her tight grip on her knees slipped a little, and her eyes started to sting and then snapped wide open. "GPS!" Eagerly, she opened her phone's map, and immediately a notice sounded. "No connection?" She stood up on her bed. "No connection! What am—" Swaying slightly, she crumpled into a heap back onto her bed. "No, Ennis, you can't stand up so fast… You know this." Panic had beaten her senseless. She sat up slowly. *No, no, no. How am I going to get out of here like this?* Her anxiety intensified inside, just like the thunder outside. *I can't afford to be ill! Not that I can help it... Oh, God, please help me...* Her situation hit her full-fledged in the chest. "I'm... I'm stuck here. Okay. Under some crazy people's roof. They think I'm a vampire. They'll kill me if they find out I'm human." She rocked herself. "I can't stay here! Maybe this is all a joke... Maybe I'm on a TV show or something." She looked around her room for a camera and noticed something black reaching out from her bathroom floor. The black cloak. Her face blanched. "I've got to get out of here..."

A slight tapping on her door, amplified from the small respite between thunder rounds, interrupted her thoughts. Her shoulders jolted to attention, and her head whipped around to look at the door. Her dresser was still in place. Letting out a small puff of breath, she padded silently over to the door. While debating whether she should say anything, the silence crept on. Finally, the thunder had had enough silence. She stood there with bated breath, clutching her neck with one hand and an arm wrapped around her front. She put her ear to the door.

Nothing.

Odd.

It took several minutes for her to be sure no one was there anymore. She started to wonder whether there had been anyone there in the first place. "I can't think about that right now," she told herself. "I need to get to my car." She stuffed her phone in her pocket and began to carefully slide the dresser aside, flinching at every groan and scrape from the stubborn lump. Reaching out to take the doorknob, her hand shook. She paused, using her other hand to steady her shaking. Unlocking it slowly, she cringed as the lock tumbled. To her delight, the door opened rather silently. She glanced back at her suitcase, but her eyes fixed firmly back on the open crevice before her. It opened slowly, and she peeked around the corner. Stepping gently down the hall over the wooden flooring, she made it to the stairs. Muffled talking floated up from somewhere below her. *Oh no.* Closing her eyes, she took a shaky breath. Her body was shuddering. *No, body, no! Not now. Not yet. You can live. We're doing this* to *live.*

After taking a step down the stairs, she waited. The voices seemed to stay in a singular location. Another step. She prayed they would remain occupied. Another. Then another.

As she crept down more steps, the voices had gotten increasingly louder. Finally, she reached the bottom of her first flight. Waiting at the stairs' last turn, she became aware that the voices had stopped. A wracking shiver harassed her spine as her mind whirled through all the horrible outcomes that might befall her if she were discovered. Building up the courage, she thrust her head around the corner, not wanting to keep agonizing in anticipation.

No one.

Her breath left her body when a man walked around the corner. Green eyes met hers. The man smiled broadly. "There's our guest!" Benedict said, opening his arms in welcome.

Her eyes showed her internal horror, and all that played through her mind was *murderer.*

His smile dropped instantly. "How are you feeling?" With his eyes probing her, he frowned. "You look really pale." He neared her, and she stood frozen, not wanting to provoke him by backing away. "Do you need some blood? You didn't touch yours at dinner."

"I-I'm fine. Th-thank you." Ennis growled at herself in her mind for stuttering. *I can't show fear! I have to tread carefully, navigate this mess, and find a quick exit strategy that doesn't get me killed.*

Benedict held out an arm in escort-fashion. Ennis looked at him, conscious of her stunned face she couldn't seem to get rid of. He dropped his arm without missing a beat. "Not the type to be escorted, huh? I guess I don't know how old you are. You could be 400 years old, but you also might be 40. Age doesn't really seem to do much to your type," he mused.

She cleared her shock and replaced it with a blank expression, but her mind was boiling. *I'm 23 and definitely not a vampire. You're wrong... again.* An agitated sigh almost escaped her, but instead, she found herself being herded towards a room.

Benedict swung open a sturdy red wooden door. A puff of book smell, musty and ancient, escaped through the open door, hitting her sharply in the nose.

"Welcome to the library," he sang. There were shelves on the walls, crawling up to the high tan ceiling. *There have to be at least a thousand books in this place...* Antique furniture slumbered around the wooden shelves, resting on more smooth wooden flooring. A draft flattened Ennis's trousers to her legs, spawning from the fireplace that was tucked into the back of the room. Benedict hovered near the right side of the library, near a wall of vast windows, leaning over a desk littered with papers and a typewriter. Looking to the side of the desk, she saw a nearly identical desk, although more organized, equipped with another typewriter. Her brow furrowed slightly. *I guess they don't like electricity here?* Remembering the lamp in her room and the lights around the house, she analyzed their meaning. She couldn't remember seeing any outlets.

Ennis stared at Benedict, her eyes glazed, perplexed.

He looked down at the wooden floor and shifted his feet. "I couldn't wait to show you this room of the house... Well, this place probably isn't as grand as some places you've seen, but it's grand to me. This is my favorite place. In fact, I love it! I get to write, read, and learn. It's my one haven. Saeva doesn't appreciate it the same way I do. He has his own after all, but this... *this* is mine," he explained, gesturing grandly to the shelves. He looked at the room with an interest reserved usually for looking upon one's bride. Such love radiated from him. *No, this is obsession...*

Ennis turned from him and pretended to assess the room, but her focus was on finding exits. The four vast windows had their black curtains pulled back, allowing intermittent lighting in. *This place could be very pleasant... under different circumstances and company.* Right now, she wanted to be as far away from this place and its people as possible.

"What are you thinking about?" Benedict asked lightly, looking at her with interest. "You've been staring into space for a while now."

Ennis tried to school herself into an expressionless state. "I like books," she said, feeling that was the best answer. *I mean... I like the idea of writing my own. Not that I'm telling* you *that.*

48

Benedict's stance straightened. He snapped a book in his hand closed, an open-mouth smile radiating from him.

"I thought you might be the bookworm type! What's your favorite book?"

Ennis couldn't help but be reminded of an animated, naïve child.

"I'm more of a modern book reader," she hedged.

"Oh, do they really compare to the classics, though? Although," his hand went to his chin, "maybe those *are* your modern books. Were you born in the age of *Frankenstein*? *The Odyssey*?" he insisted, eyes wide. "Tell me, were you alive before the first printing press?"

"No..." she said unconfidently. Benedict's smile and shining eyes faded a little.

"It's rude to ask a woman her age," Saeva scoffed.

Ennis whipped around, her heart jumping when she saw Saeva leaning on the entry doorframe. He pushed off with his shoulder and strode over to the desk where the two were standing.

"How old *are* you?" Saeva asked curiously, but she thought it rang with slight disbelief.

"Didn't you just hear yourself? It's rude to ask," Ennis retorted. Her hands were clenched into fists out of annoyance. And because they had started to shake again. Her body felt alive with electricity, but that was quickly zapping her very limited energy supply.

Saeva stepped closer to her, gave her a once over, and settled his eyes back on hers with a frown. Her hazel eyes flamed with anger.

"I'd pin you at 47. You're a bit of a young vampire, aren't you? Still naïve," he said, folding his arms and turning his nose up.

"Actually—" Ennis quipped back. She mentally kicked herself. *I can't be so quick to say anything! My life is on the line, Ennis. Don't be foolish!* Her mind churned rapidly with the best solution to her age. "It doesn't matter," she said firmly, looking unfazed.

Saeva raised his brows as she swept around him and towards the door. Benedict shot Saeva a look of irritation.

"What?" Saeva asked, opening his arms. Benedict gave a tsk, shook his head, and followed Ennis's trail.

Her feet were about to choose whether to turn right towards the front door or left towards the staircase when she felt a presence behind her. She groaned quietly, squeezing her eyes shut. *I just want to get out of here...* Benedict's steps faltered slightly.

"Ennis?" he called timidly.

Ennis whipped around and stared at him. "What?" she asked edgily.

"Please forgive my brother. He just really cares about our books, you know? Writing is our life. Vampires," Benedict began, taking a step forward with something like reverence, "are our lives." His green eyes looked like they were aching but proud.

Confusion painted her face. These brothers were insane. *Vampires don't exist, man.* She sighed, wanting to massage her head. She felt herself tense even more. "I'm going to my room."

Benedict looked panicked and reached out for her but didn't touch her. "Wait, we've not actually started getting information from you, though. This is the first time—"

"Didn't you have another vampire"—Ennis tried to say the word without sarcasm—"in your house before?"

Benedict looked taken aback for a split second but went on. "This is the first *real* time we've had a vampire stay with us. We need to know what you know!"

Ennis stared at him. "What's your motive?" she asked, her face hard. She was tired of mulling it over. Why not ask?

"Knowledge," he remarked as if it was obvious. "Proper, *accurate* knowledge. Also, to create something that we alone know is true. It's a satisfying feeling."

Ennis nodded her head, playing along.

Benedict smiled and continued. "We're writers. That's what we do. It's who we are. We can't have humans in our house. Then they'd know what we were up to, and we can't have them in on the *secret*." He winked at her. "They'd tell others. Humans gossip too much." His demeanor darkened. "But we're worthy because we care so much and would keep it quiet. We're devoted to accuracy. To the higher forms. We want the best."

"Accuracy," Ennis repeated. He nodded his head barely. "But you're writing books with accurate knowledge. Isn't that spreading secrets? The exact thing you despise?" she pitted calculatedly.

Benedict shook his head, almost looking relieved. "No, we write under the pretense of fiction. We don't share the fact that the books are actually true with anyone. *That* information can't leave the house. If we said they were true, most people would think we were crazy and deny it."

Ennis barely kept from huffing. *You* are *crazy!*

"But there would still be those who'd believe." As he looked at her, he tilted his head. "So to help make our dreams come true, we really want to learn all there is to know about vampires *from* vampires."

The question came too quickly from her lips. "And what makes you think I'm just going to give you information?" She winced. *You didn't think this question through. Don't be foolish!* Thinking quickly, she turned her nose up.

Benedict's eyes became unfocused. And she didn't like that. Panic was rising in her, and she paled. *That just cost me my life. Death and life are in the power of the tongue. Too bad I won't get to carry that lesson into my future on earth.*

But Benedict's eyes cleared, and he shook his head, his smile returning. "I thought it was obvious that we aren't giving you a choice." He held his hands loosely in front of him. "And you *will* help us write."

As he stood there, Ennis thought he looked a little apologetic with his head bent forward a bit. But her situation was clear: she was in extreme danger. Panic attacked her throat. "Not tonight," she stated as normally as she could manage. But it came out squeezed.

"Then tomorrow." Benedict sighed.

Ennis swept around him without reply and began climbing the stairs. Once she was out of his sight, she hastened to her designated room and used the dresser as a shield from her circumstances. She propped herself on the edge of her bed, curling her fingers into the short, dark hair at her ears, and groaned. "This is *crazy! They're* crazy! He didn't even give me a proper motive!"

she quietly wailed. "I hate this! I need a plan! I need to escape," she moaned, feeling panic flood her again. She released her hair and shot up off the bed, starting to pace. "Okay, if I can't escape I'll—"

She paused, feeling another wave of anxiety, and simultaneously ignored the black that had overtaken her vision. "Never mind, I'll just have to escape. I'll... wait until they go to bed! It's practically four in the morning or something. They've got to go to sleep soon. I mean, most night owls don't make it past three, right? I'll just have to wait, then slip out the front door..."

Ennis nodded to herself and then stumbled into the bathroom and closed the door, twisting the lock. She turned on the faucet and scrubbed her face with cold water. *I need to stay awake. Come on, Enn...* Her body lurched with fatigue, and her heart was set on a rapid pace. She sat on the closed toilet and waited.

Before this, she had thoroughly searched her room for a power outlet. She had even snuck out into the hall to find any form of electrical outlet, but there wasn't any as she had feared. There was a seeming lack of electronics. The room had no alarm clock, they used typewriters, and there were no corded lamps in her room. Amongst the oddness, she wondered why they didn't have that stuff around even with their vehement distaste of humans. It didn't make sense.

But these were strange people.

~

The next thing Ennis knew was that her head hurt. A splitting ache shot through her skull, and her hand instinctively flew to her forehead as she jolted to a standing position. Which was a mistake. Her body refused to cooperate. Her legs became like jelly, and she hit the floor on her hands and knees. Disoriented, she tried to piece together what had just happened. The soft light was overhead. The cream-colored walls surrounded her. A tub was to her left. She was still in her bathroom. "I fell asleep," she admitted to herself. At this point, she was so exhausted that all she could feel was slight disappointment with herself. The sink counter was a small distance from the toilet, and her brow furrowed. To be sure, she sat back on the toilet and simulated falling to the right, which produced the same location of the little red spot now gracing on her forehead. She shook her head at herself, which was another bad idea, and the world swam before her eyes. "No, no, no, not good." She pleaded with her head to get better. "I can't fall asleep. They might murder me on my bed." She looked around. "Or on the toilet." She shuddered.

Assessing her body, she felt less terrible than before she fell asleep. But she was still not in good shape. *I need to get out of here... Now.*

Standing up slowly, she grabbed her trench coat from the bathtub and slung it on. It was still damp, and she wondered if the pros of wearing it would outweigh the cons that damp and cold combined always seemed to have. She kept it on.

She checked her phone, confirming what she dreaded. Low battery. A sweat broke out over her body. She reassured herself that she'd be back in her car with a means of charging shortly. Her phone had indicated it was now six in the morning, and she walked to the door. She heard nothing but waited for another minute and then turned to look at her suitcase once more. *Sorry, you're not coming with me.* She frowned. *I'd rather live than have the necessities.*

"You can do this," she told herself firmly. "Oh, God, help me."

Before leaving, she ran to the green quilt on her bed and pulled off a loose string.

Unlocking her door, she poked her head out. Nothing. She did note, however, that all the windows that had previously been uncovered were now shielded with thick curtains and tapestries that sucked all light from the house. She placed the loose string between the door and the frame. *Just in case I come back. Which... I won't.*

Her heart thumped madly as she darted down the hall as quickly as she dared rev her heart, reached the staircase, and descended the first flight. And the second. Turning to her left to get to the front door, she hit a solid wall of something. Her gasp was muffled by a hand. Panic became her autopilot, and she began to fight the dark figure. Nothing registered at that point except the need to escape. And she needed to *now.* But then a calm voice sang to her.

"Shhh, I'm not going to hurt you. Calm down. I'm not your enemy." The voice was neither Saeva's smooth, low tone nor Benedict's eager, chipper one. Her eyes finally focused on a face and found handsome hazel eyes of green and gold. She realized that she was writhing against a mass of black fabric belonging to some dark cloak. *His* dark cloak. He peered at her but held on to her gingerly as if she might try to snap at him. Her fighting lessened. *Surely he would've hurt me by now if he wanted to, right?* She stopped fighting, but tension sung in her shoulders. He immediately whisked his hand away from her mouth, and his grip on her arm retreated. He was no longer wearing the grey vest he had worn in the hours before. Now he donned a rather covering black cloak. A black vest and white dress shirt peeked out from underneath of it.

"Please do be quiet. You don't want to alert them," he said in a low voice. Her head spun. *What does he want? Why is he doing this? Is he helping me, or is he in on their plan? I mean, he works for them!* Her mind jittered as did her body.

"I was going to the kitchen," Ennis stated robotically, her face blank.

Valentine raised his eyebrows. "Were you now?"

"To get blood," she answered.

Valentine gave her a cryptic look. "I think you and I both know that you're not a vampire."

Ennis tensed even more, feeling a prickling on the back of her neck. "You dare question me?" she retorted, radiating majesty with her chest puffed and fists clenched at her sides, her head held high.

Valentine looked as if he was calculating something. His dark hair ruffled as his hand shot out and took her wrist, latching it to the wall behind her. Ennis's eyes flashed with terror as her eyes traveled to her wrist, pinned by a strong, pale hand. "If you're a vampire, you can easily overpower me," he said. Ennis looked at her wrist again.

"Do it," he challenged.

Ennis took a quick moment to analyze whether she should even attempt to free herself. He stared her down with a cryptic gaze, but she could see something like amusement lighting his hazel eyes. He wasn't angry. Ennis gave an irritated scoff. She noticed his gaze shift to the mark on her forehead. His mouth turned down a little. Turning her head to the side, she looked away from the towering man.

"Your forehead gives you away completely." His free hand pushed her dark hair aside to reveal the mark. His eyes narrowed.

"This is below me. I won't play your stupid games. You aren't worth my time, you human," she said in a dramatic persona.

Valentine sighed, releasing her wrist. "You're a terrible actor." He had removed his grip but hadn't stepped back, leaving himself in his angled position before her.

Irritation coursed through her. *Am not.* She dropped her shoulders and let her posture normalize. *There is no fooling him.* She knew he knew. *Well, there goes that.* Peering at him, something donned on her. *Why don't I feel threatened? Is this a game? Or...* She looked down. *There's no trusting anyone, Enn.* He looked at her like he was still calculating and tilted his head slightly. *But something about him...* "I'll have you know I acted in plays once." She pushed her hair out of her face. *Stay cool and get out.*

Valentine responded with silence. Ennis continued. "Plus, there's no such thing as vampires anyway. They're just a myth. These brothers are crazy, and I'm getting out of here now," Ennis announced, scooting away from him and towards the door.

"I wouldn't do that," Valentine called, arms folded. His face was stony.

Ennis's hand rested on the front door's knob. "Oh?" she replied, pulling the door open.

Valentine stood in his same spot and beamed his cryptic gaze at her. "If you get caught trying to leave during daylight, they'll think you're human and kill you," he explained. "Not to mention, your wound will give you away. You'd better cover that up."

Logic smacked her in the face as she stood half-in and half-out of the house. *Getting caught in daylight equals death now. And my forehead can kill me. This is much riskier than I thought it was. If I get caught...* Why hadn't she thought of that? Maybe because she thought this escape attempt was an all-or-nothing shot. She hadn't planned on getting caught or staying. In any case, she couldn't fail. She had no other plan at this point as all her attempts at assessing her situation were marred by her excessive fatigue. She had a way out now and could only go so much longer without food and proper rest. Shaking her head, she took a hesitant step through the portal.

"I'll also mention the extreme security measures they have in place. Weapons are set up around the house reaching far into the woods." She looked at him through narrow eyes. "Stake guns," he explained. His face echoed old, painful memories. "I don't know how thick the barrier is. Every time I've tried..." He trailed off.

Ennis now looked at him with genuine concern. The brothers had said something about being staked if she tried to leave. Maybe that's what they meant. *This is twisted.* They *are twisted.* However, Valentine didn't seem to be like the brothers. But still, she knew she couldn't trust him. She couldn't trust anyone. Isn't that what she'd been taught throughout her life?

"And you've never been caught during daylight trying to escape?" she questioned. He looked at her with a sadness that barely registered on his body, but she could read it. "And you're human. How come the brothers haven't tried to kill you? Or have they? Aren't they opposed to having other humans around? Having them 'know of the secrets' of vampires?" She said the phrase with added dramatic flair. He looked at her inscrutably. "Why aren't you dead?" she asked seriously.

"Well..." His mouth turned up a little. He pressed his slight smile away and gave her a look to close the door. Ennis stood her ground, still half-in and half-out.

"When I first got here, it was an accident. I wouldn't have even come here had I not accidentally crossed their defenses," he explained in a low voice. He strode forward and stood before her, arms still crossed. "I was passing through the woods when stakes started flying from weapons hidden all over the forest. When I tried to get away, I ended up running straight into the safety of their inner area. My mistake. I wish I would've known." He sighed, looking as if his past had come back to torment him for the millionth time. "It was a miracle I survived getting through the barrier once." Silence overtook the entry hall.

Ennis's brows furrowed. "And then?" she prompted quietly.

"I tried to get back past the barrier, but it seemed I couldn't pull off what I had done getting in. Sadly I was very successful when I got through the first time. Getting out has proven to be much more difficult," he said. His eyes looked far away and dipped down as if he were working something out. He looked up from the floor and back at her. "If you try to leave now, I can guarantee your death. These brothers are psychotic. They might seem normal sometimes, friendly even, but I've been with them for two months now and I still haven't been able to crack their codes," he explained.

Her jaw clenched. She'd walked into a greater trap than she had realized. Not only were these people insane, but they also came with their insane, sick weaponry. *I should've trusted my gut and left when I first arrived.* But still, Ennis knew she hadn't seen any of these alleged weapons. Stake guns? That stuff only happens in movies and cheesy books. *Those don't exist in real life.*

"*But,*" he continued, "if we team up, maybe we both can escape this prison." His eyes were like steel as he awaited her answer. His body was still, deathly still, and powerful.

Thoughts overtook her. *I hardly know you! I don't know all my options at this point, but right now there's an open opportunity to get in my car and leave. There's risk involved in whatever I choose. But I know that my car is outside. I can even see it! So all I need to do is to get out there and drive away. I don't have time to go over all of my possible options. As badly as I want to.*

"I plan on driving out of here. You can come with me if you want," she concluded.

He looked at her curiously. "Drive?"

"Yes, *drive*. My car. I drove here. If those stake guns are real, my car will protect me... to a point. And I can't really trust you, can I? You could be as sick and twisted as those two or even more so," she postulated.

He looked at her with pity. Her hand firmly planted itself on the doorknob again. Obviously, he wasn't coming with her since he remained inside, cloaked. He stared at her, his tense arms dropping to his sides. She closed the door behind her.

Ennis felt a burst of adrenaline as she sprinted to her car, her black trench coat trying to keep up.

Her way was lit by the dawn's light just peeking over the looming trees. She extracted her keys from her pocket, suddenly trying to figure out how Benedict had stolen them before.

She grumbled. Her shaking hands fumbled too long trying to insert the key into the car door. "I can't get nervous," she told herself. Her heart was in her throat. *I can't run like that again.*

With a glance, she saw that Valentine was standing in the now open doorway, again, looking at her with pity. Feeling the lock finally click, she jumped into the car and slammed the key into the ignition. The car's engine let out a churning whir and clicked. "What?" She turned the key again. "No, Jay Jay! Please turn on!" she pleaded, her palms now slick with sweat. She ignored Valentine's frown.

The car refused to come alive no matter how many times she had tried turning the key. All the car did was click incessantly and blast AC in her face. No maintenance lights were on. She looked at the fuel levels, and the tank looked fuller than when she had arrived. Her brows furrowed. Her car was obviously not going to start right now. Her heart pounded, and she felt bile climbing up her throat.

"Okay, okay. But what *can* I do?" she asked. Looking at the front of the house, she saw that Valentine was still watching her escape attempt as he leaned on the doorframe, one hand on his hip. She looked away and shook her head, beginning to assess her options in her car. She took out the car manual from the glove compartment and flipped through it. "Clicking... Not starting..."

After a couple of precious minutes, she flung the manual back into the compartment and sunk into her seat.

Becoming aware of the phone stabbing her side, she hooked up the phone to the charger. Thankfully the phone was turning on. She wondered whether she should charge it now or wait until a time when she needed it more. *If* she were even able to sneak back out here again. Her need to feel safe won out over logic, and she continued to charge it for a few minutes, very aware of the time.

Meanwhile, she rifled through her glove compartment to find anything useful. She emerged with a flashlight. She popped open the trunk, keeping low to the ground as she waddled to the back of her car, and found an emergency blanket, standard jumping cables, and a lone prepackaged survival meal. She grumbled. *I had this the entire time? That was one thing that made me decide to stay!* Her stomach turned at that thought. Surprisingly, she found she wasn't hungry. And that worried her. She grabbed the bag and ripped it open, downing what she supposed was "vegetarian chili."

Within a minute, she could feel her energy levels rising. She hadn't eaten since yesterday. Her car snacks were depleted during her stormy ride yesterday.

Tucking the flashlight under her arm and wrapping the blanket around her, she decided to escape on foot. *I guess I'll see if those stake guns are real.* As hard as she tried to deny their existence, a sickening feeling weighed in the pit of her stomach. But maybe that was the chili.

She cast one more glance back at Valentine, only to discover he was no longer in the doorway.

She walked down the driveway, unable to keep her heart from beating furiously. Valentine's words kept playing in her head about the stakes shooting from all over the place. She'd yet to see anything threatening, which fed her hopes, making her step a little quicker. When she had driven in, nothing had flown out at her. The thought was becoming ridiculous. *Maybe* he's *the mastermind...*

She walked about half a mile down their driveway when it happened. A wooden dagger shot straight across the front of her shin, and she felt it catch her trousers. Her body had stopped in the road before she registered what had happened. And then she began to run.

Something whizzed past her head. A short yell blasted the chilly air. *I can't yell! I can't let them know I've left the house!*

With every couple of steps, stakes flew out from the nebulous colors surrounding her. Her heart was wild now as her symptoms rampaged to life. Nearly fainting right then and there, she knew she couldn't continue to dodge these stakes. This was a suicide mission. Just like Valentine had said... She wondered how she'd gotten so deep into the trap. They were still flying, nicking her trench coat but missing what was most important: her body. But she didn't want to continue to press her miraculous misses. *I need to come up with a better plan!*

Without pause, she turned and darted back towards the house. Again, the stakes assaulted the air around her. She screamed at the unexpected stakes. *But I've already been through this section! Why are there more!* She registered a mechanical whirring sound. Machine *stake guns?* Tears streamed down her face. Stress choked her, causing her breathing to become difficult. Stakes grazed by her skin, tattering her blanket and black shirt as well.

She collapsed onto the ground, heaving with exhaustion and an adrenaline crash. It seemed she had run far enough into their inner circle where the stake guns weren't set to go off. Her heart beat violently, and she tried in vain to catch her breath. It felt as if she was being choked. Her hands latched to her throat, her body struggling for air. The chilly autumn morning air lashed her lungs and her vision nearly went entirely black. The woodsy smell, which would've been welcomed under other circumstances, smelled like death to her. She heaved, but nothing came up. She was still hungry, dehydrated, and every bit exhausted. Her heart wouldn't slow down, and her lungs couldn't keep up. Her panic crescendoed as she passed out.

~

6

Ennis didn't know how long she lay there curled up someways off the driveway. She had had the mental capacity to move out of immediate sight should anyone go along the driveway. She ended up curled up behind a wide oak tree. Feeling lightheaded, she stared downwards, trying to ground herself. Digging her fingers into the rich soil, tears began to leak from her eyes.

Time passed, and she dislodged her phone from her pocket. It was nine in the morning now. Same day. Her body had barely started recovering, but if she stayed out here any longer, she risked falling asleep in the woods for far too long, and the brothers would surely discover her.

"Got to get moving, Ennis." Lifting her heavy, frail, damp body, she leaned against the tree and managed to stand up. "Move," she ordered her body.

It must've rained. Grey clouds were rolling above, and the orange, red, and yellow forest was dark and slick.

Each step felt like picking up a cinder block. And when the house came into sight, she nearly started crying again. But she chided herself. *You can't be comforted by a prison, Ennis.* She cast a longing gaze at her car as she trudged past it. It hit her that her flashlight was gone. *Wonder where I dropped that.* Feeling the weight of her body even more, she crawled up the front steps.

She nearly collapsed opening the door. Breathing was difficult, and she panted before moving again. Her head spun as she turned around to close it. Latching the door gently, she saw a dark figure out of the corner of her eye. Valentine moved forwards. *Does he look... relieved?* He stared at her with a stony expression.

"The car's dead," she said flatly. At that, she let out a laugh, which she stifled with her soiled hand. Somehow it was funny to her. Valentine was anything but amused. "What is it?" she asked, laughter gone. She tasted blood and looked down to see her slightly shredded hands. The cuts were paper-thin. *Must've caught on some bark.*

Without a word, he approached her. But he looked as if he didn't want to move.

Ennis looked at him, confused. "Are you okay?" she asked, seeing his face turn blurry for a second. She blinked hard.

He let out a steady breath. "Are *you* okay?"

"I asked first," she retorted stubbornly. She wanted to sit down but thought for some reason that wasn't the best idea.

He didn't answer her question, and she let out a puff of air. "I could be better," she admitted, sending a clumsy hand through her hair.

"I don't..." she started, looking down and around. She swallowed and then took a deep breath. "I think we should team up."

He studied her.

"Okay." His face was blank.

"Okay... Well... thank you." She closed her eyes and felt herself starting to fall forwards. But she caught herself before she hit his chest. His body tensed, and his eyes remained stony. Shaking her head, a second bout of dizziness hit her. She muted a groan and then stumbled around him, heading to her room. He followed silently behind her.

She dragged her body up the stairs using the railing. The hall felt like miles as she limped to her room. Opening the door, the string fell out, and she huffed. She found the room to be the same way she had left it. A little of her mental tension relaxed. She couldn't exactly explain why, but the idea of those two creeps rifling through her stuff set her on edge. Not that she wanted anyone going through her things, but the brothers doing it seemed worse.

She crumpled onto the bed and pulled up the blankets. She nearly fell asleep right then and there. In fact, she couldn't really recall traveling from the front door to her room. She sensed another presence nearby but couldn't find the will to open her eyes. It was dark and cool in the room, perfect for sleeping. Then she heard her door shut.

~

Ennis's heavy eyes opened. She looked around to see morning light but was met with near-complete darkness. The blankets on her body weighed her down, tempting her to go back to sleep. She felt something jabbing at her side. Feeling at it, she discovered it was her phone and saw that the time was eight at night. Her phone battery was on its deathbed, and she felt a foreboding creep up her spine and nestle in the back of her mind. She hadn't come up with a new plan yet. And since her previous plan had failed, she realized she now had to go through a whole day with the psycho brothers.

Her feet touched the cool wooden floor, and her body ached as if she'd tried to dodge death. Body cracking, she managed to stand up. Her boots sat by the edge of the bed. She huffed to the bathroom, eyelids heavy, and turned on the light, hissing as it scorched her eyes. It was too bright compared to the near-total darkness her room offered. She inspected the bump on her forehead and sighed. It didn't look too bad, a bit red. But if Valentine said it would give her away, she needed to do something about it. Splashing cold water on her face, she looked in the mirror and realized she *did* sort of resemble a vampire. Her dark hair and pale skin were now complemented by tired-looking eyes. She gave a hollow chuckle and then sighed, dragging her aching body into the shower. She flung out her now dry jacket, green shirt, and trousers and replaced them with her dirty, shredded trench coat, black shirt, and trousers. They were caked with mud, and she plopped them into the tub, thinking woefully of her bedding.

She looked around the bathroom and noted her emergency blanket from her car didn't make it back with her. *I guess I'll have to find it eventually.* She shook her head. *And the flashlight.*

"Okay. Survive a shower and then survive a day," she told herself, unclenching the hand that seemed to be permanently stuck to her neck. Her throat felt raw and scratchy.

She'd never been in a life-or-death situation like this before. At least she wasn't drowning or trapped in a burning building. In fact, out of all the life-or-death situations possible, she figured this one was one of the better ones. At least with her situation, she could use her brain, and she had someone else with her. She slapped herself in the face. "No, Ennis. You can't think of him as an ally. I can't even trust him yet. Be cautious, not careless."

She warred with her gut, which told her to trust him, that he was good. She looked down at her stomach, frowning with ancient eyes. "You've been wrong before," she mumbled. *But more often than not you* are *right...*

Continuing to frown, she took a deep breath. *My brain. That's how I'm going to fight.* Perhaps a mental battle against the two brothers would yield her escape.

Ennis stepped into the shower and lathered up using a soap bar she had brought, continuing with the analysis of her situation. *Benedict would be my best bet to work with... He seems fond of me.* She shuddered. Then Saeva entered her mind. With his strong build and predatory behavior, the very thought of him sounded alarm bells. He would be the formidable opponent. Even now, he seemed to be suspicious of her. She'd have to work on convincing him especially that she was a vampire. She hardly doubted that he would kill her right then and there if she were found out to be human. Which... she was. *God, I'm against lying. But... is this okay? Oh, God, please get me out of here alive! Do You have a plan? Of course You do, but could You tell me?* She frowned, not hearing His voice. *Sometime soon then?* Her hopeful face was replaced with distaste as her thoughts turned black again.

Ennis chuckled once more, but only at her ironic situation. A human mistaken for a vampire. A vampire. Gazing down, she noted her feet looked quite red and frowned. Blood was pooling in her feet. *Typical.* She leaned on the wall of the shower but quickly pushed off. *How many others like me have touched this wall? How many other humans have been slaughtered? Were they also thought to be a vampire and tried to play it off?* A shuddery breath escaped her. They mentioned they had one "vampire" before her, but they didn't mention how many humans. Did they murder them on the spot, or did they toy with them a bit before offing them? Feeling sick, she immediately scrubbed the arm that had touched the shower wall and stumbled over the tub's edge.

She inspected her forehead wound in the mirror and sighed. It looked worse from the hot water. She'd need to make sure her hair was on the right side. Thankfully only a penny-sized red circle was left. She didn't wear makeup so there was no use in checking her suitcase for concealer. With halfhearted hope, she searched her bathroom to discover that there were no cubbies or necessitates besides a bar of soap on the sink and one that she didn't use in the tub.

As she pulled on a blood red long-sleeved shirt and soft black trousers, she felt a presence. Peeking into her room, she saw nothing but the welcoming darkness and the faint outline of furniture. Once her eyes adjusted more, she found no one in her room. "Huh..." A slight rapping at her door made her jump back into the bathroom, fists instinctively rising.

"It's me." *The cloaked guy from last nigh—er, morning!* Relaxing a little, she moved for the door but was still unable to get her body's tension to go away. *We're going to be okay, Ennis. He hasn't hurt me.* A voice in her head added *"yet."*

Arriving at the door, she unlocked it. Her brows furrowed slightly. She didn't remember locking it but was thankful it had been. She smirked, thinking that even though she was practically delusional, she still had the sense to lock the door and think of her own safety.

Pulling open the door slightly revealed Valentine, dressed in a white shirt and black vest still. His green and brown eyes looked hard, yet tired as he stepped inside. She closed the door behind him.

"What is it?" she asked.

He turned to look at her, a light she hadn't seen in his eyes. "You didn't suppose we were going to proceed without a plan, did you?"

"No, I guess not." She frowned, perching on the edge of her bed.

He took a seat next to the lightless windows. The velvety green chair held his lithe form. Ennis had to admit that he moved with grace. *Too* much grace. She hadn't admitted it until now, but he was smooth. And she knew very well that that could lead to trouble if he ended up being a bad guy. She gave him an expectant look, arms folded.

"You have to fool them," he stated, fingers steepled.

"Obviously," she replied coolly.

"You have to act like a vampire," he clarified, eyeing her intently.

"That's clear."

"Now, how cooperative should you be?" he asked both of them, and the question hung in the air.

Ennis chewed her lip. "I really don't know. I don't know if any information I give them would align with what they already think they know. Should I just refuse to give any information?"

Valentine sighed and slightly shook his head. "Well... I mean, that *could* work. But you might get hurt. I'm unsure what they'll try to do to you if you refuse. But then again, you might be able to test it out and see how that goes. What sort of vampire punishments they deal you."

"Right... And it wouldn't really hurt me. Unless they try staking me or something." She laughed humorlessly.

"No, they wouldn't kill you. You're too precious to them... *as a vampire.* They wouldn't want to end their potential source of information," he paused, "or give away their bragging rights."

Ennis huffed. "Okay, I'll try and be *uncooperative*. But what if that fails and I have to give them information? What if that information doesn't align with what they think already? There are so many different ideas of what vampires look like and their powers and all that," she grumbled, feeling her head swim. She touched a hand to her red spot on her forehead. She wasn't sure if it was her head or her body that was causing her muddled thinking. Both would do it. He tilted his head. She shook her head. "Sorry, I'm not feeling well," she admitted. Her stomach was empty, reminding her how weak her body could become. *Salt.*

He sighed. "I'm sorry, but they won't tend to you as a human since they think..." He trailed off, looking as if he could see beyond the thick curtains.

"I know. But I need to eat. This—I can't... I have —" She looked at him painfully and then to the floor. "A condition," she finished.

"Would you mind telling me which one?" he asked gently.

"Ones, really," Her eyes darted to the floor again. His look was solemn, and she played with her fingers. "Uh, well, I have postural orthostatic tachycardia syndrome. POTS for short. And on top of that, OCD and anxiety, with just a dash of depression." Her face was sour as she tasted the words. She glanced at his attentive face.

He stared at her, his mouth in a slight frown, but his features soft. "I haven't heard of POTS. What is it like? Something to do with the position and heart rate, but what are the symptoms?" he asked politely.

"Where do I start? It's practically got every symptom in the book. Its main identifier is fainting. I can faint, but I actually haven't ever... Thankfully. My blood doesn't exactly circulate well. My autonomic nervous system is messed up, so I can't regulate unconscious things well like breathing, body temperature, heartbeat, blood pressure, sleep, digestion. It really messes you up. I get brain fog badly too. Like you can't think properly. The blood can't get to my brain well enough sometimes. It's very annoying," she huffed.

He frowned. "I'm sorry you've had to deal with that."

She looked away from his gaze. "Yeah, well, it gets exacerbated by not getting enough sleep, hot or cold environments, not staying hydrated, stress," at that she laughed, "not eating, not getting enough salt, exercising—"

"So running would be an issue."

"Oh yeah. I mean, I can do minimal stuff, but I'm no runner or sports player. Even walking around sometimes gets me symptomatic."

He hummed.

Ennis continued. "Also, anxiety can make it worse. My anxiety and OCD don't really help me in that aspect," she said with an ironic smile.

"I see. So your blood condition... Is that why you're so pale?"

She cleared her throat and laughed a little. "No, I just don't like the sun. My skin is kind of sun-sensitive, and I don't do well in the heat, so I stay clear of it. Not that I really enjoy being in the sun all that much anyways. I mean, it does lift my mood. But sunburn doesn't." Her mouth twisted. "Oh, and my condition makes me have heightened senses. You know, taste, smell, touch, hearing, sun and light sensitivity. And I can feel my heartbeat practically everywhere in my body. Sometimes I can see my heart beat visibly in my chest, but that's normal for me."

Valentine's frown deepened as she continued.

"I think they mistook my cold hands as 'vampire' hands," she added, feeing her palms. He looked at them and then rose from his chair, walking towards her. A dash of adrenaline hit her, and she straightened a little. But he stopped in front of her, reaching out a hand.

"May I?" he requested.

She gingerly offered a hand, keeping a steady look on his eyes, which were firmly affixed to her hands. He took her right hand and squeezed it. His eyes inspected the delicate, veiny, pale skin.

Her eyes widened slightly. *His hands feel as cold as mine! Cold, almost... clammy. Yeah, definitely like mine. I wonder if he has my condition too...*

He let out an unintelligible, thoughtful murmur and returned her hand to the bed. "You scraped up your hands this morning, but that seems to be unnoticeable now. Good." He inspected her hazel eyes. Shifting away from him slightly, she noted his eyes happened to look like her own, but with more green.

"Uneven pupils?" he asked curiously. Blinking and looking away, she nodded.

"Anisocoria. Slightly."

"Natural or causal?" he asked with medical air.

"Natural. I think. I don't remember it being due to an accident if it was," she explained.

"Hmm..."

"Is there something I should know?" Her head was getting foggier under his probing. Or maybe it was just because she was hungry. Or maybe because her life was on the line.

He took a step back and returned to his chair, his hands folded. "No, I find it odd that the brothers believe you are a vampire if they've noted your pupils."

"What do you mean?" she asked, focusing on his gem-like eyes, attempting to avoid the hysteria knocking on her head's door.

"With uneven pupils, you'd think they'd heal if they were due to an accident. But I've never met a vampire with uneven pupils."

"But I'm not—Wait—"

"I know, but I've not met a real one with eyes like yours. Perhaps the brothers will believe it to be something that vampires can have as well if it happened at birth. I mean, it truly might happen. I don't know. I've just not come across it." He tilted his head, brows furrowed.

She looked at him for a second and then laughed. "You mean you believe in vampires too?" She shook her head. "Oh great." Her shoulders sagged as her smile faded. She buried her face into the green quilt, eventually peeking out to see a lunatic.

For the first time, Ennis saw Valentine really smile. His lips turned up into something like a smirk. She had to admit he looked quite handsome with a smile but deadly and dangerous. Definitely dangerous. He looked at her with eyes alight.

"You mean you don't?" he asked, hands steepled again, elbows resting on his dark trousers. His strong, dark brows were lifted.

"No," she replied, trying to keep from insulting the delusional man. "I mean, I've not *met* one before, so I can't truly say that I believe they're real," she explained. *Am I the only sane person in a hundred-mile radius! God created humans. Vampires don't exist.*

"I'm not offended." He chuckled, letting his smile relax. She felt a little weight lift from her chest. "But you've already met one."

The atmosphere felt heavier, darker as his words clung to her ears. Her lightness of heart at having an ally was replaced with some grey mist. She wondered what had happened. *Maybe the lighting shifted?* She thought over his words but came up with nothing. Were the brothers vampires?

"What do you mean?" she asked slowly, her heart jumping into an unwelcome rhythm.

He sat there, very still as he had been, looking at her cautiously, curiously.

"I *mean* that you've already met one," he repeated, looking at the covered window now. But she could see that he was observing her actions even then.

He can't mean... "You?" she asked hollowly. He turned back to her. "I don't think you're..." Her nervous smile fell. She remembered the way he had pinned her wrist to the wall. Why hadn't she noticed his cold hands then? The memory of the touch flooded her. She latched on to her wrist at the thought. And the strength of his grip. "But they

76

don't..." *Why is all this making sense! Vampires don't exist! But... what if they did? God, how do vampires exist?*

Certainly he couldn't be. "You..." she began carefully, an edge now creeping into her voice. She froze, eyes wide on him. Her breathing accelerated.

His body was taut, yet his face was relaxed. He continued to sit very still. "Yes," he replied politely.

Ennis sat very still as well, mirroring Valentine's posture of hands on knees.

She bolted up. "In the name of Jesus Christ, get out, demon!"

He held up his hands, startled. "Whoa, there. I'm not a demon. Quite the contrary. Humans become vampiric through a virus. We're humans, not demons. I understand folklore portrays us as such sometimes, but there are no biblical accounts of demons being physical humanbeings. I am only an infected human."

After some silence and her heart stopped hammering, she produced a hollow, "Oh, right."

"And I don't plan on hurting you," he explained, his eyebrows knit together.

She nodded her head, being nudged in her spirit by the Holy Spirit that this man was, indeed, no demon, nor demonic. "You probably already would've done it if you had wanted to."

"I could have," he said neutrally. She shuddered. "But I didn't." He was right. He hadn't hurt her. Even when he grabbed her wrist, he left no bruise, and she didn't remember any pain, just a flood of anxiety.

"It's a lot to take in," she admitted, feeling her hand clutch her neck. "Sorry I'm not handling this more maturely." She took a pillow and hugged it before deciding that wasn't good enough.

Beginning to pace the room, she raked her hands through her hair, her forehead promising worry lines if she kept up her expression.

At this, Valentine laughed slightly, startling her. But the thick air in the room was fleeing quickly. "What do you mean? You're taking this extraordinarily well."

Ennis could see the humor but unfortunately didn't feel very much like joining in on the fun.

"Don't you want proof?" he asked.

"I take you at your word," she choked out. "I'm sorry to request this, but you're making me very anxious right now," she admitted. She was darting quick side-glances at him as if that would help the information feel less like a cannon ball to her understanding. "Could you just give me some space, please?" she asked as politely as her anxiety would allow.

His face was blank, but Ennis saw his expression fall a little.

"I really am sorry. It's my anxiety. I don't know how to deal... I've never been... This changes everything," she strained. All she could think about was trying not to have a bigger breakdown in front of this man. This... *vampire*. She hadn't really seen a lot of proof, but deep down she knew. Oh, she knew. Her gut was sure. She stopped her furious pacing.

He looked warily at her, eyeing her posture.

"I won't faint if that's what you're thinking." Her words sounded clipped, yet blending together. She sat straight down on the wooden floor where she had been standing. Breathing wasn't easy. She shuddered and tucked her knees up and put her head down, hugging herself. "I just need some time." She shuddered again, feeling the tears take over her eyes like Trojan soldiers. She gave him a quick glance. He was still there.

"Please excuse me for staying," he amended.

Ennis lifted her head and took him in. He looked like a normal man. A lithe, normal, tall, *pale* man. But he was much more than that. She chided herself for not being more accepting of him. In fact, she found him fascinating, but she'd been through too much and this was, unfortunately, the tipping point. *I'm doing well, though, anxiety-wise. I'm surprised I've been able to take this much horror without having many massive panic attacks. Well done, Ennis.* A sigh escaped her, lamenting about how one had to happen now. *Timing could be worse, though.*

She heard a whisper near her.

"Breathe."

She coughed a little but forced herself to take deep breaths.

"Good," he whispered. He was crouched by her side. She then felt a hand on her back, rubbing gently in circles.

The cold of his hand seeped through her soft red long-sleeved shirt. She felt her body start to relax a little, contrary to what her mind was yelling at her.

"It's not j-just you," she choked out. He continued to rub her back. "I m-mean, I feel overwh-whelmed by my sit-uation." Her voice came in hiccups.

He nodded his head. "It makes sense." The silence of the room rang in her ears. "You know, though, you and I are in the same boat," he said thoughtfully.

She looked up at him with a furrowed brow.

"We're both trying to escape from here. These two brothers are..." He paused. "Dangerous."

Ennis shuddered, thinking of what would happen if they were found out. And then thought of the fact that he, a real vampire, wasn't able to leave.

"But you know what?" He leaned in closer to her and said with a slight smile, "So are we."

As he smiled, Ennis noted his fangs. They were there but only in the form of defined canines. They looked sharp, but if she hadn't known who he was, she would've passed them off as just regular, extra-pointy canines.

With a slight revelation, she realized she wasn't afraid to think of the teeth. To think of Valentine. He didn't seem like a vicious, bloodthirsty monster. However, some part of her still told her to be wary. But he didn't really cause her anxiety when she thought of him. Unfortunately, the bit about vampires existing had pushed her over the anxiety cliff.

"I'm glad you're a vampire," she said.

His hand froze on her back. "What?" His voice was breathless.

"It's an advantage to beating them and getting out of here," Ennis explained. His hand remained frozen. She looked up and saw his stunned face. "I don't mean to be insensitive! Wow, I don't even know how you feel about being a vampire! I'm sorry." She mentally chided herself.

"No, it's alright. Don't worry yourself." He gave a little smile. "Well, yes, I suppose it's helpful in terms of speed, strength, and stealth, but there are disadvantages, Ennis. I'm not impervious."

She looked at him questioningly.

"The sunlight. That's something true from folklore. Well, sort of. It won't kill me, per se, but it can give me really bad sunburn depending on the amount of time I'm in it. Sensitive skin, you see. And it practically immobilises any vampire that gets caught out in it for too long. We, then, can't move until we're out of the sun's rays because of the weakness. Usually waiting until night or until time passes for a shadow to reach us. Our bodies just don't tolerate it well. I've never actually figured out why. Maybe our new cells can't tolerate its radiation. But having to welcome us in is a hoax. Same with garlic, coffins, counting, and the like."

"Have you ever been caught out in the sun?" she asked curiously, studying his face. His eyes held a thousand stories.

"More than once," he admitted, looking away. His eyes crinkled.

Ennis found herself wanting to hear the story. *All* his stories. But she quieted her curiosity with no small effort.

"What other disadvantages?" she asked. He removed his hand from her back, clasping it in his other.

"Drinking blood is true too. Unfortunately, I can't live off human food, so I've been doing what little hunting I can in the woods to get enough to survive on when the brothers aren't aware. I could live without blood for a very long time. But sort of like being in the sun too long, I can get extremely weak to the point where I'm practically immobilised." He shifted his gaze towards Ennis's suitcase. "I'm not at my best right now. For the past two months, I've been getting very little between here and the barrier. And in the house." Ennis shuddered at the thought of what he'd caught indoors here. "Animal blood is okay. The most ethical blood source, of course. Humans consume meat. I see us vampires as being carnivores but just not eating the meat." He looked down. "And I hate the idea of feeding off humans. Most of us do. Thankfully, most vampires feed off animals. Only a few vampires make the bad choice of targeting humans, thus penning folklore." He stared at the wall.

She sat enthralled by his words, staring a splinter close by her foot. "That's... That's good I guess that most don't target humans."

"I haven't figured out why they planned the stakes like that yet," Valentine confessed.

"Hmm?" His sudden shift of thought made her turn to look at him. Quickly her eyes found the floor again.

"They are out there about a mile from here. The barrier. It's odd..." He looked to the floor, then moved his gaze towards her. "Stakes are false as well. It's really the blood loss that's dangerous to us. Sun and not enough blood to eat or in our bodies. If we don't have enough blood, we can't heal properly." He looked at his hands. "We can sort of get to a point beyond healing because we're unable to feed. Eventually, we'll turn to dust. Like a normal human. Just... with more awareness. It's a slow death."

Ennis found her hand reaching for his arm. Just as quickly as it happened, she pulled it away, face flushing. "Sorry," she mumbled and crossed her arms. *What am I doing! Don't get attached.* "Anything else that's true? Anything else I should know about?"

"Well, we don't procreate. The only way to make another vampire is through transferring blood and our bite."

"Interesting," Ennis said.

"I'd love to tell you more, but unfortunately I hear the brothers waking up. It is nearly nine now. The sun has set more fully. As you might've pieced together, they've set their bodies to 'vampire time.'"

Ennis felt a sweat break out over her boy. She'd almost forgotten she was in a battle of life and death against two brothers. But now she had an anomaly as a partner, who came with dangers of his own.

~

7

Valentine moved to stand but squatted back down with a slight sigh. Brushing Ennis's hair back from her forehead, he inspected the bump. "Before you go out there, you need to make sure any wounds are hidden. Vampires heal quickly. Also, we have poise and elegance that comes from our athleticism. So try to be graceful." He pulled a small plastic bag out of his pocket. "Use this to cover your forehead. Make sure to have it on at all times and reapply after showering. It's flour and lotion. It should hide your wound somewhat. But be careful not to let them look too closely."

"I'll try," she managed, leaning away from his closeness and gingerly taking the bag. He leaned back and continued to frown, looking deep in thought. Smoothing her hair over the bump on her head, she took a deep breath.

A lump had settled in her throat when she thought of her usual inability to move quickly without getting lightheaded. Standing, he walked over to the bed, gathered the blanket, and placed it over her shoulders.

With great care, she stood, ignoring the black that overtook the corners of her vision. She blinked and hobbled quickly to the bed and sat down to ease the transition of being upright. Blood had pooled in her legs, and she could feel it. He moved into a crouch on the ground before her, his hands clasped between his knees.

He stared at the blanket surrounding her body. "Vampires can't sleep," he noted. His mouth turned down. "I miss dreaming," he said quietly. And she didn't know if those words were meant for her.

A pang of sympathy shot through her. *I don't know what I'd do without my dreams.* She looked away from his intense gaze.

"But what do I tell them? How will my information pair with theirs?" Her fingers found the fabric of the quilt and began to play with it. Valentine stood up from crouching before her.

"Thankfully they don't know much. I've gone through all their books here, and they hardly have anything but the mass collection of online research 'articles' and all of the books on vampires you could imagine."

She ran a hand through her hair. "That's good. I guess..." She knew her face was probably even paler than usual right now. Her stomach lurched and gave a nasty growl. When had she gotten this dizzy as well?

"So really all you need to do is keep to the basics I just told you. Anything beyond that, you can make up as you go along. Just make sure you don't contradict yourself. But try not to give any additional information." He paused his doctor-like instructions and looked at her a little apologetically. "Try not to answer any deep questions. And be yourself personality-wise. Your persona you tried yesterday... Well..." His mouth twitched. "Just stay you."

Nodding, she tried to take full breaths. *I can't do this! I'm going to mess it up! I'm going to get myself killed!*

"Okay, so remember, be elegant in action, but be you. When in doubt, act like me."

"Of course." She mimicked his low, smooth, methodical voice.

He smirked a little. "Not bad. But don't forget smooth movements."

He held out a hand for her, and she took it, standing a little unsteadily. Her stomach growled again, and her head swam. He glided to stand to the side of the door. She raised a brow at him. He smiled a tight, small smile and put a finger over his lips. Then there was a knock at the door.

She looked at Valentine, who gave her a little nod. Inhaling, she stepped to the door and opened it. Benedict stood there, smiling once he saw her, his hand resting on the doorknob. His royal blue vest, white long-sleeve, and grey trousers and shoes looked neat and tidy, very much the opposite of her thoughts. Her heart leapt, and she stuffed down the urge to push Benedict away from the room and slam the door. *Valentine's in here! I can't let Benedict find him!* But *she* couldn't even see him tucked away behind the open door. *Oh, he's clever...*

"Miss Ennis," Benedict started, bowing his head deeply.

"*Just* Ennis," she replied tartly. She always hated it when people added "miss" to her name.

"*Ennis*," he amended with a smile, "we'll be having breakfast downstairs." He opened his hand, gesturing towards the hall. She took a slight breath in and stepped forward, making a conscious effort to glide and not glance at her ally. She pulled the door shut behind her and waited for Benedict to follow behind her path. Heart thumping heavily in her chest, she wondered whether she would be able to make it down to breakfast without passing out. Let alone fool them into thinking she was a vampire for her duration here.

Without speaking, they descended two flights. It suddenly struck her that she'd made an agreement with a vampire. *A real vampire.* Her heartbeat went a little faint.

They turned their way to the dining room. Saeva sat at the head of the table near the fireplace as he had the night before, looking poised and reading a modern-looking book in one hand, the other hand rested on his chin. He had on the same brown leather jacket over a white shirt. When he saw them approaching, he gave a wide, predatory smile, and set the book down.

"Ennis," he purred.

Without reply, Ennis sat down at the other head of the table once again. The table was empty this time, the hardwood glistening faintly in the flickering light radiating from the roaring fireplace behind Saeva. He took a sip from a lone cup of coffee and set it down.

"Today we'll begin gathering *accurate*, general vampiric information from you," Saeva announced, staring at her over steepled fingers.

Ennis kept her face blank. She hoped she could skirt around the issue tonight. *Tonight.* She felt a yawn creep up on her but fended it off with sheer will. A peek out the window revealed a velvet night. Her sleep schedule was already messed up, but her body was adamant that she ought to be asleep right now, despite waking not long ago. *Stress, probably.* The thought of the bump on her forehead spiked more adrenaline into her system. She hoped her hair was covering it well. *So far it doesn't seem like they've noticed my wound... or my uneven pupils.*

"After breakfast, you'll meet me and Benedict in the library. I want to posit what info we've already gathered against yours to validate its accuracy," he went on casually.

To validate my *accuracy or their info's accuracy?* She wanted the swirling sensation in her stomach to stop, but she knew that this was anything but a casual conversation. The way Saeva held his cup of coffee too tightly gave away his true mood. He was eager. Maybe angry? But she knew for certain he was serious. And dangerous.

Despite herself, her stomach lurched with hunger, about to start rumbling. *Do vampires' stomachs grumble?*

She said hastily, "You already know I'm not agreeing to help you, right?"

Saeva hid behind a cyan-colored book cover, and only his brown hair and eyes peeked over it. His pale, blue-grey eyes crinkled, but not in a good way. Her heart hammered. He suddenly looked like a cartoon villain as he was set against a background of flames. "Of *coooooourse*. But we don't want to have to force it from—"

"I'm here!" Benedict announced cheerily, rushing in with two silver platters. For some reason, his chest looked a little abnormal, almost boxy, and she hadn't noticed it before.

Her heart lightened when she saw a silver vest come into view. Valentine followed behind him, carrying two trays as well. She mentally sighed a breath of relief. *At least I won't be facing the brothers alone.* Immediately, another part of her mind snapped at her. *Don't trust so easily! Especially right now! One wrong move and you're dead. You hear me? Dead! Now's not the time to be trusting someone else to save you. You have to save yourself! You're responsible for your own survival!* Her eyes darted away from Valentine's serious expression, which was focused on the table.

Benedict set down a tray in front of her and his own spot. Valentine placed Saeva's platter down swiftly and then took a seat next to Benedict.

Benedict sat next to Ennis, eagerly looking from her platter to her face and back again.

"It's AB positive. The rarest! We don't have much of it. I know we said we only had B, but I found some of this this morning!" He smiled giddily. With the smallest hesitation, she lifted the lid slightly.

What does he mean by "found"? Ennis tried not to breathe in the smell of iron that permeated the air. Her stomach lurched, but not out of hunger. Replacing the lid, she tried to look blank instead of the stony expression she knew she was wearing. She glanced at Valentine, who looked like he was intensely studying his own meal of eggs, bacon, and toast.

"What's wrong?" Saeva asked, a strange lilt to his voice. It was the first time she noticed him looking the slightest bit concerned. *Is it mock concern?*

Ennis's mind raced, and her palms became slick.

"I... never drink with an audience," she announced regally, yet slowly. She wanted to grit her teeth. *Too slow, Ennis!* "I require that the blood be brought to me at my room from now on. Leave it outside the door." *What kind of act was that! And you're not supposed to act, remember?*

Saeva's mouth fell open a little, and Benedict squirmed. Valentine pushed his eggs around and took a bite, not making eye contact with her.

"And AB positive? I don't drink that. Get me animal blood. Cow's blood. That's what I've been drinking. I like the taste. And it's leaner than *human* blood." She said the last sentence with displayed distaste as if she could taste the nastiness of human blood. She didn't know if cow's blood was leaner, but she thought it sounded like a legitimate reason. She then noted she was probably giving too much detail. *I should've just said cow's blood!*

Saeva smirked. "As you wish, miss."

"Just *Ennis*," she ground out.

Benedict looked dejected but returned to normal as he revealed his breakfast of toast and eggs. He pulled out a pair of reading glasses from the inside of his jacket, put them on, and started eating.

Everyone was a few bites in, except for Ennis. She fixed her eyes on the glistening hardwood. And it was quiet. Not even the elements decided to break the quiet. She then supposed it had stopped raining some point this afternoon. Benedict squirmed in his seat again slightly before interrupting the silence.

"Okay, I'm sorry, Ennis, but I just can't wait any longer! I want to know about vampires! The *accurate* facts." He pulled a full-sized notepad from his jacket and extracted a pen from an inner pocket of his royal blue vest.

Ennis shifted in her seat, eyeing the notepad. She looked over at Saeva, who studied her with a slight, cruel smile. He looked as if he was mocking her. But he also looked scrutinizing. If Ennis were in different circumstances, she might even think he was romantically interested in her, but she knew better. *What's this man thinking?*

Valentine had a slightly interested expression on his face as he waited for the questions and answers. She thought that if he were here, then maybe he'd be able to help her if she got caught up in her words. It was safer to have the interrogation here with Valentine than in the library without him. Where she was supposed to be going later...

"I told you, I'm not going to help you," Ennis stated.

Benedict's smile disappeared. "What?"

Valentine's look turned into mild surprised. She sat there silently, staring at Saeva. She didn't know what it was about him that irked her so much. Besides his murderous intent towards her.

Benedict turned an angry glare towards Saeva. "What did you say to her?"

Her attention was locked on Saeva. His cruel smile reached his eyes. "I didn't say anything, Brother. She's just not going to cooperate... *yet*," he added pointedly.

Benedict looked thoroughly put out. And furious. He clenched his pen, and the paper cried. He then turned to Ennis, a longing in his eyes. "*Please*, Ennis, you're the first real resident vampire we've ever had. You have to help us. Cure us of our incessant need for knowledge!" he begged, all rage gone.

Ennis looked questioningly at Benedict, withholding a laugh that stemmed from his ridiculousness and her growing insanity. "I won't," she said somberly. "Your books could get out to the world one day. I don't trust the three of you to not let secrets out."

"So... if you trust us, you'll help us?" Benedict asked.

Ennis thought quickly. "Well... No. Even well-intentioned people can slip up. You could always be tortured for the information. It's not safe to trust others." Saeva continued to stare at her, something moving in his eyes.

Ennis wanted to clear her throat, yell, jump out the window. "The information's not something I'm able to share with you."

"Is that because you aren't liable to share the information or because you just don't want to?" Saeva asked, lacing his fingers and letting his chin rest on them.

Ennis remained silent, staring poisonously at him.

At that moment, Valentine stood up. "Please excuse me. I need to get to my housework." He picked up his tray, and Saeva nodded to him, hardly interested. Saeva's gaze stayed glued to Ennis, a slight smile on his lips.

With a nod, Valentine exited to the kitchen, and Ennis felt fear take a vicious stroll down her throat and take up residence in her stomach. She swallowed thickly. *Oh no.*

"I think we should take this to the library," Saeva said, stretching his back like a cat as he stood, hands pressed forwards. "And you *will* be staying with us," he commanded.

"I will not." Ennis seethed behind a controlled demeanor.

"If you don't want to get garlicked, then I suggest you come with us," Saeva shot back. Ennis froze at the threat. Not that it would hurt her, and she actually liked garlic, but they were already going to try threatening her. At least this was a threat she could handle.

Benedict stood up, looking unconformable. "Well, Brother, don't be too hasty now. We don't want to give her a bad impression of us."

Yeah, a little too late, buddy!

Ennis stood up. She was eager to leave the stifling room, but not so to create a new one. The brothers motioned for her to walk before them. With an air of loathing, she begrudgingly took the silent cue.

It suddenly occurred to her they had hardly eaten anything on their plates. *Maybe they already ate?*

As they walked towards the library, nearing the stairs, a loud thwack echoed through the grey hall. Ennis whipped around to see Benedict on the floor, his face mashed into the ground. She halted, eyes wide, looking at the man. Stooping down, Saeva took him by the elbow.

"Come on, Brother. You're too clumsy. You'll get yourself killed one of these days." Saeva sighed exasperatedly.

"I'm not going to die from a fall," Benedict said, wiping off his knees. But then, a slow tapping noise began. She looked down and saw a small puddle of red. Saeva eyed Ennis, holding his brother's shoulder with one hand.

Benedict chuckled, pinching his nose. "Ah, would you look at that... bloody nose. I don't think it's broken, though," he said, feeling at the bone with his other hand. He looked at the floor and sighed. His eyes caught Ennis's stare as he looked up. "Oh, Ennis! I'm so sorry!" She turned her head away, her face strained.

"Not tonight," she stated tightly and bolted up the stairs away from a confused man holding his nose and a cryptic man holding his brother. Before she leapt up the stairs, she thought she saw the corner of Saeva's mouth tug up slightly.

8

Ennis slowed to a halt as she reached the front of her door.

It was open.

A jolt buzzed down her spine. "I left this closed," she whispered, nerves rocketing. She pushed it open the rest of the way with a light jab as if the door would bite her. It opened silently as usual. Stepping through, she closed the door, looking around. *I know Valentine came out of the room later. Did he carelessly leave the door open? Continuity!*

"Benedict followed me down, and I made sure he didn't turn back around," she mumbled to herself. "And Saeva was waiting—"

A dark figure appeared in the corner of her eye, and her heart nestled in her throat. Before she could scream, a placating gesture came from a figure. She could tell they had pale skin and were wearing a silver vest. Only the bathroom's dim overhead light illuminated the unifying grey of her room.

She clutched a hand over her heart, grabbing a fist of clothing. Adrenaline coursed through her, and she tried to slow down her breathing, taking a knee.

With his arms out as if approaching a wild dog, Valentine moved slowly towards her. "Sorry, I didn't mean to scare you," he said quietly. His eyes were trained on her. "I thought the open door would cue you that I was in here. I would've closed if the brothers walked by."

She breathed deeply, consciously loosening her grip on her red shirt. "It's okay. What're you doing here?" She had regained something akin to a normal voice now. "Won't they get suspicious? Think we're up to something?"

Recoiling, he walked towards the wide, blocked out windows. "We need to search in the morning." He pulled back the curtains, and a steady stream of moonlight floated through the glass, making his face even paler. Ennis noted his cheekbones looked good in the moonlight.

She blinked. "What?" Her vision darkened as she took a step, but she shook it off and stepped to the window as well.

"I think if we can get the password to the computer, we can turn off the guns in the woods."

Ennis shook her head. "What computer?"

He drew back the curtains even farther, enough so that Ennis was now illuminated in moonlight too. "The one near the kitchen. It's in a closet. Very locked up."

"Can't we jimmy the lock?"

"The lock isn't the problem, it's the password to access the computer. I've not found it in my time here. I was hoping with a fresh perspective," he glanced at her, "we could find it and escape."

She bit her lip. "A computer? I thought they didn't have recent technology. They use typewriters, and I've not seen an outlet here to save my life."

Valentine let out a breath. "Yes, well, this is their one exception." He turned to her. "Unless you count kitchen appliances," he added.

"Then there's—"

"No outlet, actually. They have things wired into the walls. I'm no electrician, and if I start fiddling, they'll notice. I'm guessing you're not an electrician either?" he asked.

She shook her head with a slight smile. "Not currently."

The corner of his mouth crept up a little. "Ahh, good one."

You might joke now, but you're in a serious situation. Ennis's smile fell, and the gloom of her situation sunk in heavily. She huffed and looked out the window. Multicolored trees were being whiplashed by invisible strands. Orange leaves swirled around the window before smacking into the pane and falling to the ground. She frowned. *If I weren't in a life-or-death situation and my world hadn't been shattered, I might actually enjoy this.*

She turned to him, her face blank. "We'll start searching at dawn. But I'll need to sleep at some point. I don't know how many excuses I can come up with to avoid answering their questions. The bloody nose thing was helpful though." She cast a glance towards her closed door.

Valentine's expression remained stony, still soaking up the moonlight. His eyes were focused on something far beyond the windowpane. "I don't think it was an accident," he said coldly.

Ennis surveyed him. "What do you mean?"

He cast a small glance at her, his face sour. "Saeva. Watch out for him. I think he's suspicious of you."

Ennis sighed with a groan, ruffling her short, dark hair. "I already figured."

He let the curtain fall. "And keep this window blocked. We don't want the brothers spying on you or using the excuse of their daily run around the house to 'accidentally see you through the window.'"

Ennis's eyes widened, and her mouth fell open a little. "What!"

"And I've searched your room for hidden cameras and devices and found nothing. Perhaps they don't want to anger you. But unless you show some more aggression, they might start testing your boundaries even more. Be careful. You're in a grave situation."

Her stomach heaved, growling like a beast locked in a cage. She felt a sweat break out over her body, and she knew she wasn't in a good place physically. She was weak. And getting weaker.

Valentine lifted a brow. "Right." He swept away towards the bathroom.

The bathroom light was a weak substitute for the moonlight's absence. He reemerged carrying a silver tray and set it on her bed.

Her eyes widened. "Is that your breakfast?" she rejoiced, lifting the lid. The platter held some rather cold and rubbery-looking eggs and slightly moist toast. Bacon was crumbled all over. On the side, there was a can. She picked it up with a furrowed brow, studying it. Her eyes widened, and she felt as if she could cry. "Soup!" The tomato soup label dully shined in the bathroom's light.

"You said salt is good for you, right?"

"Yes, thank you! This could be a lifesaver," she said, clinging to the can.

"You can eat that now. There are plenty more cans of soup in the kitchen. I'd hide some away in my room, but if they find them only now, they might get suspicious. I'll bring you them periodically from the kitchen." He crossed his arms, standing next to her bed.

"You know, the garlic threat wasn't too bad," he commented thoughtfully after a moment of silence.

She titled her head, mouth full of bacon crumbles. "Maybe not. It doesn't hurt you though, right?"

"No, it doesn't," he replied. "I suspect the other vampire here before me kept up the trope to save himself." He huffed a little with his eyes glistening. "Smart."

Her exhausted body whined for her to eat something saltier. Looking down at the soup, she moved to open the top tab, only to find that there wasn't one. She grabbed the fork from the tray and made to stab at the can in her desperation. Before she could make the first dent, Valentine caught her wrist.

"Whoa, hold on." He grabbed the can, turned around, and after a split second, the can had two small holes in it.

Ennis remembered when her mom had used cans of evaporated milk for baking, she'd puncture two holes in the top with a rusty piece of metal that was always magnetized to the refrigerator. A hole to let out liquid, and one to let in air.

He handed her the can. Without thinking about it much, she started chugging the cold soup.

"This reminds me of college," she admitted, catching her breath.

He squinted his eyes and tilted his head.

"Cold soup. I had it regularly when I didn't feel like going to the cafeteria."

He looked to the left as she finished the rest of the cold liquid.

She finally lowered the can, and a bit of the soup dripped down the side of her mouth.

Valentine smirked. Her brows furrowed at him, and she wiped at her mouth with the back of her hand.

"What?"

"Nothing," he answered, shaking his head. "I'll bring you your next meal. You should eat the rest of that too if you can, even though it's cold. Sorry." He gestured to the tray. "You haven't eaten in quite some time, so eat slowly, okay? Your body doesn't need the shock, and you've already had soup."

He fluttered to the door, and she jumped up. "Where are you going?" she blurted.

He bowed slightly. "I have to clean the house or else they'll get suspicious. I can do it relatively quickly, of course. Oh, and keep to the plan if they do end up coming for you tonight. I'd love to stay here and theorise, but I do need to make an appearance. They see me around the house during the night occasionally. But don't worry, I'll be back before morning and hopefully before they come for you," he assured her. He opened the door, and with a nod goodbye, shut it without another word.

Ennis stared blankly at the closed door, looked at her empty soup tin, and tossed the can into her bathroom trashcan. Then she headed back to the bed, feeling dazed.

The door opened, and a gasp shot through her. Valentine walked back in, using a placating gesture. "Sorry, I just forgot your bedding. I'll wash it." She stood up, stunned, holding the tray as he stripped the bed.

He was back out the door in a matter of seconds.

~

9

Hours dragged by, and Ennis still hadn't heard the footsteps she dreaded would come. There had been no sign of the brothers. She didn't hear any movement. There was no rain pounding on her window either like yesterday. Just silence and the storm of her thoughts.

The absence of Valentine's presence was palpable as she felt an air of loneliness sink in. He'd been back about an hour later after his disappearance with washed bedding. It took him hardly a minute to make the bed, and then he was gone. *Jesus, give me strength. I know I'm not alone with You, but it kind of feels like it right now.* She took a deep breath.

Picking up her phone, she saw it had finally given up its last remaining life. Tears pricked at her eyes, and she looked at the book in her lap, which was filled with writing in the margins.

During her hours alone, she had rummaged through her suitcase, found a pen, and filled in the journal she'd brought with her. But since she was on her last few pages upon arriving, she'd run out. Thankfully she'd brought a book with her for her weekend away. She was working on scribbling down everything that had happened since leaving her house. She had found it fruitless trying to come up with another escape plan as she had already exhausted all possible methods of escape she could think of. None of them gave her a plan that didn't involve a substantial threat to her life. Or sanity. Tapping her finger, she focused on writing out the twisted situation she was now living in. With hours on her hands and nothing she could really do but wait, it was torture.

She put her pen down and heaved a sigh, catching a stray tear with her finger. "I hate waiting." Her anxiety had been persistently knocking in the back of her mind, but she kept telling it to go away, even though it always came right back.

The knocking grew audible.

Ennis stood up quickly, becoming disoriented as the room spun. *I've gone mad!* She steadied herself using the green chair.

No, that was real *knocking.* She turned to her door, her eyes wide. Hastily, she stuffed the book into her suitcase and tiptoed to the door. Her lightheadedness made it hard to think. *Present, be present, Ennis!* She tugged at the door to reveal a ruffled-looking Saeva. Her throat tried to choke her. *It had to be him...*

"What?" she asked stiffly.

"It's dinner time," he replied, his hands folded behind his back.

"I won't eat with you. Bring my dinner to me," she insisted and began pulling the door shut. Saeva stuck his shoe in the closing gap. She reeled back as if he were a striking snake. His blue eyes looked like fire, and there was a slight smile on his lips.

"No," he stated, his hands held ominously at his sides now. He gave her a hard look, his smile gone. "You'll eat with *us*." He advanced through the doorway and a couple of steps into her room.

Ennis's heart was racing. "*No.*" She smoothly advanced towards him. "And if you know what's good for you, I suggest you leave me until tomorrow." She watched his face turn sardonic. "I can still smell your brother's blood on you. It...

101

lingers," she told him, walking around his statuesque body. She opened the door. "Leave before I get angry." She gave him a pointed look. He smirked, letting his head fall forwards, then swept out the open door.

He turned around and walked backwards as he began down the hallway, his palms open wide. "I hope you're prepared to be with us tomorrow. We're eager to get proper information... And we didn't get much today." He continued walking backwards, keeping eye contact with her, before facing frontwards as he descended the stairs. Ennis huffed and then disappeared behind her door.

As soon as she closed it, her body started shaking. *What am I going to do?* Her heart pounded, and she wrapped her arms around herself. It was maddening that she couldn't tell time here now that her phone was dead. *Why can't it be dawn already! Then I can search for a way out of this crazy house! Time passes so slowly here!* Perhaps it was because she was dreading any interaction with the brothers. She still hadn't had her first real "session" with them yet either.

Her stomach dropped at the thought of tomorrow, and she desperately prayed for their escape to happen today. In reality, she knew that even if they found the codes in the morning, they probably wouldn't be able to escape right away. And that would cost them another day at the "Psycho Killers' Inn."

An engine rumbled outside, and her pulse shot higher. She darted to the window, pulling back the black curtains. A nondescript white delivery truck was splashing through the mud towards the back of the house. "What is that?" she said breathlessly. After a split moment of wonder, she found herself

102

dashing out her door and down the hall to find a window that would show her the back of the house. Her socked feet slipped on the hall's wood as she tried to move as fast as she could while being quiet.

Someways down, she noted the adjacent hall was old and full of doors just like her hallway. Her hands itched to test the many doorknobs, but she put aside her curiosity about the new part of the house. She turned her attention to the window near the end of her hall.

Pushing back the dark curtains, she crept up to the side of the window. The delivery truck's headlights beamed rays that lit up the swirling leaves in the darkness. Some woman with dirty blond hair, a denim coat, and overalls was talking to Saeva. *Why does Saeva look so tired? And who is she?* Saeva stood with his arms akimbo and nodded. The woman walked him to the back of the truck, and they started unloading boxes.

Ennis's eyes narrowed, trying to get a better look at the deliveries. They were nondescript, standard cardboard boxes. And Ennis hated that.

"They're delivering food," a man's voice said in her ear. She leapt, turning around, and threw a punch at the voice.

Benedict raised his hands into a placating gesture as he moved aside smoothy, missing her small fist. "Whoa there, tiger. I didn't mean to scare you," he said, looking apologetic. But she could see he was analyzing her all the same.

"What are you doing?" she breathed, trying not to clutch at her heart.

He laughed a little. "You know, I should be asking *you* that." He looked at her knowingly, like a disapproving parent.

Ennis hoped her face wasn't red. *Do vampires blush?* She hastily turned around to examine the truck again. *You can't get anxious now! Not in front of him! Relax...*

"Food, huh?" she mumbled. Her brain was churning. *Who delivers at this time of day?*

"Yes," he said, putting a hand on her shoulder and pulling her gently away from the window. She stiffened and beat his hand away.

"Do not touch me," she growled.

He lifted his hands once again in surrender. "Okay. But you need to get back to your room," he countered with a frown.

Without a word, Ennis slid around him. She could feel his eyes on her as she walked back up the hallway. The itching crawled back into her hands as she passed closed doors. Swallowing her curiosity, she continued her walk.

She heard a door click somewhere in the hall behind her and wanted to turn around. It was maddening to not know which door he had closed. She felt her legs freeze, temptation beckoning her. After a split second, she reversed back and peered around the corner. Her heart sputtered as she locked eyes with Benedict, who stood with his arms crossed, smirking in the middle of the hall.

"So curious, aren't you?" His eyes were dark, but his smirk light. She took that as her cue to get out of there and quickened her way up the hall again. *Of course!*

"Do be mindful that you aren't to roam on your own. I thought that was obvious. But perhaps you aren't good at picking up what's right in front of you," she heard his voice call as her feet continued. "Starting tomorrow, you'll be with us all night."

"Wonderful," Ennis muttered. *Room confinement.*

After passing a couple more doors, she clicked her own shut. It was nearing dawn, and exhaustion slammed into her. She fell back onto the bed. "Oh no... I can't get tired. Not now." She rubbed her aching forehead. "Sleep, go away." She closed her eyes and sighed.

When she opened her eyes, she saw hazel ones staring down at her from above.

"Ahh!" Ennis quickly covered her mouth. Valentine winced, looking towards the door. "Sorry," she whispered. "But please don't do that! What about Benedict! Did he hear? He's just down the hall!"

Valentine's brow quirked. "Benedict? The brothers are both asleep." He stood a step away from the bed and looked patiently at her, his hands folded behind his back. "You were asleep when I arrived. I'm sorry for scaring you. Are you ready?" he asked, gesturing towards the door.

"I was asleep?" She jumped a little at the noise the bed gave off as she shifted to a sitting position. "I don't remember falling asleep."

"Yes, sleep can do that to you." His eyes looked far away. "I think..." She looked at him strangely. *What does that mean?*

"Let's go. They've just gone to bed about a half hour ago. Oh, and your cape." He pointed to the black mass crumpled beside the chair.

She'd nearly forgotten about the cloak. She'd also forgotten that during some point in her hours alone she'd flung it from her bathroom because the door was getting caught up in it.

"You should wear it in case they find us. Vampires usually wear covering during morning hours. Even indoors. It's safer for us that way."

She stooped to pick up the cloak and fastened the soft button at her throat. She saw a flash of movement, heard a metallic crunching sound, and then saw Valentine holding a can of soup out to her.

"Come, drink this," he said, guiding them both towards the hall. Before he opened the door, he turned around. She stopped abruptly, nearly sloshing her soup.

"What's wrong?" she asked. A tentative hand of his moved to hover near her forehead. She stumbled back a little.

"May I?" he asked.

Her brow furrowed, and he gently pushed her hair back.

"I didn't want to touch you earlier whilst you slept. But I wanted to check on your forehead." She silently watched his glistening eyes probe her bruise, her shoulders losing their tension.

"Your bruise is getting better." He hummed and let her dark hair fall back into place. "Don't forget to use the paste."

After recovering the paste from her bathroom, she smudged some on her forehead. Then they walked out into the hall.

She took a sip of the salty soup. "Thanks for the soup, Valentine," she whispered, and he nodded in response.

She peered up at him as he led them down two flights. "Is it okay if I call you Val? No, that doesn't fit..." She squinted her eyes, and he glanced back at her. He smiled a little and faced forwards, tilting his head down. "How about V?"

"Just V?" he asked curiously.

"Just V."

"I like it. People usually call me something else."
He fell silent, and she wanted to clear her throat.

"I like it," she heard him say quietly again, but not to her. She felt a smile creep up onto her face.

"So, what are we looking for?" she whispered.

"Anything that might be a clue for codes. Or *the* codes. That would do too."

Ennis felt her palms grow slick in anticipation of the task before her. So many rooms.

"I thought we'd start at the bottom of the house and work our way up." He walked to the reception area of the house and started plucking books from tables and looking through crusty potted plants.

Ennis watched him and then began pulling books from a bookcase in the reception hall one at a time.

"What exactly are we looking for, though?" she called, tapping her finger against the ancient tome.

"Well, I'm not sure. Some sort of cypher, maybe. Some code. It might be letters, written numbers, visuals. Look for patterns, writing, anything the least bit suspicious," his voice said.

She let out a puff of air. "We could be here forever going off of just that."

"If I had a better lead, I'd tell you."

She hadn't stopped staring at the dusty volume in her hands, but her eyes were unfocused. "Right."

~

Ennis was working through her 24th book when she heard a light thud. She peered around the open wall into the living room, but Valentine was analysing a red book he was holding, flipping furiously through it.

"What was that?" she asked.

107

"I checked underneath the couch," he replied, not looking up from the flying pages.

"Oh," she said and disappeared behind the divide again. She placed the book back on the shelf with a sigh. "I've found nothing," she whispered.

"Did you think it would be easy?" She jumped at the voice that spoke beside her. "They might not even have anything written down or any clues at all," he explained, eyeing through another book.

"What do you mean?" Her knuckles were white as she held a miniature book she'd found on the shelf.

"They're clever. Probably cleverer than you've yet realised. Even if they don't seem so. They've thought things through. They're thorough." He looked around the ceiling's edges. "They don't have cameras. I suppose they don't want to anger the resident vampires with invasion of privacy. Or have photographic evidence that can be stolen. A fact they have correct is that vampires are prone to liking their privacy. But they still have security measures in place." He looked at her meaningfully. "The stake fence." She paled. "They may let you think you have some freedom, yet they keep their prey inside. So I doubt they'd be writing passwords on a notepad in their drawer if they were going to keep secrets and victims in one place," he explained gravely.

She hummed. "Well... I guess we just have to keep looking and hope they're prone to forgetfulness. This almost seems like an impossible task," she concluded flatly. Replacing her miniature book, she reached for the next book in line. He turned heel and swept away. Whipping her head up, she said, "Hey, what about the delivery—"

"Truck? I've considered that. But at least one brother does a thorough check of the truck before she takes off. And they stay behind to watch it go." Valentine stood in front of her.

"But can't you just hijack the truck and leave? The stakes are turned off so the truck can get through, right?" she said, her face beaming.

"It's not that simple. Somehow the brothers must have a way of turning the defenses off and on when the woman comes and goes. But I don't know how that's done. From the five times it's happened so far during my 'stay' here, I haven't figured out how they do that, though, and whether the computer actually is causal or just correlated. One watches and makes sure the woman leaves like normal, and one is at the computer. But I could never catch the computer being abandoned whilst unlocked. I assume whatever they do for her they did for you when you first drove in. They might have cameras on the outside. Or sensors. I've thought that there might be a transmitter on the delivery vehicle that turns off the sensors as it goes by. I could never slip through alongside the truck though. I tried twice, and the sensors went off on me but not on the car."

"Does that mean they don't trust you if they watch that carefully? They think you'll use the truck or the computer to escape? And I don't get why you'd get shot at but not the vehicle," she asked anxiously, trying to figure out this puzzle.

"I suppose they don't trust me to an extent, and they switch up the delivery times so the pattern is unpredictable. I don't understand the guns' targeting system either. I thought maybe it only targeted lifeforms, but the woman would've gotten shot if that were true, even in her metal car. Metal doesn't seem to be the answer though. I've tried that theory." He placed a hand over his mouth.

Checking the floor, she sat down, sweeping her cape to the side, taking the heavy book with her. "What about tossing something into the stakes, getting rid of all the ammunition in the magazines?"

"I tried that. Small things don't set it off. Otherwise rocks would've been my ticket out of here. And a tree would be a bit too obvious. The sensors seem to detect bodies, maybe something in human and animal body compositions. But again, I don't know how the woman makes it through."

"Hmm..." Her eyes darted around the room. "Have you ever suggested leaving your 'position'?" she asked, using air quotes.

"Well, I'm a 'human,' and they don't like other humans knowing about vampires and what they're doing. They blatantly told me they'd kill me if I tried to leave and that even if I somehow killed them, the barrier would take care of me. I don't want to kill anyone, so I've left them alive. I don't need them dead to escape." He paused and became interested in his hands. After a moment, he snapped out of it.

"I've already tried escaping how I entered. And we both know how that goes." He looked at her meaningfully. Looking down, she bit her lip. "So I thought it better to try and figure out another way to leave. Which means figuring out the computer. That's the only real option I've come up with."

"But," she started slowly. Valentine drew a little closer to her, crouching down. "What if we..." Her eyes fell away from his.

"Tortured it out of them?" he finished gently. Ennis looked a little ashamed.

110

His face was solemn. "I've already thought that over as well. I could've done that a long time ago, but I don't think they'd talk. They won't be that easy to crack. No matter the pain. They're insane and serious about what they do. Obnoxiously so."

"But we haven't tried yet," she countered.

Valentine looked at her firmly. "I told you, I've already thought of it."

"Yes, but what if they *do* end up talking?"

His mouth set into a frown.

"And if they don't, we'd just end up..." Her voice fell. "But, technically, this is a battle of life and death so it'd be okay legally, right?" She fumbled her fingers into her shirt, clutching at the soft fabric. "But I still don't want to kill or harm anyone," she added hastily.

"And if they die, so would the codes if no clues existed elsewhere."

"True." She shoved her nose into the dusty volume and sneezed, then looked up again. "Armor?"

"Armour?" he asked, raising a brow.

"Yes! What about building something we could wear that would stop the stakes from penetrating though? Or build something from metal? Maybe that would stop the sensors!" she asked excitedly.

"The force would be too strong. It'd go right through anything we could make here in a limited amount of time," Valentine explained solemnly. "Even the refrigerator."

"Right..." she said, feeling her heart sink. She looked up, eyeing him. He eyed her back cautiously. "Your skin doesn't happen to be really durable, does it?"

Valentine blinked and then smirked. "No."

"Right. You would've already escaped." She once again took to the book.

"And then I wouldn't have met you," he said from around the corner. Looking up from her book, she found him gone. A slight palpitation hit her chest, and she thumped it before returning to her book.

~

Hours passed thumbing through books, shaking cushions, checking the living room, kitchen, dining room, reception room, hallway, the sitting room, the laundry room, and what seemed like a giant spare room in the back of the house.

"Nothing," Ennis concluded, setting a painting of a vase with white roses back in place.

Valentine reappeared by her side, examining the painting that hung on the wall in the hall. She yawned as she turned to him. He was transfixed.

"What is it?" she asked, rubbing her eyes.

"What's this?" He pointed to the signature at the bottom left corner.

Squinting at the painting, her mouth dipped into a frown. "S.C.?"

"Yes..." He hummed. "I've not noticed this before. This is one of Saeva's."

Her brows lifted. "Paintings? He paints?"

He bit his lip for a moment. "Yes, there's a painting studio on the fourth floor. I've smelled paint from that room. It's one of the only rooms I've not been in. Saeva keeps the key on him at all times. And their last name is Cerrit, by the way." He leaned in and smelled the painting. "The same paint, I'd say." He paused in thought. "Yes, it's the same."

"Does that mean there are clues in the painting studio?" she asked. *How would Valentine know? A foolish question.* Her vision went fuzzy. She slapped her face and shook her head. *No sleeping, Ennis! Come on!*

Valentine looked at her out of the corner of his eye. "Not exactly, but it is a place I haven't searched. I haven't gotten hold of the key. I've also not been in their bedrooms, which are located on the fourth floor on the west side. Those are other likely places they'd be hiding clues or codes. They always keep their doors locked, never letting me clean them. I've unsuccessfully tried picking the locks. Not a strong suit of mine. It's not my usual first means of entry," he stated vaguely.

Ennis peered at his face of concentration. "Well... I can give it a shot. I just need some paperclips. I've never tried it, but I've seen tutorials." Another yawn overtook her.

His brows knit together. "I'll keep that in mind. We'll search those rooms once our other options are exhausted or we have a clear opening. It's safer that way." He corralled her down the hall, and she turned around, lifting an eyebrow. "We can plan to search more tomorrow morning. Unfortunately, you need to sleep. You won't be able to outwit them if you're out of it." Giving her a look of pity, he nudged her forward.

She tried to open her eyes wider, but they wanted to stay shut. "As much as I want to continue searching right now, I think you're right." She sighed, stopping at the nearest window, and drew back the curtains to reveal an afternoon's blue sky. "It looks like I might have a few hours of sleep. Will you continue searching?" she asked, yawning again.

"Yes. Go on now. Sleep, Ennis," he said, gesturing to the steps. He walked beside her as they made their way back to her room. Opening the large wooden door for her, he then followed her in. He made some quick movements about the room that she couldn't quite catch and then was at the door. "Goodnight," he said quietly.

"Goodnight, V," she replied, and he pulled the door shut.

10

A rapping on the door woke Ennis up. Her body felt shuddery as if it were running on ethanol. "Oh no," she moaned, falling back onto the soft mattress. "I can't do this... I haven't slept enough." Her body felt sluggish as she pulled herself out of bed, nearly hitting the floor. Steadying herself on the nearby nightstand, she crouched for a few seconds before trying to walk to the door. She opened it to find Benedict, who wore a sweet look, hands behind his back.

"Aww... Not a dusk person?" His white shirt and brown tweed jacket rustled as he bent his body sideways.

"What?" she asked gruffly.

"And your night voice is so cute!" he added. She shot him a foul look. He brightened. "I have something for you! I hope I didn't make you too hungry yesterday." He tapped his nose and whipped out something from behind his back. Even though her eyes were having trouble focusing, she could tell what it was. A tall glass of red.

Blood.

Her face drained of color, which, when she thought about it, might be a good thing. She snagged the glass and slammed the door on the eager face.

"I'll be waiting out here," she heard his muffled voice say through the locked door.

Gritting her teeth, she spun wildly around the room. Her mind felt fuzzy, and she couldn't get her brain to work properly. Unsure of what to do with the glass, she tiptoed to the bathroom and dumped the liquid down the drain. Black took over half her vision, and she slowed to a halt before shuffling to the door, panting. The darkness receded slightly, and with a breath, she opened the door. Benedict's face looked expectant, and she shoved the empty glass at him.

"I wish you'd let me watch," he said, almost pouting. His eyes were full of something Ennis couldn't quite place. But whatever it was, she didn't like it.

"No. I drink alone," she stated. "And I'm not ready yet." She slammed the door, seeing him nod slightly before his image disappeared behind solid mahogany.

He waited for her to reemerge, wearing the same red long-sleeve, but her face looked slightly damp now. She begrudgingly followed as he guided her down a flight of steps. Right into the library.

"So this is where you'll be spending the night!" he announced cheerily, closing the door behind the two of them. "You'll be under our supervision from now on. I'm sorry, but since you aren't cooperating... Oh, and I apologize that Saeva threatened you with garlic. He's so impolite sometimes. But he has different ways of handling things than I do." He winked at her. Avoiding his gaze, her eyes went to his face. She saw a little red spot on the bridge of his nose. *Right. I guess he did fall on his face. I wonder if it's broken.* Her mind processed for a moment. *Ohhh, that's what he meant earlier.* His words from their current conversation finally reached her consciousness, and he was still flashing her a cheesy grin. *Maybe Saeva's way is better...*

Ennis turned away, examining the books with a well-hidden look of disgust.

"So, you're free to read anything you want. Well, not *anything*. I mean, you can't read *my* book I'm working on now," he explained, waving his hands about the library. "But I might ask you about some details later to help me!" he added excitedly.

She found a purple conversation couch somewhere on the other side of the room, far away from the desk he worked at *and him*, and conked out.

~

"So vampires do sleep?" Benedict asked. He was hovering over her, looking at her curiously.

"Ahh! Stop that!" she shouted, jumping up, now perched on the couch like a frightened bird. "Yes, we *sleep*. If we're bored enough, we can sleep. Just like—kind of like humans."

"So you only sleep when—"

"In addition to daily sleep," she added impatiently.

A sly, yet curious look overtook his face. "Ahh..."

When he straightened up, she caught sight of white pages behind his back. Following her focus, he hid the pages from her sight and caught her gaze. She suddenly felt like she'd been caught reading someone's diary. He smirked, trying to catch her eye contact again that dodged anywhere but his direction. "Well, now that you're awake— Can I just say how fascinating it is watching you sleep?"

"No," Ennis snarled. *I can't fall asleep around them again... Big mistake, Ennis.* Another knot of anxiety wrapped around her stomach. *I can't sleep around*

117

them. If I do, they might catch on that I'm human and murder me. If I don't sleep, my body will eventually kill me. The stress rolled over her in waves. *How long can I keep sane?*

"Well, now that you're awake, I was going to ask you to read over this since I know you're not one to answer rounds of questions. You can do this instead. You only have to correct our factual errors. Much less intrusive than questions, right?" He held out the manuscript to her, taking a seat beside her on the couch. With a smile, he plopped the manuscript in her lap. He looked at her, the pages, and then her again.

She stared at the papers in her hands. "Uh..." *What is* Nomen Ignotum? *What a weird title... "Name" something?* The wad of papers was bound together by thick red thread. *Looks handmade.*

Clearing her throat, she looked back up to find him still staring at her in excitement. "Do you mind not sitting next to me? You're making me uncomfortable." She scooted as far as her armrest would allow.

"Oh! I'm so sorry!" He shot up from the conversation couch and moved to stand behind her.

"That's not any better," she grumbled.

Benedict frowned, stepping back. "Well then... Hmm... Why don't I just go back to work over there, and you can read that over here?" He hastened somewhere she couldn't see and returned, thrusting a red pen at her. "Here." He wiggled it in front of her. "For corrections."

She looked at the pen and then up at him. Huffing a little with a smile, he placed the pen on top of the manuscript in her lap. He swept off, and she heard him sit down somewhere on the other side of the library. She frowned, lifting a flap of pages, her eyes finding a random paragraph.

"'You want me to join you?'

Yvette lowered her book and took a sip from a coffee cup. 'That's what I said, Danny.'

Standing, she crossed her arms and stared at the man. 'What's it going to be? You'll die either way. But what impact will you make? The war is on, lovey, and you've got to choose a side.'"

Ennis frowned. *What is this stuff? What war? What setting is—You know what, I don't want to know.* She gazed at the shelves surrounding her. She'd hoped to get time to check the library for clues. *Since he said I'm free to read almost anything, I doubt there are clues in here. But maybe that's to not make me suspicious of the library. Should I be suspicious?* She sighed. *Looks like I'll have to wait until morning to check this place.* If she couldn't sleep or search, what could she do? Nag? Sleep in the bathroom? But she paused and raised her eyebrows. *Or better yet...*

"Benedict?" she called softly.

Benedict, sitting at his desk, looked up from another manuscript and at her. Round tan glasses rimmed his vivid green eyes. "What is it, Ennis?" he asked, almost as if he were frightened.

Turning around, she sniffed. "I won't fix your manuscript. I told you I'm not going to work with you." She set the bound papers ceremoniously on the seat beside her.

"You won't—" A plastic cup of paperclips smashed on the ground, sending the wires sprawling across the hardwood. Jumping, she whipped her head to see a very startled Benedict standing with frigid limbs.

It took him a second to begin functioning again. "Whoa!" Crouching down, he began picking them up one by one. "Sorry about that. I didn't mean to startle you. I can be so clumsy... As you already know." He looked up and tapped his nose, wincing. "Saev always says I need to be more careful." He gazed at her as he picked up the paperclips, making her heart leap. She didn't understand his look, and her eyes darted to the shelves.

Within a minute, he'd collected all the clips and set them back on his desk. Fidgeting, he chewed his lip. "But... can't you look over it, please? The manuscript?"

Blinking for a second, she turned around and faced away from him. "No."

Taking a tiny step closer towards her, he wrung his hands. "What if... what if I gave you extra blood?"

She turned back around, facing away from him, but hesitated. If she *were* a vampire, then maybe that'd be a good deal. "Hmm..."

His brows raised, a hopeful smile on his face. "No."

He frowned, walking towards her. She felt his presence behind her and picked up the pages. His voice whispered in her ear. "Not even if—"

She jumped up and flung the manuscript at him. After a second, her vision blackened, and she caught herself on a tall, nearby island shelf. She blinked rapidly, praying it would soon pass. Her heart was hammering against her ribcage. She had pushed herself too much. But then again, she really didn't have a choice. *If I sleep here, Benedict might try to do some tests or something.* She couldn't let herself be vulnerable.

He rushed to her side, throwing an arm under her elbow. "Are you alright!"

"I'm fine," she snapped, yanking her elbow back. He latched an arm around her waist.

"No, here. Come sit down," he said.

"No, I said I'm fine!" she snapped again. Her head was throbbing. *But I really should lie down, or I'm going to pass out and have some explaining to do...* Benedict led her over to the couch again and eased her down.

"You need blood, don't you?" he whispered in a rush, his brows knit together. When his eyes probed her forehead, his hand came up near her hair, and, in a panic, she swatted it away. *Not the forehead!*

"No," she replied shortly.

"Yes, you do. You have the classic symptoms. You're paler than usual and sleeping more and nearly keeling over! You *need* blood, Ennis."

"No, I don't" she retorted, gripping at his claw around her side. "And get off!" she snarled.

He shook his head and pulled open his brown, tweed jacket, taking out a sharp golden letter opener.

"What are—No! Benedict, don't do that!" Ennis reached for the metal knife, but he was too fast, slicing it purposefully across his wrist.

She winced in pain at the sight and nearly fainted again.

"Drink it," he urged, shoving his wrist under her nose, blood dripping down the front of her red shirt.

"No!" She wriggled to the side, clamping a hand over her mouth and fell off the couch onto her hands and knees. She uncoordinately made her way to the door. Her body felt jerky, and she tried to focus her eyes on her escape portal. "Get that cleaned up, Benedict. And I won't tell you again," she murmured through lightheadedness. "So stop tempting me to drink your blood. I *don't want it*." She got her hand around the doorknob and felt a hand clasp around her wrist at the same time.

"You're delusional," he remarked, his eyes sad. "Ennis, you'll die. I don't want you to!"

"I won't die. That's not how it works!" she exclaimed wearily, wrenching away her wrist.

"What?" he asked, stunned.

Whoops. She sighed in agitation. "I'm going to my room."

His eyes were wide. "Ennis, you're supposed to be under supervision all day," he breathed.

Glaring at him, she yanked open the door. "I'm going." She stumbled her way towards the flight of stairs. She heard him say in a sing-songy voice, "Consequences," to her. His single word echoed through her mind. *What does that mean?* Her foot struck a step instead of stepping on it, and she clattered against the wall. *Valentine said to be agile. Ha...*

She heard Benedict call after her again. She thought she heard him say, "I'll check on you periodically!" Releasing a growl, she climbed the stairs, feeling like screaming, stomping, or crying. She thought maybe all three. But she didn't do any of them. She just wanted to get out of this snare.

~

Ennis awoke from a dreamless sleep. *Where am I? Why is it so dark?* The darkness was complete. Then her physical exhaustion slammed into her. "Oh..."

After sitting up cautiously, she chuckled. Considering that she would've been stuck with

Benedict in the library for the rest of the day, the stunt he pulled excused her—sort of—from that, and she was finally able to sleep. However, she didn't get to glean the library for clues. She frowned but remembered that she'd be searching with V tonight.

I wonder if Benedict checked on me like he said he would. She blinked, searching the darkness for her suitcase and then the door. *I hope not.*

"Be calm," she heard a voice say quietly from somewhere in front of her. She felt her heart speed up. A scream was nearing the back of her throat. "It's me." Something about the voice told her she wasn't in any real danger. Her eyes couldn't make out a figure. Someone turned on the round lamp that loomed over the headboard.

"V." She let out a held breath.

"Ennis," he said softly, taking a seat on the edge of her bed a little ways away from her. He wore his silvery vest again. *I wonder if he brought any clothes with him...* She bit her lip. *He was caught in the woods, Ennis. He really didn't* plan *on coming here. Obviously.*

She groaned, rubbing her eyes. "What time is it?" Considering her voice, she thought she must've been out for quite a while.

"It's not quite dinner time," he explained. He rose up from the bed and walked towards the door.

Ennis felt a flood of panic. "You're leaving?"

"Not yet."

She thought she heard a smile in his voice. He crouched down and returned to the bed, setting down a silver tray. She hadn't noticed it near the door.

"Breakfast *and* lunch," he told her, lifting off the cover.

Ennis saw a cold bowl of what looked like porridge and some sort of ham sandwich. She eagerly grabbed for the sandwich, but Valentine replaced the lid without a sound.

Retracting her hand, her eyes widened. He frowned. "Sorry, but you should wash up first," he said quietly. She looked at her hands and saw traces of blood on them. She felt a chill go down her spine. Her eyes traveled down and saw drips of blood splattered down her shirt. "Oh no, Valentine, I'm sorry!" She rushed to the bathroom, keeping her distance from him. "I completely forgot about the mess," she lamented. "I didn't realize how much of his blood got on me. I was too busy thinking of escape." She frowned.

A strained, noncommittal noise from Valentine came as a reply. She sighed agitatedly at herself. She hadn't brought an extra set of clothes to change into. She quickly ran out and dragged her suitcase into the bathroom like a lion hauling a carcass into a cave.

"I'll be right out! Let me get cleaned up."

She ripped her shirt off, which had the brunt of the blood on it. When her vision went black, she slowed down. *Oh yeah, right. Sick.* She said goodbye to the red long-sleeve and stuffed it into the small trash bin on the floor. She tied it closed and put it in the farthest corner of the medium-sized bathroom. "Okay..." She looked down and saw that her soft black trousers were unscathed. She frowned. "...No chances." Untying the bag, she tossed the trousers in too. She could smell the blood herself and wondered how bad it must've been for Valentine. He had seemed strained now that she thought about it. "Ugh."

She hopped in the shower, turned the water cold, and, after as good a scrubbing as her POTS would allow without passing out, she was confident that she'd gotten all traces of Benedict's blood off her. Just in case, she gave her hands another thorough scrubbing until they turned red.

She got out, toweled off, and yanked on a blue long-sleeve with another pair of soft black trousers. She opened the door gingerly with pruny fingers.

Valentine was gone.

Ennis's heart dropped. She sunk into the green chair near the window and pulled back the curtain. She doubted the brothers would be spying tonight.

The moon was sliding just above the treeline, shining through shadowy branches licked by the winds. The dark grass below shimmered as if it had just rained. She huffed and twisted the curtain to hang open a little. "This is a disaster," she whispered to herself. Her heart had been feeling strange since she had driven down their driveway, and she wondered how much more of this she could physically take. Her body wasn't even fit to work part-time at her desk job, which, thankfully, only required her to physically go into work occasionally. Usually she just worked from home.

She frowned, wondering if anyone was looking for her. Ami knew that she was supposed to be at the family reunion. How many days had it been? Two? Three? She'd lost count. Time seemed to morph here. Her mind felt like it had been knocked out of place and she was living in a dream. Tears slipped down her cheeks at her surreal situation. But she couldn't deny all of it was actually happening to her. *Vampires are real.* She shook her head at the thought. So many questions plagued her. *God, would you please explain?*

She was trapped here with two very dangerous brothers. And she had to put on the performance of her life to stay alive. She hadn't been in such a stressful situation before and felt it sapping her energy. It was too much. Too much stress. Too much at stake. Too much hopelessness. She couldn't cope. She jumped up and returned the curtains to their original position, plunging the room into a grim grey. The single incandescent lamp above the headboard shadowed the room with melding grey and blacks. She swallowed thickly, tears still sliding down. And she didn't know how to stop them.

She held her face in her hands, sobbing. "God, I can't do this. Please, help me. I can't handle this. I'm going to die here."

She heard a soft Voice in her mind say, *No, you will not.*

"How, God? I don't know what to do. What do You want me to do? What am I supposed to do?"

Silence.

Ennis sobered up a little. "Okay, Lord. But please let me know what I need to do." She stood, wadded up some toilet paper, and wiped her snotty nose on it. "I still don't know if this is classified as sinning or not." Taking a shuddery breath, she squared her shoulders.

"Okay, Ennis... We're going to get out of this. Somehow. We have to continue playing the part or we'll—" Her heart thundered. "No... We play the part, V and I find the codes, then we're free," she said, trying to console her morbid inner voice, her arms wrapped tightly around herself. "Right... Free." The word tasted strange. She took a deep breath and stroked her arm. "Now you need to eat. You need energy." She plunked down on the

126

mattress—the bedding now gone—and started chewing through the sandwich. She didn't feel hungry, and she knew that wasn't a good sign. Despite it all, she plowed on valiantly.

After she was through with the sandwich, she took a few bites of the cold porridge but stopped when her emotions resurfaced, causing her throat to clog in addition to the claggy substance. She crawled back into the chair.

Ennis wept. She didn't know how long she did, but, oh, how she wept. And she ended up crying herself to sleep in a very uncomfortable position.

~

She awoke to her neck audibly cracking as her head whipped towards the door. "Who's there?" She sensed a presence.

"It's me," Valentine's voice said quietly through the door. She stood up slowly, took some effort to loosen her stiff joints, and padded to the door.

"Hi."

"Hi. Are you ready?" he asked stiffly. He had his black cape on again, with his black vest and slacks, and a white long-sleeved dress shirt underneath. There was a mound of bedding in his arms.

Looking at something over her shoulder, he stepped around her.

"Yes." She grabbed her black cloak from the floor. He quickly made the bed in the seconds it took her to put on and latch her cape.

She looked up at him and saw he had the tray in hand.

He nodded tensely at her as they exited her room and into the hall. Her brows furrowed as she tiptoed down the stairs behind him. *He looks paler*

127

than normal. And what's with this mood? But she couldn't tell if his pale was normal, perhaps intensified due to the black clothing he wore instead of his silver vest. She tried to think back to when she first saw him in his black best. Was it yesterday?

She frowned. "Are you o—"

Valentine held up a hand. A second later, Ennis heard someone walking above them.

She shot him a concerned look, but he didn't glance back. Instead, he froze on the stairwell, one hand raised, the other carrying the tray. Turning his head halfway in her direction, he put a finger to his lips, finally meeting her eyes.

After another heart palpitation, he waved them onwards.

She realized that he didn't make any sound as he walked. She wondered if he could defy gravity since he hadn't set off one creak on the ancient wooden floors, whereas she felt she might as well have been setting off firecrackers in the house. *I don't know how the virus could defy gravity... Doesn't make sense...*

He passed the second floor and descended to the ground floor. She looked back as the second floor disappeared. Her brows grew close together. They entered the kitchen, and he quickly took care of the dishes faster than she could watch.

"In here," he said, appearing before a door in the nook of the kitchen.

"What's this?" she asked. Her hand instinctively gravitated towards the round doorknob.

"The computer room where they keep the security system."

Ennis pressed an ear to the door, and a whirring noise became evident. She tried the knob. "Locked."

With a numb look, he gestured her aside. "Yes." He took his pale, slender fingers and gripped the edges of the hinge pins and plucked them out soundlessly. Gripping the side of the hinge, he slipped the door out of its frame and set it against the wall. "This is one of only two doors in this house that have enough room in the wall to slide the door out."

"Whoa..." she murmured. The computer sat atop a lonely, dusty desk. It looked *ancient*. The kind that took up half a desk's width with its monitor. Its decrepit cream-colored siding looked like a single tap would break it. "Eerie." On the blue screen, a prompt for the password glowed. There was no hint at what the password's length should be. "Have you tried entering anything?"

"Once," he explained. "It didn't end well. Three wrong entries and it sets off an alarm. I was gone before they came, thankfully. I happened to secure my alibi by racing upstairs to dust the library. I overheard them talking together later, blaming it on a blip in the system." He rested his shoulder against the doorframe and closed his eyes. "Thank You, Lord, technology is fallible."

Her fingers wanted to try every possible combination she could think of, but she knew it'd be pointless and could even move up their death sentences. Well... *her* death. She wondered what V's fate would be if they found out the truth about him. Her heart pounded violently, and she retracted her hands from near the keyboard.

Stepping away, she cleared her throat. "Okay, well, let's see what we can find then." He nodded and replaced the door's hinges.

In a split moment, he was sweeping off towards the hall. She felt stunned at his sudden disappearance. *What is up with him today?*

She felt guilt combined with dread as she tried to keep up, taking the steps two at a time. *Why do I feel guilty?* As she followed after him, her brain spun through various potential reasons, but she didn't settle on any one theory. *This is great for the OCD. OCD... right. Stop thinking about this, Ennis.*

He'd started searching in the first room on the second floor, which happened to be a sitting room. He flipped through books, lifted furniture, and was completely silent whilst doing so, except for the soft whirring of pages. And his back was always towards her.

She huffed, crossed to the right side of the hall, and came to the door directly across from the room he was searching in. She had expected it to be locked but found easy access to a room that housed a grey pool table with a few grey pool cues on the wall. There were multiple chairs and tables in this room and a small bookshelf in the corner too, along with a stocked grey bar on the side. "Huh... They must really like grey." The floor had dull grey carpeting.

She walked a few paces into the room and then glanced down, lifting a foot. *This carpet is not soft... Wait... Not carpet. Dust.* A layer of dust had dulled the room's hardwood flooring. She looked around. *This room seems like it's not been touched for years.* She felt panic starting to rise. "Oh no... What if they notice my footprints!" She looked back through the open door and saw Valentine just leaving his searched room. She figured he must've known this room and would've said something if it were a bad idea to go in. Were all the other rooms here covered in chunky dust bunnies? Wasn't Valentine supposed to be cleaning the house? She took a deep breath and immediately regretted it, feeling the dust attack her lungs. She coughed gently into her elbow, trying to muffle the noise. Her eyes watered, and she tugged her shirt over her airway, coughing more violently.

Walking closer to the pool table, she saw the dusty pool balls racked. *How are they even supposed to play pool with these? You can't tell if they're solid or striped.* She leaned in a little closer. "Oh... They're not grey... That's dust." Scrunching her nose, she moved on to inspecting the cues and even tried to make out a foot pattern on the floor from whoever had been there last. But the dust wasn't quite thick enough. She laughed to herself. *Seems like Valentine has been doing a* lot *of cleaning around here.*

She studied the curtains in the room as well. Black, like most of the others.

After investigating the chairs and tables, inspecting the bar, and checking the bookcase, she'd come up empty. No patterns. No clues.

She closed the door behind her and moved to the next room. This one was a bedroom, and she lifted her eyebrows at the eye-searing orange décor. "Hideous..."

"Vintage," Valentine noted quietly from somewhere in the hall. Ennis felt a little irritated. Now *he decides to talk?*

"Valentine," she called quietly.

"Yes?" he asked, still somewhere in the hall.

"Would you please come in here a minute?"

131

His face was blank as he rounded the corner. "What?"

She walked up closer to him, and her brows knit together. "Are you okay? You've been off tonight." Her irritation had vanished.

He truly looked at her for the first time this morning and told her firmly, "Don't worry too much, just next time when you're delivered blood, save it. Okay?" He looked pained.

A wave of confusion stunned her. He made to leave, but her hand shot out and latched on to his wrist. "I can't help *but* worry about you, V. I'll do it, but I don't understand what's wrong with you now. Did I do something wrong?"

He sighed. His icy skin leeched the little warmth her own held. "You didn't do anything wrong. I should've asked before. It's just getting a little tough around others when I'm this hungry." He turned back to look at her again. "So please save it for me." He gave her a weary, tight smile.

Her mouth hung open slightly, and her eyes were wide. "*Oh...*" He tried to leave, and she tightened her grip. "I will. But V," she called. He sighed and without looking back, took a step. She held on, being dragged along behind him. "V, wait. Please," she said softly. She wanted to cry but firmly held back her tears.

He froze, then slowly turned his head to look at her, peering down upon her. He grasped her wrist and held it in the air. His eyes looked unfathomable. She tried to not to let the sudden increase of heart rate affect her, but her breathing quickened against her will.

"Ennis," he said softly, "don't tempt me." And with that, he vanished. She, left breathless and

unsteady, thought she heard the slight muffle of
furniture being set down in the next room over.

~

Ennis searched the hideous orange bedroom
and four more like it. "When Benedict said he liked
books, he wasn't kidding," she whispered to herself
as she snapped closed the last book on the shelf in
front of her. Valentine knocked on the room's
door. She turned and saw him vanish into the hall.
With a heavy sigh, she replaced the book and
followed him. They both made their way to the
final room on the second floor. The library.

She felt her body start to shudder. "Not again,"
she whispered to herself, panting. *Shake it off, Enn.*
He opened the solid wooden door.

He began studying the many bookcases in the
room. There were ones against the walls and some
that were freestanding in the middle. She made her
way to the purple couch and took a quick nap.

~

After another hour passed, Ennis finally broke
the silence. "Any patterns?" She stood up from her
inspection of a small book table, stretching her
tired, heavy limbs.

"Not yet," Valentine called. "Although..." He
plucked a book from the shelf in front of him.
"The books on this shelf do happen to be ordered
from oldest to newest, not by title or last name." He
peered at the book with eyebrows lifted. "I've never
noticed this before," he murmured to himself.

She walked over to meet him. "That's weird." Everything these brothers did set off a choppy feeling in her stomach.

He replaced the book. "Yes, well, they are strange people."

Rubbing her eyes, she glanced around for a clock. *None in here. In fact... I don't think there are any clocks in this house. Weird.* She yawned, turning back to him. "No notations in any of them?"

"In some of them." He plucked another volume from a high shelf to the left.

"Really?" Ennis trod over to the right and opened a book. Flipping through it revealed minute scribbling in the margins. "But these are just reference notes and ramblings of crazy people." She looked closely at one. "'Fish may cause indigestion with vampires. But can they really eat food?' This is a load of garbage."

"Fish does cause indigestion."

She lifted her eyebrows. "Really?"

With a smirk, he replaced another book. "Not really."

"I mean, they think you can only drink blood. But by reading this note, do they think you eat human food too?" she asked curiously.

He shrugged a shoulder. "I suppose. They might've been fooled by some accounts of vampires eating human food. We only live off of blood, unfortunately. We can eat normal food, but it doesn't do anything for us."

"Huh..." Since the book seemed to hold no more than nonsensical ramblings, she put it back.

~

Another hour slowly melted away by rummaging through racks upon racks of books. Ennis inspected the brothers' desks, which were piled high with untidy mounds of notes and scrap paper. Benedict's typewriter was enormous, and she didn't dare touch it to hear the sentimental chink sound, although she was tempted. Investigating the desks contents, she saw Benedict's wireframe reading glasses lying on top of a red book, and she plucked them off and tried them on. She smiled a little. "I guess he just likes the look." They didn't have a prescription and were simply glass. She inspected the brown rims before placing them back on the book.

She continued inspecting the desk, shifting her head sideways to get different perspectives. Spotting a little drawer on the inner side of the desk, she hummed. "What's this?" It wouldn't budge. She stood up and found a letter opener on the desk. She suppressed a shudder as she clasped the golden metal, shoving memories of Benedict's act from her mind. Stooping down, she popped the drawer open with it, her arms shaking. Inside was a leather binder labeled *CONFIRMED* that was stuffed with typed and handwritten notes.

"Hey, V? Come look at this," she called in wonder, skimming the detailed, yet untidy black scrawl the well-worn pages held. "This, here." She showed him the last page of the notes. He stood a few steps behind her.

"Yes, I see... Interesting. So they've added new additions of what they've learned from you in red." His mouth curled. "How fitting." He peered at it. "'Cow blood is leaner than human blood.' I'm not sure that's correct." He sounded amused.

"I thought it made sense at the time. Give me a break. I'm not an..." She blinked blankly.

He observed her pondering face.

"Incon—emp—inpro—Improv master! I'm not an improv master. I failed that audition." She took a deep breath, catching his concerned look. "Wow, that was... Never mind."

His mouth turned down. "Are you alright?"

Waving a shaky hand at him, she sighed. "Another symptom of POTS. Word blanking. Fun times. I'm okay. Just tired." She looked down. *I'm not really okay, but in a way I am.*

He was frowning as his eyes saw the shake of her hands. She tightened her one hand on the binder and slipped her free hand out of view.

"Should we call it a night? Or day, I suppose."

She shook her head. "No, not when we just found this notebook."

He hummed, looking deep in thought. His eyes returned to the script, and he huffed. "And... 'Sleep when bored'?" he asked sarcastically.

Her eyes darted away. "Yeah, uh... I fell asleep in the library when Benedict was supposed to be watching me," she said, gritting her teeth. She took a nearby book and inspected it very, very closely.

"Huh." He flipped through a few more pages. "Well, I see they haven't made any other advancements from the time I got here until you showed up, besides those two. And one about blood smell lingering." He gave a thoughtful hum, thumbed over a section she couldn't see, and then handed the binder to her. "That's a good sign."

Putting down her book, she looked through the *CONFIRMED* pages again and sighed, her shoulders sagging. "So you've seen this before?"

He nodded. "I found it whilst *cleaning.*"

"What do you do exactly? I mean, with the dust in this place you could build a sandcastle. You can't actually be cleaning, right?" she said absentmindedly. Then her head shot up from reading the binder. "Oh! Or—or do you actually clean? I'm so sorry! I didn't mean to—"

A deep chuckle echoed through the room. "Most of the rooms they tell me to leave alone. Hence the sandcastle material. I do other normal housekeeping duties. They don't let me go outside, though. Or at least, they don't *allow* me to."

"So is all the stuff they think true actually true?"

His mouth skewed. "They don't know much, considering a lot of what's in that binder is speculation. Common theories that have evidence going for their validity. I would've told you about it earlier so you could align what they know to what you say. But their *confirmations* are basic and not necessarily true. They do think vampires are strong though... I should have mentioned that earlier. Sorry. I assumed you already knew because of your interactions and conversations with the brothers."

She nodded. After a moment, her heart darkened again just like the sky was doing outside. "V... I don't feel any closer to getting out of here."

"Don't you?" He looked at her seriously. "But we are. We're eliminating potential possibilities. Eventually, we'll come to a solution. Process of elimination, my dear."

"Like... torturing them?" she said, her voice quavering. Her hand instinctively wrapped around her stomach, holding it tightly. She wandered a little closer towards him and the door. An uneasy feeling had settled over her.

"Well..." Valentine sighed, slowly stepping towards Saeva's desk. "Let's hope we find a way out of here that doesn't involve torture. Then we can send over some heavy reinforcements to deal with them." She looked over to see Valentine's face grow taut, his hands bracing against the desk.

Eyes widening, she began to close the distance between them. "What is it?"

He raised his hand. "Please keep your distance. I—I really don't want to do anything foolish," he said bitterly.

Why didn't I save the blood earlier? Ugh! "V, you need blood," she lamented, clenching her fists. However, after a second, she unclenched them and added softly, "Don't be foolish."

"Foolish?" he chuckled. "I'm not daft. You're the daft one, Ennis."

"What!" she retorted.

He smiled but regained his composure. "You're offering yourself to me when you yourself have a blood condition. You need all the blood you can get, Ennis, and more. You're already in bad physical shape. You should probably be bound to bed right now." He moved closer to her.

"Ennis." He sighed. "Thank you for your desire to help. But truly, I *will* be fine. Just like you'll be fine. Vampires don't die from blood starvation," he told her. "We just... sort of lose all energy. Sort of like what happens when we get caught in the sun. We become extremely weak, but we don't die. I mean... It'd be different if we lost a lot of blood, but that's not the case. We don't die from starvation alone."

A gust of wind howled against the window. A draft filled the place, slightly shifting the black curtains, admitting a sliver of weak sunlight behind Valentine.

"So please just save what blood you're given. That'll be enough for me," he said, wearing a slightly sad smile.

She sighed. "Okay... But if you really need it..." She gave him a meaningful look.

Valentine smiled a little more. "Thank you, Ennis." Then his face turned grave. "But please never offer yourself to a vampire. Ever."

Her heart hammered, but she said nothing. Turning, he glided towards the exit.

Her eyes caught the sliver of light in his path, and she gasped. "Watch out!" she cried, lunging to quell the stream of sun.

He turned to see a faint ray of sunshine to his left him. "Ah." Before she even made it to the window, he was there putting his hand slowly into the sunlight. "Just watch."

Ennis inhaled sharply and rushed to his side. "V! No!" But his hand was perfectly normal in the sun. Perfectly pale. Perfectly unburnt. He let his hand hover between him and Ennis. Her hand shot up but stopped, and she eyed him timidly. He nodded, allowing her to inspect his. It felt cold and clammy as usual. Brow furrowing, she searched his eyes.

He pulled his hand from her and stepped away, looking towards the door, his face strained. "I think we ought to wrap up our library excursion. You need some more sleep. Did you forget when I told you we don't die in the sun? Remember, folklore is very wrong."

"Momentarily. I guess... it's just ingrained in my mind." Rubbing her face, she sighed. "Yeah. I need sleep." She felt a nasty wave of exhaustion roll over her. She dragged herself forwards, feeling weight in her limbs as if drenched once again in the cold rainwater from the first night. She shuffled through the library door, and Valentine followed close behind a few seconds later.

They walked to the third floor, and she suddenly stopped. "Valentine, where's your room?"

"I'm on the third floor as well but on the other side of the house," he replied quietly.

"Huh... I mean... it's good to know in case anything happens."

With a nod, he bowed ever so slightly. "Of course. I should've told you earlier anyways. Sleep well, Ennis."

"Goodnight, V."

She closed her door. Then crawled straight into bed.

~

Ennis awoke to the sound of steady rain. She blinked in the darkness, straining to see any hint of light behind her curtains. Even time seemed twisted here. She groaned, rolled out of the soft bed, and padded to the bathroom. She turned on the sink and was jolted awake by splashes of icy water.

Drying her face on a linty white towel, she looked in the mirror and sighed. Gingerly, her finger touched the blue bruise on her forehead. She winced and let her hands grip the counter instead.

She gasped as her heart surged in her chest. *How long has my heart rate been this high?* She coughed to get rid of the irregular rhythm. Letting out a shaky breath, she sank to the bathroom floor and hugged her knees, hoping the quivering would stop. Her body was breaking, and she couldn't deny that. *I'm dying and in a hopeless situation. I'm practically going to die. Whether the brothers kill me or my body kills me. Whichever comes first.*

She shook her head, which exacerbated the lightheadedness and headache that threatened to restrain her to bed for the night. "No. Okay, Ennis. You can do this. It's not hopeless. You'll be fine... You're eliminating. It's part of the process. You're not doing nothing," she told herself. She ruffled her short, dark hair and took a deep breath. "You'll be fine. As always. You're not going to die."

A calm Voice in her head said, *"You will not die."*

"Thank You, God." She smiled sadly.

"Okay, Ennis. Now get up. You have a battle to win. And it starts with getting dressed for battle."

Edging herself up against the wall, she slowly hobbled to her suitcase and looked through its contents, frowning. She'd only brought a couple of pairs of clothes for Ami's family reunion weekend. Sighing, she shrugged back on her sweaty blue long-sleeve and pulled her green clothes out of her suitcase, taking them to the bathroom. Putting them in the sink, she sniffed a sock and froze. "What?"

Taking another whiff and then one of her shirt, she was convinced. *They've been washed.* She swiveled around. Replacing the clothes, she looked about her main bedroom. No one was there. No trace of anything. Her cape, which she remembered tossing off at some point whilst she slept, was hanging neatly on the back of her green chair. Her cape reminded her of her trench coat and the fact that she hadn't seen it since a few days ago. *Or was that just yesterday?*

She turned to go back to the bathroom, but something caught her eye. In the corner of the room near the door were two cans. She rushed to inspect them but slowed when her vision blackened. Tomato soup. She began to wonder if the brothers ate any other flavor. Picking up a can, she saw two fang marks on top. Smiling to herself, she looked down. She drank one can, taking the other and hiding it in her suitcase. Feeling thirsty, she stood up with great effort, panting as she reached the sink, and took a long drink of cold water. She placed the empty can on the sink counter and suddenly hoped the water was potable as she had been drinking it since her arrival. She made a mental note to ask V.

There was a tapping at her door, and adrenaline shot through her body, causing her heart to pound. Maybe it was just V, but she didn't hear his low, soothing voice with which he usually announced himself. She took a deep breath.

"Who is it?"

"Saeva," a gruff voice announced.

Ennis sighed and steeled herself, opening the door a little. "What do you—"

Saeva thrust a large glass at her. "Drink it. I'm not going to stand here all day." His voice was snippy, and he shifted his weight to his other foot.

Without another word, Ennis took the glass and slammed the door. Relief flooded her face when she saw the can of soup she'd just downed and quietly poured the blood into it over the sink.

"Oh no!" she whispered. She set down the tin on the counter again, blood spilling over its sides, dripping down her hands. Blood still sloshed in the glass. An image of V's taut face flashed through her mind, and she bit her lip, looking wildly about. Turning the faucet on slightly, she jabbed her hands under it. Gritting her teeth, she spun around the room, her head still spinning when she stopped. She thought about everything she could pull out of her suitcase, but nothing was suitable to contain this amount of liquid. She set the blood down on the ground and looked around for anything that could be of use. *How did I fail to think ahead about this!* She eyed the bulbous crystalline lampshade that was mounted on the wall over her headboard. Stepping gingerly on the bed, she reached to unscrew the glass.

The lamp's threading squeaked, and the ancient springs shrieked. Biting her lip, she gave a final twist to the cover. No noise came from behind the closed door, and she let out a breath. She gently slipped off the bed, flipped over the shade, and then grabbed the glass of blood, dumping the rest inside. The smell permeated the air, and she stifled a gag with her shoulder. She put the bowl-like lampshade behind the curtains and thanked God that the curtains were so plentiful and thick. They piled nicely at the bottom, making an adequate hiding spot.

She ran back to the bathroom, grabbed the tin, and, walking as fast as she dared, stashed it behind the curtains as well. She vaulted to the door and settled herself. *Oh no.* She panted and fell to the floor. *Pushed body too much.* Her heart was erratic, and her head felt like it would burst. *Can't breathe!* She forced air into her lungs.

Saeva sighed loudly. "Well? Are you done?"

She remained as silent as she could with her uneven breathing. After a minute, she pushed her bangs back and steadied her breathing. *God, help me.* Standing, she just opened the door and thrusted the filmy red glass back at him. A disgruntled sound came from him as he snatched the glass and sneered. "Were you sipping it? Follow me."

Keeping her face blank, she closed the door. *What's with his new attitude. I mean, I know he's mean, but what's with the irritation?*

Reluctantly, she trailed behind him as they ascended a flight of stairs and strode down a dim hallway. She was breathless and leaned against a wall while he wasn't looking. *We must've passed eight rooms in this hallway already!* He turned a corner, and she pushed off the wall. She sighed internally, thinking of all the imminent searching.

Finally, she caught up. Her thoughts were broken with a cold voice. "You're spending the day with me." Saeva turned his frosty eyes on her as his hand stopped on a door's knob. "Don't make things difficult."

Her brows quirked. *What does* that *mean?* He retrieved a golden key from an internal pocket in his brown leather jacket and turned the ancient golden knob.

"Sit," he commanded.

Ennis took a few steps in and took in her new surroundings. Paintings were everywhere. Beautiful, textured, swirling. Many easels stood freely around the light room. A red velvet chair was poised near the lone window that had drawn back white curtains. The outside sky looked like a black hole compared to the shifting variety of colors on the canvases. Even the rich cream-colored walls were bright and lively.

Abstract paintings were dotted between paintings that were recognizably scenes. She took in the handiwork of a nearby canvas, which displayed a partially finished park bench scene.

The work was incredibly detailed, yet it seemed dreamlike.

"I said sit!" His voice cut through the air like a knife to a vibrant tapestry. She turned around as casually as she could manage, looking at him unconcernedly. It became quickly apparent to her that he meant it as he strode towards her and latched a hand around her upper arm. She fought down the rebellious part of her. *If I try to fight him off, he'll find out I don't have superhuman strength... But if I go along with it, it'd show I'm complacent and maybe they'd keep testing my boundaries. Agh!* She gritted her teeth at her lose-lose situation and allowed herself to be dragged into the red velvet chair near the window. He stood in front of the chair she'd been unceremoniously thrown into, thinking. The rain drizzled outside, creating steady, musical monotony. Suddenly, she longed for fresh air. She hadn't realized the extent of the stifling nature that being in a house for so many days without feeling the sun or wind had on her. She felt like she'd been there for a week. *Maybe I have.* She moved to open the window.

"Don't touch anything," he hissed.

"I need fresh air."

He scoffed, folding his arms. "What are you, a dog?" he said. However, he didn't move when she resumed opening the window.

After the top unlatched and the window was pushed up, a gust of clean, rainy air permeated the room. She audibly sighed. *This air smells better than any smell I've ever smelled.* She leaned on the window frame, greedy for the delicious air.

After a moment, she begrudgingly settled back into the red chair and stared out the window. *This chair is uncomfortable. All lumpy.* But she smiled internally as the breeze hit her face even in her seated position.

Saeva had gone quiet, and she turned to see him staring at her. "Stay just like that."

Ennis felt a sweat break out over her body. "What?"

"Stay!" he commanded, and tromped away. She heard him gather a few things near the wall where an artist's table rested. He returned to the spot near the window with a soft chair and an easel that held a canvas the size of a bedroom wall mirror. He disappeared again and returned a few moments later with a readied paint palette and cup of brushes.

His eyes seared hers. "I told you to stay. Get back in your original position."

Blinking, she shifted into a more comfortable position. "What are you doing?'

"You're the subject of the cover of our book in progress."

"No," she stated hotly, rising. "I refuse."

"Refuse?" he asked with mock incredulity, matching her stance, his muscular body tense. "Oh, Ennis, you don't *have* a choice."

"I think I *do*," she retorted, stepping around the chair towards the door.

"No, you don't. If you don't do this, I'll make sure you don't get any more blood until you comply," he called coolly.

Ennis's steps halted, and her fists clenched. *Valentine.* She couldn't let him starve.

"Come on. Sit down," Saeva said, his tone irritatingly sweet as if talking to a stubborn child. She closed her eyes and lowered her head slightly. Lifting it back up, she turned around and walked stiffly back to the red throne of defeat. She really didn't want her face to be used for public reasons, but Valentine was disproportionately more important.

"Now, look out the window like before," he ordered, positioning his easel to his left. "Good." He whipped off his jacket, exposing a black long-sleeved dress shirt.

~

The rain mixed with the sounds of a moving brush. His paintbrush glided across the surface, lifted, and dabbed the palette, all to start over again. Sometimes he would wave a clean palette to dry his current work on the canvas. She looked at him out of the corner of her eye every so often. His face was intently set on the canvas. She figured he would be rather more handsome if he weren't a monster.

Saeva caught one of her peeks and made a sour look. "What are you looking at?" he sneered.

"Something..."

"What?" he seethed.

She turned away. "Oh, never mind," she replied.

"Do you *want* me to threaten you?" he roared.

"Would that make things less boring?"

Saeva looked at a far corner of the room. "Don't play mind games with me," he stated with a smile, returning to his painting.

She felt as though they had been painting for hours, but she now regretted stirring him up, no matter how bored she was. She didn't like the look in his eye.

"You can answer questions if you're so bored." His smile grew wicked.

She fell back into silence.

147

"How did you become a vampire?"

This question struck Ennis. *Why wouldn't he ask about the gory details of being a vampire? Why an origin story? Why this?* Her eyes were set on his.

"Tell me," he said in an almost friendly air.

She remained silent, staring at him.

"Shall I retrieve the garlic?" he questioned.

Continuing to stare, she held her body still.

He reclined back, looking amused. "You aren't going to answer, are you?"

Silence.

"Fine." He stood up and walked over to a corner near the door and opened a little drawer from another long art table, pulling out a tall jar of dried garlic cloves. He slid back into his chair, resting the garlic precariously on the easel's ledge.

She blinked.

"Why won't you talk?" he asked curiously. "Is garlic even dangerous to you?"

Casting her gaze out the window, she ignored him.

"Interesting..."

Out of the corner of her eye, she could see him staring at her. He blinked, and a smile Ennis didn't like lit up his face. She gave him a questioning look.

"You're a curious vampire," he said quietly, spreading a layer of thick red on the canvas. *Why does that sound familiar?* "However, I can't blame you for being secretive. Most are." He gave her a slightly understanding glance.

Her heart revved. *What did he mean?* She nearly sighed out of confusion, irritation, and exhaustion.

A knock at the door broke their silent communication.

A tray entered through the door first, attached to a tired but ever spritely man in a white long-sleeved dress shirt, black slacks, and black dress shoes. *Benedict.* "Saeva, this is your lunch. Sorry it's a bit late, I've been busy having Valentine assist me with our latest revision," he said politely. Her eyes were drawn to the bandages hidden under his left sleeve. She paled.

Saeva continued dabbing at the canvas, not sparing a glance. "Take it away."

Benedict sighed. "Brother, what have I told you about not eating?" He tsked. "Well, Ennis, I have something for you too," he announced cheerily. Her heart shot into her throat, and her empty stomach churned.

"No, she's not earned it, Brother," Saeva said.

Benedict's brow furrowed, and his smile flipped down. A bottle was in the crook of his arm. A *red* bottle. "But—"

"She hasn't *earned* it," he said again, locking eyes with her.

Benedict nodded hesitantly and closed the door.

Saeva glanced at the tray waiting on a table near the door, then back to his painting. "Well, I won't eat if you won't eat," he said cryptically.

Her confusion now poisoned her face, and Saeva smiled.

"And is that supposed to be a threat?" Ennis asked sarcastically.

He smirked, shrugging a shoulder. "I'm just being polite," he said innocently.

"Yes, and you'll stop threatening me too," she sneered, shaking her head.

He continued painting. "Yes, I will."

Ennis blinked, a bit frozen at his sincerity. *Did I miss something?* She scrutinized him as he sat there on his plush armchair.

"Are you hungry?" he asked.

"No," she fired back. At that, she became hyperaware of her stomach's desire to grumble.

He smiled dubiously. "Let me know."

Ennis considered his mood changes, and it concerned her. However, he was pretty consistent in his maliciousness towards her. *Cruel, rude, irritated, angry, vicious, and quiet.* She wondered why he had now decided to play nice. *Perhaps a new tactic. Well, I can handle that...* She smirked slightly and stared out the window.

"How much longer are you going to be?" she asked, toying with the white window frame.

He swirled a hint of grey into a splash of red. "Oh, very much longer I'm afraid." She couldn't help but feel as if he were laughing at her.

~

Ennis jolted up once again. The dark rainy sky had turned lighter. Her eyes felt heavy, and she repeatedly caught herself drifting off. *Don't sleep around them, Enn!* It had continued to pour, but morning light was on the horizon. She had to admire, at least slightly, Saeva's work stamina. He'd been painting all day without food or water since they had started. He didn't even go to the bathroom, which she thought strange. She had already been let out once to use the bathroom, to which she had to explain that vampires actually did use the bathroom. She shuddered at the memory of the conversation as she had left with a sentence of awkward explanation. While she was gone, she'd hoped to catch a glimpse of V, just to feel a little better. She felt alone and unsafe whenever he wasn't around. However, he was nowhere to be found.

When she returned, Saeva was still sitting where he had been and had made progress on his painting.

Throughout the many hours she sat in that room, she prayed and talked with God, knowing that His plan would happen, no matter the things that seemingly got "in the way." *Nothing can ever get in the way of Your plan because You already know what happens and have planned for things! You're the great orchestrator, making beautiful order out of the clanging of sinful people.*

She sat there, slumped, staring out the window, pondering the escape plan. The room she was in held no clues she could visibly see from where she was seated. She wondered if there was anything else hidden in the drawers or paintings themselves.

Her stomach rumbled. And she froze.

Casting icy eyes on her, his face was solemn. "So vampires' stomachs growl?"

"Unfortunately, yes," she noted agitatedly. Her words had started slurring a while back, and she'd made it a point to not talk too much. It was hard to think too. She hadn't eaten anything but the soup before they started and was feeling very lightheaded. She needed water and sustenance. Her breathing had been labored for the past couple of hours, which she hid with frequent sighing, due to her lack of calories and lack of rest.

After studying her for a silent minute, he placed his brush onto his messy palette. "Hmm, well, I suppose we can continue tomorrow."

She stood up and wanted to roll her eyes. *Another day under observation and in boredom, not getting anything done. Great.*

He swung a limb towards the door. "I'll take you to your room."

Ennis swiveled around the easel, taking a look at the painting. She tried to blink away the black creeping over her vision and calm the shortness of breath that plagued her. The canvas was roughly outlined, a base already painted, but she could see that the person being painted resembled her. A nervous jitter crawled through her body.

"It will be beautiful when it's done," he noted. "Now let's go."

Ennis, strolling towards the door, tried to take in her surroundings, checking for any semblance of a clue amidst her wracking brain fog. Nothing.

She was ushered out of the room by his corralling arms. When they were in the hall, Saeva turned around and locked the door, sliding the key into his inner coat pocket again. Her eyes latched on to the shiny golden key.

Saeva looked at her and gestured her down the hall, towards the stairs. "Go."

They walked together until finally stopping at her room. He bowed slightly. *Formality? Why now? He wasn't ceremonious this morning—er, night. Dawn? Dusk.*

"Bye bye," she said, and closed the door on him, sighing heavily once she heard footsteps creaking back up the hall. She ran her hands over her face. "Bye bye? What, brain, are you four years old? I wanted to just say bye!"

Sighing, she lugged her body towards her suitcase, stumbling to retrieve the soup can from it. Her vision turned black again from the exertion.

Plucking out the can, she found the top fully enclosed. Fully metal. No holes. She wished V were with her. Replacing the can, she made her way to the bathroom and drank heavily from the tap. "Oh, sweet water," she whispered to the spigot. "Thank You for water, God!"

Wiping her mouth, she refreshed herself before returning to her bed. A silver tray rested neatly on it. She spun around the room with a smile but found no trace of Valentine. Her smile faded, and her shoulders sagged. Sighing, she moved to the bed and uncovered the tray. A portly sub awaited her. She picked up the cold sandwich and ate feverishly. "A sub never tasted so good," she mumbled through the sliced chicken.

There was a gentle tapping on the door. She froze, chicken half-masticated.

"It's me."

She sighed in relief, swallowed, and unlocked the door with a shuddery hand. "Hi, V," she breathed, trying to blink away the black again.

"Hello, Ennis." He swept through the door, re-locking it behind him. She made for the bed, nearly missing the bed's edge as she got on it.

"Thanks for the food." She picked up the sub again.

"Sorry it's a bit old. I put it in the ice section where they don't ever really look. I didn't let it freeze though." He lithely took a seat in the green armchair and placed one leg on top of the other.

She bit into her sandwich again, chewing thoroughly this time. She had felt the last bite scrape down her throat.

After a couple minutes, Valentine elegantly stood up, walked to the end of the window nearer the head of her bed, and drew back the curtain.

The weak dawn light that barely came through made his hand look even more deathly.

Ennis blanched. "What are you doing!" she said, rising to stop him. "It's almost morn—"

"Remember, the sun?" he said.

"Right... Sorry." She clenched her teeth. "I guess my old info is still etched into my mind." Her eyes surveyed his appearance. He was wearing his black clothes again. His vest, slacks, and shoes were all black. The exception was his white long-sleeve. She noticed his hazel eyes looked more drained.

"Oh, right! There's blood for you behind the curtains. I'm sure you could smell it already though."

Pushing the curtains aside, he revealed the two containers. He lifted the glass lampshade of blood and touched his chin. "Imaginative," he remarked, turning around the crystalline, bowl-like object. It was about the size of a cantaloupe and only filled a little.

She shrugged. "Well... I didn't have any other container big enough. The can was full, and I didn't think a shoe would be the best option."

He smirked a little and added the tin to his harvest.

Valentine moved to stand near the chair, back turned. "You don't... mind?" he asked. She lifted her head, putting down her sub. *He sounds... timid?*

Shrugging again, she shook her head. "Of course not," she said lightly.

He took the can and chugged it with his back to her.

Her eyes widened. Although his back was turned, he was very obviously trying to get it down as quickly as possible. There was no hesitation.

He moved to the crystal.

"How—how does it work? I mean, what's a vampire's eating process?" Ennis asked shyly.

Valentine turned around, his face looking healthier already. "Well," he shifted his weight to his other leg, "if we have it in a container, it's consumed like humans would drink. But when biting, it never gets sucked up in our fangs like some people think. It's a little less appealing. The teeth are there to draw blood, but we... drink from that spot."

"Lapping? Like a vampire bat?"

"Well... no."

"Hmm." She tilted her head.

"You know how vampire bats drink?" he asked with an amused expression.

She tried to fight off an embarrassed smile but sorely lost. "Well, ironically, bats are my favorite animal," Ennis said sheepishly.

It was Valentine's turn to hum. "Why so?"

"They're misunderstood. They help the environment, and yet people don't like them. I think they're underappreciated," she said passionately.

"Agreed," he said, nodding. He lifted the crystal a little higher. It hung in the air for a moment. "Would you... like to see?" he asked timidly.

"Yes." She wished she hadn't answered so eagerly.

She stared, curiosity winning out over politeness as he locked eyes with her. Looking slightly grave, he lifted the rim of the glass to his lips. His canine teeth were very visible. She could see that they were at least half an inch long now, definitely longer than before. He tipped the contents, and the red painted its way into his mouth. *It's just as if he were drinking a smoothie. A very much* non-vegan *smoothie.* He lowered the crystal and stared at her cryptically.

Her heart jumped. He looked like a stereotypical vampire now. *How haven't the brothers noticed? How haven't I noticed?* However, she figured that blood lining someone's mouth and a little dribble of red down the side would make anyone look like a vampire. He set the lampshade on the chair.

He quickly wiped away the runaway blood with his hand and licked it off after turning his back again.

She couldn't help but stare. He truly *was* a vampire. Not that she didn't believe it before, but he hadn't done anything so stereotypically vampiresque in the time she'd known him.

Turning around, he met her eyes and gave her a questioning look.

She ducked her head and picked up the sub again. "Sorry for staring, I just..." She lowered her sandwich. "I'm fascinated."

He looked wary. "You're not afraid?"

She looked at him meaningfully. "No," she said plainly.

He broke eye contact with her and looked down. Grabbing the tin and crystal, he vanished quickly. The faucet's music sliced through the silence.

He returned within a few seconds, replacing the tin and lampshade behind the curtain.

"I'm glad."

"Hmm?" She observed Valentine, who had stopped in front of her bed with his eyes focused on the door.

His eyes traveled down to the floor. "I'm glad you're not afraid, Ennis." His words were quiet as if his voice might shatter if he spoke any louder. His shoulders straightened, and he turned to face her. "Thank you for saving the blood. I hadn't eaten in a while."

A thought struck her. "What *have* you been eating?"

"I... found whatever I could." He began to walk a little around the room, looking at her dresser, curtains, and nothing in particular. "I hunted what I could in the woods around here. But with the stake weapons, there aren't many animals that get through. I've only found a few birds and, rarely, a squirrel. I once found a possum, which I suppose was here before they activated their perimeter. Climbing trees doesn't get you out of the stake barrier either. The animals have learned not to come near this area of land. I'm sure they get scared off before they can even enter or die. That and there's probably a lot of dead animals near the outer edge." A hand rested on his chin as he continued wandering the room. "I wonder if someone on the outside cleans them up. I hadn't noticed any the night I stumbled inside this place... Maybe it's..."

Ennis quirked a brow, but before she could question, he continued.

"So food is scarce. But I've rarely have time to go out because the brothers keep careful watch over me." The corner of his mouth lifted mirthlessly. "They keep me busy with cleaning and this and that."

"How much blood do you need?" Her mind churned.

"We can survive forever without blood. What matters is how much energy we have. Just like a battery, we don't cease to exist if we're out of it."

She hummed.

"But truly to be of normal countenance, a litre a day would do nicely. Even one every few days is more than enough."

"Okay. Hmm... I'll do my best."

"With this much blood every day," he gestured towards the curtains, "I think escaping will be much easier. Unfortunately, I've been weak as of late." He looked across the room at something on the wall she couldn't identify. "You haven't even seen me in my prime."

She shuddered. *What kind of damage could this man really do? Has he killed anyone before? He must have a lot of horrors he's experienced in his past. His past...* "V?"

"Yes?" He turned back to look at her.

Biting her lip, she went for it. "How old are you?" Her eyes were curious.

"Oh." He smiled a little. "I'm many centuries old."

"How old, exactly?"

"I was born in 1696."

Her eyebrows shot up. "Huh..."

With a smirk, he huffed. "So I suppose I'm a fair bit older than you then?"

"Only a little..." She chuckled. But she settled into a curious silence for a while.

"You seem quite modern for someone born that long ago. I wouldn't even have guessed you were older than you look."

He smiled. "I take great lengths to blend into whatever society I'm in. I study culture, body language, vernacular, etcetera. Less questions that way."

Her mouth fell open a little in amazement. "What's it been like? Seeing the world change over so long a time?"

His demeanour became ancient, like a thousand books of knowledge laid on his shoulders, weathered by the history they held. He looked down. "I suppose you would say it's strange," he said, standing still near the foot of the bed. "But it's all I've ever known since I didn't die as I should have." He gazed at her with fondness. "The funny thing is that everything has changed, but everything is still the same. People still have the same motives. Same desires." He huffed. "'And there is no new thing under the sun.'"

"Ecclesiastes," she supplied, the corner of her mouth lifting. "And under the moon?"

He smirked. "Well, I suppose the moon is an *entirely* different ordeal." He chuckled. "Truly though, people haven't changed. They all make the same mistakes. History repeats itself. Those tropes are true." He looked at the blocked window as if he could see beyond it and out at the building crescendo of pink hidden by grey clouds and rain. "The days repeat themselves until it could drive you mad. Sunrise, then sunset, and again and again, to no end." She saw his face grow pained. "All the things you've done haunt you." He looked at her now. "They haunt me, Ennis." She wanted to throw her arms around him and hug him tightly, to relieve the ache that she could feel herself. But she didn't. She stayed seated on the bed.

"The past is past," Ennis stated. "You know, we've already handled them."

"And of crimes?" he asked solemnly.

"Crimes? Well, there'd probably be no evidence now. Statute of limitations too. What could you do?

Go to the police and turn yourself in? They wouldn't take you for something that was done a hundred years ago."

"If you told police what happened, I doubt they'd hold it against you since legally they probably couldn't." She shrugged. "I mean, they'd lock you up in a mental institution," she noted with a half-joking, half-serious smirk. He smiled and lowered his head. Her stomach twisted, and her face became somber.

"And of other non-criminal wrongs, you know, perhaps people would be more forgiving than you think.

"Funnily enough, I deal with the same worries. The same haunts."

His eyebrows went up. "I doubt that," he scoffed.

Shaking her head, she explained. "I have OCD, don't forget. Well... I mean, I haven't, um... killed anyone." She peeked up at him.

Valentine's demeanour sank. "You think I've killed people?"

She took a deep breath and let it out. "It's a possibility."

"Do you think I'd kill you?" he asked softly. His eyes steadily pierced hers, and she drew in a breath again.

"No."

"No?" He raised a brow. His stillness was unnerving, and power radiated from his form. His arms were crossed. His strong figure stood poised before her. "That's good then," he said, taking a seat on the edge of the bed, facing away from her. "And I haven't killed anyone. But the conscience is a delicate thing, Ennis. I remember things... bad things I've done."

160

"So do I. And I realize that you've had longer to live with them and make more mistakes, but that means that they're even more past for you now. You have to forgive yourself. You can't be your past because you *are* your present."

"True, Ennis." Valentine steepled his fingers together. "You know, you and I seem to have some commonalities I didn't know about."

She let out a shaky breath, raking a hand through her hair. "Yeah... Except you've got the whole... centuries thing on me." She smiled, laughing lightly.

"I suppose I do." He looked over his shoulder at her. "Strange," he commented with a slight smile. "I'm glad I've met you."

Her fingers found the quilt, and she fiddled with the fabric. "Strange?" she whispered.

"You're strange. I know it's cliché, but I truly have never met anyone like you."

She smiled crookedly. "Same to you." She noted his mouth as he smiled slightly. His fangs no longer looked as visible as they had been after he'd drunken the blood. *Do they retract or something? I wouldn't think so.* He turned around, one foot hanging off the bed. Her heart hammered like the rain on the window.

"V?" she said timidly.

"Yes?" He sat there poised, ancient and young at the same time, a hand on his propped up knee.

She swallowed, trying to word things as carefully as she could. "How did... How did you change?"

His casual tone and stance left him. His limbs tensed but then relaxed. A little smile that held many emotions alighted his face. "It was a long time ago."

He paused for so long that Ennis thought he had decided to leave it at that. But he started up again. "It was 1725 when I was bitten."

"So you become a vampire by being bitten, but you mentioned something about vampire blood?"

"Well, getting vampire blood into your system is also part of the process. We're not demons, as folklore tells it. We have a virus. It ravages our systems and turns our bodies superhuman with nasty consequences. The virus keeps the host alive so the virus doesn't die. I suppose the virus mutated over time from some other disease.

"We can pass it on through our bite, which transfers special saliva only released during a bite. The saliva's composition is only half the formula. Once it mixes with the blood, that's when the reaction happens and can infect a new host. It's the catalyst." She raised her brows. "Strange, I know."

"Oh..." Her mind raced, trying to piece everything together. Questions flooded her so much so that she found it difficult to focus.

"How many vampires are there out there now?"

His brows furrowed. "It's hard to say. There's no way to track them. Maybe a few hundred thousand. We learn to keep our heads down. Surprisingly, most of us don't draw attention to ourselves. I've seen a few serve communities through being firemen, policemen, and akin careers. Some work desk jobs. Some stir up trouble."

"So... how did it happen for you?" He gazed at her, and her face reddened. She waved her hands. "If you don't mind me asking, that is!"

He smiled. "No, it's okay. I've had so many years to come to terms with it." He sighed. "Back in 1725 when I was still uninfected, I happened to be in York, England, working as a store owner's accountant. During my time there, a man who ran a foreign business stopped by our shop to make a deal with my boss about ownership. My boss had wanted to go home early that day for his daughter's birthday. I walked in on the exchange, and he left me in charge of handling the last of the contract signing with the man and left to go home. The mysterious businessman was very wealthy and owned numerous estates all over Europe. His eyes were a vibrant brown, his hair, black. His disposition was friendly on the outside, even in his expensive formal attire. But he spoke with an undertone of danger. It's hard to describe."

"No, I think I understand." She laughed uneasily.

He smirked a little, then his face became stony. "After my boss left, the man cornered me. He looked me up and down and said, 'I like you.'" Valentine's face seemed very pale now. "And then he pinned me against the wall and bit me. I couldn't fight him off. He was so strong." His eyes were dark. "I remember tasting the metallic flavour of blood, and then..."

Ennis's eyes were wide. "And then?"

"I woke up in the same little office with blood all over me and no trace of the gash in my neck. Papers everywhere. The man was gone. The contract missing, along with all the documents and things worth any value."

"So he did it just to rob your store?" she asked bewildered, her mouth open slightly.

Valentine huffed. "I've been asking myself that for centuries. Such an uninteresting transformation motive if that were true."

"But... he said he liked you?"

"I suppose he saw something in me that he liked enough to make me a vampire instead of just killing me... or letting me go."

"What happened to you after that?" she wondered. He motioned to her tray as he went on. Absentmindedly, she took up a few of the baked potato sticks that were on the side.

"I acted normally. It actually wasn't as difficult to disguise my illness as you might believe. Nowadays it's different for newer vampires. Back then, I switched to only working at night. I bought a few cows to keep. When my boss's business went under, I travelled all over the world, holding many different jobs. From gardener to blacksmith to doctor to cook to publisher, you name it."

"That's..." Ennis was breathless. "That's really impressive."

He smiled. "Well, if you had as much time as I have, you'd be able to do all those things too."

A smile crept over her face. "I mean your resumé..." She jokingly let out a puff of air. "Must be very impressive."

He laughed. "I can't exactly give references for everything now. But the experience is important. Thankfully I'm very affluent due to investing over a long... *long* time."

Her smile faded. "But, how do you get around documentation?"

"Well, every lifetime or so I'll get my name changed to the public. Illegal papers, unfortunately, made by some other vampires I know. I'm not keen on it, but it's how I stay out of ending up on a lab table or some psycho's house. Governments don't have vampires in mind when they set up documentation." He sighed.

"I understand." She poked at the sub in front of her. "Wait! Is Valentine your real name? What's your real name?" she asked with terror. She couldn't pin why exactly she had such horror at not knowing his real name, but it shook her to her bones.

Giving her a smile, he laced his hands together. "Actually, you've caught me in the second lifetime of me using my real name. It's nice to hear my true name every so often."

"So your name is just Valentine?"

"That's actually my first name. Again, strange, I know."

"Do you have a last name?"

"Trutina. Valentine Trutina. And yours?"

"Ennis Athrú." She shook her head. "Valentine Trutina... That's quite a name." She let a smile creep onto her lips, and he looked down with one as well.

"Ennis Athrú..." He tried out her name. "So is yours," he concluded with a smile. "Are you Irish?"

"Maybe. There is never really a consensus in my family when we talk about it." Her mind swirled with unanswered questions. "So what about..." She stopped. *Am I asking too many questions?*

"Yes?" he asked kindly.

Her mind started to go into overdrive. She wanted to know more about his past, what his family was like, what his life story was, how he managed to live all these years, whether werewolves existed too, what monsters were out there, if there was a vampire hierarchy, what do fangs feel like. She cleared her throat, settling on a simple question. "What was your original home like?"

He stopped moving. And Ennis felt her heart do the same. He looked positively enveloped in

165

thought as if she had stirred up some dormant country of memories.

After what felt like hours, he finally answered. "I... was born in 1696, as I said before," he started. He took a long time before continuing as if he'd not told the story in a very long time. *I wonder if he's* ever *told this story.*

He continued. "And I grew up like any normal child back then in working class. Our family had its problems. Like all families do. My mother was an angry individual. My father, the sweetest man I knew. I had three sisters. All three were married off at a young age to men I didn't agree with. My second eldest sister, Ulin, I was close with... We were so close." His eyes dimmed. "It was hard on me when she got married to some wealthy upperclassman. I told her not to agree. She didn't want it, but times were hard, and we all did what we had to do to survive."

"Lise, the third eldest, was married off to a wealthy man. She was a dreamer and wanted to join the military when she was younger. But then reality hit her when she was scorned for her ideas, and she agreed to the marriage." He smirked. "She was still fierce though."

He took a deep breath. "Marte, the eldest, was happy in her marriage. She, too, was wed to a wealthy man. She didn't really care about love. Ulin did. Lise did. But Marte had a 'wealth is happiness' sort of mindset."

"So you're the youngest too?" Ennis asked. She stared, rapt, having long abandoned her meal again.

"Yes. You are as well?" he asked with a small smile.

"Yes, three older brothers."

"I see. Are you close to them?"

"Uh..." Ennis took a moment to think. She hadn't really considered her childhood in a while. Her mind thought it was too difficult to process. "I don't think so. I'm definitely not as close to Rodney as you are with Ulin."

He gave her a sad, crooked smile. "As I *was.*"

She felt her stomach drop. *Oh no!* "Sorry, I meant—"

"Please don't worry, Ennis. It's been so long. Please don't feel bad." Valentine stood and walked over to her and rested a hand on her shoulder. Leaning in slightly, he looked her in the eyes and said meaningfully, "You can ask anything you'd like." He smiled. "And you can't hurt me." He straightened up, returning his hand to his side. Ennis watched him dart around the room so quickly she couldn't keep up.

"I have so many more questions though." She sighed, running a hand over her face. "I could talk to you for days about everything."

A little smug smile found its way onto his face. "In time." His eyes found hers and then the wall. "Do you mind answering a question for me?"

Ennis perked up, feeling dread take hold of her stomach simultaneously. "Sure. I mean, depending on the question."

His arms were held at his sides as he stood before her. "Why do you trust me?"

Her heart shot into her stomach. "What?"

"The night we met, you didn't trust me, but you did later." He shook his head. "You were so guarded, even considering the situation you came into."

"I don't trust you, perse. How can you trust anyone but God?"

Valentine tilted his head and squinted his eyes. "No doubt God's the only One we can fully trust. But a relationship takes some trust too. However, we can't rely on others instead of God. You and I both know you trust me to an extent though."

"Then desperation, maybe." She sighed. "Well, you're so different from others I've known before. And I don't have much of a choice since my first escape plan failed." Her eyes darted to the floor and then the wall. "Isn't it normal not to trust people after knowing them for so little time?" She laughed a little, feeling unease take hold of her throat.

His brows quirked. "You've known me for only a little while."

"But you're different. An abnormal case." She looked at him as he blinked at her. "In a good way," she added. She rubbed her hands together absentmindedly.

"What..." His words died off, and his hands clasped behind his back. "What made you so uneasy around others?"

"The desire to live? You can't trust people."

"We're not all bad."

"I know," she answered as if were obvious. *But it's hard to live that out.*

"Your distrust goes beyond common sense."

A retort died on her lips. She knew the answer. She'd always known the answer. *Should I even talk to him about it?* She considered his relaxed stance, and he moved to sit in the green chair. *I think I can trust him. After all, he's not shown typical warning signs... Maybe he's just trying to help. He did just tell me his origin story.*

"I guess..." She squinted, studying the bedding intensely. Valentine searched for her eyes but

168

didn't find them. She sighed. "I guess it was back when I was in school and getting my degree. I had a series of bad friendships. Toxic people." She was silent for a long time, and her eyes swam. "I trusted them, and they let me down. It made me second guess myself. I still do. I thought we were close, but then they'd betray me, order me around, want me to do things for them out of convenience, or just wanted to be in a romantic relationship and left when I rejected them. None of those friendships ever lasted. It became so common that now I keep everyone at a safe distance. Even Ami, my closest friend." She didn't wipe away her tears but pretended they weren't there. "People can leave you with so much pain. I guess I found the pros of having friends don't outweigh the cons."

Valentine frowned, his eyes searching her face. "Do you think that's true?"

"I'm sure not for everyone." She sniffed. "Foolish emotions," she mumbled.

He smiled sadly and exhaled. "You remind me so much of myself."

Finally, her eyes lifted and found his. "How?"

"I'll explain some other time, but I had a similar outlook on people once. But I ask again, do you think that's true? Is it really not worth having friends?"

"I guess if you meet the right people. But that's difficult."

"Well, I can tell you that not everyone will be like that, Ennis. Everyone has good traits and bad, but that doesn't mean that everyone you meet will be toxic."

"I know." Her heart ached. *I do know. I just...*

"But you don't seem to live by it. However, I don't think you've given up on friends either."

How did he know? Her eyes fell. "It hurts too much. People are so mean." *Wow, I feel like a child saying that!*

A sad smile returned to his handsome face that was framed by his dark hair curling at his ears. "When we trust God first and fully, then it won't matter what others do to us. It's like we're anchored in Him, and then no wave can toss us. A boat is meant to be on the water, Ennis. We're meant to be around other people and have relationships. I don't mean to make you feel worse. I actually want you to be able to trust others again. And I hope you can start with me."

Looking up, she smiled a little and laughed, her eyes darting away. "We'll see." Patting her face with her sleeve, she tried to whisk away the remnants of her emotions. He watched her intently.

His demeanour slipped back into concern, and he rose from the chair and approached her. "How are you feeling? I'm sorry I haven't been in to check on you more. How are your illnesses? How are you holding up?" He slowly touched the back of his hand to her forehead and retracted it. A slight frown dipped a corner of his mouth.

"I'm..." She let out a puff of air. "Well, I'm hanging in there. I don't know how much more I can take, though. My body isn't doing well with the little bit of sleep thing." She sighed in aggravation, raking her hand through her hair. "And I know that when I sleep, it takes time away from searching. But without it, I can't function. And then that tradeoff means more days spent here in this nightmarish house with a pair of psychopaths." She fell onto the patterned green quilt, staring at the ceiling.

"Sleep is necessary, even if it costs you time. It's worth it. You're already at a breaking point, I can tell. I don't want to push you past it." He eyed her forehead. "Why don't you sleep tonight? We can do a little searching tomorrow."

"No, I'll help search tonight. I can't stand doing nothing." She slowly rolled up into a cross-legged position.

"You're not doing nothing. You're buying us time. Plus, won't people be out searching for you? Someone would've expected to hear from you, wouldn't they?"

"Y-yeah..." Ennis felt a frown coming on. "Ami. She's probably worried sick. By now she might've even told my parents. Are my parents back now? How many days has it been? But my neighbor was coming to check on me. I forgot to leave a note..." Her eyes grew wider, and a hand flew to her forehead. "Oh, they'll be panicking! I'm sure they'll tell me off for stepping foot in this house." But her hand fell. "That is, if I'm even alive for them to."

Valentine looked stern and walked over to the window. "Don't say things like that. We're going to get out of here. As long as they don't know the truth, they won't hurt either of us."

"Sorry, I'm just... I'm not used to this sort of thing."

"Being in mortal danger?"

"...Yeah."

"I think you're handling it fairly well, Ennis. We have a plan. So try not to stress too much."

"Too much." She huffed. "I don't think that's possible." Her mouth turned down. "And aren't we being a little suspicious, though? Won't they find out we're friends? You're spending a lot of time

171

away when I'm away too. Won't they put two and two together?"

"I've been trying to act disinterested around you." He shot her an apologetic look. "Sorry. But hopefully, that's been working. They haven't been around when I've been with you in your room, so I think it's alright. We'll just continue to keep doing what we're doing."

"Okay... I'm just so worried."

"Ennis, God is in control," he said firmly.

"Yeah, but sometimes actually grasping that fact is hard."

"Feelings don't dictate the truth or make it any less true."

Her shoulders perked up as his words connected and her smile returned. "Wait, you're a believer too?" She paused, looking down. "You quoted Ecclesiastes. And talked about trusting God. Why didn't I make that connection?" Shaking her head, her smile widened.

He smiled. "Perhaps you're used to thinking Biblically or being surrounded by like-minded Christians." His hand found the curtain, and he clutched at it. "Yes, I've been a Christian ever since I was 34. I was so lost my entire life up until that point. I didn't know where to go, what to do. And I'd been asking God why He let me become the way I am."

She blinked. He tapped his teeth, and then she nodded.

"And then I became a Christian and thought of all the good I could do with my life, how I could glorify God. I don't stay in any place long, but that doesn't mean I can't do good wherever I go and share the Gospel. I never would have chosen this longevity. But God will use the bad in my life for my good." His eyes were ancient and sweet.

"Okay," he said, taking the tray. "Why don't we reconvene here after the brothers go to sleep? They'll expect to see me for a little bit, but then I'll come back here later. Try and get some sleep in the mean time. Is that alright with you?" He gave her a meaningful look.

She nodded, biting her lip.

"Don't worry, Ennis. We're doing fine. I've got blood now, so that's even better."

"I like your optimism, V." She smiled, letting go of the bedding she hadn't realized she'd grabbed again.

Valentine looked down, smiling, and then reached for the doorknob.

"And V?"

He turned around to look at her. Her eyes were shiny. "Thank you."

He closed his eyes, his head dropping down, and then opened them, looking at her. "You're most welcome." With that, he swept out of the room, the door closing without a sound.

Ennis huffed and fell onto her back again, staring up at the ceiling, a million questions shouting in her head.

~

11

"Ennis?" a voice called. *Why does it sound like I'm underwater?* "Ennis?"

Ennis moaned, trying to get out of something that entangled her. Water? The voice was clear now. "Ennis, wake up!"

She shot out of bed, flailing her arms and gasping for breath. The blankets were wrapped around her limbs, and she wriggled them off. She grabbed at the ache in her chest. "Wh-what was that?"

"Looked like you were having some sleep paralysis," Valentine said. He tilted his head slightly. He had his black cloak on.

"Not the first time." She held her head in her hands, rubbed her eyes, and gave a groan.

"I wouldn't have woken you up if you weren't having a poor sleep." He looked towards the blacked out window. "We have some time before dusk. Are you still up for some searching or do you want to try to sleep again?"

"Yeah, let me just..." She grabbed her cloak from the side of her chair and swung it around her shoulders, yawning. "I'm ready."

He blinked, staring at her for a moment. But a second later, he waved her through the door. "The third-floor search commences," he murmured.

~

Rooms. So many rooms. Ennis wondered if this place really *did* use to be a bed and breakfast. It definitely had quite the potential.

She sighed, closing the last drawer of a dusty mahogany bureau. "How does this house even have this many rooms?" She turned around to see Valentine fluidly replace the bed he was inspecting. He had picked the whole bed off the floor.

"From the front, the full extent of the house is covered by the trees. Very deceiving. The estate is bigger than a mansion." He suddenly appeared by her side, lifting the wooden bureau with little effort. "Anything?"

She crouched to peer underneath the piece. "Nothing."

"Well, that covers this room then," he said, sweeping out of the room. The bureau was already back in its place.

Ennis trudged towards the next room Valentine had gone into. She stifled an enormous yawn with her forearm. "Maybe the seventh room will be where the clues are," she said.

She realized Valentine had missed the next door and was already in the next room over. She peered at the heavy wooden door that looked like hers. "Hey, V? You skipped a room."

"I didn't skip it. It's mine," came his response as he floated into the barren hallway.

She bit her lip and looked at the floor. "Have you searched it?"

He appeared next to her side instantly. "Of course."

"Hmm."

He motioned her into the next room, and she gave his door one last look before it vanished as she swept through the next room's doorframe.

A lonely lamp was perched by a small wooden table in the middle of the room. Her fingers slowly began to inspect an ancient floor lamp. *I wonder what his room looks like.* She touched the lampshade's serrated edging, and a shower of dust trickled to the floor. She coughed. "Dusty." Looking at the lamp, she followed its cord to the wall. The cord disappeared into the baseboard moulding. She crouched and felt a wave of breathlessness overtake her. Steadying herself on the wall, she tried to relax.

"I've checked the outside of the house. The power runs directly into the appliances. There aren't any outlets. They don't even have heating here. Just fireplaces. Even though I could meddle with the electricity, as I said before, I don't want to kill the power altogether. Their house electricity isn't wired to their stakes. I've already tested that method." He flipped a crusty green armchair around, inspecting it from different angles. She wasn't so sure green was its original color.

She picked at the bedding she'd wandered to. "I wonder how old this place is."

"I can't be sure. They've never told me, and I haven't found any documents on it. It's old though," he reasoned, casting a sweeping look around the length of the ceiling. "For you," he added with a smirk.

Ennis paused for a second, then chuckled. "Yeah, I guess you're right." She frowned a little. *I really want to appreciate his jokes right now, but I'm just so exhausted.*

He set the chair back down without a sound and darted around the room so quickly she couldn't keep up. It was like he'd vanished.

Wow, he's fast. A thought suddenly struck her. "V?"

"Hmm?" His reply sounded like it had come from multiple different places as he continued his speedy search.

"What's going to happen when we get out of here?"

He chuckled lightly. "There's some positivity." He stopped some distance before her. "What do you mean?" Even though he said it casually and from some paces in front of her, she could see something in his eyes.

"I mean I don't want to leave you." She felt the weight of her words sink into her heart like teeth. *How could I say that? I hardly know him!* But something about him... She knew she wanted to stay with him. Stay in touch, at the very least. "I don't want to never see you again."

"Oh," he said, his tone unidentifiable. He met her wary eyes as she sat on the dusty blue quilt. "I don't want us to be strangers either. I meant what I said about you not living alone, not living friendless." His voice was even, solid.

She felt her heart lighten as if a cord had been severed, one that had been squeezing it uncomfortably tight. She smiled and looked down. "Good." But something nagged at her. It felt like he was going to leave, vanish, and never contact her again.

After a few silent moments, Valentine looked around the room once more, arms crossed. Since it was mostly empty, they had already completed their search in the room.

He appeared by a window and lifted its veil. A streak of soft light lit his pale cheekbones. "Let's get you back to your room. You should get some sleep," he stated, dusting his cape off. She refastened her own with clumsy fingers. "Spending time in the library again before the third floor seemed like a good idea at the time. I think I overworked you."

"Don't worry about it. I agreed to it." She yawned. "Let's hope floor four is where we start finding some answers."

He led her gingerly to the door leading into the hall but gently put an arm out to stop her. He stood still and looked as if he was straining to hear something. Her heart was in her throat. *Are the brothers awake!* He scouted the hall and then waved her on. "Just a mouse." Surprise painted his tone slightly. She looked up and down the desolate hall. *I guess he didn't get all the animals yet.* They began padding their way back to her room.

She wondered how he could move with such stealth. *He's not even tiptoeing. He's just... walking and yet not making a sound. Is he even touching the ground?* Her eyes widened, and she felt her heart speed up as an enormous creak shrieked through the air. She felt her vision blacken and tried to press forward without passing out. *I can't get caught! Do I run for it?* As her foot lifted off the floor, there was another shriek. She looked down. Realization hit her that it was her own step that had caused a loose wooden floorboard to scream. She held her breath and looked up. Valentine peered over his shoulder at her and nodded for her to continue on.

~

Almost there. She crept into her room a few steps behind Valentine and shut the door, locking it with clumsy fingers. She slapped her face. *Stay conscious. Stay conscious, Ennis!* She was fumbling with her cape's clasp now.

178

"Are you alright? You're slapping yourself." He caught her eyes and saw her hands. His mouth turned into a small frown. "And your hands are shaking."

"I'll be alright. Just... symptomatic. I should rest."

His eyes did a once over of her, and he sighed. She knew he was concerned. "I'll let you get your sleep then." He moved to the door but stopped. "Are you sure you'll be alright?" He moved forward towards her. "Do you need me to stay? Can I do anything else to help you?"

Her heart sped up even more. "Yeah, I just— fine. Um, sleep—I mean, uh, goodnight." Her clasp finally came undone, and she flung her cape to the floor.

Valentine bowed his head slightly. Ennis could see that there was a slight smile on his face, unlike his usual contemplative demeanour that reminded her of the pensive one she wore most of the time. A side of her mouth turned up. He glided to her suitcase, and a chunking sound sliced the air. He turned around and handed her a punctured soup can.

"Goodnight, Ennis. See you tomorrow." He closed the door.

She felt a wave of dizziness hit her. She desperately needed to get out of here. And regular meals. And sanity. *I might need to be in bed for weeks to recover from this and probably therapy for the rest of my life. But if I mention vampires, they'll think I'm actually insane. So I'll obviously just leave the real vampire out of this... Yeah...* Her eyes started leaking, but she didn't bother to dry them. This situation was not normal. Nothing had been normal since she'd left her house however many days ago. She couldn't even remember how many days had passed here. Her mind felt like it was falling apart, melting like the seemingly constant rain against the window. *God, get me out of here, please! I feel like I'm dying in more ways than one.*

She hunkered with the covers over her head and sipped her soup without tasting it. She felt her eyelids closing and slapped her cheeks. Setting the partially empty can on the nightstand, she made her way to the bathroom, and with teary, droopy eyes, took a long drink from the sink. The water tasted slightly rusty and salty. "Yeah, I *really* need to get out of here," she croaked.

Looking at herself in the mirror, a sigh escaped her. Her hair was like frantic, dark ocean waves being tossed about, her eyes had dark circles underneath them, and her pallor had worsened, all attesting to how she felt.

Rebelling against her overwhelming desire for sleep, she stripped off her clothes and stumbled into the cold shower. Her eyes were closed as she washed her body.

She felt herself falling and braced her body against the shower wall. She fell to her knees, trying to decrease her rapid heart rate. "Did I fall asleep standing up? Or did I pass out for the first time?" She hastily rinsed the soap from her hair and stepped out of the tub, kneeling and shivering. She grabbed a towel and halfheartedly dried herself off. The towel dropped to the ground, and she pulled back on her blue long-sleeve and trousers and flopped onto the bed. Pulling the covers over her, her eyes fell shut immediately. A second later they snapped open at the knocking on the door.

Ennis jumped out of bed, wobbling on her feet and nearly collapsing. *V? No, he would've announced himself.* That only left two possibilities. And either one was a nightmare... Her pulse rushed in her ears. *What could either of them want during the day?* She lurched to grab the can on her nightstand and stashed it under the curtains. Stepping to the door as lightly as possible, she pressed an ear against the cool wood.

"Ennis?" asked the smooth, low tone.

Her heart sputtered out of rhythm.

Saeva.

12

"I've brought you something," Saeva said. *His words sound off. Should I wait for Valentine? Should I... just not open the door?* Her mind raced as she covered her face with her hands. *No, Saeva can't know that we're friends. I can't wait for V. Should I play dead?*

"I know you're awake." He sighed impatiently.

What do I do, God! She clutched her heart to muffle its hammering.

"Ennis!" he barked.

If I wait any longer, he might bust down the door. She let out a shaky breath. "What is it?"

"Open the door and find out."

She frowned. "No thanks." Her bed was in sight, and she was determined to go to sleep.

"Oh, come on, I brought you a midnight snack. Well, a mid-*day* snack," he corrected, his voice cold. "Since I withheld blood from you today at lunch and dinner, I only thought it would be fair. And I don't want you getting too much like an animal." He sounded a little apologetic. "I also heard the shower running, so I knew you were up."

She closed her eyes and hissed silently. Then her eyes locked with the curtains, behind which were the glass lampshade, the tin can, and her soup remnants. She gritted her teeth and let out a noiseless sigh. And taking a deep breath, she walked back to the door and opened it with a trembling hand.

Her expression was lackluster. "Thanks," she said in a dull voice, grabbing the glass. As she closed the door, his hand slammed against it, catching it.

"Ahh, but this time, you have to drink it right now. I want to *see*." His words were deathly.

She froze. *Oh no. I didn't plan for this.* She thought for a quick second and then held the glass of blood out to him. "Then I won't drink it," she said with mock politeness. He shoved the door open, but his feet remained firmly planted in a wide stance outside her doorway.

"Oh, no, sorry, but there's some suspicion going around. I want actual proof." He narrowed his eyes at her.

Ennis looked at the blood in her hand, trying not to show the fear that ripped around like a tornado inside her body. She couldn't drink it. But if she didn't, then the act was up and she was dead. *The act. Act.*

She scorched him with her eyes as she turned around and tipped the glass to her lips. *Wretched.* That was the first word that came to mind as her mouth filled with the taste of iron. What was worse was that it was slightly warm. She didn't want to know whether it was animal blood or human blood.

She was reminded full well that humans weren't meant to drink blood as a strong urge to gag coiled in her middle. But she couldn't let herself vomit. Not yet. Steeling her mind, she faked gulps, letting the blood pour down her front instead of down her throat, coating her blue shirt and black trousers in a sheet of fresh, thick blood. She accidentally swallowed some and felt her vomit reflex kicking in. She wanted to choke, to cough, to dispel it from her system as soon as possible, but Saeva was standing behind her, watching her every move. Spinning around and putting on a fury, she hurled the glass, shattering it on the wall behind him. And she ran to close the door. He recentered himself in the doorway, eyebrows high. She got out "Dishonorable!" before locking the door and bolting to the toilet. She scrambled for the towel she had just used and vomited into it. She thought she had heard him walk off before she'd thrown up, but she wasn't sure. The entire bathroom was specked with blood from her clothes and jerky movements. She felt her stomach lurch again, filling the towel with more red liquid. She couldn't decipher her dinner from her "midday snack." She wanted to puke just holding the towel. The smell was toxic.

After the heaving had stopped for a solid minute, she threw the towel into the shower and sprawled out on her back on the cold tile floor, feeling something slick on her fingers. Blood. *Oh... my bedroom floor too...* The cold from the floor soaked into her back, radiating through her body. She wiped at her sweaty forehead with her wrist. Head spinning, her vision darkened. She felt her limbs shake before growing weak and heavy like cinder blocks.

Her body was breaking. Slowly. Agonizingly. And the more time she spent here, the quicker she could feel her death advancing. Her early death seemed more probable by the second.

There was a knock at the door, and she wanted to scream. She couldn't take this. Looking up at the ceiling, she closed her eyes. *God, if this is a Cerrit brother, I'm done for.*

"Ennis?" a quiet, familiar voice called.

Oh. Trembling, she pulled herself up to a standing position and held on to the wall as she made her way to the door. She noted that she'd left bloody handprints on the walls and a dripping trail on the hardwood floor. Stepping over the splash zone, she unlocked the door.

"I smelled—" Valentine's face froze in shock as he saw her starkly pale and blood-coated.

"Are you okay?" He vanished for a quick moment and reentered her room with a sheet, leaping over broken glass in the hall, landing almost silently. His white sleeves were rolled up and dark vest was removed. Shutting the door quickly, he locked it behind him, ushering her to the bed, and folded the sheet, easing her down onto it.

"Saeva brought me a 'midday snack,'" she said bitterly. "And he wanted proof. They hadn't seen me drink blood before. So... tonight was the night."

"Oh, Ennis, I'm so sorry," he said. His tight tone caught her attention.

"V?" As she looked at him with worried eyes, he turned away.

"The blood, Ennis," he clipped out.

"Oh... Sorry, I—" She felt another wave of nausea hit her and stumbled towards the bathroom. Valentine grabbed her at her waist, keeping her upright. She fell to the toilet and vomited. Backing away, he looked down at his hands. His face paled.

"Towel," she barked. Valentine quickly provided her one from the rack above the toilet, and she vomited into it.

"To muffle the sound?" he asked.

She got out a strange squeak that sounded something like an affirmative reply and threw the soiled towel into the shower. His eyes followed the toss, and he leaned to look into the tub, nose wrinkling. He sat back on his haunches.

185

"Do you think you're finished?" he asked, patting her back and sweeping her hair from her eyes.

She swallowed. "Y-yeah. But I thought that too before you showed up. Oh, Saeva! He might be back to clean up the mess in the hall!" She wanted to curl into a ball, but the wet feeling down her front reminded her of the mess that would further ensue.

"He won't be. He went back to his room. I'm sure he'll ask me to clean it in the morning.

"Ennis, how much blood did you drink?" he asked seriously.

She shook her head, but it sent her into a dizzy session. She kept still for a moment before answering. "Two mouthfuls maybe? On accident," she managed.

He thought for a moment. "Did you vomit it all up?"

"I hope so." She paused in thought, eyes closed. "Probably."

"Then it shouldn't be too bad." He grabbed a washcloth and wet it. Then Ennis felt coolness hit her forehead and mouth. Her eyes stirred open, but Valentine shushed her. "Just relax, Ennis."

She let her eyes fall shut as exhaustion hit her very core. Her body slumped to the side. He caught her. She felt as though she had no energy left. She was entirely spent. *God, receive me now.*

He lightly wiped at her face, cleaning away the semi-dried gunk. He continued on to her neck and then stopped.

"Ennis?" Valentine whispered.

She gave a questioning grunt.

"Can you change your clothes? Do you have the strength?" he asked quietly, holding her frame in one arm and the rag in the other.

She groaned but weakly nodded once. That was easier than words. The next moment she found herself propped against the tub's edge and him gone. He reappeared with her last good set of clothes, and then took his leave.

Pulling herself up using the sink, she looked in the mirror. "Ugh." She ripped off the bloody blue shirt and trousers, then piled them into the corner of the bathroom. Her heart surged, and she took a knee, panting.

"Ennis? Are you okay?" Valentine's voice called through the door.

She took a few light breaths. It felt like she were breathing air from a paper bag. "Y-yeah." She awaited his rebuttal but, instead, was met with silence. With a deep breath, she stood up, took a new washcloth, sat in the tub, and turned on the shower. She jumped and gasped at the cold and quickly twisted the nobs until a temperature she could put up with came out. She wiped the cloth around like mad before stumbling out and whipping on her green long-sleeve and black trousers in record time. She dropped to the floor, but Valentine was there to catch her right before her body touched the bloody surface.

"Hey, let's not sleep here. Okay?" He scooped her up into his arms, and before Ennis had time to register much else, she felt her bed beneath her, the bloodied sheet gone. The semi-scratchy quilt was even welcomed now. She tucked herself tightly into a ball on her side, closing her eyes.

"I don't feel good," she whimpered. She could feel the tears starting. *Ugh, foolish emotions! I guess I'm that exhausted.*

Valentine sighed, rubbing her shoulder. "I know. I'm sorry about all this." He looked towards the window, then towards the bedroom door. She opened an eye, inspecting him. *It's not your fault.* She wanted the energy to tell him so. Turning his gaze back to her, he sat down on the edge of the bed near the window. A few moments of silence passed.

His voice was soft. "Do you want me to stay here whilst you sleep?"

Her eyes opened and blinked. *Oh no... Uh... Well, I guess it'd be okay as long as he and I stay sensible.* "Please," she whispered. "I don't know if Saeva bought it or not. I don't want him killing me in my sleep." She was breathless by the time she finished her words.

"I won't let that happen. But I don't need to be in your room to do that. So I'll ask again. Do you want me to stay?" His face was serious.

"I mean... If you don't have to be here..." *Well, I want him here, but it might cause trouble. But I'd feel more secure with him actually being here. And it's less of a distance to travel if something happens.* "But... I..."

"Yes?"

She shifted uncomfortably. "Let's just both remain respectful okay?"

He smiled.

"What?" she said, feeling her face redden.

"No, no, please don't be embarrassed." He sounded genuine. "I find that extremely admirable. And absolutely, I'd planned to be nothing less. Forgive me if I've been anything but."

She nodded, feeling her body's tension ease a little. "Thank you. And yes—I mean no, you-you've been very kind." Feeling her eyes close, she tried to keep them open but failed.

"Thank you for being virtuous."

"Thanks be to Jesus for saving me," she said, feeling sleep start to invade her mind.

"I do thank Him," he whispered, but she wasn't sure if that was meant for him or her. She hummed anyway, a slight smile briefly gracing her face. A grey haze settled onto her mind, and she started thinking of random things, not all good. She realized her eyes had closed and flung them open.

Amidst terrible things, there was still the promise of good to come. That had partially been sustaining her. She thought of what awaited her after she died. It would be sweet. Perfect. She just hoped she'd live a little longer on this earth and not go out in a horrible way. Like by the hands of the brothers. The future seemed so much nearer when death was present. Even so, she knew God would work it out for her good.

Her eyes were sealed shut again with sleep in the pitch black room, but her mind swum with a street of gold.

~

"Ennis?" she heard a voice say.

Trying to focus her eyes, she felt that her head was on something very much not a pillow. She felt at what it was and pulled her hand back, finding her fist clutching a bread roll. *Do I smell lemons?* Her brows furrowed.

189

"You fell asleep eating your breakfast." Valentine chuckled. He sat in the green chair, dressed in his black vest still, writing in a forest green book.

"I did?" She looked at her bed and saw a tray sitting on top of the blanket.

"Yes. I suppose you were half-asleep when you started eating."

Memories from last night finally shredded her sleep-riddled mind. "Oh... Wait, what about the brothers! Won't they wonder where I am? Where you are? What time is it?" Panic began to build in her stomach. But hunger shot her through with pains, and she gripped her middle. She was starving. Without hesitation, she fit the roll entirely into her mouth.

His pen stopped, and he looked at her. "No, both are still asleep. And right now I'm 'getting an early start on cleaning.' I've cleaned the house already and prepared their breakfast. It's seven in the evening, by the way. But they'll be here for you in a half-hour or so after they wake. There's no need to panic."

She looked around, coming up with no evidence of forced entry. "But... Did Saeva come back at all last night? And thank you for protecting me."

Valentine blinked, resting a hand on his chin. "No, actually. Neither of them did. I suppose you really did fool him. And you're most welcome."

He started to pace the room slowly, abandoning his book on the chair. "This is good. If they're truly buying it, it means this buys us even more time."

Ennis perked up at his tone. "What do you mean?"

He eyed her warily, hands looking disquieted at his sides. "Well, if we're out of time, we're pretty much left with one option that doesn't involve killing or torturing them."

The roll felt stuck in her throat, and she swallowed hard. "We leave," she said breathlessly.

He frowned, folding his arms. "Precisely. We leave when our efforts have been exhausted or we're out of time. I'm afraid we'd fare better against the weapons than if they see through our ruse and try to off us themselves. Don't be fooled by their personalities."

Her lungs burned, and she felt another shot of fear. Clearing her throat a little, she forced her mind to stop thinking of how she'd partially been lulled by the brothers. *Come on, brain. Think about now. You can analyse that later!* "I'll do what I have to do to survive." She paused. "But I really don't want to kill anyone."

His eyes seemed far away. "I know. The conscience is a strong force, and it can alert you of the need for change, or it can drive you mad."

"So it's agreed. If we can't find the codes, we leave. If they come after us, we fight—" Her mind was interrupted with a thought. She slapped her forehead. "V... What if we escape, and they track me down later? What if they track down my family? They'll know my name and address. My insurance info is in my car, and maybe they rifled through my wallet! They've probably already gone through them." Worry crashed over her head, sending her to her knees. Valentine eased her down before her knees met the unforgiving floor and then gave her space. She touched her eyes. Tears. The waves were too strong and massive to escape. She was dying, drowning. Drowning in hopelessness. Staring at the wooden floor, she raked her hand through her slightly curly hair. Several dark hairs fell out, and her eyes shot open. She'd been worried about her life, but what if the brothers were to find out about her family? What if they wanted to take vengeance? Her heart sped up. What's worse, what if she died and they *still* wanted vengeance? She couldn't protect them then. Could she even protect them now? She clutched at her neck, trying to control her breathing.

"Hey, hey," V said, crouching beside her. "It's going to be okay. I'll protect your family *and* you. I won't let them kill your family."

Ennis's vision blurred, and she rubbed her eyes. "Thank you, V. Thanks so much. I... I don't know what to say—" *Oh, God, please let nothing happen to my family...*

"Don't worry about it at all. I'm glad to help," he said earnestly, his hands resting on his crouching knees.

She was still for a moment, enveloped in thought. "Hey, V?"

"Yes, Ennis?"

"How long have you been alone?" She mentally chided herself, biting her lip. *Why are you asking this, Enn! A little impertinent, don't you think? But... he doesn't have family, does he? Maybe some other vampire friends?*

His relaxed hands seemed to tighten, and he was silent for a beat. "I think it's been decades. Friends aren't exactly something you want to keep around in the vampire world unless they are other vampires. Even then, secrets slip if you don't trust the right people, vampire or not. Sometimes humans can be advantageous friends, but you have to go through their deaths each time. You think you might get used to it, but... it hurts every time." His eyes were filled with shadows.

She sniffled. "I'm sorry you've had to go through that. That has to be so tough. And I'm sorry I'm adding another heartache to your list then."

He gasped quietly and moved to crouch before her. "Oh, please don't think it's that bad. Don't ever think your positives will not outweigh the pain that would come after your death. You are someone I'm proud to know, even in the few days that I've had with you," he said, staring into her eyes. "Deaths, while painful, do mean knowing people who gave you joy. And I didn't say that has stopped me from making human friends altogether." He smiled, but she could see the pain in it.

"You hardly know me though," she admitted. "But I understand the sentiment because I feel the same way about you." She half-smiled. "Logic tells me this could end horribly, but that's a risk in any relationship. Any relationship can turn sour. But we still take the chance in case they are ultimately sweet."

"That was..." Valentine started, his face visibly relaxing.

She rolled her eyes. "Cheesy."

"It was true," he added with a grin.

She gave a heavy sigh, rubbing her face and looked around the room again. "Okay... So what we *can* do about all this to get out of here is keep searching, right?" she said to him but also for her own sake.

"Yes. Although take it easy, Ennis. You're pretty weak right now. We don't have to rush just yet, but let's get ready for another act."

~

13

It was dusk when Ennis emerged damp but dressed. Her soggy hair drooped on her forehead. The washing she'd done after the vomit session hadn't left her feeling very clean. Even though she was expecting to faint in the shower, she had recovered fairly well considering everything she'd been through thus far.

She'd pulled on her forest green long-sleeve and black trousers again, her cleanest clothes. Valentine had been gone for some minutes, and the smell of lemon assaulted her nose as she stood with her arms akimbo in the middle of the bedroom. The rain beat mercilessly on her window. "How can one place rain so much?" She sighed.

Her bloody clothes had been removed from the bathroom as well as the washcloths and towels. All traces of blood on the floors, walls, and furniture were gone. She shook her head. *He really does a good job of cleaning.* In thought, she looked down at her own hands. Only hours ago they had been covered in blood. She had just scrubbed the remaining red remnants from under her fingernails during her third shower this evening. Actually, she was surprised to make it through one shower, let alone three. Looking left, she found an open soup can near the end of her bed. Two holes. She half-smiled as she took the can and drank the familiar taste. *I don't think I want tomato soup ever again for the rest of my life.* She was already full from the earlier meal but didn't know when she'd be able to eat again and knew she needed the salt and calories, which had been in deficit for too long.

A knock disrupted her meal, and her head whipped towards the door.

Silence.

Quietly, she placed the can behind the curtain and moved to open the door.

Benedict.

Standing with his head tilted, Benedict bowed slightly. She felt self-conscious when she saw that his tall, lean figure was covered with a forest green sweater and black trousers. *I hope he doesn't comment. And... does his face look abnormally pale this morning–er, night?*

He smiled with his eyes shut. "Hi, my lady!"

"My lady?" Keeping her face as blank as possible, she gripped the door.

"I've brought you breakfast." He whipped a glass of blood from behind his back.

She steeled her face. "Of course."

"Here." He handed it to her. She nodded once, smoothly closed the door, locking it, and then whirled into a frenzy. Stripping back the curtains, she splashed the blood into the glass bulb. A knock at the door made her heart and limbs jump, causing the blood in motion to splatter over the curtains and her hands. She nearly let out a roar of aggravation but tiptoed as quickly and quietly as possible to the door, opening it. Benedict looked slightly startled as she appeared before him. She shoved the empty glass back at him.

The smell of iron had already permeated the air in her room, and it mixed with the lingering lemon scent. She held back a gag. Sticking her nose in the air, she sniffed. "Thanks."

She remembered V's words to remain in her own character, but she couldn't help putting on a persona. It calmed her nerves, however slight. It made it as if this whole thing were a play. A sham.

Benedict took the glass and then smiled. "You have a little something—" He reached a hand out towards her, and she lunged backwards, feeling the urge to fight take over.

Her nostrils flared, and her heart kicked into overdrive. "What are you doing!"

He huffed a laugh and shook his head. "I was going to get a little bit of blood, right—" He took a big step forward until he was in her room and made to wipe at her cheek. His smile had dropped. And she noticed.

"No!" she barked as she swatted away his incoming hand. A stunned expression betrayed her. She stood wide-eyed.

Benedict loomed over her, and his friendly face fell back into place. But she saw something stirring in his eyes, lurking beneath their vibrant green show. Up close, she noticed the bruise on his nose was practically gone but had an odd coloration. Concealer? In an instant, Benedict backed out the door and gestured for her to follow, complete with another infuriating smile. "So sorry. I didn't mean anything by it."

Ennis tried to regain her mind. *What! Wha-what was that! Lies! He was in my room! What if- Oh! The lemons! The cleaning. Could he smell it? He'd have to have had. Did he notice? What about the blood spatters on the curtains! My forehead! He's testing my boundaries, isn't he! That was a definite test!* Her stomach churned and rolled.

Benedict stood waiting, arm held horizontally, gesturing her towards the stairs, a handkerchief in one hand. She blinked a few more times and then followed him robotically, trying to keep her panic below the surface. He let his arm fall, and stuffed the unused fabric back into his pocket. She mentally noted to wash her hands soon. They were feeling quite sticky.

As they walked, Benedict gabbed away, but she was consumed with her own thoughts, even though she knew it could be beneficial to listen. But she just couldn't. She caught a little bit of his rant as she refocused with some effort away from her mulling. "So I'm stuck with all the writing while he gets to do what he wants. Not that I mind writing, of course. It's just not my *favorite* thing to do. Maybe second favorite. But he gets to *paint*. I'm not a good painter myself. I tried, but my work didn't stand up to his. Maybe if I practice more—"

"I think we all have our strengths," she added automatically.

He stopped and looked over his shoulder. A smile returned to his face. "Hmm?" It struck her that he, like Saeva, would be rather handsome if he weren't a twisted human being.

"Hmm?" she voiced, echoing his tone. Waking up from her daze more fully, her heart skipped a few beats. "Oh... Well..." Her mind was blanking. "I think that we... shouldn't try to be as good as someone else but rather best ourselves. Comparison leads to dissatisfaction."

He nodded, sticking out his lips. "Said like a true sage." He smiled, turning around to walk backwards to face her. "Maybe you're right... I shouldn't try to be as good as him," he said thoughtfully, a finger on his chin. "And I have other talents." She thought he sounded a bit cryptic. He shook his head as if coming out of a daydream. "Well, as I said earlier, I'll leave you with my brother again while Valentine and I edit." He sighed dramatically. "Never become a writer, Ennis. The work never ends. Nothing is ever perfect as it should be."

She pressed her lips harder together and held on to her stony expression. They were at the door of Saeva's painting studio. A lump formed in her throat at the smell of acrylic.

He winked as he opened the door for her. "Maybe I'll see you at lunch."

Inside sat Saeva, already painting in his same spot as yesterday. He was wearing his same brown leather jacket as usual too, covering some black vest and white shirt. *What a combo...*

Saeva cast a glance towards the open door. "Sit down," he commanded.

Benedict gave a tsk. "Be nice, Brother. She's our guest."

More like prisoner.

Ennis stepped in hesitantly, looking over her shoulder at Benedict, whose hand rested on the doorknob. His eyes met hers with a friendly smile as he closed the door.

"Sit down," Saeva snapped again, almost sounding bored.

She huffed and walked as slowly as possible to her seat. *He's in a great mood.* If he was going to cause her torment for another day, then she would have to find a way to deal with it. His odd, slightly friendly demeanor from yesterday seemed to have vanished. And she wanted to know why. Hadn't she fooled him? Was he getting more suspicious? *Does he know?*

He glanced over at her and huffed, his expression scorching. He threw his paintbrush onto his palette, stood up, and stormed over to her. Her body froze, and he snatched her wrist. "I told you to *sit down*," he snarled. He yanked her forwards, and she stumbled behind him in his stormy wake. Not a word escaped her, and she let him throw her down into the red seat again. When he released her wrist, he looked down at his hand and then to hers.

His eyes widened slightly. "What's this?" He turned his reddened hand towards her.

"Strawberries." She gave him a look.

Anger flashed in his eyes again, and he whipped out a cloth, not unlike Benedict's, and wiped his hands of the blood. She watched him intently, and he turned his eyes on hers. His eyes traveled down from her face. With an exasperated sigh, he snatched up her hand and furiously wiped it off, moving to the next one when he was complete. She was frozen, allowing him to hastily clean off the slightly dried blood, and her mind was blank. Once he was done, he crumpled the fabric and threw the cloth across the room into a bin. She blinked, her eyes lingering on the now reddened cloth hanging on for dear life before it fell into the basket.

He turned and snapped the window open. It let out a hideous shriek against the age of its frame, and she flinched. She wanted to cover her ears but resisted, clenching her teeth instead. A gush of pure air hit her face, which made her shoulders subconsciously loosen a little. Stomping back to his seat, he picked up his brush, dabbing furiously.

So it's going to be like this today, aye? Ennis took a deep, silent breath. She could handle this. It'd give her more time to think anyways and maybe rest a little. Fewer questions and statements to dodge, but his toxic attitude was smogging the room.

Looking out the window, she caught sight of the grey night. The wind shredded leaves from

199

bony branches. The sky was full of dark clouds, quickly billowing towards the house. The rain had stopped at some point during her encounter with Benedict, even though it'd been hounding her window minutes ago. She remembered the bloodied curtains. And her soup behind them. *I didn't get to finish my soup... I needed the salt.*

"Was I too rough on you?" Saeva asked, snapping Ennis from her thoughts. She gave him a stunned look. *What?*

"I apologize," he murmured.

What lies.

Her shoulders squared. "Do not touch me again," she growled. The effort made her head swim. *Okay, no more of that. I might've been fine earlier, but I've hit a wall now.. I'm really not doing so well. Okay... God, please help me live.* Too little sleep, food, and rest. Too much stress. And murderous people. Eyeing one of the said murderous people, she knew that he could really do some damage to her if he wanted. That is, if he found out she was human and not the extremely strong being he thought she was. If she was a vampire in his eyes, then she shouldn't have to worry about them making any real power moves. In their minds, she could easily overpower them. As long as they believed that, then *they'd* have to worry about being slaughtered. If she could keep up the persona.

"Or what?" he taunted, setting his paintbrush aside. Her heart rate soared, and her eyes honed in. *Oh no...* "Will you *bite* me, Ennis?" He stood up and advanced until he was a few paces in front of her. Her breathing picked up as she clenched her fingers into the red velvet arms. "Will you *kill* me?" he challenged. She wanted to run. To jump out the window and escape. She forced her body to remain still. He looked positively predatory as his blue eyes trained on her, his head moving from side to side, begging her to make a move. His brow was furrowed in mockery. *How do I fight, God?* Her vampire façade was her defense against death. Unless Valentine was in the vicinity. But she didn't want to bet on it. *What do I do?* She wanted to chide him not to tempt her but decided against it.

"You're all talk and no bite," he spat, frowning. "You act so high and mighty, but you really are a pathetic, little vampire. So young."

She bit her tongue, but words seethed in her mind, craving escape. Then it hit her. *He's calling me a vampire! Good! Good, Ennis!*

"And yet..." he sauntered over to her, staring her down, "you don't even have anything to say to me." He loomed over her, placing his hands on the red velvet armrests. She remained seated, a determined look covering her face. "Why?"

She continued to stare at him, her mouth closed casually.

His furrowed brow released a little. "Why won't you respond?"

She let a smile creep up and broke eye contact, turning her head towards the inside of the studio. She realized that he was leaning in closer, and she closed the gap between them, pushing him away with her confidence. Both of them were standing now, and she wore a scowl. "Saeva, I won't play your games. Paint or be done with it!" His eyes were slightly wider now, and his face was blank. He took a couple of steps backwards.

Without another word, he turned on his heel and sat back down on his soft chair, looking sour. He picked up his palette, and the sounds of brush strokes filled the room again. She tried to shake her

nerves away mentally since she didn't exactly want
to shake them away physically with him watching.
Gliding back into her seat, she stared at the
welcoming floor. The nerves festered instead, and
she looked out the window, desperate for
something to gather her attention. The shifting sky
was a welcomed distraction.

The moon became completely shrouded by
thick, threatening puffs of black, and the wind
picked up, skewing her bangs. A jolt of adrenaline
shot through her, and she shifted her body so the
wind wouldn't give her away.

~

Several hours of silence passed, and she felt as
if she were the paint drying. Saeva had been sitting
there, staring at her as the paint dried in rounds.
She wanted to let out her annoyance but only kept
a plastered expression of boredom, staring out at
the dreary night, ignoring his observation and the
fact that the rain would blow into her face. And he
didn't seem to care that the area near the window
was getting wet either. What he was thinking, she
didn't know. Thankfully he wasn't questioning her
during their painting episodes, which she found
concerning. In their shoes, she thought she'd be
interrogating the "vampire" slyly. But Saeva was
silent.

Every once in a while she would turn to gaze
indoors, and sometimes this elicited a snappy
command from Saeva to get back into her original
position. But the room looked inviting. Light
compared to her dark thoughts. Her hands itched
to explore its paint-splattered wooden cabinets and
drawers. At least she was able to think about things

during the silence. If she were with Benedict, she thought she'd have a harder time getting away with that due to his exuberant talkative and *questioning* nature.

But as time passed, she could feel herself becoming weaker and weaker. Her vision blackened or took a dizzy dive every now and then when she turned her head. Sometimes it happened when her head was still and staring at a faraway object. And from past experience, she knew this wasn't a good sign.

She snuck a peek at Saeva, finding him sitting, engrossed in his painting with a face of pure concentration. He hadn't tried to rile her up in hours. She snapped her eyes back to the scenery, absentmindedly gazing outside. The sky was thick with dark clouds rolling in the distance. The larger storm had been culminating ominously for a while now some miles off. Only small bouts of rain had come off and on. *How many more days will I be stuck in this psycho house?* She looked at her hands and saw the smallest traces of blood. She frowned. *At least they're buying my act.*

Ennis's gut started screaming red alert, but she looked around and saw that everything was as it had been for the past many hours. *What's up, body?* A sudden wave of lightheadedness struck her. Looking up, she noticed the storm was fast approaching. *Storms make me feel worse. And... rain... Water!* Distant thunder shook the air, and she realized she was too dehydrated. Her energy deficit was also seeking revenge.

She stood up, squaring her shoulders. "I'm going to the bathroom."

Saeva continued to paint, not even looking up. Quirking an eyebrow, she gingerly made her way to the door and swung it open and closed behind her. *That was easy...* She let out a sigh of relief. But that sigh went straight into Benedict's chest. A yelp escaped her, and she flung herself backwards into the closed studio door.

There was a glint in his eye. "What's this?" With a smile, he squinted his eyes. "Are you trying to run away?" A tray rested in his left hand, piled high with a ham sandwich. Her mouth fell open and watered. She promptly closed it and tried to refocus her eyes, finding them unwilling to cooperate.

Her spine straightened, and she cleared her throat once. "Actually, yes. To the bathroom. Now if you'll excuse me..." Sidestepping him, she continued on but slowed her walk after a few paces and turned around. Benedict was staring at her with a slight, curious smile. She couldn't shake how creepy he looked. *What's he staring for? Is he waiting for something? Is this a test?* With a quick thought, her eyes settled on his firmly. "Do you have anything for me?"

His smile deepened, and his eyes closed momentarily. "Ahh, yes, I do. I'll leave it in the studio for your return."

"Thank you," she said, before turning and gliding a few doors down towards the designated bedroom's bathroom she'd been told to use during studio sessions. All the while, she prayed Benedict had brought her blood. And that she wouldn't be expected to drink it in front of them. She prayed...

~

Standing in front of a giant, antique mirror, her eyes followed its design. Its detailed siding was laden with golden swirls and pearls. The expansive bath opposite the mirror made her think about how splendorous the mansion might have been when it had full staffing back in the day. A sigh escaped her. *This place will probably never be like that again. If it ever was in the first place.* Now it had two insane owners. She let her hand glide over the dark brown and gold swirled wallpaper. She wondered where they'd gotten their wealth. *Inheritance or something?* With a shudder, she didn't put it past them to have offed someone just to take the person's money. *Would Benedict actually kill someone?* She definitely didn't have any doubts about Saeva. Her mind lurched at the thought of him. What was he trying to pull, anyways? Was he testing her too? Did he really want her to bite him? Was this his goal? Did he think it would make him a vampire? She knew that wasn't exactly how it worked since Valentine sort of explained it, but perhaps the Cerrit brothers really didn't know. Shaking her head, she tried to stop the circle of unanswered questions. A pressure was building in her head, like the world was bearing down on her, crowding and pressing against her skull. *Oh boy.* She filled some water into her hand from the ornate golden spigot and drank deeply.

When she figured she'd been in there too long, she took one last glance at the sweep of swirling white and grey marble underfoot. The clawfoot bathtub slumbered on top it as if it were awaiting an order to attack intruders. The grand cream-colored marble sink mocked her. In fact, the entire house mocked her. She wondered where the code hints were hidden and let out a laugh, thinking the sink and tub probably knew if furniture could talk. She blinked and looked at herself in the mirror. *Am*

I going crazy? Shuddering, she took another long, cool drink before trudging out of the bathroom, trying not to walk like she'd just gotten off a merry-go-round.

She turned down the hall, back to the painting studio, even though her feet wanted to go elsewhere. "You can do this, Ennis. Just a couple hours more..." She clutched her head and felt as if the ground had lurched to the left. "Stay conscious..."

The fresh air from the window hit her as she walked in, and her lungs were suddenly starving. Saeva was munching on a sandwich in one hand and painting with the other. *Well, I have to admit he's dedicated.*

She barely sat down in her chair without stumbling and stared out the window. *Oh, Lord, please give me strength. My body is failing. I—*

"Don't you want it?" he asked.

Her eyes were still locked on the outdoors, at the black clouds that had been rolling in, towards freedom. *Wow, it got really dark while I was gone. How long was I gone?* She tried not to move. "Huh?"

He scoffed. "The blood."

"No."

An eyebrow went up. "No?"

Her blank expression failed and was replaced with a stormy look. "I will never drink in front of you again. It's dishonorable."

"Dishonorable?"

Her eyes darted towards the trees and then the clouds. "Watching a vampire drink is... dishonorable." She knew she'd have to be wary about what she implied about vampires and their culture. Or else she'd be tangoing even closer to death. She could already smell a rose.

He eyed her silent form. "Why is it dishonorable?"

No response.

He sighed. "Well... then you won't get your blood if you don't drink it in front of me."

Her heart started to pound. *What if I can't get Valentine any more blood?* Surely they kept the blood somewhere Valentine knew, right? Maybe they could work something else out another way. She didn't want to go through another vomiting session and face more potential pathogens. She already wondered if she had caught something. Time would tell. If she lived that long...

She remained indignant, turning her face even more out of his view.

"Fine," he grumbled and picked up his paint brush.

~

How long is this going to last? How long does it take to paint me? Ennis didn't know how long it had been since she'd talked with Saeva. A half hour? An hour? She stood up and thought she heard a creak emanating from her joints.

Saeva gasped slightly, jumping as she approached. "What are you doing?" Walking over towards him, she peered over his shoulder at the painting. Her eyebrows lifted slightly, and she felt herself pale. *Wow...* It actually looked like her. Sure, it wasn't an exact resemblance, but with paintings, it could be difficult to capture an accurate representation. Her own slightly pronounced cheekbones were noticeable as he had painted her looking out the window in a side profile. The window opened up to a blazing red sky, with a few white gauzy clouds attempting to hide the fiery air.

His breathing stopped. As did the sound of the wind. Looking about, she saw the trees whipping outside the window and his shoulders moving up and down slightly. What was wrong with her ears? It suddenly got very hard to think, and she blinked repeatedly, focusing back on her portrait. Black was creeping in on the corners of the painting. *Oh no...* She felt herself fall to her hands and knees, panting. The sound of the trees rushed into her ears. Saeva shot up, eyes wide.

"Ennis?" he gasped, struck in shock. His hands undecidedly hovered between himself and her. But they didn't reach for her.

Oh no... Now now! She tried to stand up, but her body had other ideas, and she crumpled to the floor again. *Fine. Fine! Body, I could really use your cooperation right now!* She felt her heart speed up, and her head felt full of webs. *I hate this... Please go away. Lord, help me!* She held her head in her right hand, and screwed her eyes shut, clutching her left hand to her right shoulder. While she tried to ease her own body, she could comprehend that Saeva was saying her name and asking her questions, but she couldn't muster up the energy to respond or really decipher what language he was speaking. She felt like death. *I think I'm about to die. And I had been doing so well... Lord, receive my spirit.* She gingerly curled herself up into a ball on the floor.

The next moment, she heard a thunk and opened her eyes. There, in front of her face, was a glass of blood. She quickly shut her eyes, rolling her body away.

His voice made sense again. "Ennis, you've got to drink!" She could hear the anger in his shouting.

She responded by clumsily waving off his suggestion.

He got down on his knees next to her. "Then what's wrong?" She could hear actual care in his voice. *That's strange... Or is it fear of losing his prize?*

The last thing she registered before everything went black was a pair of arms scooping her up and the smell of leather.

~

After what she assumed to have been no longer than a minute, she awoke to her head against Saeva's brown jacket. He was carrying her somewhere. She squirmed, but there was little she could do without sending herself back to the black void of unconsciousness. *Agh... If he hadn't moved me, I might've been alright. Ugh.* She certainly did not want to be in his arms right now. *What is he planning to do?* Fear shot through her, and she turned her neck uncomfortably. His mouth was set, but his eyes were glistening with concern.

"I'm okay," she managed to say and hoped he'd let her recover by herself. *If I can recover.*

He kept his eyes straight. "Shhh," he hushed softly.

He's not letting me down. He's not setting me down! Struggling to get free of his grip, her voice tensed. "Seriously, you can put me down."

He held on to her tighter.

Panic had now thoroughly set in. "No, really. Put me down!" she gasped.

He froze in place. "Is my blood making you uncomfortable?"

She quickly thought over his possible responses if she told him that it was his actions and self, not

209

his blood, that caused her panic. But he'd probably ignore her if her response were anything but about blood. If she said yes, who knew what he would do.

Her voice came out flat. "No, you are."

He switched directions and walked back up the twisting hallways. Realizing that they were still on the fourth floor, her heart pounded. Where had they been heading? She and Valentine hadn't searched that floor yet. That would be tonight. *Maybe.* But what was on that floor? She wracked her brain for the answer, but her head still felt fuzzy.

Unfortunately, Saeva's nice charade was still in play. She kept struggling, but a thought hit her hard in the head. She'd imagined something like this happening. But what happened in her daydreams? She wracked her brain. *The key!* She frantically thought of which pocket he had put the painting studio key into before. Trying to keep her anxiety at a minimum, she forced her breathing to slow so she could focus. Time was running out as they descended the stairs. *This is going to be embarrassing... But it's now or never.* She flailed her arms and clutched at his jacket, putting on an act. "Put me down!"

He sighed. "No, Ennis," he said as if saying it for the millionth time.

"I don't need you. And I don't need your leather jacket either," she mumbled, making a mess of the leather, picking at it and flinging her arms about. "Let go!"

He shrugged in his jacket uncomfortably. "No, *you* let go."

"No," she said childishly, feigning a near unconscious attack. *Is this what acting drunk is like?* She gave another spurt of precious energy and ransacked his jacket, mumbling grumpily about

210

how brown and leathery it was and how the smell of leather was sickening and bad for cows.

Feeling quickly around for any inner pockets, she managed to find one, but it yielded nothing. She felt for more pockets, and he stopped walking.

He peered down at his chest. "What are you doing?"

Oh no... Quick, Ennis, think! She let her hand linger on his heart, and she mentally hissed at what she was doing. "You have a heartbeat."

He quirked an eyebrow. "So do you. Which is odd because I thought vampires didn't *have* heartbeats," he said tightly.

"Some do. Some don't," she explained, feigning delirium.

"Really?" he asked, half-skeptical, half-curious.

"Mmhmm." *Ugh! No key!* She removed her hand and wished she could vanish. She could feel her face redden. She didn't enjoy toying with him nor being this close.

He huffed and recommenced striding down the hall. "We'll be painting again tomorrow."

She was severely embarrassed and uncomfortable by the time he kicked open her door and lowered her onto the bed. She immediately curled away from his standing figure and shut her eyes. She wouldn't thank him. She didn't want to encourage his behavior of picking her up like that and not complying with her demands to be set down. But she did want to get on his good side. It was probably better to be there than on his bad side. Whatever she was doing seemed to be working. But she wondered why though. He was very confusing.

Her heart jumped into her throat. *The blood from this morning! The soup! The lemons!* She peeked at the curtains. Clean. *Valentine.* She let out a shaky breath.

Saeva stood around for what seemed to be a couple of long, uncomfortable minutes to her before the door closed. He hadn't walked around her room either, and she thought he just stared at her for a long time and then finally left.

She wanted to decipher his actions, but her head refused to cooperate. However, she knew what she needed to get her brain and body back in gear. Food, water, salt, and sleep.

~

It was about dinnertime when she awoke. And the nasty storm had made its way to the house. The pitter-patter on the window tapped as if it were trying to tell her the secret to her freedom, beckoning her outside, speaking to her in Morse code too rapid to translate.

A few clangs echoed from the stairwell. While the house was big, the stairwell carried sound very well. She groaned as another pang of clanging rang out.

She had slept but was still feeling very weak. Her body was shaking, and it seemed hard to think. *Not a good sign.* Rubbing her eyes, she sat up. A shudder ran through her. "At least I got some of one necessity out of the way." She crawled out of her bed and her heart surged. She gasped, eyes widening as she tumbled from the bed. The blanket that had gotten yanked down with her softened her fall onto the hardwood floor. Untangling her limbs from the fabric, she stopped. "Wait..." She ran the rough blanket through her hands. "I don't remember getting under the blanket..." *Was it V? Or...* She shook her head and crawled her way to her suitcase, verifying that her journal was untouched. To be safe, she had written in Pig Latin and used random words from other languages she'd learned over the years so that it added an extra layer of security. *It was foolish of me to write anything down.* She flung the journal back into the suitcase, going back to position it just right underneath her clothes and placing a string on it just so. *I need to find a place to hide that. Or burn it.* She pulled out a tomato soup can from her luggage, and her mouth watered. *V must have put this here.* Oh, how she was hungry! She knew that she hadn't consumed enough calories, and it was severely catching up with her. She felt like she was constantly being choked and could pass out without further warning. And now she needed V's fangs to puncture the metal. But he wasn't there. She wanted to cry.

Instead, she mustered up the strength and crawled into the bathroom, shutting the door behind her. Floundering to bathtub, she started working the lid against the tub's nozzle. Its sharp edges dented the top with no small effort from her tired arms. A little surge of happiness shot through her at the progress. But that progress soon flattened to disappointment as the lid denied entry. She grumbled, positioning her back against the tub's wall.

She looked morbidly at the tin. *Teeth can be replaced...* In desperation, she bit into the can, resulting in eight sore teeth instead of food. *Did I actually think that would work?* She ran a hand through her dark, sweaty hair.

Her body was suddenly wracked with incoordination, and the can slipped from her hands, rolling onto the floor with a clatter. She shot up despite her illness, grabbed the can, and stumbled towards her suitcase outside the bathroom. Her hands hit the floor before she had meant them to. Black. That's all she could see. Blinking away the darkness, she crawled the rest of the way to her luggage. She flung the unopened can into her suitcase and grabbed the only object of some heft she had in there: a shoe. She snatched its twin before lunging back into the bathroom. The rumbling of footsteps approached, and she gritted her teeth. *As expected.* She carefully placed one shoe on her foot and the other in the bathroom's corner. She silently set her old boots on the ground. A pounding ripped through the room.

"Are you okay!" a desperate voice shouted through the door. She hastily, yet clumsily, made her way to the door and pulled it open with a shaking hand.

Saeva stood there breathing heavily with wild eyes. *How tiresome.* She held up a hand. "I'm fine. I just dropped a shoe." At that moment she realized how ridiculous her plan sounded. Her eyes traveled down with his. She was wearing water shoes now. *I mean, at least it covers for the dropped can sound, right? Right?* But wearing them as normal shoes seemed ridiculous.

"Oh." He pulled his head up to face her. Once his shoulders relaxed, his brow lifted.

"I-I uh..." *Ennis! Don't stutter!* "I was concerned... with the cleanliness... of the bath. I was going to bathe." *What! That doesn't even make any sense! And I was going to* bathe? *What century am I from!*

He turned his body out towards the hall a little. "Oh? I'll have Valentine clean it tonight. But... can vampires catch... foot fungus?" he questioned, his cheeks slightly reddening. She was intrigued by his current non-dominating nature. It was startlingly caring. She suppressed a shudder.

It sunk in that she'd been standing there in silence for far too long. "Well... I don't like to walk where it's unclean." She sniffed and then slammed the door. "I'm perfectly fine!" she added, which was a lie. She needed salt and food, and she couldn't get either. She prayed to God that V would hurry with food and his can opening skills.

The clanging from the kitchen had stopped, and the rain sounded louder now, whether from the absence of sharp clangs or her intent to hear if Saeva had walked away yet. The rain splattered against her window, and she wished she could hear a tune in it. But it made a monotonous grey noise.

She sighed, slipped down the wall next to the door, and held her knees to her chest. Her vision was blackening again, and she felt like death. Her stomach was starving, reminding her with sharp pangs. And so were her lungs. She *needed* to get out of here, and she wouldn't get very far with low energy like this. She'd have to get better about sleeping and eating if she could help it. If *V* could help it. She needed regular meals and plenty of them. But she was already trying her hardest. She tamped down her tears and the choking sensation that threatened to suffocate her. Gritting her teeth, she stared at the black window. "I will not give up." Her body was shuddery again, reminding her that it was not pleased with her new regimen. "Sorry, body."

There was a gentle knock on the door. "Ennis?" the low voice called. With a sigh that made her shoulders relax, she clumsily moved a hand to the lock and Valentine walked in. "I have your—" He took one look at her and then moved so fast she couldn't register. He set down a tray and a glass of blood on the bed and a bucket of cleaning supplies before he was at her side, helping her up by the elbow. *Why is it people always help people up by the elbow? Wouldn't the waist be more efficient?* She felt a wave of gratitude as he picked her up underneath her knees and shoulders and carried her to the bed. He set her down gently and removed the tray's lid. It was a pork chop with gravy and a side of asparagus. Looking upwards, she whispered thanks to God, then dug in hungrily.

She glanced at Valentine. "Thank you. For... everything," she said between bites. She swallowed thickly and cleared her throat, pausing. "Sorry for being impolite, I just really need calories right now. But really, thank you."

A smirk crept onto his face, and she wanted to know the story behind it. "I don't stand on ceremony, Ennis." But he spoke again without elaborating. "I'm here to 'clean your bathroom,'" he said with air quotes before picking up the glass of blood from the bed. "I'm surprised they asked me to bring this to you. They must really be engrossed in their latest draft. This will be their tenth published book." He took a long gulp and gazed at her as if looking through her.

She took another bite of pork. "What?"

He shook his head. "You *really* don't mind if I drink in front of you?"

"Not at all," she said, waving her hand in a placating way.

After she swallowed, she frowned slightly. "You don't mind... me eating, right?"

He let out a long laugh. It was odd. She didn't think she'd heard him laugh this long. It was deep and rich. She liked it. Dabbing away a tear with his white shirtsleeve, he took a deep breath. "No, I don't. I... I don't think anyone's ever asked me that before." He was overtaken by an onset of giggles now.

She put her fork down. "Are you... drunk?" she asked cautiously.

He wiped away another tear. "No, Ennis, we can't get drunk. Alcohol doesn't do anything to us. It's just expensive to drink. Some like the taste though. But not me," he explained, regaining his composure. "Maybe I'm drunk on hope."

She still wondered why he found that so funny. Maybe it was weird to ask, but she didn't know what it was like to be a vampire, and she wanted to be considerate.

He straightened his silver vest, and his smile eased away. "What actually made that noise?"

Her head whipped up. "Huh?"

"That noise Saeva charged up here for."

She tried to clear the lump in her throat. "Ah, well I dropped a soup can trying to open it," she admitted.

He frowned in thought. "I see. I'll bring a knife or something for you to keep here. I'm afraid if I took their only can opener, they might get suspicious if they found it missing or anywhere outside the kitchen. I don't know how much good a knife would do you though." He tapped his finger on his glass absentmindedly.

She nodded. "Right." Her head took another reel. *No more movement for me.*

His eyes widened. "Ennis?" he asked slowly. Her heart revved. "Why do you smell like leather?"

Her stomach dropped. She'd forgotten what had transpired between her and Saeva. Her mind wasn't working properly tonight. *How did I forget that!* "Uh... Well, Saeva carried me to my room." She could see Valentine's eyes burn with fire, even though his face remained slightly confused. "I nearly fainted when I stood up in the painting studio. I haven't slept, drunken, or eaten enough. I actually did pass out, which is weird because usually I just come really close to unconsciousness, but never actually go unconscious," she explained. "I told him to put me down." Her eyes were on her plate. "He didn't."

His eyes were a thousand degrees. "V?" she asked timidly.

His intense gaze lasted a couple more seconds, although they felt like eons to her, and he took another sip of blood. "Sorry," he said shortly. She knew it was an apology for his reaction. But he gave no further explanation. *Huh.*

Looking towards the window, she resumed eating her pork chop.

~

Since Valentine's "cleaning" time was running out, he told her he'd return once the brothers went to bed. They were still up and expecting an appearance from him before bedtime.

"We'll be searching the fourth floor tonight. But we'll need to be even more careful. The brothers sleep on that floor, so it'll be a bit more dangerous." With that, he closed the door, tray in hand. Ennis felt the odd warmth of his presence pull from her bones. It swirled from her sinews before vanishing

218

like mist. She shivered, pulling the blankets around her.

She flopped down on the bed and cocooned herself under the covers, feeling the familiar exhaustion overtake her. She let her eyes close.

~

"Ennis?" a gentle voice said.

Scrunching her eyes, she emerged from the blankets. She had been dreaming. A weird dream, she had to admit, but it was somewhere far away from this nightmare. She wanted to keep sleeping to get away from her current situation. But if she kept sleeping, how could she improve her reality?

"Are you ready for our venture this morning?" Valentine asked, placing some paperclips on her nightstand.

"Mmhmm." She groaned, flipping the blankets off her. He held out her black cloak, and she begrudgingly rolled out of bed, gripping the black fabric. Flinging it around her shoulders, she padded her way to the sink. A sudden bout of dizziness struck her that sent her to her knees. Valentine was at her side as she panted on the floor.

He placed a hand on her shoulder, his voice restrained. "Are you okay?"

Darting a glance at his checked expression, she blew a breath out. "Yeah. Got up too fast. Most times I can get out of bed without a problem, but... I think... I think..." *I don't want to get him down, but I think I'm getting worse.* She eased her way to a standing position and quickly lunged for the wall for stability.

His voice came out strained. "What do you think?"

"I'm getting worse." She was breathing hard as she held onto the bathroom doorframe. Valentine's face was blank, and he hummed acknowledgement.

The sink awaited, and she drank deeply from it before wrangling her boots. She dropped her water shoes back in her suitcase. The paperclips near her bed caught her eye. "What's this?"

He crossed his long arms. "For lock picking. You said you knew how? Unfortunately there aren't any books on unlocking locks in the library or I would've tried myself."

She rubbed her eyes furiously and blinked hard. "Right." *Try to remember how this is done, Ennis.*

A few moments passed as she twisted the metal, jabbing her fingers so much they turned red. Finally, they took shape. But was it the right shape? She couldn't tell. *I think this is how they're supposed to look? It's the best I can do from memory.*

Holding up the paperclips to her exposed lightbulb above her headboard, she nodded and made to pocket the makeshift tools. She frowned, patting her trousers. "No pockets." Stuffing them into her shoe, she took a deep breath. "Ready." She stood up and held out a hand. Valentine looked at her and then at her hand. "It's for you. It's a backup set." She plopped the paperclips into his hesitant hand.

The two slipped out of her room and made their way to the fourth floor like two shadows. Their black cloaks billowed behind them as they shifted through the halls, careful not to make much noise.

At the final step, Valentine put a pale finger to his lips. "Remember, they sleep on this floor." She nodded, ducking into the first room of the hall.

Her brow furrowed as she massaged her upper ribs. "Huh?" The room was completely empty except for a fine layer of dust covering the floor like a short carpet. She wondered how many years it had been since the brothers had been in here. Or *anyone.* Valentine was now at her side.

He crossed his arms. "A lot of these rooms are empty on this floor. But there are a few storage rooms up here."

"Oh," she mouthed, shutting the door silently.

Sure enough, each door she opened was filled with nothing but dust and maybe a couple of boxes. It wasn't until the seventh door that a room took more than a few minutes. However, after a quick search, nothing but dusty porcelain dishes was discovered.

Valentine opened the next door, and a frown set deeply into his face. "The main storage room." Ennis peered around him, and she wanted to cry.

Boxes. So many boxes. The room contained piles upon piles of books, boxes containing junk, and lofty shelves housing assorted, dated items. A section near the door had carpet that was less grey and seemed to store stacks of printer paper and things that weren't aged to the color of cheese. "I guess we'd better get started." Her voice was equally grim.

~

Hours... Hours passed searching through that room. Seemingly endless amounts of dusty artifacts strewn around in boxes with old newspapers filled Ennis and Valentine's time. Odd contraptions that were probably from the 19th century passed through her clammy fingers in search of something that might yield clues.

Using her wrist to rub her sore eyes, she wiped her nose on her shoulder, sure that the amount of dust she'd inhaled could have created an army of bunnies. "I want to say we should just bypass this room. But if I were hiding something I didn't want someone to find, I might place it in here for that exact reason." She had finally broken the long void of conversation. Replacing a small box from the shelf she'd been going through, she wiped her forehead and stretched her back, which cracked mercilessly. Crouching down, she picked through yet another peeling box, simultaneously massaging her chest. *Heart pain stinks. I must be low on blood or something.*

Valentine cast her a glance as he sorted through a box of loose papers. "Plus, if you wanted to try and catch someone, this would be the place."

"What do you mean?" She set something that looked like a rectangular kaleidoscope back into its box.

His hand froze on a scrap piece of paper, and his eyes looked far away. "If I had something hidden in here, it'd take a long time to find it if you didn't now where it was. So if I wanted to catch someone in the act, I'd have a longer window."

Humming in response, she rummaged through a dusty tome. Her eyes widened, and she stopped moving. "I hope they don't realize stuff's been moved around." *Why didn't I think of this earlier!* A wave of adrenaline caused her heart to ache even more and added more breathlessness to her already long list of complaints.

"It's alright." He had resumed his searching. "I'm allowed in here and sometimes get things from the new corner. So don't worry. It wouldn't be impossible for something to get shifted around."

She felt a hefty amount of worry lift from her shoulders. *And he can hear them coming, so I shouldn't be too scared.* Her shoulders relaxed a little more.

~

Thankfully Valentine possessed the speed of a superhero due to his virus and had gone through most everything else by the time she'd finished off a tenth of the boxes.

"Nothing?" she asked, a frown forming.

His mouth was in a tight line. "Nothing."

Shaking her head, she lay down on the floor. "This is ridiculous! The code could be hidden in anything. Be any pattern," she growled.

"Or not even be written down at all." He heaved a sigh as he came and stood near her head, peering down at her. "Perhaps this level will still yield something favourable." He looked at the door. "Tonight is a good night to try their bedrooms. I've never checked them," he said as if talking to himself.

She sat up and twisted around to glare at him, ignoring the wave of vertigo. "Can I ask why we didn't do that sooner?" She felt something boil up inside her. *Why wait?* She'd trusted his judgement and figured there was a reason why he didn't want to search the brothers' rooms yet. It would've been the first thing she'd done. He'd said something about safety right? What did he mean?

Standing his ground, he kept his arms lightly at his sides. "Well, their bedrooms are risky. You absolutely do not want to be caught there. The other rooms we could play off easier, but with their rooms, it's most suspicious. Remember I can't exactly force entry there, and I can't pick locks. Replacing doors would not be easy, and I don't trust they wouldn't notice minute damage. However, since we've gotten nothing thus far, that increases the chance that something *is* hidden in their rooms, and now it's worth the risk since we've weeded out the other possibilities."

All of the irritation in her drained out as if she were leaking blood. Her vision went fuzzy, and she fiddled with a bit of pillow stuffing coming from a nearby box. "Makes sense." *Why didn't I think of that? Am I even thinking? God, forgive me.* Sighing, her eyes traveled up to meet his. "I'm sorry for snapping."

Valentine crouched down. "You're forgiven. Don't worry about it," he said with a slightly smile and picked off a fuzzy from her dark hair. He stood up and began assessing the room.

Flatting her hair down, she played with the pillow fluff again. She still wished that they could've searched the brothers' rooms sooner but had to admit that it was better to be careful since they were buying the act, which meant they had time. For now. But that time was coming to an end, one way or another. She felt her stomach roil.

Valentine glided to the windows and let their curtains down, submerging them in weak yellow light from the wall fixtures. "Let's check the last few rooms. Then only the painting studio and their rooms will be left."

She nodded, dusting her hands on her trousers, and followed his trail out the door.

After he had moved forwards, she shot a piercing look at the closed door behind them before they continued their search down the hall.

Valentine stood on guard while Ennis searched the next rooms with her fresh set of eyes. Some of the more sparse rooms didn't even have functioning lights in them. She expected to see a rat or mouse scurry across the floor whenever she opened a new door. But every time Valentine's words came back to her. *"I... found whatever I could."* She swallowed thickly. *Too bad he didn't have something better to eat then. And what about diseases? Do vampires get diseases?*

One room they came by held the bathroom she used during painting studio sessions. Her eyes brightened, and she pointed at the bed with the purple duvet, near which was the bathroom door. "I know this one. I've searched this bedroom and its bathroom already. There's nothing. Nothing but an expensive, clean room."

Stiffening, he nodded once, closing the door by its gilded handle.

The next moment, Valentine flung open a door and pulled Ennis into the darkness, closing the door to a crack.

She couldn't see him clearly through the void, but he looked like he was glancing at the door. "What?" she whispered.

"You stay in here while I go search their rooms." She could feel his words on her face.

Her eyes widened, and she glared his direction. "What about my lock picking? I can be useful!" She felt her fists clenching.

He returned his eyes to hers. "I'll check if the rooms are unlocked, and you stay in this last spare room until I return and report, okay? If they're unlocked, I'll go in. If they're locked, I'll come get you."

Her heart dropped. "But—"

His shoulders were taut. "I'll take the fall for being the creepy person trying their locks during the day. I don't want you getting hurt." She thought his words were coated with well-concealed worry. He cleared his throat. "Plus, I've been here longer than you have, so I'll make up an excuse about needing more paper towels from the painting studio. Kill one bird or I might find a stone."

Her hands found her heart unconsciously. "They'll buy that?"

He shrugged a shoulder. "I used up all the paper towels this evening after I 'spilled' a whole bottle of juice. They keep some supplies in the painting studio. I've seen Saeva carry a roll in every now and then. He's the one with the key." He looked at the door, then at her. "As for Benedict... I'll say I heard something suspicious in his room."

She could feel him willing her to comply. She bit her lip. "Isn't *that* a little suspicious?"

Smiling a little, he used her shoulders to twirl her so she traded places with him. "Ennis, I can talk my way out of it. Don't worry."

"A little late for that." Her hands wanted to do something to ease her nerves, so they found her cape and picked at it. She studied his face, trying to read it in the darkness. *His voice and face are calm, but his eyes aren't. I don't think... Kind of hard to see...* She squinted.

He put a hand on the doorknob. "I'm going to go. And Ennis, sorry to ask this of you, and I know you want to help, but if anything happens, promise me you'll stay in this room please. I don't want you getting involved."

Her face became solemn, and she shook her head. "I can't promise that, V..." She searched for reassuring words but found that she had none.

Letting out a breath through his nose, he closed his eyes briefly. "Fair enough."

As he opened the door, the little daylight that had sneaked into the hall through the poorly kempt curtains made the spare room glow. Ennis felt her rapid heartbeat throughout her entire body as she saw his black cloak vanish down the hall and round the corner. She bounced on her feet, looking back and forth between the dusty spare room and the hall. Within a second, she followed in quick pursuit to see him glide to the end of the adjacent hall.

There were four doors in total in this west hall, two on one side and two on the other. A window with steady beams of sunlight peeking through holes in moth-eaten red curtains rested at the end of the brothers' hall, acting as watchman of the halls' connecting path. She wondered where that way led. *This house is bizarre. And huge!* She saw Valentine stop at one of the doors. A pale hand delicately tested the doorknob. Locked. When he moved over to the door beside it, he looked over at her and quickly waved at her to get out of sight. She wanted to rebel, to stay close, but she knew it wasn't a smart move. She mentally sighed and returned to her lonely, dark spare room.

~

It was pure stress. She jumped at every single sound that echoed in the rickety room. She thought she heard a groan emanate from the corner of the room and shrunk back against the wall. *Nothing's there. Nothing's there. You know this. Come on, Enn...*

The dark was enough to nearly drive her mad. Waiting alone in the unfamiliar room caused imaginary things to crawl their way up her legs with spindly limbs. She involuntarily shuddered. Pressing her ear against the door, she prayed for any sound of Valentine's return. "It's been like twelve minutes. He should've been back by now," she whispered. *Oh, God, please let him be alright and find the password!* She'd been toying with the paperclips, trying to keep her stress down.

A creak crackled the air, accelerating her breathing. She stuffed the paperclips back into her shoe. *V doesn't creak. Maybe he ran into trouble?* She squished her ear harder against the door, unwilling to crack the door. But she didn't hear voices. No indicator that anything was awry besides her own gut and a sound. *Maybe it's a mouse?*

Ancient boards groaned in the hall, and her heart leapt. *Definitely not a mouse.* She tried to take steady breaths so she wouldn't hyperventilate. *V definitely isn't that loud! And he would've come into the room by now.*

It was a brother.

She wanted to peek out the door to see which brother it was. But at the same time, she didn't want to expose herself. Her logical side won out, and the door remained shut. *God, please don't let them hesitate here!* The footsteps passed by the door. Letting out a breath, she clutched the doorframe for support. *Thank You, Lord.*

She waited a moment after hearing them vanish before listening to her curiosity. *Whoever it was, they shouldn't be back for a couple minutes. And if a brother is out, that's not a good sign! V could be in trouble if he's not back by now!* Taking quick breaths, she cracked the door enough to take a peek.

No one.

She slipped through the door and down the corner of the hall the way Valentine had gone earlier. She scanned around its edge. The empty hall tried to echo her breaths, and a sour feeling bit into her stomach. The air even smelled wrong, like its usual dusty odor was gone, hidden by something more sinister. Everything was telling her red alert, and yet she couldn't tell if that warning was for her or for V.

A voice sounded from one of the rooms, and she darted behind the corner again. Staying close to the wall, she strained to hear it over her heartbeat rushing in her ears that cried for her to do something. *Quiet, heart! I can't hear!* Nothing was intelligible. The voice stopped. *Which brother? Which room? Are they talking to V?*

She swallowed thickly and then slinked down the hall. She looked at the farthest door down, the one V was at when he shooed her away. She was certain he was in that one still. Tiptoeing to the portal, she clutched her heart. With a trembling hand, she tested the door he had gone through, turning it as quietly as she could. Locked. Panic struck her, and she nearly collapsed to a crouch. Was he still inside? Who was talking? Did she need to create a diversion? Or... did V go into another room? She tested the other door. Locked. Her heart sunk even further down. Did she dare try using the paperclips to pick the lock when one of the brothers was in his room? It was a fifty-fifty chance. Either way, he was locked in one of the rooms. She removed her hand from the doorknob and let it fall to her side.

"What are you doing out this late?" a voice asked quietly. A man materialized from around the corner. "And at my door?"

Her body froze.

Saeva stood at the beginning of the hall with an arm akimbo and curious eyes.

14

"I—" Ennis's mind was blank. What excuse could she concoct to explain her predicament? What could she say? He was poised at the corner of the hall, arms folded now, with a mug in one hand.

She didn't break eye contact. "I-I wanted some more blankets." *Blankets? That's the best you can do?*

"Blankets, huh?" He chuckled, slowly pacing forwards. He leaned over and set his mug down on the ground.

Her mind began wailing sirens. She needed to get out of there.

"And were you going to steal them from... my room?" He took his time as he stalked his way towards her, his movements careful, calculated. His usual glassy blue eyes were shrouded in shadow.

She felt her fear meld her feet to the floor. Her body was rigid. *Move, body!*

"No, I thought you'd know where they were." She wondered if that even made sense. Her brain failed to compute, and she couldn't bring up her usual cause and effect thinking. *I just lied. I hate lying. Oh, God, sorry! Help me out of this situation, please!*

Finally, she was jolted out of her fear long enough to take a few hasty steps towards the other corner down the hall. The window was taunting her, beaming at her desperation. *Sunlight.*

She felt the trap clamp down on her. No wonder they had their rooms near this place. No wonder the curtains weren't replaced. In their minds, this was vampire repellant. If she walked through without being seriously harmed, she'd have some explaining to do. They obviously thought vampires couldn't be in the sun since they didn't keep reigns on their victims during daylight. Her mind darted around whether she could try to tell him that vampires didn't burn in the sun. *But that would expose—*

"Careful," he warned.

Too close. He was too close.

She felt a hand snap around her wrist, and she turned around, wild.

His eyes taunted her as he pulled her away from the window. "The sunlight."

Her heart reached a feverish pace with his tone. *Not good... Something's not right here.* "Ah, yes. Well, I'll be getting back to my room now." She yanked her arm away, but his grip didn't loosen. Her breathing became erratic. *Help me, God!*

He tilted his head. "Just as I thought."

"What is?" she squeaked. *Agh, voice! Not the time!*

With a smirk, he was looking down at her. "You don't even overpower me." His eyes were searching for a confession.

Her heart stopped. *He knows.* Her panic made her want to babble excuses, to tell him that she wouldn't tell anyone about their endeavor, this house, the vampires. But she knew she'd never keep those promises. And he would know too. *Valentine, where are you!*

"And I know exactly what you want," he purred. *Purred?* Her mind stopped. *Wait, what is he—*

"You've come to visit me this late during the day. You want to talk in private, huh? And about what?" he said, now backing her against the wall, his hand still clenched around her sleeved wrist.

She tried to steel her features, but she knew her eyes were radiating fear.

"And you don't even fight me off, even though you could throw me through the wall." He grinned.

Her stomach twisted at his words. *I was wrong... This is so much worse.*

He released her wrist and loomed over her, putting a hand on each side of her, caging her. He was over half a foot taller than she was and a wall of solid muscle. Without thinking, she tried ducking under one of his arms, but he just slid his arm down too.

Straightening up, her hand flew up to subconsciously flatten her bangs to her forehead. "I don't think we're on the same page," she choked out. He closed the small gap between them, and her hands shot out against his chest to try and keep some distance. She tried to push him away now that both her hands were free, but at that, he smiled. Glaring up at him, she raised her voice. "I don't like you, and I don't want this. I'm a Christian and wouldn't do that." She shoved her hands against his chest again and felt something come loose. Fumbling around, acting as if to find better leverage to move him, she gripped the thing and stuffed it into her pocket discreetly. She gave another push at him but then stopped. Her mind started working out how hard it'd be for her to knock him off balance even if she had a running start. Working from this close, it was hardly an option. *Outwit him or find some nimble escape. Come on, Ennis!*

"And yet you're still here," he purred, so close to her ear she could feel his breath. She shuddered, gritting her teeth. *Oh no, no, no!*

Unable to think, she sputtered the first thing that came to mind. "I don't want to hurt you!"

233

"So you choose to let me play with you instead?" he mused.

"You're not listening." Her body was shaking with fear. *I think I'm going to black out.*

"Then what are you going to do, huh?" He moved his head to her other ear. "Are you going to bite me with those little fangs of yours?"

Ennis tried to make sense of what he was doing. "Am I—No!" she yelled. Her fear stunned her mind. Her brain wouldn't think. When he moved his head closer to her ear, this jolted her to action. "Agh!" She shoved at him with all the strength she could muster, which gave her enough room to slide away from her capturer. "Leave me alone, Saeva!" she growled as she started running down the hall, ignoring her blackening vision and off-kilter inner ear. He easily caught her by the left arm. She yelled. A door opened behind him.

Saeva smirked. "Not until you—"

The sound of a punch died off in the echoey hall. Her face was hard as she glared at him, resentment burning in her eyes. She clenched her fists tighter to hide their shaking, her right hand burning and bright red. He'd hardly moved from the punch. His eyes were wide, his face a mask of shock. Turning his head back towards her, his words trembled. "Did you just—"

In a whirl of black, she vanished. Disoriented, she felt herself being lifted from the ground and smothered in black fabric. She heard a pained cry and smelled iron. And within a dizzying moment, she was back in her room, her door closed, locked, and barricaded with a bureau.

Valentine was fuming, his eyes blazing, and Ennis, for the first time, felt a jolt of fear towards him, even though she knew he wouldn't harm her.

He was breathing heavily. "Did he hurt you?" he demanded.

His cape was abandoned on the floor, and she noted that hers was as well. He'd set her down as gently as a cloud on the edge of the bed and was now crouched before her.

She stared at the floor, seeing right through his form. She tried to snap herself out of it, to process what had occurred, but she could only manage to talk. Her eyes were blank. "What just happened?" She became aware her body was shaking.

Moving away from her, he began to pace. He stared imploringly at her from the other side of the room, his shoulders strung with tension. "I swept you up and gashed that *fool.*" His anger tempered as his expression eased the longer he looked at her, but she could still see it boiling underneath the surface. And she didn't like that.

"Was that wise?" she asked, still staring at the floor.

He blinked. "Wise? I think that it proves you *more* of a vampire." Crossing the room in a blink, he returned to her. "But are you alright? I heard everything."

Her nose caught a whiff of blood. She suddenly realized she needed to get out of these clothes *now*. They felt contaminated. Gazing towards her suitcase, she remembered it was empty of clean outerwear except for a pair of jeans. All her shirts had now been soiled by blood. Floating to the bathroom in a daze, she carried the bedsheet with her. She stripped off her clothes, which smelled terrible. And despite everything that had happened, she couldn't pin down why. She wrapped the sheet tightly around her, transforming it into a toga with shaking hands, and floated back to the bed.

Valentine crouched before her again, his hands clasped between his bent knees. He looked at her and awaited a response. But she just stared. "I'm sorry for not getting there sooner. Benedict woke up when I was in there. He was talking to himself."

This roused her. "The voice." She looked up at him, meeting his pained hazel eyes with her own. "Yes, I heard a voice. That's when I thought... you might be in trouble."

His hand reached for her forehead and moved her bangs out of her eyes. "I was... If you hadn't yelled at Saeva, I doubt Benedict would've come out of his room until dusk. But he doesn't sleep more than four hours sometimes. I fear today was one of those days.

"I might've left a trace of trespassing if I'd tried to exit. Then suspicion would arise. I don't know why his door was unlocked whilst he slept, though. That's unusual." He ran a hand through his thick, dark hair, his eyes searching something unseen in the quilt. He huffed. "He stirred and locked the door from the inside. They're so paranoid that they have strange locks on their doors. It locks and unlocks with a key on *both* sides. I never knew that. I assume Saeva's is the same. I hid in his closet until Benedict opened the door to see what the commotion was. I slipped through and..."

She felt a spasm go through her. She had been pinned by Saeva, and her body reviled the memory. "I—He didn't hurt me. But..." She shuddered.

His eyes caught her right hand that was latched to her neck, and he reached for it, holding it lightly. Her knuckles were red but didn't have open

236

wounds. "I can figure as much," he whispered. "Talking about it might be good. If you're up for it, Ennis. It might help you process. But you don't have to if you don't want to."

He gently felt at her hand bones. "You got him good." He chuckled a little. She winced at the pressure but nodded. He whipped a white cloth out of his back pocket and began wrapping it around her knuckles.

Her eyes focused on some random crack in the hardwood floor. "He... pinned me against the wall," she said in a small voice. "I tried to get away, but he's strong... I couldn't beat him. He took it as *encouragement.*" She wanted to throw up saying that last sentence. A trembling overtook her hands, and he held them tightly. *Why am I so emotional about this? Why is my body reacting this way? I'm safe now. Nothing really happened.* She furrowed her brows, looking at her hands. *But... that was all against my will. And it could've gone even further.* Her breathing shifted into near hyperventilation.

Valentine sighed, his eyes sad, and shifted to sit on the bed, slowly pulling her in for a hug. Ennis didn't hesitate in accepting it. His strong arms enveloped her. Her own personal shield against all the bad that raged at her on all sides. She felt safe right now. And she wanted to stay like this. But he couldn't protect her against everything, and it was wrong of her to think he could. God was the one ultimately protecting her. *'Every good gift and every perfect gift is from above, coming down from the Father of lights, with whom can be no variation, neither shadow that is cast by turning.' Yes, God, You supply every good gift. Valentine is a good gift, a friend. Thank You.*

Valentine grew still as his head turned into her hair. He pulled away gently and vanished before returning within seconds with a wet washcloth. He handed it to her. She knew immediately what it was for. She began scrubbing at her right ear, wanting to remove any remnants of Saeva's presence. She shuddered, trying to rid herself of the whisper of his breath.

After a solid two minutes on each ear, she let the washcloth drop to the floor. She could still feel Saeva there. She rubbed at her ear and then grabbed both ears and rubbed them simultaneously.

"Ennis," he took both of her hands in his and lowered them to her lap, "your ears are red," he said softly. He let his hand float to her right ear and gently brushed it, coaxing it.

She inhaled deeply and then let out a shaky breath, her mind feeling numb. "I can still feel it."

"It'll fade," he whispered. Without missing a stroke to her ear, he was laying in bed on top of the quilt with her nestled into his side. She nuzzled into his chest, feeling her mind go fuzzy. She felt his still body. And noted the absence of a heartbeat.

"Won't they come for us?" she whispered, her eyes tearing.

Valentine stopped stroking her ear and brushed her hair from her eyes softly. "They will not make it down the hall." His tone was deadly.

~

Dusk took ages to come. Valentine had moved the green chair to the edge of the bed and sat with his back straight, his eyes on her form, with a view of the door as well. After he'd moved from the bed, Ennis had finally fallen asleep. But her rest was fitful. Her mind was jolted awake every half-hour, filled with adrenaline, adamant that the brothers would burst through the door. And each time she awakened, Valentine was there to tell her all was well, even though both of them knew all was very much not well. But this informed her that the brothers had not made an attempt at making her pay. She then would bury her face back into the shield of blankets and fall asleep, only to repeat the process.

When the morning's light finally died out, so did Ennis's fear that they would come seeking vengeance. At least for today...

She slowly got out of bed, feeling naked without her blanket fort. Her sheet toga had stayed in place, for which she thanked God. Stumbling her way to the shower, she paused.

"I won't leave you," he promised. She nodded without turning towards him and closed the door behind her.

After the quickest and most thorough scrubbing she'd ever given herself, she toweled off and was ready to dress. She'd had to sit down to shower. Her body couldn't handle standing. When she'd rolled out of bed, she felt like death was very near. She wondered how she'd made it through the night or how she was even standing after showering. Her body had been pushed to the extremes, yet she still stood. Even though she felt like death, her body was still functioning. *God, is it my time to go home? Or do You have more for me to do on earth still? Because I'm surprised I'm even alive right now.* Closing her eyes, she listened for a response but didn't hear one. Opening them, her eyes found the pile of soiled clothes in the bathroom's corner.

"Well..." Her green shirt from the daytime smelled like leather. *Weird. Why does it smell like that?* She leaned over and observed the green fabric. It held a spray of now dried blood on it from Saeva. *Ah. That's why I smelled blood.* She sighed, looking at her other soiled blue shirt and her red one that was bloodied as well. All three of her shirts were stained red in some fashion. And her shredded black one hadn't been seen in days. She suspected Valentine had burned the evidence of her escape, along with her trench coat. Items a little too suspicious to be wearing around the brothers.

She took in a deep breath and closed her eyes tightly. "Hey, V?"

"Yes?" She could hear him at the door.

"Do you think you could get my clothes washed ASAP?"

Ennis heard silence for a moment, followed by his hesitant voice. "I can try and clean them here."

She nodded and wrapped the sheet around her, walked out to grab her pair of jeans, and returned to the bathroom to put them on under her toga. Before rewrapping her knuckles, she inspected the slightly bruised skin. "Is the flour stuff really going to hide this?" she whispered.

When she opened the door, he saw the clothes that were piled on the floor, and his nostrils flared.

Her eyes widened. "What is it?"

He still stood in the doorway, frozen. "I can't stand their smell. All your shirts are now riddled with their scents. I hate the smell of *him* in particular," he choked out, and she didn't have to ask whom he meant.

Ennis lifted her brows and put a hand on his wrist, smiling weakly. "Don't bother then. I'll just trash them."

He sighed, studying the mass of fabric. "But you don't have anything else to wear."

She shook her head, walking around him. "I could always wear this makeshift toga. I'm sure they're stylish amongst... Grecians back in the day." She bit her lip, doing a terrible job at suppressing a giggle. Within a second, she sobered up a little. "I don't think they'll have clothes laid away for me." She shifted onto her other leg, dropping her gaze to the floor. "Would you mind if... I borrowed..." She tried to find the words. *This is awkward.*

She jumped as a white shirt fell around her shoulders. He was now standing behind her. Somehow his clothes had managed to come away unscathed by Saeva's blood.

"Thank you." She turned around but found the barricade moved away from the door. He was gone. She stared at the empty doorway where his scent lingered. Or perhaps that was his shirt. She picked at one of the soft white dress shirt's sleeves and smelled it. It smelled exactly like Valentine. Like an earthen, freshly rain on forest with a grate of sweet and spicy nutmeg. She smiled at this revelation and then felt quite silly. Shaking her head, she stumbled back into the bathroom, pulling on his shirt over her underthings and trousers, which, thankfully, were wearable.

She couldn't help but think of V now that she smelled like him. Thoughts reeled about what his past was like, what his favorite food had been, what his favorite blood was, what kinds of adventures he'd been on, if there was a vampire government and how he felt about it. She wanted to know all about him, and she determined right then and there that if she made it out of here alive, she'd spend days questioning and getting to know him and about vampires in general. Maybe she could be of use to God anent vampires or Valentine or both.

She felt a slight rejuvenation. Sure, the brothers were after her and now she feared for her life more than ever, but she knew she had V by her side and he would not abandon her. And she knew, even more surely, that God would be with her and that no matter what happened, whether death or life, everything would be okay. She stared into the mirror, took a deep breath and prayed, asking for forgiveness, provision, and strength. Something was stirring in the air, and she knew change was on its chaotic, merry way. But whether that change was positive or negative, she couldn't tell.

A gentle knock sounded. A lump formed in her throat, but she swallowed it back down. She strode to the door and opened it without hesitation.

"I brought you a few more things." Valentine walked past Ennis, who let out a held breath, and set down some towels, a can, an apple, a cup filled with something white, and a new black cape. He was dressed now in his silver vest and a white dress shirt. "I know my clothes will be big on you, but I don't have anything else. My clothes I wear now were given to me by them, delivered by the truck shortly after I arrived here. The original clothes got destroyed when Benedict 'accidentally' dropped them into the fireplace." He turned towards her, his brows quirked. His face relaxed as he held out his black vest.

Ennis moved to close the door, locked it, and then gave him a doleful look. "V, I can't. This is *your* black vest. The one you wear in the daytime."

He walked towards her and slipped it around her, buttoning it so fast she didn't even see his fingers fly. "No, this is the one *you* wear at nighttime."

"But—"

"I want you to have it." His look turned dark. "I don't want you wearing those bloody clothes... please. And marching around like an ancient Grecian isn't a good idea.

She nodded, shifting around in the too big clothes. "Okay..." With a mixed smile, she adjusted the vest. "Thanks."

Valentine bit his lip for a moment, then retrieved and punctured a can of soup from the bed, handing it to her. "I'm sorry. The old clothes just remind me of that evil pair. And the blood smell, I can't—"

"It's okay, V. I won't wear them."

His tight shoulders visibly relaxed some. "Thank you..."

She picked at her vest. "Silver suits you." She smiled. But her smile faltered. "Won't me wearing your clothes give our alliance away?"

He crossed his arms, shrugging. "My excuse is that there simply weren't any other clothes in the house when you asked me for some."

Clearing her throat, she tugged at the long sleeves and then slammed her arms down at her sides. "Well then! Let's get this night started. We'll have to face them eventually."

Chugging the soup, she strode to the door, but the bathroom caught her eye. "Right after I trash my clothes." She swerved left and headed into the bathroom, gathering her pile up gingerly from off the floor, careful not to riddle her new clothes with the old scents. Picking up a pair of trousers, she felt a solid lump in the fabric. "What is..."

V was at her side. "What's what?"

She wriggled her clothes around, trying to find the solid bit again. She shook out the clothing pile. "I think it's a—"

"Key..." V swooped down on it, holding the golden key lightly between his long fingers, inspecting it. He rose slowly and let Ennis see.

"The painting studio," she breathed.

He hesitated. "How?"

She shook her head. "I don't—"

The turbulent memory of her encounter only hours before smashed into her consciousness with vividity. The memories stirred anger deep within her, but it also sent her to her knees, heaving for air. "I guess I was thinking after all..." she said incredulously. Flashes of when she shoved at his chest when she was pinned by him darted through her mind. *How could I have forgotten that part? How could I forget? Is something wrong with my brain?* The memory of him breathing in her ear made her shudder and her hands to cover her ears.

Valentine put a hand on her back. "Ennis, breathe. You're safe right now."

Shaking her head a little too vigorously to rid herself of her thoughts, she straightened up to appraise the little golden piece. Her eyes held on to the metal like it was a mysterious treasure. As she flipped the key in his hand, he looked at her with a slight, lopsided smile.

"Well done. I'm sorry about how the key came into your possession, but nevertheless, it's one more place to look. Well done."

"True... But what about Saeva's room? Did you get to search it? Not that you could. I mean—" Putting a hand to her head, she sighed. *Why isn't my brain working right?* She tried to steady her increasing nervousness.

244

He, too, sighed and shifted his weight onto his other leg. "No. Benedict had awoken when I was nearly done searching, and I couldn't go out without casting suspicion on you. You're the vampire, after all. They're blamed for everything." He shrugged his shoulders. "We'll need to—*I'll* need to search Saeva's room as soon as possible." He turned the key over to her. "The paint studio we can search together. And we can start tomorrow morning."

She held the key as if it were the last tin of soup in the world. "In the morning then." She was about to pocket it in her only pair of jeans, and trousers, for that matter. "No." She handed the key back to him. "You should keep it. In case something happens to me, I want you to be able to search. Plus, you might get less suspicion from them. They might search me."

She froze. "Wait... I might be posing for the portrait today. He'll notice the key is missing if he hasn't already!" She shoved him towards the door. "V, you need to search right now if you can. He'll *know* something happened if he doesn't find his key in his jacket. Search the place as fast as you can. I'll distract them," she urged, pushing him harder as he hadn't budged.

Valentine reached for her hands and placed them at her sides, taking the key simultaneously. "Don't worry, Ennis. I will do as you say." He nodded towards the bed. "Use the paste in the cup to cover your knuckles and your forehead. Same drill. And put a little water in it if it dehydrates." He paused for a second. "Take a little time to prepare yourself." Then he zipped around the room and, without another word, was gone.

Now she just had to distract the brothers. And with what had transpired last night, she didn't think it'd be too difficult.

~

15

Ennis patted her forehead with a washcloth before drying it and applying the paste there and on her reddened knuckles. She needed to get out there and stall, but she could feel her nervous system breaking down. This was a lot of pressure.

She'd placed the apple behind the curtains for later and replaced her dwindling towel supply. And now it was time to stall.

After taking a deep breath, she snatched her new black cape that rested ceremoniously on the back of her green chair. *The old one must be bloodied or* scented *too.* She flung the fabric majestically over her shoulders. But when she reached for the doorknob, her hand was visibly shaking. "You have to do this, Ennis." She clenched her fists, and without waiting another moment, flung the door open and marched down the hall, taking the steps regally but swiftly. She hadn't thought up anything elaborate and now her improvisation skills were going to be tested. Perhaps not the most opportune time, but it was now or never. And she'd needed to improvize successfully or she might not get a chance to show her film acquaintances how she'd improved.

As she strode to the first floor, she wondered how bad the wounds were that Valentine had inflicted on Saeva. *By the bloody evidence on my shirt, it's probably pretty nasty. And... I punched him in the face...* Her steps faltered. *I punched him in the face!*

With bated breath and clenched fists, she walked into the dining area.

No one.

What? She marched into the living room and found it, too, was empty. She let out a breath. Turning around, she checked all the other rooms on the first floor. Even the laundry room.

Empty.

Her brow furrowed. "Where are they?" Feeling foolish standing in the laundry room, she just started walking. The library seemed to be the next best bet.

As she slowly climbed the steps, stopping occasionally to rest her surging heart, she wondered if they were in the painting studio. *With Valentine.*

She started running, abandoning her caution, and flung her body up the steps. Straight into the sight of the Cerrit brothers. Greater horror struck her as she saw the long gashes on Saeva's throat, running under the neckline of his white t-shirt. She swallowed thickly. An unpleasant mixture welled in her: terror from being in his presence again and anger at what he had done.

An odd moment passed between them. No one spoke. Saeva locked eyes with Ennis, burning her with fire. His eyes shot down to her apparel, and confusion flashed across his face followed by disgust.

Benedict's face was stern, although he smiled easily. But his voice was strained. "Oh, hello, Ennis. I was just going to help Saeva with some fresh bandages."

She was still, hands clenched into fists, calves tight. Her eyes, equally as cold, were aimed at Saeva. "Hello, Benedict," she clipped, not shifting her gaze.

The air was thick and hard to breathe. She wanted to clutch at her chest but remained stoic.

The deep, dark grooves in his skin took on a red hue near the edges. It looked as if a bear had swiped down his front. She was torn between wanting to help heal his wounds and giving him a "friendly" pat on the chest to send a clear message that she was not to be played with. She decided to go against her compassion, which might make her case worse, but also to go against her revengeful spirit. She clenched her jaw, her hand itching at her side.

Saeva stuck his chin out. "Do you plan on attacking me again?"

"Shouldn't I be the one asking *you* that?" she snapped, not folding her arms, even though they twitched instinctively to do so.

Benedict patted his brother's shoulder, making Saeva hiss. "Now, you two, let's get along." Benedict leaned in towards his brother's ear. "Brother, remember what we talked about," he whispered, patting him solidly as if he could somehow physically transfer his words into him. A flash of Benedict's bandaged wrist caught Ennis's eye as he clapped his brother. His sleeves had nearly always seemed to cover his wrists, but not now. Her mind flashed back to the letter opener incident, and she could feel herself pale. Saeva's words jolted her back to the present.

"Don't you feel this was *unnecessary*?" Saeva spat, glaring at her.

She barely blinked before hurling her own accusations at him. "And you think it was okay to corner me and be so close I could feel your breath? You violated me!" She longed to dig into his wounds and cause him more pain, but she bit back the urge. *Remain wise and don't listen to your flesh.* But she was sorely tempted...

Saeva took a couple steps down, landing closer to her. "*Oh?* And as if you weren't sending those signals to me," he sneered.

As if awakening out of an observational sleep, Benedict looked wide-eyed and then raised his eyebrows at Saeva. "Brother, is that what you did?" His mouth hung slightly open.

"You grabbed my waist and pulled me to you. I didn't *ask* for that, Saeva! I don't want any part of you! And I sure didn't ask for an assault!" Her nostrils flared, and her heart picked up speed. *Calm down, Enn... You're not in good shape to be having extreme emotions right now.* At the thought of her life-or-death situation, she internally gave a humorless laugh. Her mind snapped back to the present with Saeva's scoff.

"Do you really think you weren't? I know you were, just like you still are! Looking at me like that." Shaking his head, he huffed.

She threw her hands up in the air. "Like *what!*" she yelled questioningly. A thought snapped into her mind. *This is my distraction!* She internally sighed. *Why couldn't it have been a distracting game of hide-and-seek?* Then her mind started churning.

Benedict took a couple steps down and placed himself between the two fiery beings. "I want you two to calm down. How can we work effectively if you two are fighting? Hmm?" He turned to her. "Ennis, I fully understand why you did this to my brother. I sincerely apologize for his behavior." He placed a hand on Saeva's shoulder.

Shrugging his brother's hand off, Saeva glared at Benedict. "Don't apologize for me!"

Benedict replaced his hand on Saeva and put a hand on her shoulder as well. "Look, the two of you had a squabble. But let bygones be bygones. No one's perfect. I, Benedict, sincerely acknowledge this fact." With a calm expression, Benedict continued to look between them.

Saeva wiped his brother's hand off his shoulder. "Do you think I want that *monster* around me? Look at what she did, Bene!" Saeva pulled down his shirt collar, exposing even deeper gashes.

Her throat tightened. She couldn't tell how far they actually went down his chest. She guessed at least past his heart. And the farther down they were, the visibly nastier and deeper they got. She turned her head away from the bloody sight, suddenly nauseous and simultaneously getting a wracking heart palpitation. *Too much stress. Too many emotions.*

Benedict's grip on Ennis's shoulder held steady, but he seemed to wobble slightly too. Instinctively, her arm shot out to grab his. "I-I know it looks bad, Brother, but you are warranted every inch of that wound."

"Yeah, I guess she didn't kill me, right? What *mercy.*" He said the last word with spite.

I wonder how Benedict ever gets along with him. They were like fire and water. But she'd just have to keep them roiling. *Valentine's still in the painting studio.*

Benedict had started to sway again. Sighing, she shook her head. "Are you okay, Benedict?"

He nodded but soon gave up the movement. "I think... I think I should sit down. I'm not good with gore." He swallowed rather thickly, and she looked for an escape from the immanent mess. But something clicked in her mind.

Her eyes widened, and she looked at Benedict, trying to keep her expression neutral. "But you bring me blood."

Nodding slightly, he closed his eyes. "It's the flesh that gets me faint," he quavered, his voice trailing off to a whisper. Saeva grunted before making to take his brother's left shoulder, the arm Ennis was holding on to.

"Switch," Saeva hissed.

Her head whipped to Saeva, her eyes glaring. "What?"

He sighed impatiently. "My wound is on my left side. I need to shoulder his left," he barked. She took a moment before allowing it and took up Benedict's right side, being surprisingly smooth when she avoided brushing against Saeva as they passed one another.

The two helped carry the heavy body down the second-floor hall. Saeva kicked open the door to the library. "Be gentle, Saev!" Benedict chided weakly. The two of them wrestled Benedict onto the purple conversation couch. She gripped at Benedict's arm that was around her to unwind it, but he held her tight.

"Benedict?" She pulled on his arm. "Let go."

He whimpered. "I don't want to be alone."

Ennis lifted a brow. *What is wrong with him? He's not drunk. He's only faint.* She looked to Saeva for help, but he only turned and walked towards the door. A shot of adrenaline coursed through her. *Not yet!* "I'd like a warning next time," she said loudly in Saeva's direction.

He didn't stop walking.

Another shot of epinephrine coursed through her.

"Next time I won't be so generous," she sneered.

He approached the door and still had momentum. *Uh... Uh! What other card is there?* She froze. *Oh...*

252

"I'm... sorry," she said quietly with articulate vulnerability. His hand was still, clutching the doorknob now. Silence permeated the rust-colored library.

His head was tilted down as if he were staring at the doorknob in hand. "Is that so..." he ground out.

Do I detect a note of hopefulness? She thought quickly, her eyes searching the muted purple fabric.

She bit her lip. "Look, I don't want to start fights. But I will end them."

Saeva turned around, his face made of contemplative stone. His blue eyes probed her statements. "More lies, Ennis?" His voice was agitated as if he wished it to be the opposite.

Her heart pounded. *More? What does he mean?*

Glancing down at Benedict's moaning form, she then observed the dusty books. Anything but those piercing blue eyes. "I... said I was sorry, alright? Really." *I mean I am sorry that I hurt you, but it was self-defense.* She tried in vain to free herself from Benedict's arm again, so she dejectedly plopped down onto the couch beside him. "I just wish you felt the same."

Saeva shook his head and approached the couch.

Benedict groaned and pulled her closer to him. His green eyes were shut in misery.

"I know that's a lie, Ennis. You can't lie to me." Saeva's breath shifted her dark hair slightly, and a tremor shot through her.

Trying to get leverage on Benedict's grip, she turned her head towards Saeva. "Then you can't accept the truth, Saeva." But the heaviness of her words weighed down the air. When she couldn't take looking at her enemy anymore, she watched the next one.

Benedict's face seemed rather long, but it was proportional. His black hair was just long enough to touch his ears. She wanted to see his green eyes again, just to see them up close. She had to admit they were some of the prettiest eyes she'd ever seen. But they happened to grace an insane man. Benedict moaned and clung tighter to her, causing her to be unable to turn around to face Saeva. "Stop it, Benedict," she grumbled. "I don't want to hurt you."

"But you'd hurt me?" Saeva's voice shot like cold water into her mind. *This guy!*

"And you'd hurt *me*?" She was becoming quite uncomfortable in such an awkward position.

His eyes were tortured. "I didn't mean to," he whispered.

Ennis huffed in her head. *Yeah right!*

He continued, glaring at a marble statue nearby that was nestled in the freestanding shelves. "I thought you wanted it too. I thought there was a chance." He sounded so pained it could've broken a heart. Just not her heart. She turned around as well as she could still being caged in a lanky, yet very strong arm.

"Don't ever do that to me again," she said lowly. Saeva's shiny eyes looked away towards the windows. They were uncovered and letting in the moonlight. No rain tonight.

"I'm... sorry." His words sounded unnatural, and his brown hair framed tumultuous blue orbs.

"I forgive you."

He paused, looking shocked. It was as if he'd never been forgiven so easily before. Or perhaps ever. Nodding once slightly, he exited from the room in silence.

She sighed, hoping she'd given Valentine enough time to search, but also hoped that Saeva's heart would change. And Benedict's too.

Taking a deep breath, she turned to survey Benedict. His eyes flew open, giving her an eyeful of two-toned grass and forest.

"Well now! That was better than what I'd hoped for!"

"What!" Ennis's body lurched to shoot up out of her seat, but his grip was still there keeping her planted by his side. "But you were—I thought you were—"

"Unconscious? Overtaken by the faint?" he finished, closing his eyes and pulling his free hand up to his forehead dramatically.

Ennis was stunned. "What were you trying to do?"

He straightened up a little, his arm still cast around her, of which she was still very aware. "Well, I don't like the look of gore, but I was in a play once as a boy. Did it show?"

She quirked an eyebrow.

He sighed and smiled, shaking his head. "Oh, Ennis." His tone sent a shudder through her body. *Oh no...* She knew at that instant she'd been wrong. Wrong about Benedict. *Not good!*

He lifted a shoulder. "I thought you two might make up."

She jerked in his grip and tried twisting his arm skin through his white dress shirt. "Benedict," she warned.

Hissing and chuckling simultaneously, he slipped his grip up to be around her neck. "Oh, I'm not ready to let you go just yet," he teased.

Her body was screaming to get out of here. *I'm not strong enough to fight him off. If I fight, he'll know. Stay cool, Ennis. Play this out.* "Not you too."

"You don't like my brother," he stated as if he had taken no notice to the way her body had become even more rigid.

Oh no... How to play this... What's he getting at? The silence stung her ears.

He tilted his head to talk in her ear. "I'm waiting for a confirmation, my dear."

Biting her tongue, she tried to turn her head to look at anything but his piercing eyes.

He chuckled again, removing his arm and, instead, gripped her under her arms as if she were a puppy. In her shock, he placed her beside him but in the corner of the couch. She couldn't break away before his arm snaked back around her neck.

"My brother hasn't loved in a very long time," he noted as if commenting on the weather.

Why is he telling me this? Get your hands off me!

He sighed dramatically. "And it would be a shame for anyone to toy with his heart." His words were friendly daggers. She clung to his arm, feeling that he was starting to steadily choke her. "However, I forgive you. I know you have a good reason."

"Benedict," she implored, sounding a little hoarse. Vampires didn't need air, did they? Or maybe the brothers didn't know either. From what she'd observed, Valentine didn't need to breathe, but he did breathe. "I don't like your brother, and I don't want to toy with his heartstrings. I'm a terribly bad musician. Got kicked out of band class once."

He tightened his grip around her throat. "Oh, Ennis. To think of holding someone like you in our

256

house…" His meaning was ambiguous, and he paused for a brief moment. "I forgive you for what you did to my brother. He deserves every bit of it. He can be a bother." Sentiment oozed from him as he loosened his grip slightly.

He looked down at her with curious eyes and studied her clothes. "Why are you wearing Valentine's clothes, Ennis?"

She sincerely hoped he couldn't visibly see or feel her heart pounding. "My clothes are soiled with the stench of blood."

He peered at her face.

"You think you can ease up on your grip?" Her thinking was getting muddled, and she knew she needed air.

He came to himself and focused on her. "…Ah." He relaxed his grip, but it shifted down to her arm, yanking her up with him. "Today you spend with me. Saeva has hogged you long enough. Now it's my turn." Tapping his free hand against his leg, he glanced around the library.

"Now, what do you say to a game? I don't think I can make you share your secrets without torture, and I don't want to do that right now." He closed his eyes. *Wasn't he against torture before?*

Her head chimed with warning bells, and she shifted her weight to her left leg. "I'd rather go back to my room."

Opening one green eye to look at her, he smiled. "Oh, I very much think you would. But we both know that's not what's going to happen."

Her heart hammered violently. *What does he know?*

257

16

Ennis's breathing became unsteady, quickly feeding her growing hysteria. She debated whether giving Benedict a knee to the crotch was wise. Even if she escaped now, she had no where to run. If she did, someone would end up dying.

Tightening his grip painfully around her small, pale wrist, Benedict forced her along with him deeper into the library. She bit her lip to quiet the sounds of pain that tried to escape her. She was sure she'd have bruises later. *Good thing I have long sleeves.*

"Which game?" he asked, walking them over to a massive mahogany cabinet in the back of the library. She had seen the cabinet before in her escapades with Valentine. There had been a stack of games hidden inside. *That would kill time, but...*

"Hide-and-seek."

He was reaching for something in the cabinet with his free hand—the other was still latched to her wrist—but he paused. "Hide-and-seek?" He flashed a smile. "I love that game!" Closing the cabinet doors, he stood up. "I used to love to play as a child. Saev wasn't so fond of the game, but I loved it as a boy! I could play for hours! It was fantastic! He once left me hiding for four hours. I eventually came out of my spot in the recycling bin." His smile faltered. "I found him where he had started counting. He said he was still looking... as he read a book, sitting on the couch."

She grimaced. *Sounds like my childhood.* She stared at him. "Are you game then?"

"Yes!" He bounced on his heals, releasing her wrist. "Who starts?" He rubbed his hands together aggressively.

Clearing her throat, she tried to focus. "Why don't you hide, and I'll look? And I won't leave you waiting for four hours." *I hope Valentine's done by now. Saeva's already gone.*

"Sounds fun!" He galloped to his mahogany desk near the windows and pulled out a little drawer. Clinking sounds wove their way to her ears over the chest-height shelves standing between them. Snatching something, he returned to her. He grabbed her wrist, holding something she couldn't see in his hand. "Open," he commanded. Her hand stayed clenched. With an aggravated noise, he wrenched open her hand, plopping a pair of earplugs into it.

She lifted a brow at the two yellow foam bits. "What are these for?" They rolled around in her hand and left a wet residue. *Ew.*

His eyes were trained on her hand and shot to her face. "Your nose, silly. You have a very good sniffer. It would hardly be fair." He winked. *Ooohh right. The pretense.*

She shoved them back at him. "I'm not wearing them. I'm not going to go around looking like a madman. I can just pinch my nose."

He shoved her hand towards her. "Yes, Ennis, but I don't trust you enough for such a serious thing as this."

Shaking her head caused him to pout. *Does he really want me to wear these?* Then it hit her. "And you trust me not to take the earplugs out?"

His face cracked a wide smile. "Oh, you *are* a sharp one!" He looked smug. "I am a prankster." He laughed cheekily.

259

"You made me look like an idiot," she mumbled, shifting her weight to her other leg. *This guy is crazy... Why is this interaction even happening?*

"No, you did that to yourself," he said, a glimmer of something unsettling in his eyes.

Ennis tried to keep her features straight, but she felt something was very much wrong here. She just couldn't see what it was. *Why did he even do—*

"Okay! I'll go hide and you stay right on that couch and count, Count!" He pointed at the purple couch.

She remembered her old theatrics and brought them back to life, iterating her pretense of pride. "Are you insulting me?" Her voice wound through the ancient shelves.

He swept into a slight bow, losing his playfulness. "No, of course not, Ennis."

She frowned, remembering that she had to show them she meant business and would not be walked over. Plus, didn't vampires have some majestic, powerful air about them anyway? *Valentine sure does.* "Stop bowing. That's foolish to do that."

His replaced smile faltered again, and his eager hands fell to his sides. "I'm sorry. Sometimes I have so much fun with you I forget my place."

Your place? Her mind spun, and her body started trembling. *What does that mean?* She clasped her shaking hands together, nodding towards the door.

"I'll go and hide. Let's not spoil what we have." He used a placating gesture and then motioned for her to sit down on the couch. "Start counting, *Ennis*," he amended. She sat down reluctantly on the purple couch and closed her eyes, *sort of.* "To one hundred!" he shouted, and then he was out the door.

260

One, two, three, four, five, six, seven, eight, nine, I wonder where's he's going to hide... Wow, I'm really playing hide-and-seek with an insane man. Hmm... Valentine should've already had enough time, but what if he needed to fix something he messed up whilst searching? What if he found something! Saeva would've made noise if he found him, right? There'd probably be a commotion. Hmm... She sat up straighter on the couch. *Oh yeah! Counting. Hmm, how many would that be now? Thirty? I'll just go from there... Thirty-one...* She continued to count until she reached a hundred and then announced, "Ready or not, here I come," and swept off to find the hidden body, shaking her head at her strange circumstance.

First, she started in the library, but she knew she'd heard him slide into the hall before she even started counting. Despite the oddity of her entire situation, hide-and-seek had been one of her favorite games as a kid. While her love of the game was strong, others didn't seem to emulate her level of affection for it.

She crept into the hall after finding nothing but dusty corners and dust bunnies. The hall creaked at her presence, groaning under her shaky boots. *So much for stealth... Valentine would be good at this game.* She determined this little game would provide her more time to look for clues and get a fresh perspective on the house. It gave her a reason to get up and about in the massive house again and also to look for hiding places of her own. Who knew when they would come in handy? Although, this allowance of her roaming the house seemed unusual. They'd been keeping watch on her during the night. Perhaps they thought the light-leaking windows were deterrent enough for her not to roam in the day. At least not roam in the places that mattered. Her heart hammered at the revelation. Where the windows leaked more light, there must be something the brothers didn't want them to see. The brothers' rooms seemed to be one of those spaces they didn't want them to be in. She made a note to tell Valentine when she found him. But as for nighttime, she hadn't been this free in a while. And it scared her.

She peeked into all the rooms on the second floor and found none of them held Benedict. She hadn't sensed his presence either. Plodding up the stairs to the third floor, she scanned through those rooms as well. She tentatively opened her own door and looked down. Before leaving her room, she'd started mentally noting a little string in the doorway. Its placement changed minimally when the door opened and closed, but she actively avoided treading on it. A sigh escaped her when she saw it unperturbed, but she checked the room just in case, prodding at the curtains. No one. She closed the door, noting the string again, and made for the other rooms.

There was one door she hadn't been in before on this floor. *Valentine's room.* Her heart hammered. *Why am I nervous? It seems too private. But Benedict could be hiding in here.* She swallowed. *I hope he's not.*

Opening the wooden door that looked like her own, she stepped into what was probably the darkest room she'd ever been in. Even the light from the hall's wall lamplight was sucked into the void that was his room. She felt along the wall for a light switch and found a chest instead. A hand clamped over her mouth.

17

A muffled scream echoed in the hollow room. "No need to scream," a laughing voice chided. *Benedict!* Ennis shoved him away.

"What are you doing!" Her hand clamped over her heart, and she felt for a light switch and found it but didn't flip it on. Instead, she grabbed a clump of his dress shirt's front, and flung him into the hall and closed the door, stomping into the light.

He was thoroughly amused. "I *think* I'm hiding. But I guess I didn't win." He shrugged with a smile, his hands in his pockets.

"What is that room anyway?" she asked, already knowing the answer.

He scrunched his face, shaking his head. "That's Valentine's room. He won't mind. I tell you, I had to fix his curtains though. Some light was leaking through. I should tell him not to let it happen again. What if you entered in there during the day?" He shuddered. "I don't even want to think about it." Shifting onto his other leg, he waved a hand over his body. "Plus, it's easier to hide in complete darkness!" He tilted his head. "Do you talk to him often?"

Ennis looked around the hall. "Who?"

"Valentine, silly!"

"Oh, not really. No," she lied. *Sorry, God!*

He hung his head and then looked up dramatically. "Neither do I. Shame, really. I mean he's not an enthusiast like my brother and me, but he's still willing to work for the cause. I'm glad I found him! Can you imagine it! He walked up to our doorstep, and we took him in right away despite what he is. Wonderful worker." He paused,

263

eyeing Ennis with an air of friendliness, but she saw she was in an interrogation. His eyes slipped off her and onto a nearby, uncovered window. The night had turned cloudy, dusted with fog now. "Even though he's human, he still knows how to choose correctly." His eyes were on hers now. And she didn't like his smile.

Why did he say that just now? Why tell me? What does he mean? Valentine hadn't been specific on how the brothers had taken him in, but she knew threats had been a part of it. *But wouldn't they know he made it through the barrier? And they think a human can make it through that?* She remembered her encounter with the stakes and suppressed a shudder. *Maybe they took pity on him? Thinking a human wandering through the woods fell into a vampire trap?* Pity? She took in his watchful eyes, his shoulder too high strung. *I don't think so.* Shifting uneasily on her feet, she glanced down the hall. "I guess it's my turn."

He crossed his arms. "You ended up cheating."

"What?" She stared down the hall again.

"When you came into my room, you weren't pinching your nose."

Her shoulders tensed and then sagged. "...You caught me. I wasn't able to find you," she lied.

He jumped into the air and pointed at her. "Aha! I knew it! I win by default!"

"Whatever." She continued to study the hall, up and down, sweeping her gaze over it.

Following her eyes to the corner of the hall, he peered over her shoulder. "What is it?"

She leaped away from him. "Thinking of where to hide. Now start counting." She shoved him into an empty room opposite Valentine's and closed the door.

Quietly, she slipped into Valentine's room before she could overthink it even more. She flipped the light on and examined the room anew.

His bedroom was quite plain, holding the same furniture as her own: what looked like a wooden queen bed, a bedside table, a chest of drawers, and a lamp stand. There was no armchair, however. A connecting bath was present as well, but he had a wardrobe. She opened the latter to find one pair of black slacks hanging. Her mouth tipped into a frown. Her fingers idly picked at her black vest. Turning off the light, she pulled herself into the wardrobe and sat down under the hanging trousers. She waited until she heard Benedict's unmistakable words of "Ready or not, here I come!" and his disappearing footsteps before opening the closet, turning the light back on, and inspecting the room. She wondered when Valentine would return, *if at all*, and hoped it would be soon.

The floor was wooden, as most everything in the house seemed to be. She didn't root through his furniture, but instead, settled herself on the floor, looking around curiously. His bed was lined with a thick night-blue cover that was weaved with silver. *Pretty.* His curtains were black and drawn, blocking out the night's festivities.

She heard a small plink, then another. Before long, the rain was pelting the glass, causing a comforting monotony to overtake the house. That way she didn't jump at every creak, thinking Benedict was coming down the hall. After turning the light off, she took a seat and rested her back against the wall, waiting in the darkness. She longed to pull back the curtains and take a look. After what felt like 20 minutes, she did.

Her knees cracked as she stood, and she let out a low groan. Stepping slowly to the window to avoid the blackening of her vision that came anyway, she pulled back the curtains and gazed at the rather drab outlook. The watery panes from unrelenting sheets of rain obscured the side yard. She sighed, noting the grey and orange strokes that she did manage to make out.

The room felt strangely devoid of Valentine. Her fingers played with her too long white shirtsleeves. Letting the curtains rest slightly open so that a little night light came through, she moved to the bed and picked up a pillow, sniffing it hesitantly. *Oh, he probably never rests...* She replaced the pillow and folded her arms. *What does he get up to during the day?* With a sigh, she resigned herself back to the wall and waited.

~

It felt like an hour had passed when she finally got up and opened the door, peeking into the hall. A creak sounded from above. *Saeva or Benedict?*

She didn't know how much time had passed, but she was done with waiting. She crept into the hall. Silence. Her gaze swept up and down the length of the hall before her feet moved for the stairs. She stumbled down a flight and pushed open the library door, exposing a figure sitting casually on the purple couch reading a book. Her heart dropped. Then her mind caught up. And then disappointment.

"Ah," she said flatly.

Benedict turned a page. "I'm still looking." Glancing towards her, he settled his open volume on a nearby side table. He took off his glasses, which Ennis knew very well he didn't need, and set them on the newly closed book. "You finally caught on." His smile was gilded with cheer but was made of hate. Her breath was sucked out of her. She had never seen him like that before. Her pulse sped up. *I've really misjudged him.* His weird behavior tonight had already set off warning bells. She made for the door.

"You forget that we're spending the whole night together." His voice rang clearly through the dusty shelves. "And it's not even halfway through. Don't rush off so soon."

Her feet were planted facing the door. She didn't turn around. Instead, she kept a steady focus on the open doorway and her hand resting on the knob. "I don't entertain liars."

He smirked. "Nor I."

Her heart plummeted. *Oh no. This can't be good... How much does he know! Or maybe it's a trick? Is it time to call in backup? Oh, please get me out of here, God!* Her mind spun deftly into untidy circles. She replied by striding through the door and down the hall. She stumbled up the stairs while Benedict called her name. He raced down the hall to catch up with her. On her fourth step, Benedict caught her wrist, flinging her around. Her mind raced wildly as she tugged to regain her limb. "Let go!" she shouted as loudly as possible, mustering up as much anger as she could. Surprisingly, she found it very easy to summon and that scared her.

Benedict's face flickered with fear but schooled into worried agitation. "Whoa! Are you trying to wake up the whole neighborhood?"

She wanted to punch him. "So what! There's no one within a hundred miles of here, and you're telling me to be *quiet*?" she roared. "I said let go!"

For a second, she thought she might ruin her vocal cords. The familiar scratchy feeling was starting to surface, and she was already out of breath. *POTS, this is not the time!*

His expression changed, and he chuckled as if he'd just gotten a funny joke, but there was darkness in it. "Oh, Ennis." A shiver ran down her spine. Had she been wrong? Was Benedict the one she should've been worrying about all this time rather than Saeva? His demeanor had altered. Sure, she still saw his friendly face and lively green eyes, but today, today there was a definite shift. And she didn't like it. She prayed that Valentine had found something to help them escape tonight. Otherwise, these were someone's last breaths.

"Do you think my brother and I are so daft? For different reasons, maybe. But on this, you haven't fooled me." She heard a thump from upstairs and continued to hope. He yanked on her wrist, his eyes cold but coherent. "Look at me!" he hissed. His cool voice returned. "You know you could've torn me to shreds. But you didn't. You're not killing me right now." He tilted his head and smiled. "I wonder why that is."

Before she could pass out, a crash of footsteps descended the stairs like she had loosed a stampede. Saeva's livid presence shocked the air. He was breathing heavily, and she could see the rapid pulse in his neck after her eyes finally tore away from his red and bruised cheek. It seemed he had fresh bandages on underneath his white shirt and usual brown leather jacket. She couldn't help that her eyes widened a little. *Well... Not what I was expecting.*

Her eyes turned desperate as they found Saeva's face. "Saeva," she began, thinking quickly.

"I'd rather spend the rest of the night with you instead of your brother."

Saeva blinked, his hand was frozen on the railing beside him, and it took one twitch of Benedict's shoulder to shake him out of his shock. His eyes found Benedict's grip, and Benedict tightened his hand around her wrist.

Benedict straightened his shoulders. "Ennis, you're mine for tonight," he announced crisply, reminding everyone in the vicinity. Then his gaze caught Saeva's. "Brother," he acknowledged.

Saeva looked like he was about to attack. "What did you do, Benedict!" His eyes now locked onto his brother's.

Benedict's face flipped back to amicability. "We were playing hide-and-seek, and she cheated."

Saeva found Ennis's gaze again, and she communicated silently. *Get me out of here.*

"Let her go," Saeva growled deeply. Benedict blinked, looking taken aback. Saeva seemed unmovable. Benedict sighed and tossed her wrist towards Saeva. Her arm fell lifelessly back to her side, and Saeva stepped between them.

Benedict waved a hand. "I was just messing with her. No harm done. We had a good conversation, didn't we, Ennis?" he leered, directing his words behind Saeva's back where she shook. Her lips were firmly pressed together, and she held on to the railing for support. "Come *on*, Brother. I didn't do anything." He looked at Saeva, his brow up, and waved his hand toward Ennis. "You'll be won over by *this* girl?"

Without looking, Saeva's hand latched on to her arm. "No, but I know you, Brother." Turning around, he began dragging Ennis behind him. *Well...*

269

She could guess where he was taking her. And as she suspected, within a few moments he was at the painting studio door. Her head was still reeling from what she'd just discovered about Benedict, even if his cryptic language hadn't made sense yet. She saw Saeva's free hand lift up and go into his jacket. Her heart leapt into her throat, and her world went blurry. *The key!* Reaching into his pocket, he dug around for a second. She felt like she was about to faint again but resisted propping herself up against the wall. He extracted a key and put it into the lock just as her vision darkened. *What!* Her chest threatened to cave.

He lugged her through the door by the arm, which he still hadn't released. "Get in," he barked.

He threw her farther into the room, letting her go, and locked the door behind them. He was facing away from her, his shoulders rising and falling quickly with heavy breaths. "I have the only key," he said lowly, stuffing the piece of gold back into his inner pocket. *I wonder how Valentine got the key back in there.* "So don't think he'll be coming in to get you." He smacked the light switch, illuminating the room. However, it almost didn't need light because of the color of the walls and the open window that seeped in night light and rain. He moved to face her now, wounds peeking around the bandages in all their glory, glistening in the bright light. She swallowed again and turned her head. If she looked at it any longer, the compulsion to help him would grow. She decided to take an interest in a painting in her line of vision. It was a field of tall grass speckled with wildflowers, almost abstract. She tilted her head, shifting her angle.

He hadn't stopped staring at her. "What did he do to you?" She turned around, keeping her face as disinterested as she could manage. Striding forward, he looked down on her. But she didn't back away. Instead, she puffed her chest a little and held clenched fists at her sides. His gashes looked so much worse up close. *And his face. I did that...* Again she felt the push to help him, to help him heal, but stuffed it right back down alongside her desire to punch him again. His teeth were clenched. "Tell me, Ennis."

Her mind ran through a billion thoughts. What could she tell him? How much should she tell him? She snapped out of it when she became aware she'd been staring at the gash on his throat for too long. "You saw it." She looked away. "And he's conniving. Does that count?" *How should I play this?* She blinked. "He's—I don't want—" *What would benefit me most here?*

His shoulders sagged. "Ennis," he said softly, tilting her chin up. Her eyes widened, and she felt a shot of adrenaline at her error, jerking away from him. His hand still hovered close to her face. *Oh no! I forgot he likes me!* "I'm sorry."

Her brows knit together ever so slightly. "For what?"

Sighing, he looked at a painting on his right. "For all of it. For what I did last night. For what my brother has just done to you now. No vampire should be treated like that. You deserve so much more respect," he whispered.

She frowned. "What about humans? Wouldn't you give them the same respect?"

He dropped his hand. "They deserve to be treated like the scum they are."

271

Wow. This guy is a pendulum! And a hypocrite! "Do you include yourself in that?" *God, how could he think so lowly of humans? Your image-bearers?*

He glared at her, but she couldn't help but feel it wasn't aimed at her. "I do. That's why I want to become a vampire so badly. I can't be my old self. I want another life. A new start." Letting out a heavy sigh, he massaged the right side of his neck. Then his hand fell and smacked his leg. "But you've rejected me." He shot her a dark look, not stepping away from her.

Rejected you? When was I asked to make you a vampire? She swallowed and wandered her way to another painting, away from the wall of his broad shoulders. This one held a very strange depiction of a baby lamb, alone in a field under a pink sky. She quickly moved on to the next painting. "You know, you don't really get to start over."

He stared at her as she moved about his painting gallery, observing in silence.

Flashes of her own sin assaulted her mind, and she tried to push them away, reminding herself that she was saved through Jesus, and that her past was no longer against her record. *But the OCD lies really get to me still. But they're lies. Lies. They're not Truth, God.* "You have to live with all the things you've done in your past. It's not a reset button, Saeva. It's a *repeat* button. You live your mistakes over and over again." She continued to wander, overcome by her deep thoughts. "Like with a painting. You can try to paint over it, to scrape it clean. But the original canvas is always underneath. You can't undo time and history." She stopped at one painting. "You have to become a new person. You have to die to your old self. Otherwise," she turned to him and stopped, "you just keep painting over the original. Only God can wipe your slate clean and replace it with something unfathomably beautiful."

"But you've died to your old self."

Her smile was bittersweet. "Yes." *But not in the way you're thinking.*

"That's what I want." He was pleading now.

Frowning, she shook her head. "Then you're looking in the wrong place. Look to God. Look to Jesus Christ. I guarantee He's what you are looking for."

He blinked at her, something glistening in his eyes. "I don't—I can't—" His hands were shaking at his sides.

She bit her lip and looked away, praying for God to change his heart. *What more should I do, God? Anything?*

Voice quavering, he was breathing unevenly. "Tell me it gets better, Ennis."

She looked at him, really looked at him. His blue eyes were a stormy grey. His arms hung limply at his side, his shoulders hunched as if he carried a weight too heavy. A burden he couldn't handle. Both brothers were giving her cause to worry. They were both so volatile. But Saeva was admittedly broken.

Frowning, she shook her head. "I can't tell you that," she said quietly. A tear now trickled down his face into his wounds. He didn't flinch. "We can't change ourselves. Jesus Christ changes us. We can't erase our past. But we can become a new, better person through Him. He's done that to me. He lives in me. The feeling is beyond words. I thank Him for doing so. That's my new life. Vampirism is definitely not the answer. It's not the answer to anything." She looked down, a slight smile on her lips. "I can guarantee through Christ that if you believe in Him, it'll get better. The best. If you're feeling condemned, it's because you already are if you don't trust Jesus. But that's the beauty of God's offer: He's offering you eternal life freely. All you have to do is accept it solely through faith in Jesus Christ. Then you aren't condemned if you're hidden in Christ! It's not about what we do. It's about what He's already done. It's beautiful, Saeva."

His eyes took on a new look, and his brows furrowed as if trying to solve a complex riddle.

She shrugged a shoulder, eyeing him. "Relying on God is all we *can* do."

After a moment, she added, "We can't really do life on our own."

His eyes cleared. With a mixture of emotions on his face, he advanced towards her. *Is-is-is he going to hug me!* She braced herself.

Saeva brushed by her and squeezed out too much tubed color on a sterile palette. He mashed more tubes and began mixing quite violently. A held breath escaped her.

"Sit. I don't want you to preach at me anymore. We're going to paint."

"Saeva, this could change—"

He turned on her. "I said I don't want to hear it! I've heard it before, and it's a bunch of lies."

With an ache in her chest, she shook her head. "But this is true and life-changing."

"Yeah, and so could my torturing you, but I'm not going to do that right now."

She sighed, resigning herself to the all too familiar red velvet. *Lord, get through to his heart, please. He's not listening.* She heard a Voice in her head saying, "*It's in My hands.*"

As she stared out the window, the fiery trees shook and lashed each other, some near barren now. The rain had stopped, and the torrent of wind had shown up. *I guess another storm is on its way.* Holding her chin in her hand, she adjusted her elbow on the windowsill.

She hadn't had any contact with Valentine tonight to confirm any hints at escaping in the morning. She tried to think of a way to get out of the room. This house. This entire situation she had stumbled into. Shifting her focus back indoors, she studied the many paintings.

The room looked just the same as it had yesterday. *Valentine must've done a pretty clean job of searching... Not that he doesn't always.* The paintings were all in the same order, easels lining the room. *Nothing looks out of place.*

She gazed out the window again at the shiny grass, wishing to be far away from this place and these chaotic brothers. Valentine, however, was another story.

A leaf smacked the window, causing her to jump. Saeva glanced up and shook his head, returning his full attention on getting some red color to his liking.

"You won't change me," he stated.

Ennis didn't follow her eyes' desires to look at him, so they stayed glued on the thrashing trees. *Why is he bringing vampirism up again? And now? When did he even ask me to make him a vampire? I don't get it!* "No."

Sauntering to the soft chair near hers, he plopped down with a palette in one hand and a set of wetted brushes in the other. "Well then... I guess you'll be trapped here forever. Or can vampires die from blood loss?" He smirked.

She turned to him pointedly. "No, I'll just wait for the—" She held her tongue. *Why would I even give away something so clever! Do they have the electric bill set on automatic payments, even for the future? Their money could run out too. Because if the power is cut off... Or maybe if lightning fries the system... If they have generators, they can only go so long... It'd probably be a long time though. Maybe a year or more before someone finds out something's wrong and kill the power to the stake guns?* Her head spun. It wasn't a quick escape plan.

Saeva cleared his throat overly loudly, and she glared at him. "You'll just wait for what?"

She sniffed. "I'll just wait for the pair of you to die from how boring it is sitting here, painting me."

He chuckled, picking up a brush and dabbing it in red. "Maybe for you." He dabbed at the stretched canvas. "But I quite enjoy painting and think my subject would be the *first* to die of boredom." He smirked again.

She grumbled and turned to examine the wooded scenery yet again. Their backyard was stout, with short grass and no fence. Well... they did have a fence, but that was far into the woods and unlike any other fence she'd ever encountered. She wondered if Valentine had tried the entire perimeter... *He must have...* She sighed.

"If you have something to say, then say it, Ennis," he snapped. She glanced over at him, still leaning her cheek on her hand. He clicked his tongue. "You're sighing again. Stop it." She could see a little vein on his forehead above his flaming blue eyes that blazed her. His look traveled down. "And why are you wearing Valentine's clothes?" With wide eyes, he snapped his look back to her face.

276

Shrugging a shoulder, she sniffed. "Because the smell of blood won't come out. And you guys don't seem to have any extra clothes for me."

He huffed and continued painting with an annoyed expression on his own canvas. "I'll get you some," he mumbled.

She caught herself before she sighed again. It was torture being here. And even more so because Valentine would tell her the verdict of the painting studio recon later. She sighed away the rest of the night with Saeva.

Until finally dawn was near.

~

18

Ennis was delivered back to her room and told by Saeva not to open the door for "that devious fool." She shut the door and desired a long, cold shower. But first, she removed Valentine's vest and placed it carefully on the bed, smoothing it out, followed by his white shirt. She stumbled to the bathroom, ready for the refreshing, yet slightly sulfurous water that awaited her.

After getting clean and dressed again, she heard the timely knock of yet another bloody delivery, reminding her that she hadn't eaten human food in quite a while. Her stomach hadn't given any hunger signals, which was not a good sign. She quickly ran to the curtains and pushed them aside. To her relief, glinting surfaces caught the dim light above her headboard. She made her way to the door and opened it a crack.

Valentine. Her brows lifted. Then her eyes trailed down to the full glass of blood in his hand. "Your dinner," he announced.

She blinked but took the glass and shot him a questioning look. *The studio, Valentine! How'd it go!*

He gave her a tiny smile, and she returned a curt lift of the corner of her mouth. Her eyes darted to check up and down the hall. Slamming the door, she raced to her filling station and poured as carefully as her eager, little hands could. As she poured the thick liquid into the glass, a distinct thunk sounded. A gasp escaped her, and her eyes shot wide open. *Oh... Ohhhh!*

Leaping back to door, she quickly tried to school her beaming and palpitating heart before pulling the door open. "Thank you," she said neutrally, turning her back on him and closing the door. *Ahh, Valentine, you found something! Thank you, God, for giving us whatever that clue is!* Looking over her shoulder, she pounced back to the curtains and waited for her blackened vision to go away before she shifted the curtains and found the glass lampshade. Sticking her hand in, she fished for the key, ignoring the warmth surrounding her hand. She pulled out a key that was unlike the shape of the painting studio's. Scraping off as much blood as she could back into the glass, she then washed the key and her hands thoroughly. *I don't know what this unlocks, but it has to be important!*

She began jumping into the air but quickly told herself to stop. If she was going to be escaping tonight, she was going to need all the energy and rest she could get. She padded to the sink again, downed some water, and then flung herself under the covers for a good dawn's sleep.

~

Ennis awoke to light rapping on her door. Sitting up, she swung her feet over the edge of the bed and inched back the window's thick fabric. Weak sunlight met her face.

"It's me." The low voice was oh-so-familiar and calming.

She carefully made her way to the door, squinting through the dark. She unlocked the door to find an eager-looking vampire. With a tray in hand, he stood, wearing his same black cape but his silver vest instead of his usual black one, which she was now wearing.

"Here's your meal. Please eat quickly. I'm going to try all the locks while you eat, okay?" Valentine handed the tray over to her.

She gestured to the curtains. "And you?" Looking over her shoulder, he glided towards the curtains. Some light clinking echoed through the room, and then he was standing back in front of her.

He wiped a bit of red from his lip, a small smile there. "Done." In his eyes, she could see something working.

She grinned. "I haven't seen you this eager before."

His eyes crinkled. "Well, I haven't been this close to escape before."

Her smile went sideways. "Hmm..."

Taking a seat on the bed again, she stuffed in as much food as she could. Waffles today.

Her eyes found the curtains, and her mind sparked. "Oh, V! I had an idea!" She waved her hands about wildly, gesturing to things that weren't there. "The curtains, V! The curtains! The sun. And how they shine means they don't want people to go there."

Crouching before her, he tilted his head. "Slow down, Ennis. What do you mean?" His eager demeanour was overridden by his desire to understand. Her mind was fuzzy from not eating or sleeping enough lately.

She took a breath. "I thought about it today, or was it yesterday, when I was playing hide-and-seek. What if the curtains, how they're positioned, indicate places they don't want vampires to go? What if it's a clue? The places that leak more sunlight might be the places they don't want vampires to go near or search. That means they might have something valuable there."

His brow furrowed, a long finger touching the tip of his chin. "You have a point, Ennis. I hadn't thought of that. I'll search those areas then, especially trying to find a lock in those vicinities." Standing up, he looked at the half-eaten pile of waffles. "Okay, well, you eat, and I'll be back soon. I won't be away long." He vanished into the hall after a smile of hope aimed her way.

~

She was munching on the last of the cold, salty bacon when there was another knock followed by Valentine's call to open the door. As she unlocked it, a dark head of hair that was blown out of sorts rushed in. The man looked crazed, but his face was set.

Valentine's cape fluttered as it caught up with its hurried wearer. "Sorry, I forgot to tell you the key I found in the painting studio was in a tube of paint. But I just opened up a small chest in the laundry room that was on the backside of the washing machine. *In* the back of the machine actually. A pull out box. Unfortunately the curtain theory was incorrect related to this key. But still good thinking."

He held up a piece of paper.

Shaking her head, she tried to focus and reached for the note. "What's that!"

Valentine handed her the paper and began pacing. "I think it's the code we've been looking for. I'm surprised they even kept this in the house."

She examined the wrinkled white paper, eyebrows lifted. After taking a couple of tries to read it, she sighed. "It's gibberish." The scrawl was nearly illegible. She squinted, turning it this way and that. "'xc tabx'? But those aren't even real words!" She slapped her forehead, turning over the shoddy parchment. "This is a code? Is it the password for the computer? Did you enter it in?"

Valentine nodded, arms folded. "I've already tried, so no need to worry about that. Remember, three failed attempts set off the system. I've already used two attempts. I tried it in reverse as well. It's a cypher, I think. I've tried working on it already with the alphabet backwards and forwards. It's gibberish."

She huffed and ground her teeth. "Maybe they're just messing with us?" She turned the small note every which way. "Can you get us some paper? It looks like we're going to be busy today. But I think it's almost pointless at this point to try and figure out the computer password. Even if we decode this, it might just be a hint to the real password. Or a hint to the hint."

Valentine nodded, his hand to his chin, head tilted. "I suppose it could be, but I think it wouldn't hurt to try to figure it out today. They aren't breaking down your door to stake you yet."

She huffed again. "Yet." A sigh escaped her. "Benedict's getting suspicious. I'd hoped we'd find the password, not just a clue." Shaking her head, she continued. "I guess we'll give decoding a shot, and let's pray for God to give us what we need." He nodded before vanishing.

She glanced at the paper again, sighing and rubbing her face. She figured her eyes must have looked like a raccoon's by now. "What kind of twisted puzzle is this?" She lifted it to her face. "Well, at least we have a repeat letter. That should help," she whispered. Sniffing the note, all she could smell was the smell of the ink-penned letters. *Pen ink and paper.*

Cracking her neck, she sighed. "Roman numeral theory doesn't work. 'Ninety tab ten'? What's that?" Holding the paper to the light on the wall. "Invisible ink? Doesn't smell like it." Her hand fell to her side, the paper along for the ride.

Creeping to the window, she peeked around the curtain. The sun was just barely beginning to lighten the slate grey clouds. "Just one more day..."

She couldn't deny that she was beginning to feel hopeless in her situation. Only finding another clue instead of the password had resurfaced her depression, causing her to have so many negative thoughts on top of her already fragile mind. Her chest ached, and she rubbed at it. *How can you hope when things seem impossible?* A Voice sounded in her heart. *Because I'm with you.*

"Thanks, God." The corner of her mouth lifted ever so slightly. She let the curtain fall, and paper and pencils rustled on the bed. She gasped, her hand flying to her chest. "You're so quiet. Sorry," she said, trying to settle the rapid beating in her ribcage.

He half-smiled, his eyes slightly sad. "No, no. No need. I'm sorry I startled you. I'll have to remember that."

She felt a small smile find its way onto her face.

The nearly illegible paper on the bed taunted her. *This is practically impossible to solve.* She sat on the green quilt and twisted the fabric with her fingers.

Picking up a sheet of blank paper, he began to scribble. "Come on, we've got to break this code as soon as possible. God is with us."

She nodded and picked up a pencil and sheet of paper and began a methodical scribbling of the alphabet. *God, we need You!*

~

Valentine, sitting on the green chair, glanced up at her from his scrawling several minutes later. He frowned and rested his paper on his knee. "Are you okay after what happened today?" His voice was low and calm.

She was pulled from her deep concentration, frowning slightly. His eyes looked deep and caring, and she looked away. "I'll be okay." Clearing her throat, she shook her head. "Benedict seems really suspicious, V. I think he's getting close to figuring me out, if he hasn't already. He's so cryptic when he speaks, like he knows what I am. I used Saeva as an escape from him today." Her face was etched with guilt. And V definitely noticed.

Before his paper hit the ground near the chair, he was standing before her. "You know normal decency doesn't apply here, right? This is war, Ennis. This is self-defense."

"Yeah, but I hate that I can manipulate." She looked down at the quilt. "I don't relish it." She sighed in aggravation towards herself and flipped onto her back. The paper she had been writing on settled on her face.

He sat on the bed and tried to find her eyes. "Ennis, what you're doing is allowed. This isn't manipulation. You're being *clever*. This isn't normal, everyday life. We're on a battlefield. It's just taking place in the mind." He glanced at the window. "Although, we really are on battlegrounds.

"I feel like a sociopath," she admitted, a lump in her throat.

He shifted the curtains with a long arm. "You're not a sociopath," he said gently. "You're at war, and it's life or death. You don't want to hurt anyone. That's not your goal. Your goal is to get out of here alive."

A retort died in her heart as she contemplated his words. She was, after all, only fighting to survive. This *was* war. And she *was* fighting for good reasons. But spiritually, was it right? *God, is this right? Please, tell me. Everything is so confusing.* Her sigh propelled the paper up a little, allowing her to catch a look at Valentine. He was looking at her cryptically, his eyes partially squinted.

Standing up, he tied the dark curtains in place. Dulled sunlight illuminated the dusty air. Taking a glance at the cloudy sky, he tapped a finger at his side. "If Benedict is getting suspicious, I think we ought to hurry."

She lifted the paper with an aching hand and gave him a look.

He smirked. "Hurry even more."

She returned his smile and resettled the paper.

With a sigh, he frowned and tilted his head. "And I'm glad you're holding up physically as well as you are, even if you aren't mentally. We can deal with that later even though it's vital to your health, but right now we have to escape alive." His voice was gentle, his eyes trained on her trembling hands.

She nodded, and they both fell into an uneasy silence.

~

"This is infuriating!" Tossing another darkened sheet on top of her growing mound, she slapped her face gently. She'd fallen asleep a couple of times, and Valentine hadn't awakened her. She could still feel the pencil's imprint on her shoulder from how she'd fallen asleep. But now, she'd been at the riddle for quite some time. She opened and closed her hand and shook it out.

Valentine's crumpled mountain beside him was comparable. "Don't give up, Ennis. We still have more cypher keys to test." He inspected his current sheet of paper as he was perched on the green chair. "Well... at least there are a fixed number of possibilities."

"But there's something like a million, right?" She huffed.

"Only 4 to the 26th power. Roughly..." His pencil rested against a playful smile.

Ennis looked at him, just staring. She wore a small, plastered smile, but her eyes looked crazed.

He smirked. "Yes, that does create a problem, doesn't it?"

She returned to her writing, her smile disappearing with an exhausted huff.

He steepled his fingers, watching her scribble furiously and count off letters and glanced out the drawn window. A frown found him, and he folded his arms. "Ennis?"

She spared him a glance. "Yes?"

"There's always another way."

She looked up from her paper and slowly set her pencil down. Her eyes were far away, and her face paled. "I know... I mean with this code, I think we'd run out of time before we finally solved it. *If* we ever solved it." She frowned, but her mouth twitched. "Armor?"

His head fell back as he laughed out loud. "No, not the armor." His smile faded. "You know I mean leaving, though. We can alert police about this deathtrap once we're on the other side. I'm sure they'll be interested in you, but I should probably stay away. I don't want to be *poked* at. But since you have a normal life waiting for you, you're much less suspicious than I am."

Her brow furrowed, and she leaned in towards his direction. "Suspicious?"

Moving to sit on the bed beside her, he let his eyes trail along the grey walls. "I don't exactly have a job or friends that can vouch for normalcy. And I'm not exactly the picture of an unsuspicious civilian. The forged documents. Going about at night. A loner most of the time. People have thought of me as shady." His eyes went far away, replaying old memories. He shook his head. "Also, I'm sure they'll want to contact me during the day, and I don't want to have them think I'm an *actual* vampire."

Ennis chuckled. "Because you definitely aren't."

He returned her smile. "No, of course not." He clasped his hands together.

She was laughing still, but his posture caught her eye. Even though he was sitting up rather straight, his shoulders sagged a little. Frowning, she began to worry more about him. *Is he tired? He looks tired. Can he get tired? Is he sick? Can he get sick too?* Her mouth opened, but when she caught sight of his eyes, her words died. He was smiling at her, his eyes brighter tonight than she'd ever seen them. She returned her attention to her paper, the furious scribbling hardly making any sense to her. Her eyes had long been going blurry.

After a moment passed, she looked around the room. "Well, I guess we're going to make a run for it after all." Her mouth turned down. "After all that searching..." Sighing, she shook her head. *Is this the right decision, God? Maybe You'll allow us to escape. Please helps us to escape alive!*

When she glanced over at him again, Valentine's smile had disappeared as well, and he rested his hands on his knees, his eyes focused on a speck of white lint clinging to the curtain.

"When?" she asked hollowly. She could feel herself tensing already, her body aching with built up fatigue. *I can't run. I physically can't. But I'm going to have to or I die. I might die from running. But I guess that's better.* Her heart revved up just at the thought of exertion. Her heartbeat was already high from the constant stress, but would their escape attempt be enough to kill her? This was not living, and she didn't dare to entertain the idea of staying here under the brothers' "care." She swallowed thickly. *Leaving is the only option.* She nodded her head, her hazel eyes steeling.

His head snapped up, and his face looked tired. "At dusk. If you're up for it." He looked at her with concentration, scrutinizing her. She looked away, her body feeling jittery. *Best to end the stress as soon as possible.*

Tossing her paper aside, she stood up slowly, allowing her blood flow to adjust, and peeked out the curtains. The sky was a hazy orange. Clouds were sweeping off in the distance, escaping from the house, and the lawn shimmered in the low sun.

"Alright, so about an hour?" Glancing around the room, she tried to put off the panic of packing. "I should down some soup and water, and maybe we can take some with us. Who knows how long it'll be before we find civilisation so we can call for help." She caught sight of his slightly sagging shoulders again, and her words were no longer silenced. "And what about your blood supply? How will you be? Are you feeling well enough? I don't mean to be rude, but... you don't look well."

Without thinking much, she slipped a hand to his forehead. He recoiled slightly at the sensation but allowed her to touch his face for a second before catching her hand and easing it to her side with a chuckle. "It doesn't work that way."

Her eyes went wide. "Oh, sorry! I thought maybe... I mean it's a natural... Uh... the... I don't even know what I'm saying." She chuckled and darted her eyes away. She had found out his forehead felt the same temperature as her cold hands. Even though he looked better now than he had when she first arrived, she was still worried about him. He seemed too pale, and his eyes looked tired. "You can't get sick? Fevers? Any illnesses?"

Shrugging a shoulder, he placed his hands loosely around his knee. "Not that I know of. Our weakness come from the sun, blood loss, and mental griefs. But beyond that, none that I know of."

He stood and observed the glittering and shaking landscape in silence for a moment. "But you're right. I do look unwell. I haven't eaten enough lately. But I think if we get past the border, I can find some animals. That'll be fine for me."

Shifting, she let her feet hang off the bed. "Are you sure you're alright? Can you make it? You really do look sick."

He smirked and crossed his arms behind his back. "That's generally how we vampires look. I don't mean to be rude, but I think that's a reason why the brothers first mistook you as one."

"I don't get much sun." She smirked too.

"Neither do we."

She bit her lip. "Well... Don't they have a blood supply we can take with us? I'd feel better knowing you've had something substantial."

He cast his gaze on her and then let it drop to the floor, his body still. *Is he smiling a little?* "Yes, I could pack a bottle, and I guess I could go drain their supply since we don't plan on staying here any longer." He was smirking again.

"Okay." Rising to her feet, she gave him a light shove. "Go have yourself an evening snack. We leave at dusk."

~

Ennis sipped water from her hand as she leaned over the sink. She huffed, clenching her hand to stop the shaking. Her stomach was roiling, and she couldn't stop her body from vibrating. Valentine had been gone for a couple of minutes, and she had already finished her preparations for what was to come. She heard a rapping on her door and moved to open it, and Valentine burst in, holding a black backpack.

"How was dinner?" she asked lightly.

He set down the backpack on the bed at lightning speed. "Quite unfulfilling, actually." He unpacked some contents that were in it and laid them amongst the other things that she'd set out on the bed.

Dread seized her insides. "What do you mean?" She started walking slowly towards him, tripping on the floor. She dashed to the chair and steadied herself. *You can't be clumsy now, Ennis. This is the time for stealth and speed.*

He paced around the room. His nervousness rubbed off on her as she fiddled with her long white sleeves. "The blood supply is gone." His face looked even paler.

Her heart raced even more quickly. Subconsciously, her hand shot to her neck. "Then... what's going on?" Her mind began to make connections, and then her whole body tensed. And she really hated her conclusion. "No..."

He nodded, eyes darting to the window and then the backpack. "Yes, Ennis. I think they know. Or at least they're suspicious enough to get rid of the blood supply." He looked irritated but then sighed. Appearing at the bed, he speedily packed the backpack with carefulness. "Well, it could also be a foolish stunt of theirs to try and make you hungry enough to bite one of them." He paused his hands and tapped his finger on the bed. His eyes looked faraway. "Or me."

She shook her head, and her hands darted out to help him pack, only to resettled at her side and then repeat. "Well, regardless, are you going to be okay?" Her voice quavered.

He turned to her with soft eyes. "Ennis, don't worry about me. It would have put me more at ease if I had been able to though, but it's not like I'm on my last reserves." He glided forwards to stand at her side. Her fingers were digging into the green chair as she swayed slightly on her feet. "The only thing I'm worried about is not being able to protect you. I want us *both* to get through that barrier and away from this insane family. But..." He shifted onto his other foot and looked down. "I won't deny I fear losing lots of blood. That's the thing that could really be an issue for my body. The sun's not going to kill me, but the weapons might make me lose too much blood and kill me." He rubbed his fingers together at his sides. "And you," he added quietly.

Ennis shook on her feet and, her hand flew to her heart. "Okay, Valentine." She gulped and closed her eyes for a moment, saying a silent prayer. And then her eyes flew open with fire. "We're going to do this. I think they're already too suspicious of me." She looked at him shyly. "But you don't have to flee right now. You can wait. It's me they're suspicious of."

He closed the gap between them, his face like stone. "Ennis, don't even think that I'd leave you on your own. I will gladly run with you."

She shrugged her shoulders with a tired smirk. "Well, you'd beat me."

A slight smile broke his serious expression, and he pulled her in for a hug. "Yes, I can run faster than you. But you misunderstand. You don't need to run. We'll run together," he said over her shoulder. He pulled back, keeping her at arm's length. "Well... I'll run *for* you." He chuckled.

At that, her heart lightened, and she ran a quaking hand through her short hair. "Sounds good."

"Alright then." His tone was serious once again. "Let's make sure you're ready, and we'll be off."

And a lump she couldn't clear was stuck in her throat.

~

Ennis checked the backpack one last time. Inside was her wallet, two bottles of water that were really an olive oil bottle and a whiskey bottle drained out and filled, matches, her journal she'd kept whilst there, the book she'd used as a second journal to double as paper for fire starting, two pens, two bars of soap, a portly bottle of whiskey, four cans of soup, some bread and sandwiches that hopefully wouldn't spoil quickly, a cord of rope, and a kitchen knife wrapped in a couple towels. They also wrapped towels around the glass bottles to keep them from smashing into one another. She added in her phone and charger and then shouldered the bag. She could feel the contents settle heavily, causing her to shift to the side and push the air out of her lungs. She frowned. *I'm against stealing. Please forgive me, God.*

Valentine shifted the cape's clasp at his throat. "I can carry the bag you know," he said again.

She felt slightly breathless under its weight and tried to shrug the bulk to a more comfortable position. Waving her hand, she tried to hide the fact that her body was trembling from exertion already. "I told you. This is in case we get separated. *I* need these things. Fortunately, you don't."

Blinking, he heaved a sigh. "Fortunately..." he mumbled. His shoulder twitched. "In the *off* chance we do get separated."

She shot him a knowing look. "Yes, the *off* chance."

Turning in a circle, she took a mental picture of her room, which had become a strangely homey place for the past however many days she'd been locked up here. She really wished her phone had power but shrugged. Her eyes caught her suitcase near the bathroom. *Goodbye, Suity. You served well.*

Adjusting her black cape, she took a deep breath, which caused her heart to beat unevenly. She thumped her chest before clearing her throat. Valentine, near her window, watched her carefully. Their hazel eyes connected, and then hers darted away. "I'm ready," she said.

19

Valentine peeked out Ennis's bedroom window and nodded once. The orange sky was fading into a pale grey with intermittent clouds, taunting them with dusk. "Let's go now." He turned to look at Ennis, seeing her shaking knees. He snapped his eyes back to her face. "Remember, I won't carry you until we get out of the house in case we need to split up if they catch us."

Ennis nodded, breathing rapidly. "Let's pray." After he nodded, she began, lifting her gaze to the heavens. "Thank You, God, for being righteous and good and for being with us this far. We're worried, and we know You know this. God, I know this seems impossible, but You can make the impossible possible. Help us escape and give us strength please, if it be Your will. We love You and ask You to help us feel Your presence. In Jesus Christ's name, amen."

"Amen." Valentine opened his eyes, and she saw a light in them. And she knew exactly where that light had come from and felt it in herself. It was God's light. Even though her anxiety was overwhelming, she knew all was in God's hands.

He silently pulled open her bedroom door and stepped into the hall. She could feel her heart speed up. *Shh, please don't act up now. It's not the time!* She couldn't help but feel the tremors that shot through her and the dizziness and unsteadiness that upended her balance. But adrenaline spiked her body, giving momentum to her steps as she burst into the hall. *God, please be with us and help us make it out alive.* She followed closely in Valentine's shadow as he glided slowly enough for her to be at his heels. Their black capes morphed them into one dark shadow. They slid through the hall and to the stairs. She wanted to shush her backpack, which made odd shifting sounds with every step. The house was silent, unnerving her even more. Valentine's head shifted side to side as they swept along, making his dark hair ruffle.

An indistinct noise sounded through the house, and she whipped her head up to look at him, her hands twisting together. However, he continued plowing down the stairs, taking the steps two at a time. She plodded along behind him, watching her feet carefully again. His cape was scarily close to her falling steps. But the two never met.

They reached the first floor in the shadowy house, welcomed by tired-looking grey walls and the many windows of the hall. The slim cracks in the drawn curtains let in streams of orange that lit their path. Ennis squinted as Valentine led them through the hall and reception area, all the way to the front door. Her brows furrowed. *We're going out the front door?* Without hesitation, he turned the golden knob and pulled the door open a gap. He slid out, and her heart surged with a wracking palpitation. *This is it...* His hand reached back through the ajar door. Ennis took it, and he pulled her effortlessly through.

The cold air sucked the warmth from her lungs, making her want to cough, but she quelled the desire. They made it four steps off the porch before a chuckle echoed through the chilled air. Her heart died and revved up at the same time. Slipping on the wet grass and leaves, she landed hard on her backside. Valentine's eyes widened, and he was still for a split second before he snatched Ennis's hand, hauling her to her feet. The leaves whipped about their idling legs, dancing an ode to chaos around their frozen bodies. *What do we do! Valentine's frozen! Is he thinking about what to do like me? Oh... I'm going to die.* She craned her neck to look at the house.

"Going somewhere?" Benedict was leaning on an open, third-story window frame. He held a gun that had a massive cylinder, and it was pointed straight at them.

"Let's go!" Valentine said, swooping her into his arms. His feet had barely moved before Benedict cocked his gun.

"No!" she screamed. A hideous screech sounded behind them. BANG! She thudded to the ground, rolling apart from Valentine. Her backpack spilled some of its contents on the ground. Behind them, a maniacal voice, which was a mix of shrieking laughter and rage, shouted at them. "We're right behind you!"

She shook her head, her vision blackening, and scrambled on her hands and knees towards Valentine. "What is it!" she wailed.

Valentine clutched his leg, hissing. A foot-long wooden stake protruded from his thigh. He blinked hard.

His teeth were clenched. "Keep going." Yanking the stake out with one quick motion and putting a stray soup can in her backpack and rezipping it, he scooped her up again. "Sorry."

She shook her head in astonishment. "No need to apologize." Trying to catch her breath and stop the panic, she gripped her neck. "I can run. I don't want you to hurt. Your leg."

He took a very brief moment, gathering himself. "That'd be illogical," he said, before

297

breaking into a run again. But she noticed he was going at a slower pace.

Within seconds, they made it through the side yard and were in the woods. She had just barely made out her car's blue hood before it vanished. Something thundered through the trees behind them, and she couldn't make out what it was through Valentine's chest.

He glanced down at her, and his voice was whipped away as he spoke, but she thought she heard him say, "Don't look back."

The hauntingly familiar screech of bullets ripped through the air, tree bark shattering madly about them. She could feel something shove Valentine forwards. She pressed herself into his chest and squeezed her eyes shut. A powerful bang made her ears ring, and a scream tore through her as something shoved into her left side. Valentine let out a breath and stopped, leaning her against an oak tree. Standing back, he yanked out another large stake that had gone straight through his middle. He threw the spike weakly into the woods, which Ennis thought was still a pretty amazing throw. She didn't even see or hear it land, but she wasn't sure if that was because of his unnatural strength or because she was in so much pain. She clutched her left side and pulled a hand back. Blood. Looking down, she probed the new gouge in her side with a finger and noted, with gritted teeth, that the wound was about half an inch deep. *Oh, that's probably not smart. Don't touch the wound, Enn. Infection.* She clutched the tree for support. Tears and sweat blurred her vision as she looked at Valentine. Something dark coated his middle. He was very pale, but his eyes were focused, and he crouched down beside her. She'd slumped to the ground. *When did I get here?*

He slicked his hair back, which gave her a clearer view of his worried eyes. "Ennis! Ennis, are you okay?" He frantically pulled her shirt up a little to inspect the wound.

She stared at him and shook her head. "You're gushing blood, V!"

"I'm okay for now. I'm unnatural. You aren't." He looked behind him. And she noted his dark hair was riddled through with leaves and debris. His worried eyes were again on her wound, and his hands soon followed, gingerly touching the oozing area. "This..."

She tried to smile, but she looked stern. "It's only half-inch. I'll be fine. But I'll certainly die if we stay here any longer." A wail escaped her lips as she forced herself to stand. She teetered as she clutched the tree, her eyes falling shut.

In the distance, voices slipped through the trees. The wind carried them like worried messengers. The voices were warped as they wove around bare, spindly branches, but their message was clear. "You're not getting away!" It was distinctly Benedict's tone. But it no longer held any sort of friendly cheeriness like it had. No. Now it was colder than the air slicing through her exposed skin. She shuddered and tugged at Valentine's arm. "Come on!" She stumbled a few steps deeper into the forest, breathing raggedly.

Valentine huffed, half-exasperated. "What are you doing?" Again, he scooped her into his arms and pounded over the fallen floor. The woods encroached them, pressing in on them. Even though his movements were smooth, pain shot through her side as the cold air and motion

299

aggravated it. The urge to vomit surfaced in their attempts to avoid the oaks, pines, and vines that appeared out of nowhere.

The shouting no longer reached them now. Her heart was acting weirder than usual, and she clutched her neck and heart.

V glanced down. "Ennis?"

"Fine," was all she could get out. Her voice didn't want to work. She felt a wet spot on her side, and her brows furrowed. Reaching down to feel at it, she realized blood was soaking her shirt. Or was it V's blood? Her eyes didn't want to focus. Her head spun and she moaned, tucking her head against his chest. The wound had begun to burn wildly and unmercifully as if a stake of fiery ice had decided to have a go at her. Instead of panicking, she tucked her head even tighter into him and focused on what she heard. Or didn't hear. No heartbeat thundered back at her. He wasn't even breathing. She supposed, lightheadedly, that he didn't need to.

Then the forest awakened with a whirring noise.

No, not the forest.

The guns.

20

Something caught Valentine's right arm, and he backed up. He growled, sloppily setting Ennis down beside a tree. "The barrier," he groaned, yanking out a stake. His eyes broke from the stake barrier to look wildly about him. Trying to watch him, she moved her head.

The world tilted sideways, and she shut her eyes. "No, no, no," she mumbled to herself. "Not now."

His hands were uneasy at his sides, and he huffed, turning to tend to her. "Ennis, we're going to have to charge through the barrier." He flung his arms around her, standing her up simultaneously, and held her like a penguin protecting its young by wrapping himself around her like a shield. And he'd aimed them straight at the stake perimeter.

He advanced two steps and then halted. A lethal silence punctuated his words. "We're too late."

"What!" Ennis felt herself being shoved behind a tree just as a spray of bullets shattered the bark. She heard them rip through fabric and shuddered.

Her voice quavered as she peeked out from behind the rough trunk. "V?"

"I'm fine!" His face was stony, and she could see him sway a little as he stood. "Stay there." He searched for her eyes, and, after finding them, he nodded once, seeming satisfied. Whipping away towards another oncoming spray of bullets, he ran out of her sight. She peeked around the other side of the tree and saw Benedict reloading his massive stake gun, with some type of automatic gun resting against his leg. Saeva was on his brother's right side, wielding what looked to be some sort of automatic shotgun and another oversized, automatic gun she couldn't identify. Both of the brothers were breathing heavily and didn't bother to wipe away the sweat that trickled down their reddened faces. They were bedecked in ammunition like overzealous gun enthusiasts, magazines strapped around them like they were going to an all-out war. Her stomach felt weightless. *This* is *a war.*

Benedict sent another spray of bullets towards them. However, Valentine walked straight through the bullets, and Benedict's eyes widened with curiosity. All three of the men stood in about a thirty-foot triangle. Benedict slowly began to wear a wide smile, and his words carried to her on the wind.

Benedict huffed, his eyebrows high. "Valentine, you can hold your lead." Valentine was silent, pressing forward towards Benedict in a silent stride, his hazel eyes flaming green. Benedict turned to his brother. "Find her."

Saeva nodded solemnly, marching off in the direction Valentine had come from. Ennis's eyes widened, and she stripped off her backpack, ripping it open with clumsy fingers. The pack felt lighter than she remembered but decided to figure out why later. Digging around the backpack, she found the knife wrapped in a towel and freed it, gripping it tightly with white knuckles. With a trembling hand, she swiped at her palms with a loose towel. Sweat and crimson blood had slicked her grip. Her heart beat so fast she felt like she could go into cardiac arrest at any time. Looking down at her wound, she saw red staining her left side too. Her face was blank as she tried to understand why she wasn't feeling its searing pain right now. "Adrenaline," she mouthed.

Benedict's voice was still being swept to her on the wind, along with the rhythmic crunch of his brother's approaching footsteps. "To think that all this time *you've* been our vampire," Benedict said, shaking his head that hovered just above the aimed stake gun.

With a face of stone, Valentine stood poised before him, his head leaning forward. His hands were hovering near his sides, slightly out away from his body. His legs were apart, grounded firmly on the damp soil. It was almost as if Valentine were menacingly waiting for his food to finish cooking.

Benedict looked him up and down. "Quite a lot of blood you got there," he said over the barrel of his gun.

Without comment, Valentine dashed forward.

Benedict yelled as he pulled the trigger. "Let me add to it!"

The stake went straight into Valentine's heart. A sickening crunch ripped through the cold air. But he didn't stop. He barreled forward into Benedict, crashing into the man. Both were knocked to the forest floor. Flailing, Benedict took a stake from one of many on his belt and swiped at the furious being. Both righted themselves, taking a split second to poise for another attack.

"You still wish to kill me?" Valentine asked calmly, dodging another attack and landing a nasty clawing down Benedict's right side.

Benedict shrieked, switching his stake to his uninjured left side. "You *and* that girl! She's human, and you're too unruly to work with." He spat. "You both die."

Valentine eyed him with glassy eyes. "Oh dear. You shouldn't have said that," Valentine murmured icily, blood dripping out of his heart cavity. His hazel eyes blazed, his fangs visible, and his arms flung out and grabbed hold around the brother's shoulders. Benedict wrestled in his grip, landing a stake to Valentine's thigh and stabbing over and over.

"No!" Benedict yelped. With a single twisting motion, Valentine now held him by his throat using a single pale hand.

21

"Where are you?" Saeva sang, his gun raised. His brown hair shifted as he took in any signs of movement. His blue-grey eyes looked pale in the dying light. Ennis was thankful for the leaves that added movement to their surroundings. But she could still hear his crunching steps get closer. Her breathing became erratic, and she held her mouth open slightly to breathe as quietly as possible. The cold air pierced her lungs, making her chest ache. Or maybe that was from the stake wound. Guarded by the towering oak, she shuddered to a standing position, panting. She shut her eyes against the noise she was making.

"I couldn't believe you were human... But you've convinced me now." His voice was full of disappointment.

She clenched the knife tighter. *Why is he talking now? Taunting? Drawing me out?*

"I was suspicious at first, but then you drank that blood." His voice was colder than the air. "You *fooled* me." He spat the word with rage. "I didn't believe him. You were so good at your role. But, now, who turns out to be the vampire? *Valentine?*" He gave an aggravated growl. But something had changed in his voice just then, something Ennis didn't like. She could understand anger. In fact, that might have even given her an advantage due to him being distracted by emotion. But there was something else there, and she couldn't pin it. A bubble of laughter formed in his throat. She swallowed thickly. That was it. Hysteria. And that was much worse. "And you really believed we wanted to write those books just for personal satisfaction? Hardly." He laughed with scorn. "They're a signal, Ennis. A signal to vampires to tell them that we *want in*. And they'll come. And if you get away, which you won't, they'll come after you. And if they don't get you, someone else will. Someone always will. After all, they're a secretive bunch. Can't have just any human with their knowledge."

The crunching sounds were louder in Ennis's ears. She held her knife to her chest. *Why is he telling me this now!* Her body wanted to run, to walk, to get out of there. She felt the familiar compulsion to move around to stop from passing out. *No! I can't do any of those things right now!*

The wind tore at the trees and a rain of leaves enveloped them all in fiery reds and bloody oranges. She closed her eyes for a brief moment. *Now.* She darted out from behind the tree with the knife clenched in her hand and snagged Saeva's right arm with its blade. A scream tore through the woods, and one of his guns crashed onto the shifting ground. She looped around and caught his other arm with the blade before he had a chance to pull the other trigger. The second gun fell from his grip as she zipped around him, leaving him dizzy. Her heart surged and she stumbled to a halt. Yanking free a stake from his belt with his good arm, he bolted at her, raging.

She flung herself to the ground, avoiding the rampage. Catching herself with her hands, she stood up using a tree. Everything was moving so fast. She knew at any moment her life could end. *Oh, God, help me!*

His body turned towards her, and her mind snapped to attention with more adrenaline. He barreled at her, catching her arm in his slick hand,

and wrestled her to the ground. She screamed as she felt something disconnect as she hit the ground hard. Her right shoulder denied her command for it to block her face. Her vision blackened, and she felt her consciousness slipping away. But she repeated to herself one thing. *Hold on to the knife. Hold on to the knife.* Before she could do much else, he slashed his stake at her, holding her down with his right arm across her chest. A scream tore weakly from her throat, causing the gruesome sight of Valentine's recent work to go black. Her middle seared, and her lungs were being crushed beneath his weight. Sweat poured down her face and stung her eyes. Her lungs heaved as she sliced the knife blindly with all her might.

Then sounded the scream that she supposed would haunt her for the rest of her life. His gut-wrenching shriek pierced the misty air. His grasp faltered as he clutched his face instead. She righted herself on her hands and knees and scrambled back. Straight over his left eye there was a nasty slice. He gave another haunting wail as he struggled to his feet and began blindly running towards where Benedict and Valentine had been. Her breath hitched, and her eyes widened as she saw his trail veer right. *Isn't that where the—* He was too close. Her mind quickly spun through what was about to happen, and whether or not she should warn him or let him go. And she only had a split second to choose.

"No!" A scream lurched in her throat just before the stake guns went off. It was too late. Her eyes were frozen, staring at him as the stakes continued to pound away at his body. Numb and unable to move, she watched as his body fell limply to the ground, and the guns whirred back to silence, tired but content in their work. The body was motionless.

Ennis turned around and threw up. Her breathing came only in shuddery jolts. Waves of emotion wracked her, but which ones she couldn't tell. Her mind was not processing. It refused to turn like it usually did, to an even lesser extent that it had been these past however many days.

Becoming aware of the darkness covering her vision, her mind snapped back to where she was. And she hadn't realized she'd stood up while she watched the horror. Her body gave out, and she fell. Her hands and knees pressed into the moist leaf bed beneath her bloody fingers. Her arms quivered, her right shoulder giving out. The knife glinted slightly in the dying light, coated in dirt and red beside her. Her body violently shuddered, and she pulled herself into a ball away from the knife.

She heard nothing, and the trees seemed dark grey. *Where was Valentine?* Her mind could only think small, simple thoughts. Straightforward, but not complex. She focused on hearing the trees. They rhythmically danced to and fro, at peace. *They're taunting me.* Her adrenaline was wearing off, fatigue crashing into her. She couldn't remember how long it'd been since she'd heard Valentine and Benedict fighting. *Fighting! They're fighting!*

Her mind snapped out of its daze, and her body got up automatically, set on a mission. She stumbled back to the tree, stuffing everything back into the bag that had come out during her knife extraction. She let out a growl of aggravation as she clumsily packed everything back in. Her hands didn't seem to be working properly. Once the bag was stuffed and painfully adjusted over her limp arm, she grabbed her knife, and another shot of adrenaline coursed through her. Bile shot up into her throat. The sticky knife was red. Swallowing back down her feelings, she trampled over the crunchy, dead foliage. The sickly sweet and musky smell of decaying leaves attacked her senses.

Another strong gust sent a cascade of orange, red, brown, and yellow raining down. There, some ways off through the shower, she could make out a dark figure. Her good arm pumped at her side as she moved as fast as her weak body could manage. But she slowed to a halt when Benedict slipped down before the vampire, still. Her eyes made their way up the vicious-looking frame, black cape whipping in the wind. A grey vest was visible in the thin light. His eyes... His eyes were filled with something wild. Blood dripped down his mouth and neck, and his chest was heaving. Then the figure turned towards Ennis, catching her stare. Her eyes remained fixed. A small smile lifted his face before he closed the distance, appearing before her.

Pulling her into a tight embrace, he let out a breath. "Ennis, are you alright!"

A subconscious wail escaped her lips. Her arm hung limply at her side, swaying from his jostling hug. Her knees gave out, and the knife dropped to the ground. Lights twinkled before her eyes.

He followed suit, crouching next to her, his eyes wide.

Blinking away the black, she blanched. "My shoulder," she whispered.

Valentine's eyes fell on the bloody stream seeping from the side of her shirt. He tore his eyes away. "Not good..." he whispered to himself. Turning to her again, a different light was in his eyes. His hand gently prodded her joint. She felt something wet on her neck. *Oh, I'm crying. Tears.* His eyes were soft. "Ennis, I'm going to put it back in. Stay with me, okay?" He put a hand on her elbow.

She whimpered. "V..."

"Shhh, I know, Ennis. It'll be over soon." He set her down gently on her back before he took her right elbow and moved it away from her. Her cries of pain were swallowed up in the vicious wind. He moved it behind her head slowly. She hissed, feeling a solid resistance. He moved it a little more. And a little more. And then she felt it pop back into place with a snap. Her eyes shot with silver, and she closed them immediately, seething through clenched teeth. Fresh tears stung her eyes. Through the pain, Valentine's ragged breath reached her ears over the wind.

"V?" she whispered, wishing blood would return to her head.

His hazel eyes met hers. The agony was tangible.

Her eyes widened. "Are you okay!" She reached to touch his forehead with her left hand.

His body shook like hers, and he collapsed next to her, propped up by a tree. The rough, dark bark began getting darker.

Her brows furrowed. "V?" Within a second, it clicked. "V! Blood! You're bleeding out!" She looked down and saw a fresh coat of blood covering her body and knew it wasn't her own. "You're badly hurt!" She crawled the little distance to his side, wincing at the pressure on her right arm. Her hands moved to staunch the leaking, but the blood kept coming. Her eyes caught the puddle of blood pooling at his thigh.

310

He turned away. "I'm not stable right now, Ennis," he breathed, his lips tight and face pale beneath a coat of blood.

Shaking her head, and regretting it as the world tilted like a funhouse, she clutched at the tree. The bark bit into her palms. He turned his face away from her.

She looked at the back of his mottled hair. "Valentine..." His chest was rising and falling rapidly, shallowly, and a steady stream of blood flowed out. Realization smacked her in the face. "You're *dying*."

When he didn't respond, her heart shot out of rhythm, and she gripped at his shoulders. "V!" She turned his head towards her. His eyes were shut, his face pained. "V, I'll..." Her mind churned for ideas. "I'll go get Benedict." A sick feeling warped through her at the thought of seeing his dead body, let alone dragging it here. She wondered if she would even have enough strength to do that.

Shaking his head, he murmured. "It'd leave a trail. And not enough time. No good." He opened one eye, looking at something beyond. "We're going to have more bad company soon. I know their scents. I know them." His voice was labored, and his shoulders sagged.

She stared past him, into the oddly grey orange color of the forest. Her heart hammered, but her mind was clear. "Then take me." Her voice was firm. She wouldn't be getting out of this alive if Valentine wasn't with her. He could smell trouble coming, and they were out of options. Shaking his head, he opened an eye and looked at her. "Ennis, you're too weak. Your illness. And you've been through too much—"

She sighed. "You know it's our only option." She dug a hand into the dirt at her side. "Please, V. I'm willing," she said more quietly. Exhaustion was hitting her hard. *Greater love hath no man than this, that a man lay down his life for his friends.*

She crawled into his lap and rested her neck against his lips. "Please. Just get better," she whispered.

With a resigned sigh, his arms wove around her. "It'll hurt."

She gave a small noise of assent, her lips tight and face pale. A fresh rain of leaves flittered through the air, red dancing before her eyes. Then she felt his fangs press into her neck. The sharp, thorn-like pain wrenched a cry from her, but she quickly grew accustomed to the pain, and it melted away. Things were blurring, but her pain was becoming less and less. She could feel her blood leaving her, slipping away through her veins. Her consciousness was being sucked out of her. *What an odd feeling. But... it...* Her eyes relaxed and fell shut. Valentine's grip became tighter around her, but his fingers were gentle. His strength was returning, and her heart lightened at that. Or was that the loss of blood? The world faded to black.

~

22

Ennis felt her feet hitting something and an arm around her stomach. All around her, multiple thunks sounded off. Her body hung limply over the arm, but she was too weak to turn to see what was going on. On top of that, her eyes didn't seem to want to open. Something repeatedly bumped into her head, and she smelled sweetness every so often. Working an eye open, she saw the ground moving beneath her as her legs dragged over a blur of colors. *What happened to the floor?* Someone was hissing. *What is...* Then she realized both she and her carrier were moving incredibly fast. Whoever this person was, they were hunched over. *What a weird way to travel.* A moan escaped her as pain ripped through her consciousness. She didn't want to know what her body looked like. *Guess I didn't die. Yet. There's still a chance to live. Thank you, Jesus.*

"Ennis? Are you awake?" Valentine's voice said.

Valentine! Her voice didn't cooperate. Instead, only a slight chirp escaped her, lost in the wind howling around them.

He hissed. "Well, if you are, we're currently going through the barrier."

The thunks were still mercilessly pounding away. She noticed she felt new stings across her legs and arms, surprised she could feel anything beyond the crippling pain from her side. *Barrier... Right. Stakes. Travelling through the barrier. Overkill... Ow...*

A couple seconds passed, and her eyes were overtaken by a long bout of blackness. This was the most pain she'd felt in her entire life. Her side ached like the dagger was still in it. *How are we*

313

surviving these stakes? With no small effort, she billowed her lungs that felt like they were being crushed.

He dodged around the surrounding trees. "You'll be okay. We just need to get out of here." His voice was steady, but he was obviously concentrating on the task at hand.

Ennis felt something hit her face again. She opened her eyes long enough to see what was smacking her in the face.

A human arm.

She wanted to scream, but her body wouldn't allow the use of oxygen for that purpose. Again, the arm smacked her face. And she saw what the arm was clothed in. Brown leather. *Saeva was wearing a jacket that was... Oh...* Nausea struck her. The sweet leather mixed with the musky scent of dead leaves made her want to gag. *...We're using him as a shield.* Her eyes closed again, her body too weak to swat at the flailing arm.

~

When her eyes opened again, the erratic thunking noises had stopped, and she was propped up against something hard and uneven. She turned her head ever so slightly and felt bark chip through her matted hair, pressing into her skull. *Tree.* She opened her heavy lids slightly and saw shadowy trees and two giant spiky porcupines. Or were they dinosaurs? And they were only four feet away from her. *How do dinosaurs live out here?* Her eyes fell shut against the split-second wave of unconsciousness that struck her.

She tried to open her eyes again. Her head hurt, but the night's dark blue washed over everything, creating a strange blue peace. Thankfully it wasn't day, lest her head split open as her eyes told her it would if she saw any bright light. *I must've hit my head sometime during the fight.* She tried lifting her hands, but they rose up strangely as if attached to puppet strings. Her movements were clunky, uncoordinated.

Shifting around a little, she realized how sticky she felt. She touched her left arm with her right and felt a sticky residue. *I could bottle myself with all this maple syrup on me. This tree really has a goldmine. Syrup factory material.* She felt the tree behind her, nearly impaling her hand on a piece of sharp bark. *That's weird. Why isn't the tree all sappy? It got this much on me...* Her eyes opened again, this time a little wider. No, she wasn't in the company of porcupines or spiky dinosaurs. They were Saeva and Benedict.

Her stomach rolled. It was too brutal to continue looking. *How is this happening! This isn't supposed to happen in life!* She wanted to turn away and put distance between herself and the bodies, but she was so weak. As she tried to move, she caught sight of her own body. It wasn't syrup. It was blood. She closed her eyes and wanted to scream. And she didn't even know whose blood it was.

She wondered if she even had the strength to stand, let alone walk. Oh, how her body ached all over! Attempting to move a leg, she felt it wobble profusely. *Stupid leg...* She tried her other one, and it gave way as well. *I guess I'm dead meat if someone comes to kill me.* Her mouth thinned into a grim line. She winced as she poked at her wounded side, causing her a sharp inhale. *The stake... Valentine!*

She twisted her head suddenly, and a grunt ripped through her. *Slowly...*

She tried her voice. "Val-ine." Her voice was weak and raspy.

She didn't hear any response over the wind that ruffled her matted, dark hair, which was crusted against her pale, bloody face. *Again.* "V?"

"Ennis?" The voice was weaker than hers, pained. Pain or no pain, she was going to find him. She only had to struggle on her hands and knees to the backside of the tree. "D-don't come over here. I'm I'm n-not—"

Whatever the reason, she didn't care. Stumbling forwards on her hands and knees, she found Valentine riddled with holes. Her eyes immediately felt unfocused. A pile of glistening stakes lay strewn to his right, alongside a discarded, ragged cape. Her heart surged, and she instinctively rushed to stop the bleeding again, trying to plug up his heart space. These wounds weren't like the ones before in his chest. These were actual *holes*. She could see the tree behind him through various-sized holes in his middle. Entirely drenched in blood, his body was a gruesome sight, but she resolved not to turn away.

She pressed harder on his vitals. "No, no, no, V! What can I do!"

Slumping against the tree, her own weakness warred against her consciousness. She fought for energy, ignoring her vision that was going in and out of black. Grunting in pain, he clumsily put his bloodied hand on hers to push it off but didn't have the strength to go through with the motion. Instead, it rested there on her hand. Her adrenaline kicked in again, and her eyes widened. *He's too weak. He's going to die!*

"Live." His voice was quiet.

She didn't have the strength to shake her head. "What?" He wasn't making sense. Well... she didn't *want* his words to make sense.

"Live," he repeated in a whisper, holding his hand on hers.

She scoffed. "I'll live." She stood to her feet. "And you'll live with me." She fell immediately back down to the ground, panting in a wave of breathlessness and black. Her body desired for her to sleep. *No sleeping!* She'd caught herself on her wrists and felt the shock go through her body. Her right shoulder shot through with pain, and she cried. Her limbs were clumsy, but her heart was set.

Looking to the sky, she cried in determination. "God, please help me." She dragged herself up slowly, her legs shaking. Catching herself against Valentine's tree, she prayed. "Please." He wasn't breathing and worry taunted her that he might really be dead. His eyes were closed, his face smattered with blood, and his vest no longer silver.

Analysing her surroundings, she breathed hard. There *had* to be something he could drink. She knew she might never wake up if she offered more of her blood, and she knew he wouldn't accept it anyway.

A little ways off in the distance, her eyes caught sight of a small mound. Hardly thinking, she stumbled towards it. A bubble rose in her chest. *Hysteria?* Using the trees as crutches, she launched herself between them as if she were in a sad, slow pinball game. Her heart surged, and she shook her head, feeling leaves scratch her face. *I'm on the ground.* Blinking away bits of dirt, she felt like she would never get up. *Fainted.*

Panting there for a moment, she felt another surge of adrenaline, and it kicked her body into motion. Clawing onto another nearby tree, she continued fumbling through the starlit forest. She fell onto her knees, tripping over something hefty. And stared straight into the eyes of a dead fawn. Its large, dark eyes were open. There was a fresh stake in its side, blood still trickling out. She fell onto the deer, and tears streamed down her face as she wept. "Thank you, Jesus!" Laying a hand on the animal's light brown skin, she felt its rough hair slide between her fingers. The body was still warm. While she didn't like that the little guy died, her heart bounded excitedly in her chest. So much so that she could actually see her heart pumping when she looked down at her now heavily damaged, no longer white shirt and black vest. Standing, she tugged the small beast by the hooves back towards Valentine, careful not to head in the direction where she supposed the stake guns slumbered judging by the direction the stake had struck the deer.

She soon discovered the deer was *heavy*. "How can a little deer weigh so much!" She huffed, lugging the deer inch by inch. *How do I even have any strength right now? I think this might kill me, but it's worth trying.*

She thought of the holes in Valentine's chest and torso and sped up as much as she could without causing herself to faint again, which she did multiple times. She had long abandoned her worry that she'd stop breathing. If she was going to die, she was going to die trying to help Valentine live. She didn't care about saving her own life at this point, figuring she was beyond healing. She only wanted to stay alive long enough to save Valentine. "Please let him be alive," she prayed. Her eyes were focused on the deer's limp body.

It felt like forever had passed when she practically dragged the deer into Valentine's lap, collapsing onto her back on the multicolor bed by his side. He started at the sensation, and his eyes lazed open. "Wh—Ennis?" His voice shook with disbelief. The dead deer's head hung limply in his lap. "You..."

"God provided... everything." Her world was spinning, and she couldn't see. "Drink." She wanted to hug onto his side, but she didn't have the strength. Her lungs felt like they'd collapsed, or at least what she reckoned collapsed lungs felt like. She twisted her head to watch him lean down and pick up the deer's head. He was moving so slowly. *This must be what he's like in the sun. Drained. Weak. Like me.*

As his fangs dug slowly into the deer's neck, his eyes began to widen. She wondered if he even had used enough strength to bite through its skin, but he began to swallow little amounts. But a minute later, he was taking large gulps. Regaining some strength, he sat up and pulled the deer closer. Her eyes moved to some motion in his chest, finding that she could physically see his wounds closing up. The tree behind him was disappearing. In amazement, she watched his sinews stitch together. "Whoa." *That's one tough virus.* Then her world blackened.

When her eyes opened again, he was just finishing his meal and stood up to replace his cape. He picked up the backpack from the other side of the tree and slung it over his shoulder.

Walking over to her, he knelt down, pushing her hair to the side, and placed a kiss on her forehead. "Thank you so much," he whispered. He lifted his head to the heavens. He smiled. "Thank You."

All she could do was barely lift the corner of her mouth. Her body was fiercely protesting her little excursion with the deer. *I legitimately think I might die right now.* Fear accelerated in her as her head whirled again. *I want this sickness to stop.* But a stillness reached into her heart, and her fears were struck down. *Right. I'm saved. No need to worry.* She let her body relax. *God, receive me now.*

Valentine frowned, seeming to contemplate for a moment, but finally pulled out a towel from the bag.

She opened one eye at the sound. "Oh no."

"Oh yes," he countered, unwrapping the towel that was wrapped around the whiskey bottle. She could see he really didn't want to do this, but she knew it was necessary if she lived after all. "Now stay lying down."

She huffed. *As if I'm going to stand up.* She lifted up her shirt a little.

He caressed her face with his hand. "I won't let you die."

She nodded once.

"It's going to sting." Setting the bottle to the side, he bit his lip and retrieved another loose towel from the bag. Her brow quirked. Catching her confusion, he smiled slightly. "I'm not going to pour alcohol on you. That's an old way of doing things. I'd rather treat any infections later than cause further harm right now."

Her face relaxed. *Oh, that's good.*

The front of her shirt was a mangled mess, covered with a variety of blood. Sighing, he frowned, taking in the sight. "I'm going to dress your wound. Not to worry you, but I don't want you getting any more dirt in there, increasing your chances of infection. I'd use the water, but you might die from dehydration first before infection."

Nodding in her mind, she clumsily felt at her clothing. As she pulled her shirt up again, a new sting seared her when the fabric touched her skin.

She instinctively reached for her stomach, for the wound she hadn't remembered she'd gotten, but he clasped her hand in his before she could touch it.

He brushed her sweaty bangs out of her eyes. "Ennis, it'll all be over soon." His words felt deep. She thought they meant more than just this momentary pain. Trembling, she nodded. *He had been a doctor once, right?* He propped her up in his arms and ripped the bottom half of her shirt apart.

What era was that, though? She looked down at her new crop top and modestly moved to cover her midriff with her arms. He stopped her before her arms hit her wounds. "Sorry, I'll do my best not to look, but please don't touch your stomach. I don't want more bacteria to be introduced"

She swallowed thickly. *Neither do I.* He grabbed the second towel and the rope that was in the bag. With a brief thought, she noted there was a lot less rope than they'd packed. Taking the towel, he pierced it with his fingers multiple times. Then he pulled the rope through, creating a crisscross. She marveled at the thing that looked like a corset, as he slipped it around her and tightened the piece, creating a little pressure on her wounds. She hissed at the contact again, shaking at the pain, but the burning quickly wore off into aching. Her eyes slid shut, and she felt her body go limp. He rested her head back on the ground.

When his eyes caught her neck, he looked startled. Turning away, he let out a breath. "I'm sorry." His bitterness was almost tangible to her, and he dared to look at the sight again. His fingers hovered over her neck, inspecting the two holes.

"Don't be. You were just trying to help," Ennis corrected in a whisper, her eyes tight against another wave of pain and exhaustion. *I still think I'm going to die.* All the movement had caused her to go breathless again and her world to dip back and forth like a bobbing boat on a discontented sea.

He shook his head, retracting his hand. "No, I don't mean the wound dressing. I mean your neck. What I did—" His voice broke.

Opening her eyes, unwelcome tears leaked out. "V... Valentine..." She closed her eyes, her brow furrowing. "You don't need to be sorry. I offered. It was an efficient..." she took a labored breath, "way out of our predicament. I'm not sorry." She turned her eyes to the sky. Stars burned in the clear night, the clouds long gone. "It was the right thing to do." She shrugged, or at least she attempted to. "Better you to live than both of us die."

He shook his head. Instead of a retort, she was met with a soft reply. "I would be so broken if you died."

She tried to shrug her uninjured shoulder again. "You've known me... what? A week?" However, she knew she meant it. *What am I saying, though!*

He scoffed, tightening his grip around her body. "And you wouldn't feel the same if I died?"

It was hardly a question. She knew he felt the same way about her that she did about him. And she knew he knew. *Foolish me.*

She frowned. "Sorry."

His face relaxed a little, looking drained, but more at peace.

Biting her lip, she looked at a nearby tree that faded to black and back to life again. "But really, we haven't known each other long."

He smiled sadly. "We've been through a lot, though. You can know one person more in a week than another in a lifetime. Suffering can grow people closer together, you know."

She closed her eyes. "I know. It does. Sorry I mentioned it. It's the truth, though."

She panted. *Okay, let's try not to talk so much, Ennis. Too many words for my state right now.*

Her eyelids felt heavy, and they wanted to stay closed. And they did. She'd stopped shaking from the new pain, but now the chill of the night was eating at her, and her trembling began anew. When had she become so cold? She guessed the adrenaline had run its course and dissipated from her veins. She was exhausted even though she'd already slept for however long their run through the barrier had been.

"You have nothing to apologise for. Sorry for my harshness. I just... don't want to lose you," he added quietly.

Her heart hammered as his eyes screamed his pain.

Looking around the forest, he scooped her up carefully and studied her face. "We're going to get out of here. I'll be alright now. Sleep. I'm going to get you some help."

She closed her eyes and tightened herself against him, preparing for launch. They shot off, but it only whipped her hair around her face. Once she settled her face against him, she could tune out the sounds, the movement, the rushing, the pain, everything. Their traveling was smoother than it had ever been.

With her face pressed into his chest, she smelled the blood on his clothes. But beyond that, she could make out the scent of the forest and that spicy nutmeg she loved. She breathed it in until she fell asleep.

~

Ennis's eyes opened to see a dense, moonlit forest. She yawned, hiding her mouth using Valentine's chest. That yawn sent a sharp slice of pain through her jaw and down her neck. And oh, how she felt like death. She began shaking again.

He squeezed her lightly in his arms. "We're far away from them now," Valentine soothed.

She closed her eyes. "They're not going to find us then?" She yawned, which pained her neck again. She wanted to ask who "they" were but didn't have the energy nor the brain capacity to comprehend the answer right now. Her eyelids felt like bricks, but she fought to keep them open. Likewise, her limbs felt like lead, and she decided to fight to move her arms another time. *Such a horrible sensation...*

He was traveling slower now, gliding over the ground, even though he was indeed taking steps.

He came to a standstill. "No, not anytime soon. And definitely not in these woods."

Ennis looked around. "What's wrong?" She winced as she turned her face towards the surrounding area. As she did, she caught sight of one of her hands and noted the thin wounds on them. They had been pelted with leaves during her sleep, and her body was feeling their little slices.

Valentine scanned the scene. The winds were whipping the trees violently. Tiny cyclones swirled to life and died. One of the cyclones sent a splash of leaves their direction, nicking her temple. With another stronger gust, her hair blew about in the musky air. But she didn't see anything surprising in the vicinity, neither good nor bad, and wondered what he had sensed.

He kept her in his arms as he looked at the sky. Her eyes followed his and found the moon some ways above the horizon looking fairly full.

With a sigh, he shifted his weight to his other leg. "We've still got some hours before it starts to turn to day, but it's a bit pointless to continue on right now."

"Why?" she asked, feeling her body jump to life again despite her undeniable weakness. *Thanks, adrenaline.*

He subtly sniffed the air. "I can't catch the scent of any civilization out here. We could be travelling *away* from help. The wind is making things difficult." He sighed, watching the trees dance. "It is a beautiful impediment though."

Ennis watched the trees and murmured agreement. It *was* absolutely gorgeous the way the trees danced to the whistling wind as if they heard a tune she could not. Her side and stomach ached. A reminder that despite the beauty close by, reality was closer. She turned to look up at Valentine and blinked. Feeling her stare, he held her eyes for a moment and then turned away and placed her against a tree.

Her body was overcome by a set of trembling. "I think these mountains go on forever."

Instinctively, she clutched at her wrapped side. She was thankful her shoulder was in place now, but her other wounds weren't exactly in the best conditions. Since they'd stopped and she'd had some sleep that seemed to give her a little bit of energy, that allowed her to finally inspect her body a little more fully. Dread flooded her as she debated whether to look. She grimaced and sighed. Then she looked down.

Her entire body was covered in scrapes, and she could see bruises forming on nearly half of her visible skin. She felt an ache in her neck and touched the spot, finding two indents. ...*Oh.* She sighed, leaning her head back against the bark. The world swam, and she surged to sit forwards to make her body pump blood to her brain better. Her symptoms were worse than she wanted to believe. She couldn't deny the way they made her feel. When the familiar choking sensation attacked her, she fought to stay conscious. *I need rest. Sleep. Food and water good...*

Valentine, framed in moonlight, swung around, and in one swift motion, stooped to her side. His eyes were wide. "Ennis, are you okay! Stay with me!" Two of his fingers shot to the side of her neck, feeling under her jaw, and she groaned.

Her eyes opened, and she noticed that his eyes looked very much like giant black pearls in the starry light. She imagined hers looked similar. "Pearls."

His brow looked even more worried. "Ennis?"

"Tired," she said, laboring with the word.

He nodded gently, taking a seat beside her. He pulled off the backpack and whipped out a can of soup, piercing it quickly. He tipped the can to her lips. She had difficulty swallowing and coughed weakly.

Shaking his head, he continued studying her face. "I don't think it wise to continue moving tonight. We should wait until the wind stops blowing in all different directions. It's mixing up scents."

She nodded. "Makes sense. Scents sense." She took a deep breath, and her back jerked up straighter against the tree in a spasm. Her body was fighting for survival. *This is embarrassing...*

He pushed the can up towards her mouth again, and she took a small gulp. "If the wind doesn't get sorted out before day, then we'll stay around here until the sun sets."

Too weak to nod, she lazed open the other eye and found his concerned face. Her eyes caught sight of his clothing. "Capes?" She mentally felt for the fabric that should have been on her back. It wasn't there.

Unclasping the cape at his throat, he removed his cape and swung it around her shoulders. "You lost yours during your fight with Saeva. And mine has more holes than poor logic." He smiled a little. "I can't move about in the day with this rag, and your wrapping is using most the towels." Her mouth moved to speak. "And I won't take those, even if you offer." Her mouth fell shut.

Despite her pain and anguish, she managed a smile, letting her eyes fall shut. But her heart lurched as did her stomach. *Ugh.* This prompted her to take some more gulps of soup. *At least I don't feel* as much *like death right now.*

There was a pause. "Ennis?"

She shook her head. "I'm okay." She thought she could sense him retract his hand from midair

327

and return it to his knee. His eyes didn't leave her form.

She thought she could hear a lullaby in the wind as sounds softened around her, but Valentine's voice sliced through the welcoming fog of unconsciousness. "No, don't sleep yet. You need to eat." She complied as he lifted the can again. "I'm going to find us somewhere to sleep tonight." He looked around, surveying the area. "I'll build one if I have to," he added in a murmur.

She closed her eyes again. "And *no* sleeping, Ennis." Her eyes flew open, and she sniffed. "Count how many trees you see," he suggested.

With that, Valentine was off into the night, leaving the can in her hand. She couldn't hear him, and a shot of fear coursed through her blood. But she didn't fear him running off without her. She feared what might happen while he was gone. In the night, she felt naked as if her shredded clothing were nothing more than strips of air. *What about wolves? Are there wolves in these mountains? Bears?* She even feared a run-in with a nasty raccoon or porcupine. Did porcupines even live around here? Her mind flashed back to the bodies, and her stomach lurched. *No, no, no. Don't think about that.*

Large thuds sounded in the distance, their echoes swallowed up in the rushing winds. But when they stopped, she could only hear the thunderous winds that assaulted her ears. Usually, she loved the wind. But since it hindered their search for help, she prayed it would cease.

She sighed, staring at the ground before her, thinking back to the people he mentioned were coming after them. Who were they? Why had they shown up only then? Why hadn't V mentioned them before? Had the brothers called for backup?

Were they a part of some vampire group? *Were* they vampires? She stared at the trees, but they only shook their hands at her. Her eyes lifted to the heavens. "Thank you for getting us out of there, God. Both of us." Then her eyes closed.

~

Ennis felt her shoulders shake. *Am I that cold? In shock?* She realized someone's hand was lightly shaking her. "I told you no sleeping," Valentine said gently, scooping her up, making sure the cape was encapsulating her but leaving her head free. The backpack was already on his back. "Come on. I've built us a little shade for the day."

Valentine whisked her through the cold night to a structure made from fallen trees.

When her eyes found the massive thing, her mouth hung open slightly at the sight. "Little! You made a tree teepee! A tree-pee!" It looked like a giant teepee of towering trees, all leaning against a single sturdy rooted tree. *Thankfully they look fresh, not riddled with grubs and fungus. Or wild animals...* How he'd managed to get them all standing at the same time, she didn't know. Ripped off branches enveloped the exterior, creating more protection. It looked like a festive autumn cone.

He walked her inside, through the tree-trunk-sized gap, to where there was a bed of dried leaves. "Wow," she croaked. There was probably a radius of six feet inside with the brush cleared away and a fresh bed of leaves laid out. Glancing down, she saw there was some bare ground too with rocks in a circle and sticks inside the shape.

He smiled. "It'll do."

The leaves made a soft crunching noise beneath her weight as he set her down. Swinging off the backpack and the cape from around her, he unwrapped the two bottles, wrapping the last two towels around her. He took out the matches and started a fire, which sizzled to life, casting the tree tent in an eerie orange glow. The shadows fled and regrouped over and over. A howl wailed in the distance.

Her hazel eyes widened and sought Valentine's. "What was that?"

He scooted her closer to the fire. "I don't know. Certainly not a person. Maybe a coyote, maybe an owl. It doesn't matter to you either way. I can take it down easily." He paused. "And maybe it'll be my breakfast," he added with a slight chuckle.

Tension eased out of her shoulders. She was in the presence of a very powerful ally. And she didn't feel so afraid anymore. *God, I thank You for sending Valentine. You're the One who provides and the One I can rely on. Help me to see more clearly what You've done. You work through others too.* She shivered and hunkered nearer to the flames, pulling the towels snuggly around her in an attempt to keep her warmth from escaping. So much of her skin felt exposed.

She followed the smoke upwards with her eyes, watching it funnel out the top where a gap had been left in the roof, escaping to the highway of the winds. "This is really something you know."

He hummed in response, but his eyes were on her. "Sleep, Ennis. We'll be safe. God is good. While the wind is our enemy, it's also our friend tonight. It'll erase our trail, if we even left one."

She turned to lie on her side and stared at the fire. "God will come through. He always does," she whispered to herself.

~

Ennis awoke to a chill in her bones, the towel and her shredded clothing not doing much to protect her from the elements. She hadn't even thought of how cold it would be in the mountains.

Little spears of light blinded her as she opened her eyes as daylight seeped through the leaves on their shelter. *Light!* Panic swept over her and her hand grasped for Valentine. He was studying something in his hands when she, still half-asleep, grabbed his red and white shirt, tugging at him. "The sun!" Her voice hoarse, she scrambled to act as a barrier between him and the sun speckles. Her muscles immediately protested her quick movements, and an ache ripped down her side.

Valentine caught her by her middle and eased her back down to the leaves. "Whoa, whoa, calm down, Ennis. This much sun won't incapacitate me. I'm fine. Take it easy or you'll reopen your side." He gestured at her towel-wrapped middle, frowning.

Blinking for a few seconds, she was still in a sleep fog and shook her head gently. Letting out a breath, it visibly swirled around her, and her nose ached. And then it hit her like a slap in the face. All the memories... Shrieking Saeva falling lifelessly to the ground. Benedict's still body slipping down Valentine's front. Valentine's fangs.

At that, she clamped a hand instinctively over her neck, the ache still present. Valentine looked away, his eyes downcast. She remembered the stake guns. *Oh, the stake guns...* The dead arm slapping her in the face. The holes riddling V's body. The staked deer. And then the pain in her own body. She lurched onto her hands and knees, gasping for air. How had she taken it all in stride yesterday? Her mind flooded with too much noise from within. Everything flashed randomly, sending one grotesque image after another, violating her mind. Her body shook tremendously.

Valentine placed his hands on her shoulders. "Hey, Ennis? Breathe." His voice was calm and empathetic. "We're okay. We're going to be okay. We did what we had to do to survive. But I need you to calm down now. Those memories aren't happening right now. They're past. Stay here with me now."

Her arms quivered as she held herself up, her right arm aching furiously. When dizziness struck her, she rooted around for a repurposed water bottle and ravenously ripped off the cork. She nearly choked on the oily liquid. Perhaps she just hadn't acquired the taste of olive oil flavored water yet. As she drank, she worried about how their water supply would run out soon. They needed to find help ASAP. They had been through so much. Survived so much. She felt tears prick her eyes and realized just how hard it was to breathe. This was too much. Her head spun with all the things that had happened in the past week. But every challenge they'd faced had been solved, and the ones that remained would be taken care of as well. "V..." She suddenly felt like laughing. Something had clicked, and she clutched a hand to her forehead, hoping she wasn't resigning to hysteria.

He moved his hands to rest on the tops of his legs. He'd been rubbing her back after letting go of her shoulders, and she hadn't noticed. His eyes were trained on her, a slight frown on his face.

Her eyes found the fire that still crackled with moderate life, and she shook her head. "I can't do this alone. I never could." She looked him full in the eyes. "I wouldn't have made it out alive had it not been for God. He planned this all out. Don't you see it? You, you were already there at the house. He's freed both of us."

Valentine's eyebrows raised a little.

She gave a dumbfounded smile. "God provided a way out. I couldn't do it alone. I've done that my entire life. Feared that others would just let me down. That it wasn't worth the pain." She sighed, sounding frustrated. "I've been so daft... But this..." she gestured around her, but to nothing in particular, "*this* just tells me how much I can't do everything on my own. For a long time, I've tried to do things all by myself. I trusted God, but I didn't trust Him completely. I trusted my own capability. But even the strength I thought I had, that wasn't even mine. God gave me that strength. He's giving me strength now. I'd be dead in both body and spirit without Him. Every challenge, every trouble, He made us a way out. He's solved everything for us. He orchestrated our escape! He gave me you, and we needed each other to escape. In everything, He's provided."

Valentine stared at her, his eyes becoming softer. A slight smile was on his lips.

"And I know this," she continued, nonplussed. "I'm not planning on living life alone again. Or only in my own strength. I want to live in God's strength, not my own. I'm too weak. Even without my illnesses. I can't do life alone or fight alone. We weren't made for that." She wore a small smile, but a blaze burned gold in her hazel eyes.

Valentine tilted his head, smirking. "And I'd love to aid you in that quest of not living alone."

She smiled even more at his amused expression.

When his face relaxed, he leaned back onto his hands. "I realised the same thing, Ennis. But I figured that out the moment you wanted to team up. I know it's God's strength, not mine. The Holy Spirit teaches that to others in His timing. Indeed, it baffles me at times, but He has the best planned and works in mysterious ways." Picking up a stick, he poked at the fire and wore a bittersweet smile. "You know, God worked on me by using you." He met her curious eyes. "You don't know a lot about my past, Ennis, but since I've known you, I've changed. God used you. 'And we know that to them that love God all things work together for good, even to them that are called according to His purpose.' Just as He promised. He's faithful, and He'll keep His promises."

She beamed. "God always has things planned out for His children. He brought you and me to the same place, overlapping our time. He's so clever."

A steady silence followed. And the two were content with each other's company. When the wind whistled through the entrance of the tent, the noise broke the silence.

She crawled towards the backpack, and he swiftly handed her an opened can of soup. She took a few swigs. "Did anything happen last night?"

He sat back on his knees again. "Not even a moth decided to join us."

Ennis sighed. In the moment of stillness that returned, she listened. "The wind's died down some." She tapped on one of the fallen trees that had been righted to make the tent. "Can you smell any civilization?"

His mouth curled into a smile. "Can I smell civilisation?" Turning his eyes to the tent's entrance, he shook his head. "Not yet, but I might be able to smell other humans when they get closer. We'll have to keep moving once the sun sets."

Frowning, she downed the rest of the soup. "Waiting all day…" She sank back into the leaves.

"Just a few more hours actually. You've slept most of the day." He looked into the fire with an unnerving depth.

She sat up straighter, setting down the can. "What is it, V?"

Turning towards her, he peered at her. "You know, I really have to thank God for how this turned out. We're nearly clear of this diabolical chapter, and I'm just so thankful to Him. He can use even the worst for good. We've been through a terrible ordeal and survived." Pausing, his eyes dipped to the fire again. "He's already taught us through this, but I wonder if He'll use it even further." He shook his head, smiling. He resumed poking at the fire with a small smile.

Her eyes slipped shut as her head found the wad of leaves she'd used as a crunchy pillow. "He's faithful."

She opened her eyes after a bit and observed Valentine once more, taking in his appearance. He was caked in blood, his pale face still smeared with red and bits of leaves. His clothes had holes, and his dark hair was matted. But his hazel eyes held something that even their survival situation could not snuff out. *Peace.*

~

23

Ennis awoke to two hands slipping underneath her. Startled, she looked around wildly, nearly punching at the assumed offender. But then a familiar presence and the smell of nutmeg swept over her, easing her fear. She let her head fall against Valentine and noted that they were moving again. Quickly.

She also realized that she'd weakened considerably more since her last wakeful moments in the tent. Her heart seemed to beat irregularly but too fast as well. When she tried to speak, she realised her mouth stuck together. *So thirsty! And my lungs! Am I even breathing? I feel like I'm dying!*

It was now dusk and the teepee was nowhere in sight behind them. His running was steady, unlike her heart. She likened his pace to an unrelenting racehorse but with the grace of a shadow.

They ran and ran for what felt like a couple of hours.

~

Eventually, Valentine slowed to a stop and put her down on the springy forest bed, uncorking and handing Ennis the last bottle of water. She choked on the slightly alcoholic beverage as it burned her throat on the way down. The fit of coughing that followed caused her to moan since it made her chest feel like it was being crushed. He turned in a circle, stopping intermittently, his nose in the air. The forest looked the same as it had since she'd first driven down the Cerrit Brothers' driveway—a heavily wooded green and orange jungle.

His head snapped to the left. "I've got something!" Her brows rose, and he swung her back into his arms simultaneously, racing off through the trees.

Within a few moments, she smelled the smoke. "Woodsmoke! We're close!"

Within another moment, they reached a clearing. And on top of a small hill, in the weak light of the moon, a tiny house was nestled against the backdrop of a multicolored forest. It leaked smoke like an old pipe, and its dilapidated yellow walls were mostly hidden with ivy. A muddy truck rested in the drive, and Ennis's heart surged with excitement.

Valentine glided them up to the front steps and set her down. She clung to him for support, and he steadied her. Looking up at him, she noted that he looked energised, happy, and somewhat nervous. With slight hesitation, he knocked on the door.

A woman, who Ennis thought to be in her 50s, answered the door. The woman was wearing a white t-shirt, her dirty blond hair was pulled back in a ponytail, and she had a phone to her ear. She dropped her hand to her side, face paling, and the phone gave a nasty crack as it landed on the dull wooden floor below. Her hand shot up to cover her mouth as she looked upon two ragged and bloody, yet smiling souls.

Discussion

1. What do you think is the main theme of this book?

2. How do you think Ennis changed as a person? Did Valentine change? How so?

3. Can you see yourself in Ennis's decisions? Why do you think she made the ones she did? What did she focus on when making decisions? What should she have focused on? What would you have done differently?

4. Most of the names in the book stand for something in Latin. Benedict and Saeva's roots mean kind and cruel. Cerrit means crazy. Do you think kindness can also be a cage, just like cruelty? How can kindness be twisted? Is it truly kindness then?

5. The setting primarily takes place in one bound location like a prison. What sort of prisons do you need to escape from? How do you plan on escaping from them?

6. Fortunately, there's One who can help you live a better life. Jesus Christ died so that you might have life. "For God so loved the world, that [H]e gave [H]is only begotten Son, that whosoever believeth on [H]im should not perish, but have eternal life. For God sent not the Son into the world to judge the world; but that the world should be saved through [H]im. He that believeth on [H]im is not judged: he that believeth not hath been judged already, because he hath not believed on the name

of the only begotten Son of God" (John 3:16-18, American Standard Version).

Jesus Christ—God the Son—lived a perfect, sinless life, born of a virgin, being both fully human and fully God. He willingly died on a cross as a perfect sacrifice for all the world's sins, including yours, to save you from your sins. (Sins are actions that rebel against God's commands; they are actions that are disobedient to God's commands). And all you need to do to have eternal life and not go to Hell—which is just punishment for your sins—is to accept Jesus Christ as your Savior. He asks you to repent of (turn away from) the bad things you've done and work with Him to live by His ways, making God the King of your life instead of anyone or anything else. He's the only One who can save you. You can't save yourself through works, or any other way. The idea that there are multiple ways to heaven is a lie. Faith in Jesus Christ is the <u>only</u> way to avoid the immanent Judgement. God is a loving God, and He sent His Son because He loves you and wants to have a relationship with you! Will you accept Him and put your faith in Him to save you and give you eternity in His love? Let me tell you, this is the best deal there is! And this is the way to live the most fulfilling and purposeful life you can ever live!

7. There is sacrifice that happens at the end of the book. What do you think Ennis's sacrifice symbolizes here?

8. Ennis has OCD and POTS. If you have chronic illnesses, how do you see yourself in this character?

9. Ennis thinks quite a lot, and you get to read her inner thoughts. Why do you think thinking was emphasized in this book? Do you relate to her inner struggles?

10. What is your main takeaway from this book?